P9-CBW-416

The Anvil Stone

Also by Kathleen Cunningham Guler

Into the Path of Gods
In the Shadow of Dragons

Edited by Kathleen Cunningham Guler

Offerings for the Green Man
The Spring of Nine Hazels

Published by Bardsong Press

The Anvil Stone

Book 3 of the Macsen's Treasure Series

Kathleen Cunningham Guler

Bardsong Press

Steamboat Springs, Colorado

This book is a work of fiction. Names, characters, places, and incidents either are products of the author's imagination or are used fictionally. Any resemblance to actual events or locales or persons, living or dead, is entirely coincidental.

ISBN-13: 978-0-9660371-5-9
ISBN-10: 0-9660371-5-4

Library of Congress Catalog Control Number: 2005935989

Printed in the United States of America

First Edition

"That which we are, we are;
One equal temper of heroic hearts,
Made weak by time and fate, but strong in will
To strive, to seek, to find, and not to yield."

— Alfred, Lord Tennyson

AUTHOR'S NOTES

ONE of the questions I am asked most often is, "How did you get into writing about Arthurian Britain?"

Usually I mumble something about how it comes out of my Welsh and Scottish heritage and that's probably true. People of Celtic descent seem to always have an eerie connection to the past as well as a need to express it through writing, music, dance, art, or some other form of creativity.

Or maybe it's just one of those fascinating benchmark eras where one sector of society clashed so painfully against the encroachment of other sectors that the quest for freedom became paramount. It is also a time so hidden from history that any writer seeking to portray it is faced with a monumental challenge to intuit the era's mindset. That it involved the people from whom I descend makes it personal.

The goal of a historical fiction writer is to meld fact and imaginative storytelling into a seamless tale, at once fresh and exciting as well as timeless and realistic. My intention in writing this series was not to merely retell a portion of the Arthurian legend. That has been done many times. Rather, I wished to bring alive a period of history through the eyes of Celtic people who could have lived then and blend the events that led to Arthur's rise to power as an influence upon their lives. Though based on a broad array of fact drawn from archaeology and other resources, the series is also based on legend and should be regarded solely as fiction. Each book can be read alone; the prominent characters, chronology, themes, and background tie them together.

In working with eras such as the fifth century Britain to which King Arthur likely belonged, historical accuracy can be notoriously difficult, given that very little documentation survives. The Macsen's Treasure series is loosely based on the combined history and legend of Geoffrey of Monmouth's *The History of the Kings of Britain (Historia Regum Britanniae)*. Geoffrey was a cleric who attempted to write a history encompassing nineteen hundred years of British kings, from the first, Brutus, to the last before the Saxon conquest. However, while some of Geoffrey's figures and events probably were historical, his work includes many blatant inaccuracies as well as outright patriotic and ecclesiastical posturing. His narrative ultimately served to popularize the legend more than provide an accurate account.

The legend as it pertains to *The Anvil Stone*—according to Geoffrey—includes the story of high king Uther Pendragon's infatuation with Ygerna, and how Merlin helps the king fulfill his desire to win her. The result of their union is Arthur. Geoffrey's history also tells of Uther's battles with the Saxon leader Octa. Geoffrey mentions that Uther suffers from a vague illness that seems to come and go. For *The Anvil Stone,* I chose not to bring this in at this point in his life.

Historically, we simply don't know how much of the legend is true. What we do know is that as the Roman empire began to falter in the late fourth and early fifth centuries, the legions gradually evacuated from Britain, the last of them leaving around AD 410. This left Britain open to invasions, first from Picts from north of Hadrian's Wall, Irish from the west, then Germanic tribes (Angles, Saxons, Jutes, among others) from the continent.

Much debate has gone on about whether the Germanic people were invaders or settlers. They were probably a combination. Either way, their settlements continued to encroach, which caused a great deal of tension. Then around AD 500, it appears that they were pushed back, and a period of peace and prosperity ensued. This stability is attributed to an improvement in British leadership that may have been the legendary King Arthur. In the mid-sixth century, however, British strength fell apart and the Anglo-Saxons methodically conquered the land that is now called England.

The Anvil Stone continues the saga of spy Marcus ap Iorwerth and his beloved wife Claerwen, begun with *Into the Path of Gods* and *In the Shadow of Dragons*. The principal characters of Marcus and Claerwen, as well as Handor, Tangwen, Blaez, and minor characters, are fictional. The named kings and other nobility (e.g., Uther, Ceredig, Budic) are possibly historical. The Saxon, Octa, may also be historical. Myrddin is of course the legendary Merlin the Magician. In the legend he is probably fictional, though it is believed he may be a composite figure of several historical bards. For the purpose of the series, I have fictionalized him as the last "high druid."

Welsh names for places and people in Britain have been used in the book as much as possible in the attempt to evoke the sense of language for the era, although the tongue actually was a precursor of Old Welsh. Of course the Roman influence is there as well. For example, Marcus ap Iorwerth's name is as paradoxical as he is himself; while his given name is Roman, the structure of his full name is purely Welsh. The word "ap" means "son of," hence, Marcus, son of Iorwerth. In contrast, Winchester is an Anglicized place-name, and was probably not used until after the Saxon conquest that led to the creation of England after Arthur's demise in the sixth century. It is used in this form because of its familiarity to the reader. I have used names in the Breton language for the sections set in Brittany (Breizh).

To give a sense of Celtic beliefs before Christianity's conversion was completed in Britain, I have chosen to instill a bit of spirituality through a Celtic visionary mysticism called "fire in the head," as well as Druidry. To some, the visions may represent an element of fantasy; however, I believe it belongs within the historical belief system that was still in practice among more remotely located native Celtic people of the time.

The dates used in the chapter headings are meant to simply be guideposts for the passage of time and are pure conjecture on my part. According to historian Geoffrey Ashe, "it would usually be pretentious to give even a 'circa' date." Dates found in source materials, when they are found at all, vary astonishingly from one source to the next.

Claerwen's vague vision of a battle in the mountains of Gwynedd is a reflection of a Welsh tradition that Arthur's final battle at Camlann occurred near a place called Cwm y Llan. Another tradition says Arthurian treasure is concealed in Marchlyn Mawr, a mountain lake that is now a reservoir. For those who recognize the story of Arthur's knight Bedwyr throwing Excalibur into a body of water, these two traditions put together give the notion that Excalibur might lie at the bottom of one of Gwynedd's mountain tarns.

Marcus's swords are likely quite a bit larger than what was normal for his time. However, as a clever, inventive man and a blacksmith to boot, he very well could have created his own swords that were more suited to his needs and nature.

And lastly, within the context of the series, Macsen's Treasure is a five-piece set of ceremonial symbols sacred to the high kings of Britain. Consisting of a crown, torque, spearhead, sword and grail, it is purely fictional and does not exist in the Arthurian legend or in history. However, trappings of kingship such as special crowns, scepters, and swords have been held dear by monarchies throughout the centuries. Couldn't it be possible that this notion speaks to the question of where the famed sword Excalibur and the Holy Grail came from?

Sometimes it's those little questions of "what if?" that prompt a story to be told. For some, to find the answer can become an obsession. In my case, that may be true, and perhaps it is also that the spirits of my ancestors have chosen me to tell their tale as much as I have chosen to write about them.

Kathleen Cunningham Guler

Pronunciation Guide/Glossary

This list should help with frequently used names and places that are difficult to pronounce. Pronunciations are approximate. Where useful a translation or notation is provided.

Blaez (Blaze) Frankish political prisoner in Breizh
Breizh (Brayz) Brittany or Armorica
Brezhoneg (Bray-ZON-eg) Breton language
Budic (BEE-dic) King of Breizh
Caer Luguvalos (Car Loo-goo-VAL-os) Gwrast's stronghold
Ceredig (Ker-RED-ig) King of Strathclyde
Dun Breatann (Dun BRET-an) Ceredig's stronghold
Gododdin (Go-DOTH-in) Northern British kingdom
Gorlois (Gor-LO-is) Lord of Tintagel
Gwrast (Grahst) King of Rheged
Hywel Gwodryd (Heeool GWO-drud) Court bard of Rheged
Meirchion Gul (MARE-Kee-on GEEL) Prince of Rheged
Myrddin (MUR-then) Merlin
Rheged (RHAY-ghed) Northern British kingdom
Tintagel (Tin-TAJ-el) Stronghold on Cornish coast
Uther (Ü-ther) High King of Britain
Y Gwalch Haearn (Uh Gwalch Hayrn) The Iron Hawk

The most noteworthy differences between Welsh and English are as follows:

The Welsh "dd" is like English "th," as in *them.* A "w" is either a consonant or a vowel; as a vowel it has an *oo* sound. A "ch" is hard as in the Scottish *loch.* The "ll" is not found in English but can be approximated as a very rough combination of *hl.*

And "Celtic" is correctly pronounced with a hard C: *Keltic.*

Macsen's Treasure

Torque of gold, born of earth
Turned by strong and calloused hands
Heavy grace on necks of kings
Returned by blood, torque of earth.

Spear of wind, born of air
Chased with lines of twining life
Swallow-swift in soaring flight
Removed by stealth, spear of air.

Sword of light, born of fire
Forged with strength of ancient magic
Cries both with life and with death
Cast to stone, sword of fire.

Grail of life, born of water
Deep and wide to hold the source
Empty but for time and memory
Forever lost, grail of water.

Crown of kings, born of gods
Bind torque and spear, sword and grail
So walk in honor, before the shadow
And journey into the path of gods.

— Myrddin Emrys

1. Ynys Murrin
2. Dun Breatann
3. The women's colony
4. The farmstead
5. Caer Luguvalos
& Uxelodunum
6. Dinas Beris
7. Tintagel
8. Ynys Witrin
(Isle of Avalon)
9. Roman Temple
10. Winchester
11. Verulam (St. Albans)
12. Ector's lands
Alba
(Pictland)
Gododdin
Strathclyde
Brynaich
Ireland
Ebrauc
Rheged
Elmet
Linnius
Gwynedd
Powys
Dyfed
Ceint
Cornwall
Saxon Shore
The Narrow Sea
13. Hermitage
14. Villa
15. Plouguer
16. Promontory Fort
Breizh (Armorica)
Gaul
Morbihan
The Small Sea

Prologue

THE boy stared into the chamber's dark interior. Night had fallen, but starlight shined crisply outside compared to the abandoned building's womblike recesses. Rats scurried before him as he entered, their feet like whispers across the flagstone floor. The creatures escaped through other doorways and holes in the Roman fort's crumbling structure, then the sound faded. It was silent. Too silent, as if the sea beyond the mists had forever drained away.

The boy crept from the chamber into the larger hall he'd explored perhaps a hundred times before. In time, his eyes adjusted to the deeper darkness. It stank of rotting flesh. A predator must have dragged in prey somewhere, he guessed, and he wiped his nose against the stench.

The hair on his neck lifted. The ceiling seemed to sag more than usual, a shadow too many above, the gloom utterly still. But did it sway, ever so slightly? Strange. The boy edged inward in a circle towards the disused fire pit, a pace, then another, and another. In the cold of the night his breath steamed, the only thing alive in the building. Or, was it?

The smell grew stronger; it was more than rotting flesh. Near a narrow shaft of starlight that spilled through a crack in the roof, his boots crunched on snow, old snow, mixed with blood and filth.

The boy looked up into the roof again. His stomach lurched. Not one shadow drifted before him. Many. Hung like bats. He could hardly bear to look, but in spite of their pitiable condition, neither could he bear to look away. The one with the imbedded Saxon axe, the handle shattered, was the least hideous. Sweat broke on his brow, yet he shook as if he had been standing on ice for hours. His ears buzzed, roaring like the relentless sea, and he was certain he was going to faint, but he could not move, could not scream, could not think.

The worst was that he recognized them. Every raw one of them. Even the woman he had heard scream in words he could not understand. Though he squeezed his eyes shut, the shadows remained, burned into his soul.

The man sat up, bile in his throat. He swallowed to force it back down, but the stale, metallic taste remained. He twisted around to drop his legs over the bed's edge and faced the banked fire pit's glow in the center of his warm, comfortable house. Each breath shuddered. Control, he willed himself, face in his palms. Control. If only the sound of the sea would stop roaring. It was only a memory, a dream, a terrible dream, but…

They had been there again. Upside down. Hung from the rafters like drying deer meat. The filthiest butcher's stall in a marketplace came nowhere close to the putrid smell. A battlefield strewn with death was nothing in comparison. So bloody retched—

He strangled off his thoughts.

The house was still, thank the gods. He snatched up his loincloth from where he had dropped it on going to bed and stood, tied it around his hips. A few strides over the plank floorboards brought him to the leather drape that separated the house's interior from its anteroom. He pushed through to the door to the outside, jerked it open, and thrust his face, his shoulders, into the winter-fresh air. It washed over his near-nakedness and cooled the sweat that invaded his scalp and dripped beneath the hair on his chest.

The dream would come again, like all the other dreams and memories. He stared at the snow on the ground, dim in starlight. How many times had he seen blood soaking into snow? How many more times would he see it dripping from the end of his sword, the weapon now clean and polished and hanging from pegs above the bed? Disgusted, he crammed the memories once more into the iron-clad part of his mind where he kept them. If only he could find a way to stop them from escaping.

With a harsh sigh, he raked his fingers through his long black hair and turned back. He softly shut the door after himself.

Inside again, seated on the fire pit's hearthstones, the man picked up a small ceramic pitcher and drank a long swallow of ale, then another, and another. When there was no more, he licked the last drops from his moustache.

His gaze came to rest on his wife. Undisturbed, she slept on, curled next to the dip in the bed where he had lain. He had no wish to waken her, yet to see her light, iridescent green-blue eyes would have been so fine indeed. Compassion. Empathy. Never patronizing. She could see down into his soul and beyond and ease some of that plaguing disquiet. How could he ever burden her with this?

He conjured the image of her eyes and let it soak all through his mind. Gradually his jaw unclenched. With painstaking care to be quiet, he set the pitcher back on the hearthstones. "By the gods," he murmured to her sleeping form. "You are my only freedom."

Chapter I

Winchester
Spring, AD 471

THE argument began with the first call of the ram's horn.

Deep within one of the palace buildings, voices erupted, loud enough to carry out through an open window. Two men and a woman, their words unsuccessfully hushed, grew insistent, cruel.

Marcus ap Iorwerth paused beneath the window on the rear side of the building and shook his head. For days he had expected the clash. Uther Pendragon, high king of Britain, had once again been caught giving too much attention to a woman, this time the wife of his highest-ranking military commander.

The ram's horn called again. A long, unwavering tone, it signaled the beginning of another day, as they were counted from sunset to sunset. Its lonely howl, a summons to the evening's celebrations as well, seemed more like a warning to Marcus. The haunting strain faded. Winchester's vast, walled compound remained quiet, unresponsive, as if in shock. Not even the brightly colored streamers atop the ramparts fluttered.

Marcus resumed his stroll of the palace grounds. Oh, to be anywhere else, he wished as he started to rake his fingers through his hair then caught himself. He detested the annoying stiffness the coating of beeswax gave it, but it was the only way to keep his thick, more than shoulder-length hair swept straight back and in place instead of letting it fall free in its usual disarray. To wash it out was something more to look forward to upon leaving. So was changing out of his fine wool tunic, breeches and cloak—all nice in rich deep blue with fancy silver decorations but too formal for his taste. And too noticeable.

The ram's horn called a third time.

The squabble between king, commander and woman ceased. Congenial banter gradually replaced it, ringing out from the other side of the building where the main courtyard lay.

A sardonic smile gripped Marcus's mouth. At sunset Uther was scheduled to conduct the ritual in which fealty would be sworn. In the king's eyes, this ceremony was more important than the coronation held several days earlier. Every nobleman, from the highest rank to the lowest, was required to swear. Uther, from the sound of the aborted argument, would be in no mood to forgive anyone's absence.

Ah, well, Marcus told himself, only a few more days…

On his way to the courtyard, he strode into the narrow alleyway between the great hall and the building next to it. A lantern dropped a circle of light onto the flagstone walkway. Placed in the middle of the light, so centered it had to have been deliberate, lay a doll-like bundle of rags stained with black ink.

Marcus halted just outside the pool of light. In that same instant, he recognized the bundle was an effigy fashioned to look like him. The ink imitated his black hair and thick, drooping moustache. Roman letters were scrawled on a narrow piece of cloth tied around the chest, and a slim dagger resembling a sword impaled the figure. Deep red splotches, smeared in places, looked like blood.

"*Mid flæsce ond blode ond bane,*" a raspy voice hissed from behind.

The words, in Saxon, tore through Marcus like spikes of ice. He jerked around. An unkempt man with reddish-brown hair glared from the shadows, his face like a snarling wolf.

The man fingered a small rock hung on a cord around his neck like it was a talisman. His snarl deepened, teeth showing, dark eyes full of anger. "*Mid flæsce ond blode ond bane,*" he repeated. He spun back out of the light and fled.

Marcus snatched up the effigy. By the gods, he had never wanted think of those words again, let be hear them. So many years had passed and he still did not understand their meaning, but their sound he remembered well, far too well. He swore. With the effigy gripped in his hand, he raced after its deliverer into the darkening yards behind the palace.

The ram's horn blared once more.

Claerwen of Dinas Beris waited in the center of the courtyard. The last time she had been there was in winter, and the yard had been stark, cold and nearly empty except for soldiers. Originally an enormous Roman villa that had long been neglected, it was now in the midst of the high king's renovations. He was bringing it up to his standards—actually a display of his taste for ostentation. Around her, all dressed in the grandeur of their finest clothing and gleaming silver, gold and pewter jewelry, people gathered in clumps. Gossip rippled like heat waves.

"Claerwen?"

She barely heard the voice call her name above the growing din of talk. On tiptoe, she stretched up to search for its source. Lord Ceredig of Strathclyde, the most powerful ruler among those of the northern kingdoms, strode towards her. Towering and husky in spite of his six-and-fifty winters, he threaded his way easily through the crowd.

She greeted him, received a light kiss on her cheek in return.

"Where's your husband, lass?" He pushed aside his faded red hair, blown across his face.

"Marcus?" Claerwen frowned at the concern in Ceredig's warm brown eyes. "He told me to wait for him here. Something is wrong?"

His voice lowered. "There's been an argument."

Claerwen half-smiled. "Between Lord Gorlois of Cornwall and Uther, about Gorlois's wife, Ygerna?"

"You've heard?"

"It was bound to happen, no? We've all been here more than a fortnight. Could anyone have missed how the king's eyes constantly wandered to her? And how she smiles in return, ever so willingly? He will tire soon enough, once he finds another pretty face."

Exasperation curled Ceredig's lips. "I've been told he and Gorlois have argued several times now. The king refuses to leave her alone. And she won't even try to avoid him. This last argument was not the usual nonsense. It was serious."

"Enough to break with Gorlois?" Claerwen's smile faded. Uther had been declared high king only recently, soon after the assassination of his older brother Ambrosius.

Ceredig exhaled as if to rid himself of the facts. "Uther is livid. He's ordered the gates locked. His excuse is to force Gorlois to stay here and swear fealty. In truth, it's to keep him from removing Ygerna from Winchester. But Gorlois is absolutely outraged. He vowed he will never swear."

A riffling gust of wind set the gauze veil Claerwen wore over her tawny-brown hair to swirling. She caught the ends and shivered. "Why would Uther squander alliances after all the work Ambrosius did to build them?" she asked. "Especially this one? It's too important."

"Gorlois controls most of the war bands Ambrosius built," Ceredig added. "And they don't respect Uther the way they did Ambrosius. With his temper, Uther could easily lose that control."

Discomfort pervaded the air. Claerwen draped the veil again and wished she had worn a light cloak. Her lamb's wool gown of deep teal-green was warm enough, but she still felt chilled.

"Then this could be why Marcus hasn't come yet," she said. "You know him…he would try to forestall the break…or at least make it less severe."

On the dais before the great hall, the high king's tall and lanky nephew, Prince Myrddin Emrys, strode out from behind a screen of drapes. "Merlin, the Enchanter," the whispers began to haunt across the courtyard. Claerwen remembered when the epithet, prompted by his uncanny gift to foretell the future—a mysticism sometimes called "second sight" or "fire in the head"—had begun among the common people and spread throughout the population. Because of it, he was both admired and feared by peasant and noble alike. When she had first met him, she discovered she possessed the same gift.

Claerwen watched Myrddin thrust out a steady gaze of omniscient, all-knowing trust that the coming hours would pass as they should. "He is worried beneath that mask of certainty," she said.

"You've known him a long time, haven't you?" Ceredig asked.

"As many years as I've known Marcus."

"And you are worried as well?"

"Marcus is late." She scanned the thickening crowd. "Will the ceremony proceed?"

"Uther will not lapse in this. To not have every one of his nobles swear fealty, here and now, he will consider disloyalty, and tonight he will be in no mood for forgiveness. Marcus will be no exception, regardless of what he has done for the king."

Claerwen looked up into Ceredig's lined and weathered face. Distantly related to him through her mother's family, she had met him but twice before and then only briefly. Yet she felt comfortable with him. Marcus had known him for nearly twenty years; his fosterage had been spent in Strathclyde's main stronghold at Dun Breatann. Though Ceredig was thirty years older than Marcus, they had remained not only allies but close friends as well, and Marcus always had a ready story about the robust and sometimes outspoken king.

She *was* worried. Though Marcus could invoke Uther's wrath in missing the ceremony, that could be rectified later. Worse, far worse, she could not guess how many of the courtiers were already aware of the connection between his name, Marcus ap Iorwerth, and that he was a spy. To be publicly identified before most of Britain's important leaders, a face put with his name, could severely compromise the necessary secrecy of his work. Uther knew this, and she could not understand why the high king insisted Marcus must swear publicly rather than in private, especially after he had already proven his loyalty by thwarting another assassination—that of Uther himself.

Several ram's horns blasted, this time in a fanfare, and Uther emerged from behind the screen. The crowd stirred into a cheer. As tall as his nephew but more solidly built, he stood next to a high-backed chair of intricately carved oak and surveyed his nobles.

Claerwen recognized the jeweled gold torque that lay around his neck, the crown of matching design on his brow, and the ceremonial spear in the crook of his elbow. Macsen's Treasure—hidden for safekeeping many years before and subsequently lost—was a collection of sacred symbols of the high kingship. Of the original five pieces, these three had been rediscovered. The remaining two, a sword and a grail, had yet to be found. The grandiose way in which Uther displayed them, Claerwen thought, seemed to cheapen them.

"He won't let the king's recklessness ruin..." Claerwen started with a grimace.

Ceredig laid a comforting hand on her shoulder. "What's that, lass?"

"Not after all he's been through..." Her words drifted off a second time. She had seen Marcus suffer so much—far beyond the boundary most men could endure. For years, in his dangerous ongoing quest to deter foreign attacks and encroachment, he had sabotaged the importation of Saxon mercenaries during the reign of Ambrosius's predecessor, Vortigern. At the same time he had manipulated scores of feuding British factions to unite behind Ambrosius and establish him in Vortigern's place. Marcus's reward? Betrayal to Vortigern, then imprisonment, torture, and abandonment to die of injuries, illness or starvation, whichever would have come first. Claerwen glared at Uther. So many times Marcus had come close to death. And all he had ever wanted was to see Britain remain free.

On the dais, Uther nodded to Myrddin, then to his seneschal, who in turn nodded to the man with the ram's horn. A long prelude unfurled, a signal to begin the homage ceremony.

The king's seneschal unrolled the first of many parchments that carried the nobles' names, each identified by a title, a given name and up to three direct ancestors. The first noble was announced. That man extracted himself from the crowd and walked along a designated path towards the dais, his wife and retainers in tow. He halted at the foot, pulled a sword, then moved up the steps to kneel before the king. He offered his weapon flat across his hands, the symbolic gesture of submission to a higher authority.

From where she stood, Claerwen gazed from one face to the next of those she could see. If only Marcus would suddenly be somewhere among them. Name after name was called. She recognized the most well known—kings, princes, queens, clan chieftains—representatives of Britain's more than fifty petty kingdoms and important regions within each. Of those she could not already identify, she tried to memorize. Some names reflected the lingering Roman influence; the remainder bore the older Celtic heritage that had never been wiped away. A few, like Marcus, who had been named by an insistent half-Roman grandmother, carried a mixed name.

The ceremony trudged on; an hour passed, then another. Restless, the crowd grew tired of waiting for the long list to be completed. Alone since Ceredig had been summoned, Claerwen bowed her head and drew a deep breath. What could she do when Marcus was called and not present?

Someone jostled into her from behind. A light tug on her hair brought her around with a ready glare, but her annoyance abruptly faded. Marcus, face tilted low, brushed the tress with his lips. He stood so close she felt heat radiate from him.

Relief flooded her. "Where—" she started, but when cold, hard nerve flashed in his deep-set black eyes she went silent. Flushed and perspiring, he was also a bit disheveled, his hair loose from its beeswax coating. The disturbing cast in his eyes deepened. Claerwen recognized the same raw grit she had seen in him whenever he was faced with death or the need to take a life. Troubled, she let her eyes ask what was wrong.

The seneschal's voice interrupted. "Lord Marcus ap Iorwerth ap Sinnoch, Prince of Dinas Beris in the lands of Eryri, the Kingdom of Gwynedd!"

Air hissed through Marcus's teeth. He flipped back the front edges of his cloak and exposed a baldric. Slung loosely over his left shoulder, the wide leather strap held his sheathed two-handed sword.

Claerwen felt his hand slide around her wrist. Narrowed under his heavy brows, his eyes swept from her to the dais. She knew he hated this. His face looked as if he were braving a tribunal in which the only verdict was execution. He started forward with her past hundreds of curious faces.

At the dais's foot, Marcus kept his hand twined around hers. She hesitated, then he nodded—he wanted her to come with him instead of leaving her to wait like all the other nobles' wives. Defiance of tradition, she wondered? Or a show of unity to Uther? They marched up, steps in unison. At the top, Marcus pulled the sword.

They knelt together. Marcus displayed the weapon across his work-calloused palms. With lowered faces, they waited.

Even with her head bowed, Claerwen felt Uther's eyes shift from Marcus to her and back. The king leaned forward. "Must you always do things your own way?" he said with quiet menace.

Claerwen lifted her head a little. Marcus was glaring at the king, and she hoped to find a hint of mischief in his eyes. None was there. Breath held, she cautiously slid her gaze to Uther. Anger convulsed below the surface of his face, but he said no more.

The ritual proceeded. Afterward, Marcus sheathed the sword. Claerwen slid her hand into his and held on tightly as they sifted down through the voluminous waves of courtiers and escaped the yard. With swift steps they crossed the wide portico of the building where they were lodged and went inside, climbed the stairs to the second floor. The corridor there was lined with guardsmen, all heavily armed. Most were men from Uther's house guard. Others wore the personal markings of their clans and guarded the doors of their chieftains or patrolled the hallway's length.

A man bearing the insignia of Dinas Beris saluted when they approached.

Marcus returned the gesture. "Report, Gwilym?"

Gwilym bowed and opened the doors. "All is quiet here, Lord Marcus."

"So be it."

Inside, and with the doors shut behind them, Claerwen ran the locking bolt into place. "Thank the gods, that's done," she said and removed the veil, tossed it on a chair. She watched Marcus move an oil lamp from the anteroom to a table in the chambers' spacious common room. He leaned on the table's edge and stared into the lamp's hissing flame.

Claerwen followed him in. "Marcus?" She squeezed his arm but the muscle and sinew were hard as stone, and she was unsure if he even felt her fingers. His eyes smoldered as much as the black soot that rose from the lamp. A sudden chill swept up her spine. "Why you were so late?"

His mouth opened and clamped shut again.

She had never seen him so. Bluntness, cynicism, and a sardonic wit that stung, she was accustomed to in his serious moods, but this cold brooding alarmed her. She waited.

No response. No movement.

"What happened?" She brushed her fingers affectionately through the hair that hung over his eyes. Color still flushed his high, wide cheekbones. "Are you ill? Or was it a fight? Are you hurt—?"

"No," he said. One hand came up and clutched her fingers. "Don't ask."

CHAPTER 2

Winchester
Spring, AD 471

BRISK knocking rattled the outer doors. From the corridor, Ceredig's voice joked loudly with the guards.

Marcus exhaled sharply, swore under his breath and released Claerwen's hand. As much as he admired Ceredig and enjoyed his company, an interruption was not what he wished right now.

"Let him in," Marcus said. "Please." He moved back from the table and listened to Claerwen's footsteps glide through the curtain to the anteroom. Before she reached the door, he whisked through another set of drapes behind the common room and strode into the dark bedchamber. He heard the outer doors open. Ceredig's voice filled the anteroom. Marcus swung off his cloak and tossed it onto the bed; the baldric with the sword followed, and from the back of his belt, the effigy. He rolled the last inside the cloak.

Control, he told himself in a stolen moment of stillness. Keep control. A long, narrow table stood against the wall to his right and he felt for it in the dark. A small pitcher of wine sat on it and he poured a cupful, gulped it down. Keep control. He faced the doorway to the common room, maneuvered congeniality onto his face and passed between the drapes.

Ceredig stood next to the table with the lamp. The casual turn of his head showed he was assessing how dark the chambers were. "I'm intruding," he said, mischief in his voice.

"Not at all," Marcus countered with a smile. At a Roman-style sideboard, he poured three goblets full of strong wine from a tall ewer while he watched Claerwen light more lamps. Though calm, her face masked worry.

"I reckoned you would have no taste for the reveling after the ceremony," Ceredig said. He took a goblet and drank.

"You cared not to stay yourself?" Marcus matched his long swallow.

"No. Not this time." A faint frown ruffled Ceredig's brow.

"Something is wrong?"

Ceredig nodded. "A message…from my son."

"Trouble?"

"Irish…again. I'm leaving at first light."

"Ah well, if it's not the bloody neighbors, it's the Irish."

Ceredig downed another mouthful. "Aye, I think it's time I gave them a bit more than they're accustomed to."

"You need a bigger pair of boots than normal to kick their collective arses?" Marcus grinned and caught Claerwen glancing at him. She looked away, paused, then gazed at him longer, surprise in her eyes.

Ceredig laughed. "You've got a pair like that with you? Ach, we've been preparing for this for some time. Now's when we'll act on it. I have one request of you."

"Name it."

"Uther's called for a high council meeting on the morrow. Wants all the kings there. Probably to discuss Gorlois, as if that would mean anything by now. Can you stand for me?"

Marcus stalled, his jaw clenched involuntarily. He felt Claerwen watching.

"I know what you think of council meetings," Ceredig said. "You can say 'no' if you want."

Marcus glanced at the drapes that led to the bedchamber and the effigy. Would it be a curse if he and Claerwen stayed? Or opportunity? Perilous either way. He downed the last of his wine. "'Tis fine enough, but I have no rank to vote."

"Not a necessity, Marcus. I merely want your ears there. I would trust no one else."

"So be it then. I'll send a report as soon as I can. In the usual manner?"

Ceredig eyed him. "You're certain? I'll understand if you can't do it. If something else is in the offing...?"

Marcus held his gaze steadily and nodded his assurance.

"Well enough." Ceredig drained the rest of his drink. "I will tell Uther's seneschal. Apologies for the interruption, lass." He half-bowed to Claerwen, winked, clapped Marcus on the shoulder, and strode for the door.

With the latch clicked into place, Marcus bolted the door again and returned to the inner chamber. Claerwen moved towards him. "Come," he said before she could speak. He took up the lamp again and lit the way into the bedchamber.

He set the lamp next to the pitcher and withdrew the effigy from the cloak. Without curling his fingers around it, he held it flat across his palms, as if to touch it more than necessary would leave evil on his skin.

Claerwen's eyes snapped up. Their paleness glimmered eerily in the lamplight.

"It's a warning," he said.

Her blanching, disbelieving face asked from whom.

He pulled out the dagger and twisted it slowly under the light. Decorative lines etched into the blade, a common practice Saxons used to identify a weapon's owner, showed dimly.

"Octa?" she breathed the Saxon leader's name.

"Aye, it has all the signs."

"But he's in prison. How could he—"

"Prison means nothing," Marcus cut her off. "Guards are too easily bribed. Even the high king's."

The image of the effigy's deliverer came to him again. The man was an assassin—Marcus was sure of it—not a mere messenger. All the markings were there, the cold hatred, the meanness. He suspected the words that had been spoken were akin to a Saxon war oath, but the amount of malevolence in them put them far beyond that. In truth, their vehemence sounded like personal hatred rather than part of an assigned task. But why had the man not attempted to kill? The opportunity had been perfect.

"A man about my height and weight," he said, "with reddish-brown hair, left it where I would find it. I gave chase, but I lost him.

It was inevitable Octa would have spies within the court looking to identify me." He willed the image to fade from his mind.

"But Octa already knows what you look like, who you are, what you are. You were in one of his camps only a few months ago, the one you sabotaged. Revenge, I would understand. But why a warning? Why here? Why now?"

Marcus wondered that himself. For years Octa had been pressing more aggressively towards a full-scale challenge against Britain's high kingship, first under his father Hengist, now dead, and since then with his kinsman Eosa. Originally from Jutland, and like his father, Octa had become an effective leader of the Saxon, Angle and Jute immigrants the native Britons collectively—and derisively—called Saxons. But as to why a warning, and in such an odd manner, he could not answer.

He watched her stare at the cloth strip. She knew the letters and could read because he had taught her since their marriage, but she did not understand Latin. He pointed at the last group of letters. "I don't know this word. The rest is not quite written correctly, but I think it says, 'Death to you. Two sons of the north or two of the White Dragon. Your choice. Beware...Excalibur.'"

Confused, she mouthed the last word and imitated his pronunciation. "'Two sons of the White Dragon' are obviously Octa and Eosa. But who are the two sons of the north?"

Marcus laid the effigy on the table, closed his eyes and fingered a torque at his throat. The heavy, twisted gold neck ring signified his status as a prince. He wished he were anything but a nobleman, regardless of how minor, and had not been required to come to Winchester.

"What aren't you telling me, Marcus?"

He opened his eyes again. His Claerwen, strong-willed, capable, and full of unwavering faith in him. How an implacable, hard-headed loner like him deserved her calm patience, he had never been able to reckon. She was staring at the grotesque figure, oddly fascinated, and still trying to decipher the Latin. She reached towards it then withdrew her fingers before touching it.

"We are targets, Claeri. Both of us—equally this time." He seized the effigy and stuffed it into the bottom of one of their leather traveling pouches that sat on the floor under the table.

"Ceredig can't leave Winchester," she said. "I just remembered. The gates are locked. He said so. Uther is trying to keep Gorlois from leaving. That means the man who left that—he couldn't have escaped."

"The order was rescinded," Marcus said. "Gorlois left before Uther gave it. The king misjudged how quickly he could move. Regardless, the man I followed could still be hidden here, somewhere."

"That's why you took me onto the dais?"

"I couldn't leave you out there. If he *is* still here, you could have been snatched out of the crowd...or worse. By being with me, over all the days we've been here, you've been publicly identified as well as I have."

He held her gaze. He knew that to apologize for drawing her into his realm of intrigue would only bring a response of self-sacrificing humility. They had followed that path many times, for many years. She had never once expressed doubt or regret for remaining with him.

The silence that followed grew oppressive. He turned to retrieve the sword and hang it from a decorative finial on the bedstead. The cloak he tossed onto a chair.

"It's not even Octa that worries you, is it?" Claerwen asked, her voice barely above a whisper. "It was that man you chased. I saw your face when you described him. It matched the way you looked when you came to the courtyard. Who is he?"

He could not answer, even if he knew. Control, he prodded himself. Shackle the memories and let the past be forgotten in the darkness of forever.

She moved close. The scent of lavender drifted from her, and when he felt her hand on his face, he met her green-blue eyes. By the light... She was beautiful. Her classic features refined from a thousand generations of Celtic ancestors put the finest marble statues of Roman goddesses to utter shame. He lifted a handful of her hair and caressed it between his fingers. Suddenly he smiled.

Her voice softened but she persisted, "You're trying to protect me."

"Always," he said and slid a hand along her neck, up into her hair.

"What happened? What aren't you telling—?"

His mouth found hers. He circled his other hand around behind her and pulled her close. Her drive to ask questions dissolved and she curved into him, her arms tight around him. She gave in to his long, crave-filled kisses.

Only then did his tension begin to unknot. He drew on that beginning; the feel of her hands on him and her warmth pressed against him overwhelmed his dark side. Only Claerwen ever brought him the peace he needed, the freedom from his memories. No one else ever could. Clasped together, he moved with her towards the bed. His last thought before his mind emptied was a prayer to all the gods that he would never lose her.

CHAPTER 3

Winchester
Spring, AD 471

"THIS is an insult!"

The high king's voice tore across the courtyard from the great hall's open doors and shattered the cool morning quiet. Its loudness was not what carried so well but the intensity of its discord. A definitive silence followed.

On the hall's front steps with Claerwen, Marcus listened, grimaced, and studied the yard from one side to the other. Except for slaves few people were about after the late night of dancing, music and drinking that had followed the homage ceremony. The overcast sky made the buildings and yard, even the people, look grey and cold.

"Do you see the strange man?" Claerwen whispered.

"No, but he could be disguised. Have care." Marcus squinted disapproval at the row of small arched windows to the left of the hall's front doors. Through the milky glass, he discerned the nobles' movements, their outlines defined by the light of torches behind them. Their voices began to rise in reply to Uther's complaint, their gestures full of anger and frustration.

"Come." Marcus twined his fingers around Claerwen's hand.

They strode up the steps and entered. Inside on the right, a few early-rising people looked for a morning meal and new gossip. On the left, an area had been partitioned with wicker screens to separate the council from the rest of the hall. Several heavily armed guards stood in a row along the partitions. Uther's seneschal, backed with more guards, directed all who entered.

Marcus disarmed in accordance with the rules of courtesy that had been strictly enforced throughout the coronation festivities—with the exception of the homage ceremony. Duly noted, his sword and the large dagger he kept in the back of his belt were placed with those of the other noblemen. Then, after giving a mild admonishment for being tardy, the seneschal waved him and Claerwen towards a gap in the screens.

They slipped into the space. Extra torches ringed it, needed in the hall's smoky gloom. Trestle tables were set up, two facing each other, a third across the nearer end. The noblemen sat around the outer sides. A pair of half-grown boys circuited with trays of drinks, serving and refilling cups.

Additional benches stood against the walls. Intentionally late, Marcus chose one in a corner made by the wall towards the courtyard and one of the screens. He sank onto it with Claerwen. The voices continued without interruption. Only Uther, seated alone behind a fourth, smaller table on the opposite side, had noticed their entrance. His glaring eyes stopped, narrowed, then swung back to the other attendees.

"You must reconcile, I tell you," insisted Cadell Gleaming Hilt of the kingdom of Powys. He poked a thick finger at the plank tabletop in front of him.

"I will reconcile only if Gorlois returns and swears fealty."

"This is madness, Uther." The king of Linnius stood. "The Saxons have overrun my lands for years. You know this. It's getting worse again. I shouldn't even be here. I should be home and fighting. Can't you see we need Gorlois?"

"Can't you understand he *must* fulfill his duty?" the king said.

The entire body of men groaned. Linnius's ruler sat down again.

"He's not even Cornwall's king, not even a prince!" Aergol Lawhir of Dyfed pointed out.

"Aye, only a distant relation to my brother," Erbin of Dumnonia, older brother to Cornwall's king, confirmed. "Why is he so important?"

Uther scratched the ears of a wolfhound lying next to his feet. The dog yawned, stretched and rolled onto its side, obviously in enjoyment of the warm floor heated by the Roman-built hypocaust below. The king's scowl eased, and Marcus thought it revealed Uther's wish to be as unconcerned as the hound.

The king withdrew his hand, the scowl returned. "Wouldn't you say my highest ranking military commander should be among the *most* loyal?" he asked.

Marcus leaned on the wall, his arms folded over his chest. The council was proceeding as he expected. He counted eight-and-twenty kings or princes. A few minor nobles, such as he. No queens, but two princesses, probably daughters brought to bargain for political marriages. While he reckoned who was present, he knew Uther had already done the same and had especially noted absentees. No Pictish ruler was there. Neither was the king of Rheged, though that was to be expected. Gwrast had been sickly for years. But of his two sons, Meirchion and Masguid, one should have stood in his stead. Neither had come.

Marcus frowned and leaned forward, elbows on his knees. By ancient custom, Rheged would be split between the sons upon its king's death, a long-anticipated event. Masguid, the younger son, was to inherit the southeastern region called Elmet. The elder son, Meirchion, would receive the rest of the kingdom. Though Elmet was much smaller, its lands were more valuable for the cattle and crops it could produce.

Two sons... Of the north... The warning echoed in Marcus's mind, and he started to calculate. Rheged was a kingdom of the north. But so was Ebrauc. King Mor had two sons as well. Marcus swept his gaze across the assemblage. Mor was there and grumbling his displeasure along with the others. Ebrauc was powerful, nearly as powerful as Rheged. But Mor's two sons were not so wont to be at each other's throats. Ebrauc lay on the eastern coast and was easier for landing Saxons to breach. Rheged had a longer coastline, but lay to the west in a much less likely landing site. But if Octa looked for an internal weakness, Rheged had it.

Marcus knew that weakness all too well. Meirchion and his brother had squabbled over their territories for most of their adult lives, even though their father still had firm control of both regions. Five years earlier, Meirchion had plotted an uprising in Elmet, an attempt to oust, perhaps even kill, his brother. At their father's request, Marcus had secretly sabotaged the scheme and preserved Rheged's unity. The animosity between the siblings continued, he was certain, a viable reason for their absence. In truth, given Meirchion's devious behavior, Marcus had expected the prince to one day have his ailing father assassinated.

But why, he wondered, if Octa had his eye set on Rheged, why would he send a warning? Other than being a trap, it made no sense.

Marcus cast a sideways look at Claerwen. Her blank expression masked the interest in her eyes; they darted from one arguer to the next. Then they stopped and stared across the room. A slight frown ruffled her brows.

He saw her gaze had landed on Myrddin. The prince had slipped in with little notice from the opposite side and was moving slowly along the wall. He came to a halt in an empty corner, arms folded, face indecipherable.

Marcus leaned back again. Baffled that the high king would so completely defy all his under-kings for another of his short-lived pursuits, he also found Myrddin strangely quiet. The prince showed neither support nor criticism of his uncle. Likewise, no one had the nerve to simply say the truth, that the problem lay with Uther's lust for one particular woman. Yet it was one of the few times those kings were actually united—and strongly. A faint sardonic smile crept onto Marcus's face. In the moment the crisis would be resolved, the nobles would return to their bickering as if nothing had happened. The irony and insipid hypocrisy astounded him.

The argument went on like a slowly played board game. The room grew stifling, not from heat but from the choking stubbornness, as thick as the smoke rising from the torches. From the way their talk had descended into a deadlock, Marcus suspected—and hoped—the meeting would end soon.

It didn't.

Disgusted, bored, he dug a fingernail between two laths of wicker in the screen next to him and peered through. Still late morning, he gauged from the dim shadows on the hall's tessellated floor. The two serving slaves were on their way back with another round of refreshments. Except for the guards, the hall had otherwise emptied again. Still no sign of the man he had chased the night before. Too public. For now, that was good. He envied Ceredig's necessity to leave, though not its purpose.

Claerwen pressed her shoulder against his. "Myrddin is coming," she whispered.

Marcus grunted. When he pulled away from the screen, he found one of the boys offering a cup of wine. Not interested, he waved the boy on.

The Enchanter took a seat on the other side of Claerwen. To Marcus, he seemed locked within himself, as if he needed to devote all his concentration to maintain an aloof demeanor. To ask his opinion on the depth of trouble Uther's insistence would cause in the long run, Marcus would have liked, but he sensed no answer would be forthcoming.

The king's voice drew his attention again. Uther was loudly proposing Gorlois be forcibly brought back to Winchester. He received little support. Half of the nobles called for him to leave the man alone. Others advised to give the commander more time to regain his temper; perhaps he would change his mind and return on his own. The animosity clung in the air so thickly Marcus was sure it could be scraped up like chunks of cold, rancid grease.

Then Uther stood and pressed his fists, knuckles downward, on the table. His face darkened. "Yesterday," he said, "I sent a courier after Gorlois with a demand for his return. The message reached him before he got more than fifty miles away. He ignored it. I've sent another demand, by a relay of couriers, day and night, to his stronghold at Tintagel. The answer will arrive tonight—"

"What good is this? We need you to fight Saxons, not one of our own!" Cadell of Powys interrupted.

Uther grappled with his temper. "If Gorlois ignores it again, I will send one more demand. Only one. If that is refused, I march, with or without you. That is my last concession." His fist pounded the table.

Intent on the exchange, Marcus felt Claerwen start. She nearly spilled a cup of wine she was holding, and he realized he had missed when she took the drink from the slave. Apparently no longer interested in it, she set it on the floor.

Uther's face remained cold and unmoving, his eyes now locked on Myrddin in a clear test of his nephew's loyalty. "This council will reconvene tonight when the answer is received," the king finished. In a swirl of robes, he disappeared through a door behind him.

Seconds later, the nobles boiled out from the meeting in a flurry of crude remarks.

Myrddin, silent all this time, turned his thin, pale face to Claerwen, nodded towards the empty tables. "Some things," he said, "must be as they must be, no differently in Tintagel than in Caer Luguvalos."

Marcus shifted on the bench and stared at him.

The Enchanter smiled briefly and pushed aside his grey-streaked brown hair. Then, as if summoned, he rose and followed the king out.

Another mark on the hour candle dissolved into a pool on the table. Marcus frowned alternately between the flame and the effigy. Next to the candle, the crude figure appeared as dead as Octa wanted him to be. The two black ink dots meant for eyes stared at the ceiling.

He turned Octa's dagger slowly around in his fingers and read the Latin words on the cloth for what seemed like the hundredth time.

"Caer Luguvalos..." he muttered and slouched back in the chair again. Once a major Roman fortress called Luguvalium, Caer Luguvalos lay along Hadrian's Wall—in Rheged's lands. So, Myrddin and Uther were concerned with Rheged's missing nobles as well, enough that Myrddin saw fit to put a voice to it.

He let his head drop back and gazed upward into the darkness. The quiet was exquisite, even if it was the result of the court's sullen mood. He thought of Claerwen, napping in the bedchamber. He wanted to share his speculations with her about the sons of Rheged, but he thought he should wait until he could make a more conclusive connection between them and Octa's warning. And after his reaction to the effigy had unnerved her, he did not want to stir up more questions. He was in control now, and though she was still giving him puzzled looks, she seemed to have accepted his bizarre mood as only temporary.

He rose and began to pace, the rhythm of steps an aid to regulate his pondering. Two sons of the White Dragon—obviously Octa and his kinsman Eosa—as Claerwen had said. Imprisoned in Caer Lundein. Marcus shook his head. Uther never took prisoners. Prisons were too easily breached, guards too easily bribed. And hard-arsed warriors like Octa neither understood nor cared a spit in the way of negotiation or punishment. Only the sharp end of a sword. Perhaps Uther had another use for them and they were in truth hostages. That made more sense.

Knocking rattled the doors. News, Marcus hoped. He swept the effigy back into the pouch and tossed it under the sideboard, beyond the candle's globe of light.

At the door he met Uther's steady blue-eyed gaze. Must be more than news, he thought. He backed and led the king inside.

Seated in the central room, Uther quietly scanned the dark space. Marcus lit a pair of oil lamps then brought goblets and wine to the table.

"My wife's resting," Marcus said. His mouth pressed halfway into a smile. He and Claerwen had secretly infiltrated Winchester the previous year. The king had become infatuated with Claerwen—until he learned her true identity. Marcus handed a full goblet to Uther.

The king nodded wearily. "I have need of your bluntness," he said and leaned his elbows on his knees, the goblet clapped between his palms. He watched the wine's surface swirl.

Marcus waited.

Uther looked up. "Am I doing right?"

Marcus dragged another chair across and sat where he could assess Uther's face. He found no ploy, only a man needing plain talk. "I kept silent this morning because I have no voice in the matter," he said.

"You came to listen for Ceredig, the most powerful man in the north. He probably has more power than I do, or more than I am supposed to have. And he chooses you to stand for him because you will tell him the truth like no one else will. What say you, Marcus ap

Iorwerth? Am I doing right?"

"Politically? You *should* reconcile with Gorlois. Without him you could lose control of the war bands, and if you do, you will lose all of Britain as well. I don't think you're ignorant that they follow Gorlois because of his connection to your brother. By breaking trust with Gorlois, you break trust with them as well."

"I have no desire to compete for popularity."

"Popularity?" Marcus snorted. "Men follow those they find capable and admirable. It's their nature. Ambrosius earned that, and you can as well, but a leader, any leader, must have a certain portion of charisma. It's in you, Uther, but sometimes it's lost beneath a lot of bluff and insult and too little temper."

The king scowled at the words. "Ambrosius was good with the soldiers. Even those who were trouble. I suppose there will always be those. As were those missing from the homage ceremony. Do you know why?"

"I never would expect any of the Picts to come," Marcus speculated. "Those close to the Saxon Shore, the same. You're thinking of Rheged."

"You noticed?"

"Myrddin made mention as well…" Marcus twisted his hand in a questioning gesture.

"Rumors," the king sighed.

"Anything specific?"

"Only guesses. The truth is elusive. And I like it not."

Marcus thought of Meirchion's past duplicity and gave a wry smile. "Aye, midden heaps of lies and stupidity and ignorance have been accumulating for more years than you would ever want to know. You will have need to thrash your way through it all to find even the first grain of truth."

"And it's in every one of those kingdoms out there," Uther said, sarcasm in his tone.

Marcus met the sarcasm with a bitter smile. "You'll need to play both the military and political sides, and play them well and hard. Ambrosius never had the chance to engage the political side—he died too soon. You've got the chance now, but not the way you've begun with Gorlois."

Again the scowl. "I asked you before to be a military commander or a councilor for me."

"And I will refuse again, should you ask, because I'm a spy, nothing more, nothing less. My work will continue—when and where it's needed. It's how I'm most useful."

The king grimaced at his wine.

"You did ask for bluntness," Marcus reminded him.

A sad smile crossed Uther's face then he gulped down the entire contents of the goblet. Marcus matched him; they poured again.

The king slowly rocked his head back and forth. "Aye, I asked. And you and your wife saved my life. I have no right to ask anything of you." Then his eyes came up again, their blueness vivid. "What of the reasons that are not political? Am I doing right?"

"You have doubts?"

"My doubts are not about the woman."

Marcus straightened on his chair. Here was the king's true reason for coming. "Tell me."

Uther drained his goblet halfway. Again he leaned on his knees. He tipped his head towards the drapes Claerwen slept behind. "I've seen how you care for her," he said. "Quiet, intense, like no one I've ever seen. And she returns it in kind." The king's teeth clenched and unclenched, like he needed to grind his thoughts into shape enough to speak.

"And it is so between you and…the lady?" Marcus finished for him.

Eyes closed, Uther winced. "Am I imagining this? Am I merely wishing—"

"She is married," Marcus interrupted.

The king grunted. "To a man I've made my worst enemy. Even if she were not married, what kind of life could I offer her? I'm no more than a glorified warrior, no better than Gorlois."

Marcus drank deeply. He sensed Uther's eager anticipation of a response and indulged in a few moments of thought before looking up from his wine. He gave a grin of self-deprecation. "The only thing worse than a warrior is a spy," he said.

Uther's mouth twisted, not quite into a smile. He waited patiently for more.

Marcus tilted his head towards the drapes. "From the first time I saw her, I told her I am a dangerous man, too dangerous for her to become entangled with. Over and over, I told her that. Then I walked away."

"But…?"

"She had been contracted to marry a military commander in the north. I discovered he was involved in importing Saxon mercenaries for Vortigern. I discredited him, which also broke the contract. At the same time she fled before she knew what I had done. I didn't pursue her. But four years later, out of revenge, that man took her captive. I saw it happen and was barely able to get her away from him before he harmed her worse than he'd already had. I hid her in a safe place with the hope she would make her own way in time. I tried so bloody hard to stay away."

"And you couldn't."

Marcus shook his head. "Myrddin has a saying, something about placing yourself into the path of the gods."

"Ah, I've heard that." Uther smiled. "A lot, lately. He talks too much in riddles."

Marcus grinned at the reference to riddles, the exact word he associated with most anything regarding Myrddin—and the gift of fire in the head. He wondered if the Enchanter had seen something in the fire that had prompted the strange remark that morning. He glanced again towards the bedchamber. Claerwen had the same gift—or curse.

"Myrddin's riddles," Marcus said. "The path of gods. Neither makes a decision easier."

Quiet settled between the men. Minutes later, a ram's horn called from the palace gates.

Uther looked up. "The courier has arrived. I told them to bring the answer to me here."

The bedchamber door opened, and the curtain before it moved. Blinking, Claerwen stood between the drapes. "I heard the…" she started then dipped in a curtsey.

The guard knocked. Uther rose and waved away all formalities, then Myrddin was announced. With the courier's parchment in his bony hand, the Enchanter entered and passed it to the king.

Uther broke the document's seal. His eyes raked over the parchment, but his grim face remained unchanged. Wordless, he turned it around.

"Oh," Claerwen said and looked at Marcus.

"Shit high, wide and proud," he read. "Well, that's descriptive."

When Myrddin added no comment, Uther rolled the parchment together. "How is the dog?" he growled at his nephew.

"It will recover."

"Fine enough. See it's taken care of, will you? That wolfhound is worth more than clumsy slaves." He thrust the parchment at Myrddin, its middle crushed, and turned for the outer doors.

"Dog drank something spilled on the floor over there," he said to Marcus. "Made it sick. I will leave immediately—"

"The council is waiting to meet again," Myrddin protested, following, Marcus close behind.

"Cancel it," Uther said. "I know. I said I would send one more summons. I will, but this I deliver myself." The doors slammed shut after him.

In the unlit anteroom, Myrddin stood motionless at the closed doors. Behind him, Marcus sensed a mood of satisfaction. He folded his arms. "So, is he bringing back a woman for you as well or have you got a frog stuck up your back?"

Myrddin turned, restrained annoyance on his face. Marcus grinned. The annoyance deepened and Myrddin brushed past, headed back for the inner room.

Marcus caught his arm. "He's had his personal war band ready to march since this morning, waiting for that answer. What are you planning with him?"

"You already know what he wants." The reply was smooth, unconcerned.

"Your reaction to that," Marcus tapped the rolled message, "was too vague. There is more. With you there is *always* more. What are you planning?"

Furniture in the common room scraped the floor harshly. Marcus spun around. Through a narrow gap in the drapes, he saw Claerwen sit down hard on the chair Uther had vacated. He slapped aside the curtains, and in a few strides he was kneeling at her side.

"What is it, Claeri?" He touched her forehead for fever, but she was cold, and her hands shook when he took them in his own.

Myrddin dropped onto his knees on her other side and peered into her face. "What did you see?"

Frowning, Marcus stared into Claerwen's eyes. He saw no evidence of fire in the head, no sign of the barely visible glow that lingered as it departed or the headache that always followed. Rather, she looked ill, as if she had eaten tainted food. "Are you sure it's the fire?" he asked Myrddin.

The Enchanter nodded. "Can you remember any of it?" he asked her.

Her eyes came up, first to him, then to Marcus. She shook her head.

"Nothing at all?" Myrddin tried again.

She held Marcus's gaze, shook her head once more. "I'll be fine enough. I just want to lie down." She squeezed his hand.

That was a warning.

"Please, I just need to lie down. I'll be fine enough." Her eyes, full of bewilderment, moved to Myrddin's face. Reluctantly, he rose, bid goodnight, and departed.

"Are you—?" Marcus started.

She slid off the seat onto her knees and embraced him. "I'm not sick," she spoke closely. "It *was* a vision."

He took her face between his hands. "Why didn't you want to confide in him?"

"Because I want to know first if it has to do with the warning, the effigy."

He frowned, his head cocked.

She sat back on her heels. "It was only for an instant. The image of a single stone—one of the sacred ones. And something about water. Like a…pond, a lake, perhaps. I can't say where it is, but the land looked vaguely familiar."

"A standing stone you've seen, like a *menhir*?"

"No, not a tall stone. It was strange. You've seen some of the ancient stones are short and thick? It was like that, but it distinctly looked like an anvil."

"Because I'm a blacksmith?"

"I don't know...but, I think, and I'm not sure why, I think it's somewhere in the north." Her face took on a questioning slant.

"What are you thinking?"

"I'm wondering," she whispered, "is it related to the prophecy?"

"Myrddin's prophecy?"

She nodded.

Marcus pulled on his moustache. Did it make sense? A vision, possibly of the north. A warning, definitely of the north. Connected to a prophecy Myrddin had made years before? The prophecy of a great king to come, one who would create a golden reign, a man who would at last have enough strength, charisma and perseverance to unite Britain's factions and drive out the ever-encroaching Saxons? The king's name had been revealed in some of Claerwen's visions, and though she had never prophesied in the way Myrddin had, she was certain that one day the name "Arthur" would be as familiar as each day's rising mist and remain so into the distant future. But Marcus could not tie the threads together with logic. He wondered, was this a time when a matter of faith was needed instead?

Claerwen's face was so pale that he touched her cheek. Her skin was warm now, but she still shook. "Did you drink from that cup in the hall?"

Her arched brows dipped downward. "No. Why?"

"The sick dog Uther was concerned for—it may have drunk from that cup. You put it on the floor. It could have easily overturned."

"Poison?"

He smoothed his moustache again and nodded slowly.

"The slave was rather insistent I take that cup," she said then gripped his arm. "He handed it to me, instead of letting me choose. You suspect the man you chased is still here, and he bribed the boy to bring that drink to me?"

Marcus's eyes narrowed. "If so...if that drink made the dog sick but not enough to kill it, then he might have wanted to make you sick, perhaps to make you stay in these chambers for a while."

"Expecting you to go out alone?" Her mouth dropped open. She drew away and rose, picked up the goblet Marcus had left on the table. It was still half full. She lifted it to her lips, wrinkled her nose at it, then abruptly set it down again with a smack. "Does he wear a tan cloak?"

Marcus rose, his eyes sharpened. "You saw him? When?"

"Late in the afternoon. I heard birds squawking outside the window, like they do when they defend their nests. So I went to look. They were diving at a man in the courtyard. He was staring up at the window, and he wore a ratty tan cloak, almost like a monk's robes, so broad and draped about him. I didn't see his hair—the hood was up. But his *face*…"

"Could you see him well enough to describe him?"

"He was a little far away, but I could see his eyes were deep-set, dark. Brows that slant downward in the middle, like yours, only straight instead of bent, and thinner. A long, straight nose, broad at the bottom. His face might have been rugged once, but it's gotten a bit saggy. He had several days of beard, I couldn't tell the color."

"Could you see if he wore something around his neck? Like a rock on a cord?"

Claerwen's eyes pinched as if peering into the past. "A rock? I don't remember seeing… But he had his hand like this." She pressed a fist against the base of her throat. "It was his expression, Marcus. He was so hard, so filled with stone-cold hatred. Like life meant nothing to him."

"Like a wolf," Marcus said, his lip curled bitterly. "I'd wager he was looking to know if you had taken that drink."

"Do we stay and learn who he is, why he's here? Or would it be better to slip away and avoid him?"

Marcus opened his mouth to answer but held onto his thought. She had said "we," and he knew she truly meant it no other way. They had grown accustomed to working together and trusted their lives to one another, and even with no other choice open to her—now she had to remain under his personal protection—she fully intended to help him. By the light, he marveled, the woman had courage. He felt a smile creep into his eyes, partly of joy, partly of calculation. He let the smile fill his face. "We're going to do both."

CHAPTER 4

Winchester
Spring, AD 471

"ARE you sure of this?" The question escaped Claerwen involuntarily.

Torchlight streaked through gaps in what was once the floor of the palace's bathhouse. Barely able to see Marcus, she could not believe he was dunking his face in a mud puddle.

He straightened up, dripping, and spit away drops that fell from his moustache, then spread the cold, liquid mud through the full length of his hair.

"You *are* mad," Claerwen whispered.

"Absolutely," he said, his teeth oddly white against the darkness of his face. "Once this dries, it'll look like bare tree branches in winter. Are you ready?"

"I hope this holds together." She reviewed her frayed and filthy gown, the two equally forlorn undershifts beneath it, the piece of thin rope that served as a belt, and the scrap of moth-eaten wool that was meant to be a cloak. All had been mysteriously collected through Marcus's efforts over the day and night since Uther's departure, as well as the clothing he wore now that matched hers in grubbiness. Her hair, in a disheveled braid, and her face, were about half as mud-smudged as he was. She nodded.

"One more thing." He pulled a metal flask from a rip in his tunic, took out the stopper and passed it to her. "Careful, it's strong."

Claerwen saw mischief in his eyes. "What is it?"

"Just drink a little."

She shook the flask. Only a small amount was left. She sipped and returned it.

He was waiting for her reaction. She frowned and realized his eyes were mildly out of focus, then…

"What *is* this?" She gagged for air, tears in her eyes.

Marcus grinned. "The Irish, according to Ceredig, call it *uisge beatha*. It's made a different way than wine—makes it stronger. Always has some of it around and left this for me. Bloody good, no?" He upturned the flask and drank the last of it.

She grimaced at the burning taste in her mouth and felt like sulfurous fumes were rising in her head and about to make it explode. If the flask had been full and Marcus had drunk most of it… She gazed at him. He had always liked to drink—and a bit too much—but with this, how could he do what they had planned?

He hid the flask inside his tunic. "Remember," he said. "Keep at this all the way out, or they'll find an excuse to make slaves of us. Shout, sing, argue, anything you want, just make it look real. Ready?"

She nodded. He seemed in control, though he spoke a little slower than usual…

He suddenly crawled to a ragged split in a wall that opened onto the long-empty pools. Claerwen followed. At the opening he pointed out the positions of each guard behind the palace and picked the one he wanted to approach.

She thought she had been prepared, but when he lifted her up the pool's side and rolled her onto the level ground, she felt as if she had been dropped into a vat of cold water.

Marcus vaulted up beside her. "Hoo, if I were the high king, now, wouldn't you know." His voice was loud, slurring, and imitated the local peasants' accent. "I'd see that this is mended."

Momentarily stunned, Claerwen stared up at him then lurched onto her feet. "I don't think there'll be too much mendin' of this," she returned the tease in the same style of speech. "And if you were of his high king and lordships himself, you'd be too busy runnin' after a hundred women. Maybe more."

The guard glared at them. "You! What is your business here?"

Marcus ignored him and draped an arm around Claerwen's

shoulders. "And how would you know, woman? Has he been after you?"

She stumbled against him. "Oh, an' wouldn't you like to know now, wouldn't you?"

"Halt where you are!" The soldier approached with his spear lowered. Two other men followed, several paces behind and to each side.

"Eee!" Claerwen squealed and playfully pushed Marcus. "See? Now the king should be more alert or he'll lose his opportunity."

"Oh, opportunity, eh? With you?" He slipped on a patch of loose stones and muddy ground.

"That's enough from you two!" The guard halted a half-dozen paces from them. Marcus continued to ignore him. Annoyed, the man flipped up the spear and advanced. He grabbed the front of Marcus's tunic and pulled him away from Claerwen. "Ach, man, you stink like an ale barrel. Both of you. What are you doing here?"

"We're a-visitin' the high king, wha'd'ya think?" Marcus howled proudly.

Claerwen dropped to her knees and giggled. She swayed as if on the verge of passing out.

"Quit yapping like a pup," the guard complained to her. He turned Marcus around and checked for weapons. He found none but came across the empty flask and confiscated it. "Bloody thieves."

He pushed Marcus away and turned to Claerwen. "What are you hiding, mistress?"

"I'm not hiding anything," she shot back. "What are *you* hiding?" On her feet again, she backed a few steps and hunched over, ready to fight.

"I wouldn't cross her, man," Marcus warned. "She's a dangerous one."

"Keep out of this," the guard ordered. "This shouldn't be too difficult."

"Ah, but she's got a nasty kick. And she's fast. And she's not afraid. Especially when she's had a bit of the drink, believe me, you'd better be keepin' track o' your balls or she'll take 'em home for a trophy." He drew up a knee and groaned.

Claerwen fell into another round of piercing giggles.

The guard's eyes rolled. "Ach! That's enough with ye. You're not worth it." He jolted his head at the other two men. "Take 'em to the town patrol and have them thrown out of the walls. Ish, they're filthy." He shook out his hand as if permanently defiled. "Must have wriggled in through one of those breaks in the wall. Get 'em out of here. They belong with the pigs."

"Swine!" Marcus cheered.

One man took Marcus by the back of his tunic and shoved him towards a postern gate in the palace wall. The other guard tried to grip Claerwen's arm. She jerked out of his reach. With a flourish she hugged the dirty cloak around her shoulders and strutted after Marcus. At the gate they were transferred to two town patrollers.

"Ah! More swine!" Marcus laughed and started a rude song about pigs. He loped before the guards on wobbly, limp legs.

Claerwen followed him through the streets. Within a hundred paces, she turned on him. "Will you stop that infernal singing? What's so bloody funny about pigs?"

Marcus halted. "I'll sing if I want, woman!"

"Just not about pigs!"

The two patrollers looked at each other. "How did these get into the palace?" one muttered. He prodded Marcus with his foot. "Get on with ye!"

Marcus swung a fist. He missed—deliberately—and nearly fell. Instead, he stumbled into Claerwen. "Oh, beggin' your pardon, m'lady." He laughed loud enough to draw stares from the few people still awake at the late hour.

"Quiet!" the soldiers ordered.

Claerwen clung to Marcus. "You're drunk, I'd say. But, so am I."

"Ah, and a bloody fine woman you be…" he purred and hugged her.

They reached the gates at last. "Get out of here, the both of ye," one patroller shouted.

The other man reinforced the command. "And if you ever bring your filthy faces here again, ye'll be sold to the Saxons!"

"And a fine bit of manners you've never learned!" Marcus spit back over his shoulder.

His reward was a shove that propelled him into the roadway and dropped him facedown. Claerwen ran after him. The gates slammed shut, the thick barricading metal bar rammed into place on the inside. Quiet quickly settled, broken only by the song of frogs in the defense ditches that ringed the town.

Claerwen dropped onto her knees. "Are you hurt?" She pulled back Marcus's hair that had fallen over his face.

His eyes were open, but he remained motionless. "Turn me over," he whispered. "Drag me off the road if you can. Quickly."

Though not tall, he was solid and heavy for his size. To roll him over was the easy task. She gripped his wrists and strained, backing, one slow step after the next. Each scraped in the dirt but she kept on.

By the light, he was heavy. She caught her breath at the road's edge and peered down the steep embankment of the first defense ditch. The shadowy shapes lining it were mostly thick weeds and grass, though the bottom probably held brambles. She glanced up at the gatehouse ramparts. Though she could not see them, she was sure the guards watched, and she reckoned Marcus wanted them to think he had passed out. One more tug and she pulled him over the side.

Marcus's weight sent him into a skid down the slick turf. Unbalanced, Claerwen lost her hold on him and fell halfway down. She rammed into a thick rowan bush. Caught awkwardly, she struggled to right herself, but the scratchy branches pricked through her ragged clothing each time she moved.

Then she froze. The rhythmic drum of a cantering horse neared. Now she understood why he'd had her move him off the road. He must have felt the vibration in the ground.

Claerwen's skin crept. Marcus lay midway up the slope, flat and unmoving, this time on his back. The road above, broad and evenly surfaced, was the main thoroughfare out of Winchester to the west. A narrow path that led around the town next to the wall joined it near the gates. She caught her first glimpse of the horseman when he turned off the path and onto the road.

The horse passed close to the end of the ditch, and Claerwen saw the rider was a man. His face turned for an instant, almost as if he had been startled, but his features were invisible under a courier's heavy cloak. He continued westward without pause.

Claerwen stared. The beat of hooves faded quickly, their speed increasing.

"Well, that went fine enough."

She drew a sharp breath, then relief swept her. Marcus squatted just above her, a jaunty grin across his face.

"You *are* mad," she whispered.

"The only way to be." His smile broadened and he lifted her out of the rowan. But instead of setting her upright, he pushed her down into the grass. He indulged in a kiss.

With a low purr-like hum she kissed him back. Then she squeezed his arms. "Something must have happened," she said when he lifted his face from hers.

The humor in his eyes drained. "What's wrong?"

"The rider…that was Myrddin."

"Disguised as a courier? You saw his face?"

She shook her head.

"No?" His eyes pinched tighter. "Then…how? Oh…the fire again."

"He was alone," Claerwen said. "If he was following Uther—you must be right—they're planning something."

"Aye, but what?"

He took her hands and pulled her to her feet. Without another word, they climbed the embankment towards both the next ditch and escape from Winchester.

Daylight began to illuminate holes in the roof. Claerwen watched them for the occasional drop of rain she had heard during the last two hours of her vigil. Seated on the cold, damp floor, she caught sight of one and followed its silvery plunge into darkness.

She felt Marcus's head shift in her lap. Uncomfortable in his sleep, he was dreaming. Soon, full daylight would arrive, and she could wake him.

Her gaze skimmed upwards again. The roof capped a small forsaken temple from the early days of the Roman occupation. Though it had been pitch black when she and Marcus arrived in the night, they had found their way around easily enough, having been there before. The square, tower-like central chamber gradually lost its night gloom, and in the light the walls revealed chipped plaster and stains of age. A cracked font stood in the center of the floor, a puddle of filthy, leaf-filled rainwater in its basin. Decayed vegetation filled every corner and crevice.

Marcus stirred again and his breath roughened as if he had been struck in the chest. Claerwen watched his eyes fling open. He stared straight up past her, focused on some unknown and distant plane of time and space. The same unnerving cast claimed his face as it had at the homage ceremony. Was he awake? She reached a hand towards his shoulder, an offer of comfort.

He sat up before she could touch him, his fists clenched, his face bowed.

Claerwen waited. This was certainly not the first nightmare that had invaded his sleep. At home she had known him to get up in the night and go outside for cool air or drink a good amount of ale. Once she had dared to ask what he dreamed of, but he had walked away without a word. Now, they seemed to come nearly every night.

"It was that dream again, wasn't it?" She tried to muster as much compassion into her voice as she could.

He remained silent for several moments. His hands slowly loosened. "You know of them?"

Claerwen slid closer. "I've known for some time." Her voice dropped another level and she took hold of one of his hands. "I know how you try to hide them from me. They come from your imprisonment, don't they? You dream of the…torture?"

He let out his breath but said nothing and tilted back his head. His eyes turned cold. Claerwen followed his line of sight. What was he scowling at? The roof was empty, plain except for its holes, not forbidding at all, the same as the last time they had taken refuge there. Still, something had evoked the nightmare and his reaction this time was different, more volatile.

He withdrew his hand. "Gwilym will be here soon with the horses and gear," he said and rose, paced to the doorless entrance.

Glad for the growing daylight, Claerwen watched him pass through the doorway out onto the open portico that skirted the temple. She could see him study the low sloping roof there as well. The tile that covered it was broken and weed-infested and the decorative cornice over the steps missing. The surrounding forest had encroached right up to the portico.

Claerwen padded to the doorway. Marcus was listening to the sudden increase of rain tapping on leaves and the earth. Morning birds sang. There was no other sound. He moved midway down the stone steps. Head tilted back, he let the rain flowing off the roof wash the mud from his face and hair.

Claerwen followed him onto the steps. He opened his eyes and watched her pull her hair free of the ragged braid. Though the water and the early morning air were cold, she held out her hands to each side. The rain streamed over her.

Marcus caught her hand. His eyes ran over her appreciatively, down, up again.

The curves of her womanliness, she realized, showed clearly through the thin, torn garments, soaked and clinging. He seemed captivated, as if she were naked. She smiled—she was willing to be a convenient distraction that could brush aside his nightmares.

Stepping close, she kissed his palm. "There is such a sadness in you."

"Ah, Claeri," he breathed and gently pulled away. He squinted with the growing daylight and leaned a hand on one of the portico's columns, his face on his arm.

"Aching head?" she guessed.

He grunted.

"No more of that…what did you call it?"

"*Uisge beatha*. It means water of life."

"More like water of pain," she said with a hint of mischief. She wrung rain from her hair.

He turned his head.

Claerwen saw laughter start to creep up his throat. The humor worked its way through his headache and the stinging remnants of the dream until he finally gave in to it.

Grinning now, she linked her fingers in his and drew him back over the portico until he embraced her. How she savored the feel of his arms clutched around her. She squeezed him back, and his mouth came down on hers in a kiss so heated it could dissolve stone.

He backed her to the temple wall, and she knocked against its cool stones. His fingers traced down her throat and hooked into the fragile cloth of her gown and shifts. A light tug, the fabric gave. His fingertips moved down between her breasts and Claerwen shivered with pleasure. Fierce warmth rose in her, and with her hands up under his tunic, she deepened her kisses.

The plod of horses on soft ground broke the spell.

Marcus groaned. "I should have told Gwilym to come later," he said. His eyes dropped to the deep tear he had created in her clothing and he pulled away.

She glanced at the bump in his breeches. "Always thought it might be fun to tear off each other's clothes," she teased with a naughty grin. "Don't be long."

With the cloak wrapped around herself, she watched from the doorway. Shortly, their head guardsman emerged from the thick foliage, two plain but husky horses on leads with him. He rode up to the portico.

Marcus greeted him. Gwilym was obviously relieved he had been able to find the abandoned temple. Peering out from his cloak's hood, he remained mounted and returned the salute. "They're not fast, but they should have good stamina." He tipped his head at the other animals, one bay, one roan. He tied their leads to the column.

Marcus nodded. "Any trouble?"

"With your plan—all goes well. Winchester was quiet when I left. But there is news, Lord Marcus." Gwilym twisted around in his saddle and removed a sheathed sword and its baldric from behind him. "Your sword," he said.

Marcus took the baldric by the strap. He lifted an eyebrow in question.

"Octa broke from prison," Gwilym said, "as you predicted. Word came just after you left."

"It was bound to happen." Marcus buckled on the baldric. It hung the sword across his back diagonally. He reached above his right shoulder and gripped the hilt, a test that the weapon was in the right position.

"The reports say he disappeared into Ceint," Gwilym went on.

"Rumors have it he's going back to his homeland and will return…soon, but not where or when. Many boats of warriors, they say."

"Well, I'm sure no jest lies there. And the man I told you to watch for?"

Gwilym handed over a small leather pouch. Metal clinked inside it. "Daggers in that. Nothing. None of us has seen him."

"Not surprising." Marcus opened the pouch, inspected the contents, and hung it from the rear frame of the roan's saddle.

He descended the steps and walked around the animals. Each horse carried pouches filled with clothing and dried food, skins of water and wine, and an oiled-wool cloak that would also serve as bedding. He opened and closed each pouch for inspection.

"You've instructed the others of the escort to wait as long as they can and not to pack the belongings we left?"

Gwilym nodded. "There is no reason for anyone to believe you are not still in Winchester. As you instructed, I continued to set out the rumors you started that the Lady was still ill."

"Good. Go on." Marcus lifted one side of the cloak draped over the roan. Beneath, a long, narrow bundle, tied at intervals with thick leather thongs, was lashed onto the animal. In two places chains took the place of the thongs. A small, cylindrical iron lock was attached to each. He examined them closely.

Watching him, dread filled Claerwen and she sucked in her breath. Marcus glanced up, his eyes intense, the expression in them somewhere between the strange look left from the nightmare and something akin to madness. The look was already gone when he let the cloak fall back into place; apparently he was satisfied no one had tampered with the bundle.

"One man remains in the chambers," Gwilym went on, "acting as you, accepting food, drink, supposedly watching over the Lady. The guards keep their shifts at the door and are to watch for the man you described. When the ruse is no longer useful, they will pack and leave, one by one, disguised. We will all go home by different routes."

"So be it." Marcus saluted him. "Go now, and be of great care on your way. See you're not followed. May the gods watch you well."

Gwilym saluted again, pulled his mount around, and retreated into the woods.

Claerwen clutched her clothing together and started across the portico, but Marcus stopped her at the top of the steps. He waited for the hoof beats of Gwilym's horse to fade.

"Marcus—"

"Come," he interrupted.

"No… Marcus—"

"I have something to show you," he insisted. He stood on the edge of the portico and untied the flap on one of the pouches. "You know how we've used horsehair in disguises before?" He removed an object wrapped in a thin cloth and flipped the folds aside. "Glued to hang from the inside of sheepskin caps? Two of those are in there as well, one with red hair, another with dark brown. But this…is a *galerus*."

He held up a thick hank of hair, grey and excessively long—human hair—and it looked like it was still attached to a scalp. "Several years ago I came across a Roman grave in the south that had been robbed. The thief left this behind."

"A *galerus*?" She frowned.

Marcus smiled. "High-ranking Romans wore wigs, women to enhance beauty, men to hide baldness."

"This was a woman's?" Claerwen knew Roman men rarely kept long hair, but women, like anywhere else, did.

"Aye, they usually wore their hair and wigs all curled up and dressed with fancy pins. But when Christianity came into the empire, wigs fell out of favor, considered to be vain and sinful by the church."

"It's from a grave?" Though repulsed, Claerwen touched the hair. It was silky, clean, not coarse and grimy like horsehair, nor was it greasy and stiff from the goat's fat or beeswax commonly used to maintain curls. Then she saw the hair was attached to a piece of pliable leather, not a scalp. "Odd that someone would choose grey hair," she said.

"Blond and red were highly prized in those days, so I've heard." He returned the *galerus* to the pouch.

Claerwen pressed her lips together. She wondered what else he had stashed in the pouches. Obviously, he was full of plans. She lifted the cloak's hem to show the wrapped and chained bundle beneath. "I didn't even know you had brought it to Winchester."

"I had hoped it would be unnecessary…that we would simply go home. Everything has changed now."

"*Y Gwalch Haearn*?" She winced when she whispered the name.

"I very likely will need his…services."

Y Gwalch Haearn, she repeated the name in her mind. They only spoke of the ominous warrior as if he were a separate person, though Marcus had been the owner of the identity for many years. Only she and Myrddin knew he was the Iron Hawk—the elusive, unpredictable and brutal avenger whose name alone caused whispers of terror. A small number of the atrocities associated with him were true. She had seen some of them. Many more were merely rumor, but more than anything else, she dreaded when he took on the warrior's persona.

She stared at the bundle as if she could see through the wrappings to the gear inside: the thick armor-like leather tunic, breeches and tall boots, the masked helmet of formed leather. All were dyed black, meant to hide the warrior in the dark. And wrapped inside the armor rested the enormous two-handed sword, its iron pommel shaped like a hawk.

Claerwen's eyes lifted. Marcus's face was calm, steady. As a warrior and a swordmaster of the highest degree, he was a paradox, and had always called himself so. He hated to kill. It showed in the sadness she witnessed every time he was forced to take a life, either in his work as a spy or in battle. Yet when he took on the Iron Hawk's identity, he grew distant, grim, cold, as if needful of danger. She had never understood why. She dropped the cloak's edge.

Marcus eased closer. His gaze held her eyes, and he slipped his hands onto her hips. "I have one question of you. If you knew the courier last night was Myrddin, because of fire in the head, then he likely knew that you were in that ditch as well, no?"

She nodded.

"How sure are you that he will not betray us?"

"Myrddin? No. He will not. Unless the fire tells him otherwise, he only knows we escaped Winchester in secrecy. Even if he knew of our intentions, he will not betray us. I am sure of this. Marcus..."

She hesitated, then her thoughts picked up a quicker pace. She glanced again to where the gear hung beneath the cloak. He had distracted her with talk of disguises, just as she had drawn him away from his nightmares in her own way. He was shielding her, as always, not only from danger but from distress as well, and although he sometimes grew overly protective, his gift of making her feel safe had become precious to her. Safe. Even in the midst of danger, he could make her feel at ease.

A smile crossed her lips. "You've decided what comes next, haven't you?"

He nodded.

"To follow Myrddin and Uther? Or to return to Winchester, to find the man of the effigy?"

"Neither. I'm fairly sure that man's gone back to Octa. Perhaps he even helped Octa escape. No...we're going north."

"North?" She puzzled at his reasoning. "The warning mentions the north. And there were concerns about Rheged. Are they tied together? Is it reason enough?"

He turned and gazed at the horses. "As Gwilym said, the rumors are running. We know Octa's been controlling his accomplices from prison. He could be controlling the rumors as well. I would say he wants us—and that includes Uther and Myrddin—to believe we have time to wait and prepare. But what if he has *not* left Britain? It's only spring. Why would he wait until next year to invade? What if he already has his war bands aligned for a landing—now?"

"Then...you're thinking he could land somewhere in the northern kingdoms, and the warning was meant to draw you there? Into a trap?"

Marcus ran his fingers through his wet hair. "That man who delivered the effigy is probably an assassin. If he is with Octa now, I'm sure we'll meet up with him again. Aye, a trap is most certain. I'll just have to remedy that."

When he turned back to her, his eyes were intense again, this time in the way she knew he was ready to take on the challenge. And he was challenging her to accept it as well.

"You saw something in the fire, Claerwen," he said. "Something in the *north*."

Chills raced over her skin. His concise logic had snapped away, exchanged for pure faith. "It was only an image," she warned. "I don't know what it means."

"It matters not," he said. "You know to trust it, just as I've learned to trust the fire all these years." He gave a sardonic smile. "Much more than men."

Chapter 5

Caer Luguvalos, Rheged, the Northern Kingdoms
Early Summer, AD 471

"FOUR hundred and forty-three thousand paces," Marcus said. Several steps inside the timber gates of Caer Luguvalos, he halted and tossed the long ends of the Roman wig's hair back over his shoulders.

Claerwen shoved aside her cloak's hood to peer at him.

He nodded towards the Roman fort, a short distance along the road that had brought them through the town gates.

"Rheged's main stronghold," he said. "Leveled and rebuilt several times during Roman days. Not long after they left, Coel Hen seized the Northern Kingdoms, became king and made the fort Rheged's capital. You saw the smaller fort, in ruins?" He pointed over his shoulder, northward, back at the gates and the broad, richly green vale beyond.

"On the other side of the river? Up against Hadrian's Wall?"

"Auxiliary fort." Marcus studied the sprawling marketplace to the left of the road, then caught sight of an inn to the right. With one fist on the knobby top of a hand-cut walking stick and his other hand around Claerwen's elbow, he hobbled through the flow of the crowd towards the inn.

"Aye, there's a lot of paces, indeed," he said.

Claerwen matched his slow gait. "What are you talking about?"

They passed through the inn's doorway and paused to let their eyes adjust to the dark. The common room, as expected, was packed with patrons to its corners like a mattress stuffed with too much straw. Marcus shambled up to one end of a long trestle table near the hearth. He eased onto a bench.

"This has been scratching me the last bit of walking," he said as Claerwen sat next to him. He pulled off one ankle-high boot and dug a finger at the innersole of mashed sedges. At the same time, he watched the inn's keeper slip through the press of bodies in a practiced slither, fast and well balanced. The man's mouth ran at an equal pace, mostly in complaints on how tired he was, tired of demands for more of this, different of that, how people should make up their minds and be content with what they got, and that even pigs made fewer demands. One large hand gripped the handles of three pewter jugs, the other clamped the edges of five wooden cups.

He came to a halt before Marcus. "Ale, old man?"

"Four hundred and forty-three thousand paces," Marcus said with a congenial glint in his eyes aimed at the landlord. "That's how many paces the Romans calculated it took to march from Caer Lundein to Caer Luguvalos. My grandfather told me that."

The innkeeper stalled at the strange comment.

"The fifth *itinera*," Marcus went on, "the longest of the marching roads for the legions. Caer Luguvalos here, was the northern terminus, and it, along with all the other forts on Hadrian's Wall, were called entrenchments." He pulled his hand out of the boot, a tiny grain of stone underneath his fingernail. "Ah, there it is. And, aye, ale it will be, fine enough."

Marcus pulled on the boot again then slid a bit of copper next to the jug and cups the innkeeper had clunked down. He leaned to Claerwen and winked. "Four hundred and forty-three thousand paces. It's bloody long enough without a rock in your boot, even if you're only coming from where we have."

"And I was only counting days," Claerwen murmured. "A mere four-and-twenty."

The man stooped and snatched up the copper. "Are you sure you both wouldn't care for a fine stew of lamb, now?" He spoke loudly against the clank and jangle of the room.

Marcus filled the cups, a deliberate shake in his hands for the innkeeper's notice. "The ale is fine enough, landlord."

"We're lucky to have plenty of food here," he persisted. "Not like other places where there's naught but roots for digging or lichens to scratch from rocks. You're welcome to eat something." He straightened when a younger man in a dingy apron twisted his way through the crowd. "Here, nephew, take these." He passed the remaining jugs and cups to the younger man along with instructions of where they should go.

The innkeeper smoothed the few strands of brown hair left on top of his round, shiny head. "You must have come far, so it appears. I've no rooms left here today—the market you know—I could put you up in the stables. I wouldn't even ask for payment."

Marcus drank long and thirstily. "Ah, very fine indeed." He refilled the drained cup. "No need. We'll be moving on. We simply came for the market."

He had the innkeeper's curiosity hooked. The man studied the wig's cascading silver locks then glanced at Claerwen—a judgment of the seeming difference in their ages. Marcus knew she appeared a lot younger than he did even with her hair hidden beneath a kerchief. At six-and-twenty winters, his face was easy to age in a disguise; years of harsh living and long treks in all seasons had etched deep lines around his eyes and mouth. Secretly amused that Claerwen might have been mistaken for his daughter, he fingered his moustache and the beard he had been growing for nearly a month, both greyed with ash to coordinate with the wig.

"A good day for business." Marcus studied the faces he could see from his seat. A good day for gossip as well, he hoped.

"Landlord!" A man from the other end of the long table held his cup high. "More!"

"Ah, Sion, you've had more than enough already! Get home with you!" the innkeeper shouted back. "And so have most of them," he confided to Marcus. He slid onto the bench on the opposite side of the table. "Have you any news?"

That was the question Marcus wanted. Any traveler was fair prey to news-hungry townspeople, and from talk came gossip. Several heads turned. The banter subsided within a narrow radius of where he and Claerwen sat. "We have traveled from the east," he lied.

"From Ebrauc?" one man asked.

"Nay, Brynaich." He leaned closely over the table. "They worry. They say a new Saxon landing is coming. More than the usual raid."

"Ah, that's always a rumor," broke in another man standing behind Marcus. "There's no reason to believe one over the other anymore. The next raid's always bigger than the last."

"Perhaps so." Marcus nodded slowly, unperturbed by the speaker's contrariness. Apathy he had expected. "However, I saw the courier arrive. A royal courier, mind you."

"From which king?" a third man sneered.

"Why, the high king, of course. Sending word to the kings along the eastern coast, all the way to Gododdin. I saw the Pendragon seal myself."

"And how would you be allowed near enough to see the dragon seal?" the landlord questioned.

Marcus stretched up a bit straighter on his seat. "Well, you see," he deepened his voice into its full, rich resonance, "I'm a *chwedleuwr*."

The innkeeper's hazel eyes brightened. "A storyteller? From the courts of kings?" His eyes narrowed and he tipped his head in the direction of the fort. "Why aren't you up there? Why be here with the likes of us?"

"I'm merely an itinerant teller, not a court bard."

"I thought there weren't *any* storytellers left," the standing man interrupted again. He took a seat on the hearth's edge next to Marcus. "There hasn't been one here in years. Not since Hywel Gwodryd was killed. He was the king's resident bard. Did you know him?"

Hywel Gwodryd? Hywel of the Flowing Verse. The name set off alarms in Marcus's memory, but he could not place it. "No. What happened?"

"Eh," the innkeeper snorted. "Caught in the usual bickering between the two princes. Their father was so outraged he almost banished Meirchion."

"He caused the bard's death?"

The landlord shrugged. "Never could reckon out the truth of it, but the rumor was that Hywel'd learned of some nasty scheme of Meirchion's and tried to stop him. Meirchion insisted Hywel's death was an accident. Of course, no one believes that. His brother accused him outright as a murderer."

Marcus had heard whispers of a murder when he sabotaged Meirchion's uprising plot against Masguid, but he had come and gone so quickly he'd paid it no mind. He had not heard of this connection to Meirchion. Hywel Gwodryd? Why was that so familiar? Think, think.

"They said you're a storyteller!" The drunken man stumbled to the table. He thunked down next to the innkeeper on the bench, nearly upsetting it. "So tell us a story."

"Go home, Sion." The landlord tried to push the man away.

"Leave me alone, you've been talking about Hywel the bard. It's true, you know. That slow-worm Meirchion *did* kill him, I say. But I heard it was for a different reason."

"This is Meirchion's horse master," the innkeeper told Marcus. "Or he *was*, before the drink got to him. He spends more time here than anywhere else. Don't you, Sion?"

Laughter rippled around the table.

Marcus glanced at Claerwen. Her eyes darted from face to face over the rim of her cup. The talk had not gone the direction he had intended, and he wondered if she realized the scheme mentioned was the one he had aborted. He turned back to Sion. "So, tell me, what *did* you hear?"

"Oh, pay no attention to him, *chwedleuwr*," another man said.

Patient, Marcus offered his full attention to the drunken man.

Sion, encouraged, leaned forward. "Well, you know Hwyel and the king were good friends, like brothers. I saw it myself, as horse-master. When Meirchion was getting himself in too deep with some of his bad bargainings a few years back, Gwrast had to find a way to stop it. The whole of Rheged would have been up in war because of Meirchion's plots against Masguid. And it's going to be the same again, I swear it."

He sloshed down a mouthful of ale.

"Well, go on, now that you've started," the man sitting on the fire pit stones urged.

Sion obliged. "Gwrast wouldn't take sides. He's too smart to goad his own sons. So he hired someone—don't know who it was—

to ruin the prince's plans. Trouble was, Hywel found out who this man was and tried to meet with him, but not…not for…" He drifted off, his next thought forgotten.

Stunned, Marcus again searched his memory for a connection to Hywel's name. He could not gauge how much the drink had skewed Sion's memory and waited for him to gather his thoughts.

"And Meirchion stopped Hywel…?" the innkeeper prompted.

"Mphmm." Sion stared into his cup, now empty.

"Would you know why Hywel wanted to talk to this man?" Marcus asked.

Sion looked up, his eyes half-crossed. "I have not the slightest notion." He leaned heavily on his elbows, hiccuped, and slurred, "You should go to the fort and give the king a couple of stories. He'd like that…after all these years…" Sion's elbows slid apart, and he drifted forward until his head lay on the table. His empty cup tipped over and rolled towards the innkeeper like a riderless horse coming home to its barn. Loud snoring erupted from him.

Laughter broke out again. "Old Gwrast Ledlwm may have tottered on the edge of life since time out of mind," the man on the hearth said, "but his iron fist has never failed him. If his sons had half as much sense…well, then Rheged would not always be on the edge of splitting. It's true, there will be trouble again, soon, and not necessarily from Saxons."

"Bickering seems to be the brothers' favored sport of late," someone muttered.

"Of late?" the landlord scoffed. "Those two princes won't end until they're both dead." He turned to Marcus. "So…do you agree this new raid is going to be a bit more than the usual?"

Marcus's eyes leveled with the innkeeper's. "Traveling through parts of Brynaich, we noted the foreign settlements have spread out even more since the last time we were there, and that hasn't been so long. I was told—I don't speak their languages—word spreads among the Saxon settlers that Octa plans a landing with more keels than any Briton can count."

"We heard Octa had escaped, but that he went back to his homeland."

Marcus's head slowly rocked back and forth. "I would not take that for certain."

Those around him hushed at the thought, then talk gradually started up again and blended into the murmur of the rest of the room. The daily gossip returned. Marcus finished his ale and set down his cup, a signal he was ready to leave. Claerwen followed his example.

The blare of horns rose outside. Marcus lifted a questioning brow.

"Competitions, every market day," the landlord said. "Races, wrestling, mock battles. Most players come for the fun and are not very talented, but they give us a bit of a good laugh."

Marcus smiled and held out his arm to Claerwen. "Then we shall go have a look." He pushed up onto his feet with help from her and the walking stick. "Aye, four hundred and forty-three thousand paces. It was a bit easier years ago…" He nodded farewells to the innkeeper and the other men, and let Claerwen guide him out into the road.

They wound slowly through the marketplace, stopping at many of the stalls to inspect goods and chat—a pretense to gather more news, but personal gossip dominated the talk. Marcus suspected that people had simply become tired of Rheged's internal problems and the Saxons as well. He decided to move on to the small game field beyond the last row of stalls.

In the field's center two men practiced for a mock swordfight with wooden wasters. Around them, a thick circle of cheering onlookers had gathered.

Behind the crowd, Marcus moved slowly, head bent low. He shook as if suffering from a mild palsy and kept a hand hooked around Claerwen's arm. People made way for them, he reckoned more out of avoidance of a sickly old man than sympathy, but it also allowed him and Claerwen to choose a place on ground high enough to see the participants clearly as well as most of the crowd.

One corner of the fort's high wall of stone marked the farthest edge of the field. Marcus stopped a few paces below it in a fairly isolated spot.

The practicing men finished and were bowing to the audience's praise. One swapped his waster for a real sword. His partner retired from the field, another competitor entered. The new man was dark-haired, bearded, and so abnormally thin his clothing sagged. While he spoke to the other man in low tones, the crowd reacted to his arrival with sulking distaste and curiosity rather than cheers.

"Well, now…isn't that fine indeed," Marcus said and glanced at Claerwen. He received a questioning look. "Meirchion *Gul*," he whispered.

"*Gul*?" She stifled a laugh. "*Lean* is his epithet? Perfect. But is he any good at swordplay?"

The men began the mock fight. "He has no weight to put force behind his blows," Marcus said. "Though that's not entirely necessary for a good tactician. Which he is not."

The staged battle lasted only a few minutes and stalled when the prince was quickly backed against the ring of spectators.

Marcus grunted. "Not even he is usually so…distracted." He touched Claerwen's wrist. "Look where he's watching." Meirchion's gaze had swept up over the spectators, his eyes on something past the wall's corner.

Marcus shifted his weight and turned slightly as if to ease discomfort in the way he stood. He glanced along the south-facing wall that ran back from the field. A recess jagged inward a few paces beyond the corner. In it, a hooded man waited. Again Marcus shifted and returned his gaze to the field. Meirchion bowed his concession of the match, then strode towards the fort's entrance in the east wall. The crowd cheered loudly as another man took his place.

"Should we follow—?" Claerwen bit off her words when Marcus touched her wrist again.

Meirchion's strides were slowing. Though not truly hesitant, he appeared wary of the flow of people. In a gradual arc, he swerved from his apparent original destination and walked along the wall behind the spectators.

Marcus felt tension increase in Claerwen's arm as the prince neared. "Watch the games with interest," he whispered. "Ho, look at that man," he called out and pointed at the participants. "How he works his sword. He's good, he's good!"

Meirchion passed between them and the crowd below without a glance. Seconds later, he veered towards the south-facing wall and the niche.

Marcus tugged lightly on Claerwen's arm and edged with her up against the corner.

"What news have you?" Meirchion could be heard from the other side. Though he kept his voice low, it carried along the wall's stones.

"The Pict agrees to meet," the answer came.

Marcus stiffened. He knew that voice. It was the same harsh, whisper-like hiss he had heard in Winchester the night he'd found the effigy. By the gods, he wished he could see through the huge, thick stones, but in truth he had no need to see the face to be sure this was the same man, and from his glimpse of the hooded figure, he now recalled a tan cloak—one with the supple flow of a monk's robes, the description Claerwen had given it.

"Where and when?" Meirchion asked.

"Sunset, at the old farmstead to the north. Three days from here. You remember where it is?"

Octa's assassin began to give directions. Marcus wanted to spit. The man was no Saxon. He was British with an accent fitting to Caer Luguvalos. But he obviously knew the Saxon language and knew it well. The words spoken in Winchester had sounded as natural as any native Saxon's.

"You will have need to leave immediately to reach it in time," the assassin finished. "This warlord will not wait." Steps brushed on the grass. He was leaving.

"How did you get here so quickly?" Meirchion stalled him.

"You haven't learned by now Saxons are the greatest of sailors?"

"Octa's landed?"

"Not yet. I came ashore on Brynaich's coast. He meets the fleet farther north. Soon. Be ready."

His steps moved away again. Marcus imagined the snarling glare, a match to the sneer in the voice.

"And the spy?" Meirchion asked.

Silence. Marcus held his breath.

"I'm looking," the assassin said.

"You'd best find that man, Handor," Meirchion warned. "And the woman he's got hidden away."

Marcus scowled. A woman? Hidden?

"Watch your threats. I said I'm looking."

Marcus listened to the steps trod away. A Pictish warlord he could reckon as part of a plot between Octa and Meirchion. And the effigy had been the set of a trap—he had expected the assassin to be looking for him. But a hidden woman? Who? Claerwen?

Beside him, Claerwen drew breath, sharp enough to hiss between her teeth. He met her eyes. They were pinched and he realized he was squeezing her wrist so tightly that he was crushing it. "Forgive me," he breathed and let go. Her horrified gaze held him.

"The man he called Handor," she whispered. "The assassin?"

Marcus nodded.

She pointed at herself. "The woman?"

"Perhaps," he said. "Please, take extraordinary—"

Loud singing interrupted. It reverberated along the wall from the opposite direction. Marcus glanced past Claerwen and spit a curse. "It's Sion. Come, before he sees us. I want to see where the assassin is going."

"I thought Sion was sound asleep at the inn."

"So did I." Marcus ejected another curse. The disguise of an old storyteller had won important information for him but it hindered his mobility.

The singing wailed louder, yet it was Claerwen's face that drew Marcus's attention. He had seen it like that before, with thoughts behind her eyes that churned. Be wary, he told himself, and when she made to move towards Sion, he gripped her arm. "What are you doing?"

Her lips parted enough to show her teeth clenched together. "I'll distract him then catch up to you," she spoke closely.

He shook his head, vehement disapproval in his eyes. The silvery hair of the wig swung over his shoulders. "Too dangerous. Come."

He took two shambling steps and abruptly halted. Before him stood an astonished Meirchion, also stopped short.

"Storyteller!" Sion's slurred voice rang out. He wobbled up to them, his arms in a grand wave of greeting. "I have an idea. You should go to his lordship the king and tell him a story. He would like that—"

"Now, Sion." Marcus clamped a hand on the drunken man's shoulder and pushed him back a few steps. "You wouldn't want to annoy Lord Meirchion, would you now? Forgive us, m'lord." With his hand still on Sion's shoulder, Marcus bowed stiffly to the prince.

Sion stalled, his watery eyes unable to focus on the prince. His mouth opened and closed several times but only an awkward "mumphm" came out. Marcus guessed Sion had not realized into whose presence he had trespassed and now could not decide whether to apologize or make the insult he would rather give.

Meirchion frowned in disgust. "Go home, Sion."

Sion straightened like a snake about to spit venom. Marcus tightened his fingers. "Go on home," he said, comfort in his voice. Head lowered, Sion swayed on the verge of passing out again, then slinked away like a disciplined dog.

"And don't show yourself until you're sober," Meirchion added. "I've told you this enough times by now."

Bloody arrogant bastard, Marcus thought of the prince. Not one whit of a change in five years. "Apologies, m'lord," he said, slipped his hand into the crook of Claerwen's elbow, and started with her down the slope.

"Wait." Meirchion caught up to them. "If you truly *are* a storyteller, my father would appreciate a visit."

To replace the dead bard? Marcus caught himself thinking. Again he bowed. "Forgive me, m'lord, but we must take our leave. We came but for the market and must be on our way."

"So late in the day?"

Marcus's smile took on a crooked slant and he nodded. He let go of Claerwen's arm and shuffled closer to the prince. "Aye. Late for a reason," he lied. "To visit kin nearby…the later the better."

"Ah…" A smile broke across Meirchion's bony face. He looked like a cadaver. "The less time spent, the better? So be it then. Perhaps another time."

"Aye, perhaps," Marcus agreed. He stalled as if another thought had entered his mind, but after giving the prince a swift assessment, he bowed once more. "Good day, m'lord."

His shaking hand lost its grip on the walking stick. It fell with a thump onto the turf and rolled to Claerwen's feet. Off-balance, he pitched hard into Meirchion.

"Careful, old man." The prince steadied him. Claerwen retrieved the stick and handed it back to Marcus.

"Ah, clumsy old man that I am." Marcus smoothed his tunic underneath his cloak. "Many apologies for my infernal awkwardness."

"Not at all. Good day." The prince strode quickly towards the fort.

Marcus watched until the figure was out of earshot. "We're going back to where we hid the horses," he said to Claerwen.

"Too late to find the assassin now?"

"Aye. And we've something new to attend to." He flicked his eyes to Meirchion's receding figure.

"Follow him? To the meeting?"

Marcus nodded. He faced the wall for privacy and held out the front edge of his cloak. Inside, stuck into the cloth of his tunic, a large gold pennanular brooch hung, the kind used to hold a cloak in place.

Claerwen studied it, first with curiosity, then with wide-eyed shock. "That's his. He was wearing—"

Marcus grinned and showed her a small, silver-hilted dagger slipped into the side of his belt. "Clumsy old man that I am," he repeated and folded the cloak about himself again.

"You mean to say you filched those…right off of him?" Her eyes widened even more. "Oh…you've got something planned, don't you?"

"You will see." His grin took on a glint of feigned fiendishness.

CHAPTER 6

Rheged, two days north of Caer Luguvalos
Early Summer, AD 471

MARCUS reined in. Tired, he dismounted and stretched his cramped back and legs while he gazed through the treetops to the overcast sky. "Little more than an hour of light left, I'd guess. Hard to tell."

Claerwen pulled up near a brake of hazel and slid off her horse. "Should we go farther?"

He scanned the hazel thicket, the last truly dense undergrowth on a gradual downward slope of thinning woodland. "We're close enough now," he said. "From here on we can move faster—it will be open ground again, mostly. This will make a good camp for tonight."

He was pleased they had come as far as they had. After crossing Hadrian's Wall on the first day of travel, they had ridden unhampered through open hill country into the northwest and covered nearly twenty miles. The second day had gone more slowly with the hindrance of thick forestland. Marcus preferred the closed-in protectiveness of uninhabited woods. He also knew that circumventing the forest would have added even more time than the direct route. By late afternoon, they had nearly reached treeless fells again.

He pointed down the hillside. "By midday on the morrow, we should reach a wide river, hopefully well before Meirchion arrives. If the instructions were accurate, the farmstead lies on this side of it."

"You must know every scrap of this island," Claerwen said.

"Ah, but 'tis appropriate, no? For nomadic hunters such as we are?" He plucked at the string of the bow she carried like it was a harp string and grinned at her deerskin clothing, identical to his. So many years of tramping across Britain, so many disguises that had gained him access to places he'd never dreamed of as a boy. He scratched at his beard, washed clean of the grey but kept in case a return to Caer Luguvalos as the storyteller became necessary.

He listened to Claerwen lead their horses into the hazel brake while he gazed again down the slope. The woods were eerily still, as if the land had taken a deep breath and was holding it. The hair on his neck tingled. He squinted through the dull, flat light cast from the lowering sky and scanned from one side to the other. Nothing was there, but his warrior's sense continued to pulse.

Claerwen's soft steps approached. "What is it?"

He hushed her. Motion, far below, where the last of the woods began to thin out, caught his eye, the kind of motion that was not natural to the woods. With his hand on Claerwen's arm, he retreated noiselessly into the brake with her.

He pointed down through the hazels, but at that distance and in the poor light, Marcus could barely see the source. The movement gradually increased. A man, hooded and mostly obscured in the surrounding greenery, leaned against a broad tree trunk for a moment of rest. The stranger fumbled through a small pouch and removed a chunk of dried meat. Unhurried, he ate. Then, nearly finished with the makeshift meal, he moved a little away from the tree to take stock of his surroundings.

The cloak was tan, and when the hood fell back, reddish-brown hair was revealed.

Marcus spit a single expletive. His fingers curled like talons. He could not help himself, and he didn't even know why. The man had a name now—Handor—and he wondered, shouldn't a name make an adversary a little more human than beast? But the churning inside went on. Why? Why every time? Because of a few words that evoked bad memories and nightmares; a few words he couldn't even understand? What was claiming him?

He felt Claerwen's head turn, brush against his beard. Concentrate, he told himself. Control. Observe. Don't let Claerwen see this. He clenched his teeth and noted that Handor carried only two small pouches besides his weapon. Why would anyone travel with so little to sustain him? And to have come so far and so quickly on foot? Impossible. A horse must be hidden somewhere, and the assassin was now scouting for tracks.

Marcus pressed his face to Claerwen's cheek. "That man *cannot* interfere," he whispered through his teeth. Then he pulled away and pushed through the thicket to the roan horse. There was no other way to be rid of Handor, and it had to be now. He felt Claerwen's eyes on his back. She knew what he was going to retrieve, and he knew her heart was cramping as much as his stomach was. Without a pause, he flipped up the cloak's edge, unlashed the gear from the animal, and removed the ties and chains. In minutes, he had donned the leather armor over his deerskins, exchanged boots and buckled on the two-handed sword.

When he turned back to meet Claerwen's eyes, she looked as if he had struck her. "If I let the Iron Hawk do this," he said in a taut, quiet voice, "it will be quicker, more certain." He glanced down the slope. The assassin was readying to move on.

"Do what?" Claerwen's face drained its color. She took hold of the black tunic.

"Scare him, not kill him." Marcus gently pried her hands loose. "He cannot interfere with the meeting, not even to listen."

"It's a trap."

Marcus gave no response. He pulled on the gauntlets, flexed his fingers to settle them comfortably inside.

"It's a trap…for you," Claerwen insisted. "He wants to catch you at that meeting. He'll still go there in spite of what the Iron Hawk does."

He considered her comment while he watched Handor take his first few steps downslope. It could be a trap. But how could he risk allowing Handor access to this meeting, a meeting that could result in a conspiracy between Octa, the Picts and the rogue prince of Rheged? Whether the Iron Hawk drove away the assassin or he did it himself made little difference, but the Iron Hawk could stir up far more fear and perhaps keep the assassin at bay long enough.

Marcus noted the sky and recalculated the time. Still an hour of daylight left. He glanced again to the assassin then held Claerwen's gaze. "Stay here, but don't set up camp until I return," he said. By the stars, he hated to leave her alone. Behind her beauty was a resilient toughness and keen sense that made her as capable of taking care of herself in the wild as he was. But he still didn't like it, not with Handor so close. He touched Claerwen's face with his gloved fingertips. "Promise me? Stay here?"

She nodded, but when he started to pull away, she caught his wrist. "You have no fear…like this." She touched the baldric that held the sword. "Do you?"

There was no place for fear, he thought. No place to consider living or dying. "If anything should happen to me," he said aloud, "go due west to the Roman road and cross the border into Strathclyde. It's another day from here. Tell the border guards at the fort who you are. They'll take you to Ceredig in Dun Breatann."

Her fingers tightened on his arm.

He slid a hand along her cheek. "I'll be back by nightfall." He kissed her, brief, rough, then drew on the masked helmet. He whisked away like a dark, twisting spirit.

The oppressive clouds lowered as if to swallow the forest. Featureless, they offered no rain, not even drizzle, but held the land in a choking humidity that seemed to make even the soil sweat.

The Iron Hawk bounded down the slope with light, swift, noiseless steps over the soft decay of the forest floor. The grim thrill of the hunt rose in him, and at a level equal to Handor, he swung to his left and slowed. After a glance up the hill to confirm Claerwen and the horses were not visible, he focused fully on the man.

Handor walked slowly downward. Well hidden, the Iron Hawk slipped a hand around a sapling's trunk and shook it. Handor's head swiveled at the rustling, one way, then the other.

The Iron Hawk moved forward a step. The assassin's wolf-like stare widened then narrowed on the defensive. He backed, his eyes on the hawk-shaped pommel rising over the warrior's right shoulder. The Iron Hawk moved in another pace. Again Handor backed.

At least the man had some fear behind the perpetual snarl, the Iron Hawk mused. Advancing, he drew his sword. The assassin bolted in a weaving, uneven run into thicker woods.

The warrior followed. At first he kept the man in sight then gradually let the distance between them lengthen. For most of a mile, he tracked Handor easily by footprints, broken twigs and torn leaves. The trail twisted southward in the direction of Caer Luguvalos. After several more minutes of pursuit, the Iron Hawk halted to catch his breath.

Crouched in thick bracken, he listened. No footsteps in any direction. A glance to the sky. Another half-hour until darkness fell. He faced south now and reckoned he had made a long, wide bow from where he had left Claerwen. If he went straight east, he would find her.

But had he succeeded in scaring away the assassin, or had he merely driven the man around in a half-circle? He cracked a dry twig. Nothing reacted. He threw a small stone that struck a tree trunk. Still nothing. Again he rustled small branches of leaves.

Beneath the helmet, the hair on his neck rose as before, and he considered the possibility that Handor had sensed the trap's reversal. Worse, the man could have come across Claerwen in the hazel brake. With her reliable mount she could easily escape a lone man on foot, but the cold-faced assassin most likely had a horse hidden nearby. Damn, he hoped Claerwen was not the woman mentioned in Caer Luguvalos, but in his gut he knew she was the only possible choice.

He rose from the bracken; his warrior's sense rankled again. No evening birds sang. Like a pall of damp smoke, the oppressive overcast hung, and the light was beginning to fade.

A brief, soft swush from behind told of a sword being drawn, the sound enough to judge how close it was and how far it had been lifted. The Iron Hawk whipped around, and his sword clanged hard against the edge of another weapon that arced straight for his neck. His blow jarred all the way up his arms, into his shoulders.

Curses wracked the air. Through the helmet's mask, the warrior stared into Handor's belligerent face. The power behind the attack told the Iron Hawk that the assassin had spent a good amount of time with a high-ranking swordmaster. From the combined hatred and fear in the face glaring back, he also knew every nuance learned in those lessons would be used to its fullest.

Recovered from the stunning blow, Handor charged in. The Iron Hawk dodged sharply to his right. A well-controlled slice missed his shoulder and chopped into fronds of bracken. He swept to the left and crossed his weapon under the other sword. They locked together at the cross-guards, and he lifted, circled up, around, down. He pressed hard, trying to force the blades to the earth, but the man withdrew out of range.

Lunging, the Iron Hawk hacked again high under the cross-guard, the hit meant to sting his adversary's hands and break his grip. Handor grimaced but kept his hold and swung back with the same maneuver. The warrior shifted in anticipation, and the strike glanced. Whipping on around, he used the speed of the full turn to drive his foot into the man's hip.

Off balance and in pain, the assassin dropped to one knee. Another stream of curses ejected, and he lurched onto his feet, glaring, panting, his teeth barred in rage. He raced forward.

The Iron Hawk evaded another hissing slash aimed straight at his throat. He dropped and flipped over backward to come up on his feet again. Holding ground, he thrust his sword's tip skyward and began whipping it right, left, back, forth, hard, fast, confusing. He drove Handor backward and gained equal footing on the hill-side.

In an abrupt change of tactics, the Iron Hawk swung the blade down, around and underneath. He struck another jarring hit. The steel rang like out-of-tune bells. Sprung free, the other weapon skit-tered into the bracken.

The warrior grabbed a wad of Handor's tunic and slung him up against a tree. He held him there, sword tip to throat.

Hatred boiled up in the warrior. To unleash its power grew more insatiable the longer he watched Handor struggle to focus, fear vis-ible in the man's brown eyes. But Handor, desperate, wrenched sideways. In the same motion his bent elbow jerked up at the flat of the blade with his cloak-protected arm. With a fierce shove, he broke the Iron Hawk's hold and leapt after his dropped sword.

The Iron Hawk chased after him. Now he would have to kill.

But the assassin suddenly twisted before reaching his own

sword, fists locked together.

Path blocked and unable to stop, the warrior took a pounding blow straight in the gut. Pain and nausea cramped his stomach and at least one rib gave. Doubled over, he took another hit that knocked the sword from his hand. A third caught him in the hip. Pain tore through his left knee. He fell awkwardly.

Through the haze of pain, he could hear the assassin's hard breathing coming closer. Roll, he willed himself. Only seconds would pass before the man picked up one of the swords. The breathing grew louder, harsh, almost like a grunt. Then hurried footsteps. Roll, the Iron Hawk berated himself. Groaning, he turned over onto his belly.

His eyes focused on a moving black shape in the gloom of the forest floor. Low to the ground, tiny peevish eyes stared back at him between a pair of curved tusks several inches long. Grumbling snorts blew from a snout.

The Iron Hawk froze. A great black-bristled boar, ten paces away, considered whether it should charge or ignore the creature lying in its path. Gods of the earth, the warrior swore silently. The steps had been the assassin's flight and the breathing belonged to the ominous beast. Sick with pain and vexed at the irony that he had posed as a hunter and had not even a bow with him, he shifted his eyes to the place he thought his sword had fallen.

Too far to reach. He could try to wriggle across, but the boar could run faster than he could scrabble to the weapon. He felt the weight of his big dagger, still in the back of his belt. He began to inch back his right hand.

Another snort. He stopped. Bloody ugly brute. It was old, evidenced by the excessive length of the tusks and the heavy protective cartilage grown on its shoulders. He had seen cartilage like that before; it was thick enough to stop a spear. How long would he have need to wait? All in black, he would disappear from sight as night fell, but the boar's poor eyesight made that irrelevant. The animal could locate him by sound and smell in pitch darkness. Patience, he told himself, but gods, his gut hurt.

The wind soughed, low and moaning. Once. Twice.

The Iron Hawk listened to the forlorn sound. But the trees above were still.

The whistle soughed again. "*Gwalch Haearn,*" was called softly, and he realized in his muddle-headedness he had heard Claerwen. She had used their private signal.

"Stay where you are," he hissed.

The boar lowered its snout to the leafy decay and began to root back and forth in its nightly search for grubs.

The Iron Hawk heard the creak of a bowstring being pulled. Claerwen was an excellent shot, but this was futile. "Don't try," he warned. "You won't even be able to wound it."

Silence followed and he counted off minutes in his head. Finally, the beast wandered back the way it had come, its movement fading into the dark undergrowth. Relieved, the warrior sat up.

Claerwen ran to him. She dropped the bow and fell to her knees at his side.

He untied his chinstrap and dumped the helmet on the ground, then removed his gauntlets. Pain stabbed at his belly, and he pressed his fingers to it with a soft groan.

Claerwen's hands ran down his arm in search of what he probed. She slid her fingers underneath his palm. Marcus drew breath sharply. "It's only bruises."

"What happened?"

"What are you doing here? I told you to stay in the hazels."

"I heard noise—a lot of rustling, grunts, swords. You weren't far. Then I saw him run. He had a horse a bit farther up."

"Which way did he go?"

"Towards Caer Luguvalos. Moving fast."

Marcus groaned again, his hand under the tunic and spread over his lower ribs. "This will be more colorful than spring flowers by morning," he said and decided the bone hit hardest was not cracked, only bruised. Movement worsened the pain. His knee ached nearly as much, a reminder of when he had been shot with an arrow there years before. Ever since, he'd had a slight limp. He got to his feet, testing. The limp would be worse for a while—nothing new.

"Bloody boar did a better task of scaring him off than the Iron Hawk did," he said. "Let's hope Handor doesn't circle around to the farmstead." He bent for his sword, paused halfway. A lump different than the rest of the humus-littered ground loomed next to the weapon.

It was one of the pouches Handor had carried; the strap had been cut during the fight. Marcus scooped it up. Facing west for the last of the daylight, he examined the contents.

"I don't know who this Handor is," he said with a grim face, "but he's bloody fierce." Among several personal items he pulled out, a brooch cast in bronze lay in his palm. He turned it over several times.

Claerwen remained silent and he looked up. She was studying the items in his hand, her eyes deeply serious. He slipped his other hand along her cheek and brushed the softness of her skin with his thumb. "I didn't mean to be harsh," he said, "but you should have stayed where you were, even if you saw him run. I have no reason to think the woman he and Meirchion spoke of is not you. But *why* you, except to get to me, I simply don't understand."

She stared at the bronze ornament, a strangely peaceful look on her face. With a fingertip she traced its carved pattern, a swirling of hounds amid traditional knotwork.

Curious, he slid his fingers under her chin and turned her face to him. "Claeri?"

Her eyes came up. "Hywel," she whispered.

He stared at her, one eyebrow lifted.

"Do you remember?" she questioned. "My father said the name of the man given Macsen's sword for safekeeping was called Hywel? He was from somewhere in the northern kingdoms. Marcus...my father has one exactly like this. He showed it to me when we were home, before we left for the coronation. Hywel gave it to him when they were fostermates."

Marcus held her gaze. Claerwen's father had been a fostermate of Uther's oldest brother, Constans, during the time their father Constantine was high king. With the escalation of civil violence in those days, the five pieces of Macsen's Treasure were split and hidden for safekeeping. The crown had gone into exile with Uther and Ambrosius. Claerwen's father had been entrusted with the torque.

He dredged his mind for every part of the conversations they'd had regarding the Treasure. The talk had been extensive, an attempt to help her father remember long-forgotten details of names and homelands of the caretakers.

"I remember your father saying Hywel dreamed of training as a bard," Marcus said. "What if Hwyel Gwodryd of Caer Luguvalos was the same Hywel? If it's true he tried to contact me before he was killed, if he knew who and what I was, perhaps it had to do with Macsen's sword."

Marcus swore softly. Claerwen had closed her eyes and exhaled, long, slow. He knew she was tired, but had she heard anything he'd said? Blindly, she continued to trace a fingertip over the brooch's surface.

"Excalibur," she breathed.

Discomfort wriggled inside Marcus. Fire in the head—no matter how he trusted it, no matter how many years he had seen it in Claerwen, it always caused him unease.

Her eyes opened, confusion in them. "Did I say something?"

"You said, 'Excalibur.' What did you see this time?"

She tapped the brooch with her fingernail. "This reminds me of water rippling in the light of evening sun—burnished, smooth, mellow—like its finish. Then I saw a lake, deep and narrow, nestled in trees, lush green hills. So tranquil. Same lake as before. No stone this time. Just that word." The pain of a headache crossed her face. "The sense of peacefulness is already gone."

"Is Excalibur a place?" he asked. Again he slipped his hand along her cheek. He saw comfort come into her eyes.

She shook her head and shrugged. "I don't know. But why? Why would an assassin from Octa carry this from Hywel?" Then, as if she no longer wanted to touch it, she withdrew her hand.

"It means this man called Handor is more than just an assassin." Marcus raked his fingers through his hair. "He is conspiring with Meirchion as well as Octa. It means they're not only looking for you and me, they're looking for Macsen's sword."

Chapter 7

Rheged, three days north of Caer Luguvalos
Early Summer, AD 471

"I know. I should expect this by now," Claerwen said in a hushed voice. "But it's so dangerous. Are you sure he'll be late?"

Marcus followed her with his eyes. She was picking soggy leaves from his cloak. "He was always late. It's the only thing about him that can be trusted. Even the assassin knew it when he told him to be on time."

With the cloak leaf-free at last, Claerwen draped its front closure across Marcus's chest and over his left shoulder. She slid the sharp point of Meirchion's gold pennanular brooch through the two layers of cloth and rotated the ornament's circular piece to secure it in place. "I just hope he doesn't arrive when you're in the midst of this ruse."

"Can't be sure," he said. "But I can switch from prince to warlord and back again quicker than Myrddin's magic." Marcus gave a crooked smile and raked back his damp hair. "Though in this mist, either of them finding this place at all will be fine luck indeed."

He arranged the cloak to fully cover his deerskin tunic and breeches. His sword, hung from his belt this time, and Meirchion's dagger, were hidden beneath as well. With his dark coloring similar to the prince's, the mist, and the dim, diffused light of near sunset, he hoped his face would be unrecognizable, more so once he lifted the hood. Except for Meirchion's gaunt figure, a general description could fit either man; the cloak would hopefully disguise Marcus's more solid build as well. He had never seen a secret meeting in which wary participants unknown to each other stood too close.

"I'm going now, just to be ready," he said. "In the center, there, where the buildings were." He pulled up the hood. The motion caused pain to shoot through his ribs. He pressed a hand to his middle and winced.

"Are you going to be able to do this?"

"I will," he said. "Stay here in the woodbank. It's so overgrown you should be safe, as long as you stay here."

Claerwen nodded.

He peered into her face. Her penchant for taking her own initiative sometimes helped, but he wished she would remain in the place he expected her to be. Should anything go wrong, neither could afford additional time to track the other. "Promise me. Stay here? Then I can find you."

She nodded again, this time with more conviction.

"It's time to go lay a trap," he said and turned into the mist.

Fifty paces inside the circular embankment that surrounded the farmstead, Marcus settled between two thick timbers. One still held up rough planks that might have been the door to a house. Silence fell.

Though the air was nearly windstill, masses of grey-white dampness swarmed as if in a half-hearted attempt to escape. It thinned twice while Marcus waited then closed in again, the smell of wet air choking to breathe.

From his post, he studied what little he could see. He and Claerwen had scouted the farmstead earlier, and had memorized its layout and what was left of its structures. They had discovered not only was it abandoned but had been burned as well, apparently quite a long time before. He had also kept vigil for Handor, but there had been no sign of the assassin.

A quarter-hour passed. Marcus listened to a blackbird's melodious whistle calling at intervals behind him. The mist continued to move. He was reminded of the aftermath of a long drinking spell or having been unconscious—as if the eyes of the mist were opening and needed time to focus. Staring into it, he saw a darker grey form take shape: a man on a horse. The rider drew closer and the mist descended again, but from the squat, short-legged profile of the animal, Marcus was certain this was the Pict, not Meirchion. Luck, he smiled to himself, was good.

Marcus rose and stalked in a partial circle around the approaching rider. He heard him rein in and dismount. Footsteps that followed softly swished over the wet turf.

"Meirchion of Rheged?" The voice was loud, rough, accustomed to shouting orders.

The blackbird launched up into the trees with a shriek of discontent. In a slow swirl the mist languished, then suddenly floated on a new current and revealed a lone dark-haired man as harsh as his voice. Marcus eyed him. Aye, this was a Pict for certain. Slightly shorter than himself and thicker-set, the man was dressed in richly furred skins. A short sword hung from his belt. The face that appeared was creased and browned from living wild and free and always within a blade-span of death.

The Pict started when he realized he was no longer alone.

Marcus moved in on long, slow strides meant to show power and cause discomfort. Halfway across he halted, folded his arms, and gave a long, arrogant, prejudicial assessment.

"Talk," the Pict commanded in his own tongue. "I have little time to waste."

"I don't know your language," Marcus lied. He knew the tongue fluently but reckoned Meirchion did not. "Who are you?"

The warlord switched to heavily accented Cymraeg. "It matters not."

"Perhaps. Perhaps not," Marcus riddled. Without knowing Meirchion's exact reasons for the meeting, he had no sense of where to begin other than the obvious. "You have news of Octa?"

The Pict's eyes stared icily at Marcus's half-hidden face. "You have done as required?"

Marcus stretched to his full height and glared back. "Of course." He had not an inkling of what the warlord meant.

"So be it," the Pict said. "Then all will be set into motion. You shall have it as you wish."

Though spoken with assurance, an underlying distaste stained the Pict's tone. This disturbed Marcus. "How do I know this will happen?" he pried.

"Proof will arrive soon enough. The Saxon will reach Hadrian's Wall in six, perhaps seven days, depending how much resistance he meets."

Six or seven days… Marcus kept his face aloof and blank in spite of the knot that grew in his stomach. He had been right all along—Octa would not wait to land. But *so* soon?

Scowling, the warlord took a step closer. "Why are you so hesitant? If you've done what was required, you— Eh?" His scowl turned into a questioning squint. He lunged and gripped Marcus's arm, stared into the hood. Then a half-smile split his leathery face.

"I know you!" he blurted in his own language. "You're not Meirchion Gul of Rheged. You're Marcus ap Iorwerth."

Marcus silently swore.

The Pict shook his arm. "Don't you remember? Dun Breatann, all those years ago?" He pounded a fist on his chest. "Nehton mac Aedan."

Marcus studied the weathered face. Nehton mac Aedan… The name was familiar. Then a grin crept onto his face and he dropped back his hood. He had known a Nehton mac Aedan in Dun Breatann late in his fosterage, a wily young man a few years older than himself and of a long bloodline of noble Pictish ancestors from western Gododdin, close to Strathclyde's borders.

"Eh, heh!" he started to laugh. Now he recognized the face. Years of wear had considerably marked the man. Equally comfortable in the Pict's tongue, he switched languages. "By the gods, Nehton mac Aedan… A warlord? True?"

"So say the rumors." Nehton gave a sly grimace. "What's this about?" He flicked a finger at Meirchion's gold penannular ornament. "Ah…you're still winding the 'unbelievers' up in knots, aren't you? And to what trouble are you leading Meirchion of Rheged *this* time?"

"This time? You've been tracking me?"

Nehton grinned. A line of crooked, brownish teeth showed between his lips. "Your name was mentioned once, so I started to give some attention. Your doings…have always had a certain…mark to them. Impressive. What did you do with him?"

Marcus's mouth twisted. "He's still coming, as far as I know. He summoned *you*?"

Nehton glanced at the sky in judgment of how long they had to talk before sunset. "You still like good strong ale?"

The Pict didn't wait for an answer. Marcus grinned. He knew Nehton wanted no answer unless it was positive. The Pict went straight for a wineskin hung from his horse's saddle then cocked his head at a place to sit and talk.

"It's true," Nehton said and handed the skin to Marcus. "He summoned me. Why *me*, you're asking."

The glimmer in the Pict's dark eyes gave Marcus reason to suspect the meeting with Meirchion was not as it appeared. He took a full swallow of ale and matched the hint of mischief. "Aye…you. What does he want from you?"

Nehton leaned forward, a smirk on his lips. "Not from me. From Octa. Aye…I thought that'd wrinkle your brow a bit. He wants to secretly hire a small war band from Octa's forces. To capture Elmet from his brother. So he says."

Marcus handed the skin to Nehton. He scrutinized the Pict's eyes and mouth, gestures and tone of voice, whether truth or lie lay in his words. "And…" he speculated aloud in following the logic, "the Saxons become an easy blame for Masguid's death, should it occur. Then Meirchion rushes in to defeat the invaders—*if* he is strong enough—and becomes the hero to the people of Elmet and his own as well? Even though Elmet is still in truth under their father's control?" Plausible, he told himself, but not likely. "And what does Octa want? Beside fresh land, as always."

"Revenge for his time in Uther's prison." The Pict poured more of the drink down his throat.

Marcus took the wineskin again and drank while he considered Nehton's answer. Revenge. There was always revenge. But to make an alliance for a smallholding like Elmet would not be worth the Saxon leader's time. He would take it by force along with the rest of Rheged and anything else he could overrun. And all this in return for what kind of requirement performed by Meirchion?

"And why are you making yourself the go-between for Octa and Meirchion?" Marcus challenged. "What's the gain for you?"

Nehton snorted laughter. "Meirchion *thinks* he summoned me.

You see, I learned a bit from you, all those years ago, you and your interest in the past. You remember the lesson of the tribes from the distant east? Hordes of warriors? Huns and others like them?"

Marcus nodded warily. From the amount of drink the man had taken so far, its effects should have begun to settle in enough to loosen his tongue well. Marcus did not want him to become unintelligible. He held onto the wineskin and finished the lesson: "Invaders from the place called Asia spread west, seeking to capture the lands of Constantinople. But the people of Constantinople were wise and bribed the invaders with tribute of gold and food to go on westward. Unlike those of the eastern empire, the western kingdoms under Rome's rule were—and still are—in disarray, fighting amongst themselves, making it easy for the warriors of Asia to gain control…"

The image of a map formed in his mind. Unless Octa drove straight south into Brynaich, he would pass through Strathclyde and into Rheged…

"*You're* diverting them through Gododdin. In truth?" Marcus passed back the wineskin.

Nehton laughed and drank a long swig, then another. "Such an alliance I've made. Bribes of weapons and men for a good swift ride through to the Wall."

Marcus leaned forward. "You lie, Nehton mac Aedan," he said, a faint hint of menace in his voice. "Octa won't make any more alliances."

"How would you know? He has before."

"The last pact he made with a Briton was last winter. He lost a huge stockpile of weapons when one of his camps was burnt—set his plans back for a long while. He blamed the Briton. You should have heard the rant when he broke off the alliance. He won't trust anyone ever again, especially after sitting in Uther's prison for a bit."

"You had something to do with the burning of this camp?" Nehton queried.

Marcus gave a coy shrug. "You could say…I contributed to it."

Nehton's smile faded, and he squinted with a shrewd eye. "Bribes of weapons and men. Good, strong warriors of Gododdin.

To go with Octa to the Wall. Where Brynaich will join us from the south side." He held up a hand and clenched his fist. "We will crush those bloody horse turds." He passed the skin again. "Now that you know my game, what are you doing here, in this costume? Sabotage of your own?"

Marcus held up the skin in a salute, gave a wicked grin, and drank.

Nehton threw back his head and gave a full-hearted laugh. "You're right," he said. "Octa won't align with *anyone*. Not even among his own people. Could be, if rumors hold true, Meirchion's toying with the Irish instead…"

Marcus nearly choked on the mouthful of ale he had taken.

Nehton nodded with satisfaction that he had surprised Marcus. "Aye…Irish. Can't tell you how deep it runs, or if it's even true. Just something to bear in mind."

Marcus swore. "It's not Elmet that Meirchion wants this time, is it?"

Nehton shook his head.

Meirchion's requirement. Well, wouldn't that just reckon, Marcus thought. If Meirchion had instigated the Irish raids to keep Ceredig's forces busy on Strathclyde's western coast, the eastern lands would be left with little defense and the stray war band from Octa would find easy work. The land between Rheged and Strathclyde had been in dispute for decades. Meirchion had seen opportunity.

"I see the wheels of understanding grind," Nehton said. He got to his feet. "And by now you realize I'm not a warlord. Like you, I needed to know if I could trust you. You haven't changed. But a word of warning…"

Marcus stoppered the wineskin, rose and hung it from Nehton's horse. He lifted an eyebrow in question.

"I'd guess you've seen the man who arranged the meeting with Meirchion? Beware of him."

"You know who he is?"

Nehton shook his head. "Only that he's an assassin and he has a hatred for you I would not want to be the target of. I wish I could tell you why."

"Well, I'll learn soon enough, I'm sure. What will you say to Meirchion when he arrives?"

The Pict eyed Marcus appraisingly. "Nothing," he said. "There's no need. If you were playing him to me, I'd wager you were going to play me to him as well. I've kept my part of the bargain, haven't I, Lord Meirchion?" He poked a finger at the gold brooch.

Nehton walked to his horse and mounted. "And you," he said, "you know what to say to him now. Or best, you could walk away. The war band Octa chose for here will come anyway. Let Meirchion pay for wondering with his own sweat."

Walk away? The thought appealed to Marcus. He and Claerwen could go on to dispatch the report to Ceredig along with others to Uther and Gwrast of Rheged. And if Meirchion were left unmet at the farmstead, it would damage his dealings with Handor. A fine thought indeed, he mused and started to laugh, harsh and bitter.

Nehton joined in, then turned his horse into the mist and rode off to the north.

After Marcus had vanished into the grey wall of dampness, Claerwen heard nothing more but rustling leaves and the occasional shifting of the horses a few paces away. She resigned that she could do little but wait and sought a more comfortable place. A granite boulder, about half a man's height and gently curved, was embedded in the woodbank's surface. Thick moss padded the earth around the rock's base. Curled up against it, Claerwen folded her cloak around herself and settled in as if she were one more clump of foliage.

From the creep of dim shadows cast by the dull light, she watched nearly an hour pass. The mist had lifted enough to lighten the sky to a paler grey, but its vaporous curls remained. Tired and sleepy, she absently smoothed the surface of the moss, amazed by its wool-like softness.

The mist shifted again. A thin beam of sunlight nearly broke through and for an instant it seemed to Claerwen that something shined from under the moss. She dragged her fingers through the tightly packed growth, but no glint showed. She repeated the motion over a wider swath. Still nothing. She tried a last time. Again no sparkle, but her fingernail scraped on a hard surface. Just a rock, she thought, but tiny flakes of rust had caught underneath her nail.

Curious, she tore a hole in the moss and discovered a small metal object, perfectly round, slightly domed, its entire surface corroded. Must have been dropped, she guessed, and lain there a long time. After much prying, she succeeded in forcing the thick, marly soil to release it.

Pain struck Claerwen's hand, and she dropped her newfound prize. The ungrateful thing had stuck her with a sharp metal point. An old brooch, she saw now. She squeezed blood from a small puncture in the heel of her hand and packed fresh mud on the wound to stop the bleeding and draw out any rust fever.

Why couldn't she have simply left it alone? Yet she could not. She picked it up again and rubbed dirt off its badly deteriorated face. The pattern carved into it gradually grew visible.

Claerwen's breath caught in her throat. She recognized the design. In the same instant she felt herself being sucked backward against the boulder without her consent. Fire in the head—it was coming on. Not now, she prayed and fought it, but the choice was not hers.

White clouds thrashed across her sight—not the mist of moors and fells and the sea, but the veil of vapors from which images were spun. It swirled and slowly parted to show a pair of eyes, huge, startling green eyes, wide-set and surrounded with thick, curling lashes—a woman's. They blinked once then melted, like soft butter running down the sides of a cauldron. Hissing drops spilled into the fire, spattered up and out onto hearthstones, hot and searing.

The pain in Claerwen's hand ached. She was conscious of it, but she drifted and blackness closed in, then cleared out again, and she was lying on dark, rich soil. The pungent smell of it comforted her, a reminder of the earthy smells of home and the mountains. How fine it would be if the lands of Dinas Beris were there beneath her hands, but she heard her own wavering breath sigh like a lonely whimper, and she knew this ground was not of home.

Voices spoke in the distance. A woman's voice that Claerwen could not place. Another voice softly answered. Myrddin's. The images raced on.

More water appeared. A lake this time, long and narrow and deep. A woman, different from the other with green eyes, Claerwen believed, drifted just beneath the surface as if guided by thoughts alone. She wore brilliant white, a gown of an exquisitely fine fabric never seen before. As graceful as a selkie from the sea, the woman glided in concentric half-circles from one side to the other and back. She was drawing inward in the pattern of the sacred labyrinth. At the center, she dove deep below the sapphire surface.

Then Myrddin stood across the water on the opposite shore. Smiling, his familiar face seemed comfortable, benevolent, but from the shoulders down, he had the body of a bird covered in sleek black feathers. He watched the place where the woman had dived.

The water's surface stretched and smoothed, became so flat it looked solid enough to walk upon. Already quiet, profound silence drew in, oppressive, stifling. Claerwen struggled to breathe. Her throat tightened and tears welled behind her closed eyelids. The clouds of fire in the head drew across and shut off the link to the Otherworld. Adrift, she could not find her way back to consciousness.

Then light burst inside Claerwen, firing magnificent and hot and raging, and from its center she saw a hand ram up through the water's surface. It was the woman of the lake's hand, and her graceful, slender fingers clutched a sword's hilt as sure and as strong as any warrior's. The blade, long and slightly tapered, was forged of fine steel; the hilt, pommel and cross-guard of brilliant, chased gold. Light radiated from it, too bright to bear.

The light turned gold-green and blurred everything until all else was gone. Then a vast sea of topaz water spread out before Claerwen. As if rocked by an earthquake, a heap of jagged grey scree rose from the golden water. The heap expanded higher and wider, beastlike, shaking, then wrenched itself free of the land to push its way into the sea. Blades of grass sprouted all across its rocky surface. A gale crashed in, determined to destroy the rock, but the wind was unable to blow away even a single blade of grass. The storm passed. When all had settled, a shimmering red-gold dragon appeared. It brandished the same sword in the claws of its right front foot.

Too fascinated to be frightened, Claerwen tried to hold onto the vision and memorize every detail, but the dragon dissipated like mist in the sun. She grabbed for it, straining up, but she had no strength and slumped down again. Myrddin was calling in the ancient druidic tongue of his kind. The last word he spoke echoed over and over—the name of "Arthur."

The call faded; a soft roar replaced it. Was it the sea, rushing in with one long wave instead of many, growing louder, closer? Claerwen felt the vibration in the earth. Foreboding gripped her. Then it struck, water from everywhere. Its cold streaks swept through her hair and she was falling, tumbling without control. Pain lurched all through her, agony to breathe, water in her nose and throat, no escape. It carried her away, lungs on the verge of bursting, the pain in her chest unbearable. By the gods, she was drowning…

More pain seared through Claerwen's head as the vision left her. She groped for control of her senses, clarity in her mind. Voices still reverberated, one sounded like Marcus. Twisting, she crawled around the boulder, her fingers hooked into the moss to pull herself along. The mist had partially lifted, and through slitted eyes, she could see him. He faced away. If only she could get to her feet, if only she could find her voice to call him…

She tucked her fist over her heart. The pain in her head matched that in her chest. She curled into herself and it grew overwhelming, then the blackness closed in once more.

Marcus listened to the hoofbeats fade into the distance. So, Nehton mac Aedan had become a spy. Ceredig would laugh enough to rattle the walls when he heard this. Marcus grinned and started for the woodbank. Claerwen would find it interesting as well.

Footsteps. Marcus halted. The first pair crunched straight behind him. A second pair moved in from the right. Then a third, farther behind. Instinct as much as experience told him it was already too late to reach for his sword. He turned around.

Three men slinked out of the burnt ruins. Two were nearly a head taller than Marcus, the third and most distant appeared shorter and much younger. Although their clothing was so nondescript it did not define their origins, each man carried a large single-edged knife hung from the belt. Called a *seax*, it was the dreaded weapon favored by Saxon warriors.

The man on the right, lanky and thin-faced, eased his knife from its sheath. With each step he took, the cracked leather of his shoes exposed his muddy feet, and his blond hair was so filthy it spiked down over his eyes. He halted, crossed his arms in front of his chest with the knife pointed upright in his hand, and took a stance meant to radiate invincibility.

Unperturbed, Marcus eyed the strangers coolly. None of them were warriors, he knew, not only from the unsoldierly way they stood, but also from how they had confronted him from a disadvantage—if the mist should suddenly lift, the setting sun would blind them.

Though focused mainly on the knife, Marcus glanced from face to face to the blade and back again. A flinch or indrawn breath would foretell of a coming attack. The blade wavered slightly, yet the man held his position.

"Shall I guess you are looking for me?" Marcus questioned, his voice heavy and full of arrogance. He doubted they knew his language any more than he knew theirs. If they had overheard his talk with Nehton mac Aedan, he could not guess whether they had understood. Both he and the warlord had spoken solely in Pictish.

The knifeman grunted and returned the challenge in Saxon. His words sounded like a taunt, loud and contemptuous.

A distinct order? Or something else? Marcus could not guess. The only exception sounded like a name—Tangwen—a woman's name from his own tongue, spoken twice. He was unsure. It could have been just a word that sounded similar. "Come now, man," he said. "I thought you wanted a good fight."

The man spoke again with thickening malice. The words were identical.

"So, am I to presume you're not interested?" Marcus shrugged then moved to stride away.

The second man sidestepped and blocked his escape. Though more muscular than the first man, with a rugged face, a deep cleft in his chin, calm ice-blue eyes, and remarkably cleaner blond hair, he did not pull his *seax*. Instead, he withdrew several braided leather thongs coiled around one shoulder.

That was why no other weapons had been drawn, Marcus realized. These were not strays looking for a kill they could rob. He ripped off the cloak and launched himself at the thinner man like a rock from a slingshot.

Marcus narrowly avoided the knife's biting edge and crashed into the first assailant's legs. The man sprawled facedown, and the weapon sprang loose. It stabbed down into the turf.

The second man jerked into motion. Marcus was already up and running and snatched up the *seax* before it could be reached. He whipped around furiously and pounded the stranger in the throat with a stunning, sharp heel. The man hurtled backward onto the stone-like roots of a tree.

The thin-faced man, on his feet again, leapt, but Marcus bent over hard. The intended grapple missed, and he vaulted over Marcus. The momentum carried him through the air. On landing, he scraped a ragged furrow in the grass and flopped to a halt just in front of the other Saxon.

A dark shape thrust towards the side of Marcus's face. He dodged. The contorting motion threw him off balance, and he fell, rolled twice. Up again, he found the third Saxon closing in, a short, thick wooden club in one hand and a dagger in the other. Both weapons swung wildly. Marcus dropped into a tight crouch, and the club swished through the air just above his head. He charged upward, caught the wrist with the dagger and shifted his weight. He rammed the *seax* under the young man's ribs and twisted the blade expertly. The Saxon gagged, doubled over, then slid off the blade onto the ground.

With the bloody *seax* still in one hand, Marcus ripped his own sword from its scabbard. He advanced on the two dazed men. The huskier man had already thrown aside his knife and held up his hands to show they were empty. Unyielding, Marcus swung his blade's tip from one to the other. Neither offered to move.

"I will *not* be taken prisoner," he hissed through his teeth. "If you understand a single word of this— If you come from Octa— No prisoner! Now, leave!"

He backed, wary that they might attempt revenge for their companion's death. Still neither moved. He flicked the sword at the dead man. "Take him with you," he ordered.

The man with ice-blue eyes muttered something. His tone betrayed fear. He and the thin-faced man stared at their slain cohort.

Marcus then realized Handor might have sent them. How else could they have known to come to the farmstead? He pointed again at the body. "Take him back to Handor as a warning! Leave! Now!"

The two men stiffened at the name. Finally the notion that deliverance was theirs sunk in. They edged past Marcus, and the husky man lifted the body across his broad shoulders. They hurried off; their footfalls quickly faded.

Marcus threw down the *seax* and struck his sword's tip into the earth. Out of breath, he bent over, hands on his thighs. The pain in his bruised ribs punched at his gut, his heartbeat pounded in his head. He was glad he had not drunk more ale with Nehton than he had.

Blood had pooled in the turf where the dead Saxon had fallen. Marcus gazed at the place. The man had been young, barely old enough to even call him a man, and like the others, had been dressed in frayed and filthy clothing like a poor farmer. The pale eyes, staring blankly, had seemed too innocent to harbor the hatred needed to kill. But hatred was not always necessary, Marcus knew, only the need to survive. He straightened slowly and turned away; his hand slid down over his face as he swore at himself. Gods of the earth, the killing and the hatred and the guilt kept sliding more often between his fingers, out of his control.

Sickened, he snatched up his sword and cloak. The drumming of blood in his head was easing, but when he turned towards the woodbank once more, his gut cramped. With all the scuffling and shouting, he would have expected to see Claerwen running to help or at the very least to watch in spite of her promise to stay in her hiding place. He saw nothing of her. Were more Saxons out there? Or had Handor regained his courage and come back?

Marcus swore at himself again. He tightened his grip on the sword and ran for the woodbank.

CHAPTER 8

Rheged, the farmstead north of Caer Luguvalos
Early Summer, AD 471

CLAERWEN'S head felt heavier than an anvil. So did her legs. Stiff, like they were filled with molten iron that was cooling and beginning to harden, they would not straighten. Her arms, indeed the rest of her as well, seemed embedded with more weight than she could bear.

Was she even alive?

Her mind still thrashed with images left from the vision, repeated so many times that now she wished she could forget. She rarely remembered any once the fire had gone, unless they were triggered by another image or word or thought that brought them back in vivid detail. This time they continued without pause.

A soft moan drifted in her ears, like strained breath. Her own sigh, she realized in time. One hand was clamped to a wad of her tunic so tightly her fingers ached. How long had she been there? Was this even the same day?

A voice spoke, its closeness or distance indistinguishable. Abrupt rustling in the overgrowth followed, then fingers gently pressed on her shoulders, pulled her up and took the strain of weight from her. She fell back against something solid, alive, and that smelled of leather and horses.

The voice, warm alongside her face, called her name.

Thank the gods, she thought in relief. Marcus was there and spoke with equal relief in his voice. So comfortable now, and safe.

"What's wrong? What happened?" he asked. He was pulling

open her cloak.

Cradled in his arms, she heard him question whether she had been hurt or become ill. He was looking for injuries, she knew, but she could not muster the strength to stop him. If only her mind would clear, but it was barely beginning to, a stage at a time.

"The fire," she said, her voice thin and scratchy.

Marcus tensed. As always.

She opened her eyes. With his help, she struggled to sit up. Dread and questions clouded his face.

"What's this?" he asked. He touched her clenched hand.

She spread her fingers. Forgotten in the turmoil, the rusty brooch lay in her palm. Staring, she waited for the scattered bits of her thoughts to come together.

"Another of Hywel's?" he said before she could find the words. His brows jagged downward. "Where did you find it?"

"Here…somewhere." The muddle-headedness dragged at her and she rubbed her face. "Then…it started." She studied the moss then pointed. "There, that hole there."

"Are you saying this triggered a vision?"

"Some was the same, like before. The lake again. But there was more…Macsen's sword. And a lot of other things that don't make any sense. Myrddin, except he was…a rook…or a raven, I think. I don't understand."

When Marcus remained quiet, she looked up at him. He stared at the hole, then the boulder, then at the section of the woodbank encompassing both. Kneeling over the hole, he slipped his fingers inside and rummaged. The single expletive that spewed from his mouth was particularly foul.

"What is it?" she asked.

He drew the big dagger from the back of his belt. With long, careful strokes, he cut twice into the moss, one pass upright, the other sideways. The midpoint of each crossed at the hole. From there, he slid the blade beneath and peeled the moss back like it was thick skin, then scraped off a thin layer of clay-like soil. Before long his fingers brushed a narrow, slightly curved and smooth brown object. He swore again.

Claerwen watched his eyes lift and fill with grim resolve. She frowned.

"It is as I thought," he muttered. He continued to dig away more soil and small rocks with the knife. A second brown piece emerged, a bit lower and shorter, a scrap of moldy cloth stuck to it.

Claerwen lurched backward when he reached a third piece. Ribs. He was digging up ribs. Right where she had been sitting. Eyes closed, she felt Marcus grab her hand, and she told herself to breathe—in, out, steady, steady.

She calmed and when he let go, he continued to remove soil. She had seen dead bodies, freshly killed, partially decomposed, and she had even been forced to kill more than once with her own hand, but the closeness of this earth-stained skeleton buried in the woodbank made her turn away. Why, she didn't know. She crawled up the embankment to wait.

"The neck was broken," Marcus said after many minutes.

Claerwen braved another look. He had exposed a skull, neck and shoulders.

"I can tell from the angle of the head," he went on. "I suspected something like that. The way the neck was crushed…it was not from an accident. This was murder. It looks like he's been here a few years, no longer."

"It was a man?" Claerwen tried to keep her eyes on Marcus, but they fell again on the brooch in her hand. "This is Hywel's grave, isn't it?"

He picked up one rock, broader and flatter-surfaced than the others. Like the bones, it was stained. He wiped its face. "I believe so. Look at this."

Letters had been scratched into the surface. "Latin?" she asked.

"Hic jacet…" he read. "Here lies…and the rest is illegible, except this." He pointed at the last word. "Gwodryd."

Claerwen met Marcus's eyes. "Then… If this was Hywel Gwodryd, that means Sion was right. Meirchion murdered him. And if this was the Hywel my father knew, and the keeper of Macsen's sword, then we know why."

Marcus shook his head. "Meirchion killed Hywel to keep him from talking to me about his schemes. If he knew then that Hywel was the swordkeeper, killing the bard would be the last thing he'd have done." He held up the stone. "This tells me that this land was probably Hywel's, and that someone else knew what happened and cared enough to bury him here secretly. Meirchion never would have returned his body to his home or have left this marker to be found one day."

Claerwen touched his hand. "Do you think he hid the sword here?"

Marcus shook his head again. "Doubtful. Too obvious. If he were like your father at all, he would have been far more careful."

"If they're looking for a woman they think you have hidden," Claerwen added, "and if that's me, they probably think I know where it is. Could they know my father was the keeper of Macsen's torque?"

"And hope you would know something about the sword as well? Possibly. I don't know." He tossed the stone aside with a thud. "Damn Uther and his bloody homage ceremony. He's put you at such risk."

He began to spread the dirt and rocks over the skeleton again. Once the grave was packed down, he pressed the marker over the skull, then unfurled the layer of moss. With care, he arranged the grave to appear undisturbed. Several rocks still lay scattered, missed in the refilling, and he flipped them away.

"There's nothing more we can do here." Marcus wiped dirt from his hands. "It's time to go on."

Claerwen heard his voice, but her mind hazed over again. The fire was stirring once more like seeping mist. This time, though, it was not within her, but hovered close like a separate entity. Curious, fascinated, apprehensive, she could not pull herself from it.

A single image flashed across her vision. The pair of wide green eyes, calm, sad, solemn, the same eyes as before, stared down at Macsen's sword. The blade was shattered. Tears fell from the eyes. Then as quickly as the fire came on, it subsided.

She lifted her face. Marcus was standing, still talking.

"We can't wait any longer to send news to Ceredig," he said. "I need to send a warning to Uther as well. Then we need to get back into Caer Luguvalos. I'll have to talk with the old king himself. Are you strong enough to ride? Claerwen? What's wrong?"

Claerwen stared past him into empty space. Was this merely another memory from the earlier vision? she wondered. Or a new one to stamp a deeper impression within her?

"We must find the sword," she breathed aloud.

"Claerwen?" Marcus pulled her onto her feet. "Claerwen, what's wrong?"

"We must find the sword."

He peered into her face. "What is it? Another vision?"

His words broke through the haze. "I…I'm not sure. I think…no. It was like…a presence. Or…or someone with it."

"You felt someone else here with the fire?"

"Unmistakably. But no one is there."

"Could it be Myrddin?"

"No, not Myrddin." Her head pounded with pain again. "It must be nearing sunset. So much time has passed. Meirchion will be here…soon."

"I'm not waiting for Meirchion."

She winced in confusion. Why was he so urgent to leave? Her gaze dropped again and passed over a blotch of red on his tunic's sleeve. Blood. Fresh. Streaked on the deerskin. Her eyes snapped up to his face.

"I'm not hurt." Though fatigued, he spoke with calm. "You heard nothing? The Pict? The Saxons who came after?"

Fear clutched her. "Saxons?" She shook her head. "I remember nothing. What happened?"

Marcus laid his hand gently along her cheek. "I'll never understand how the fire uses you, but, Claeri, we have need to leave, now, right now. For the outpost fort on Ceredig's border."

She saw pain in his eyes and realized the blood on his sleeve meant another fight had happened and likely worsened his bruised ribs. She shuddered, the confusion stubborn in her mind. If only she could understand what the gods were trying to say.

"Can you ride?" he asked again.

"No, Marcus, we must find Macsen's sword. Before it's too late." The words were out before she could stop them.

"It must wait. There is no choice. Not now." Again the dread crossed his face, but it softened. "I understand. I do. Believe me.

When we go back to Caer Luguvalos, I will try to find out everything I can about Hywel from Gwrast. I hope he can give us a clue about the sword, but there will be little time, perhaps no time. Claerwen, Octa has landed. He could be here in less than a sennight. Do you understand?"

It was that bad. She could see it in his eyes. He was not trying to scare her. But the gods tugged at her as well with whispers in her soul. How could she ignore that? Yet when she locked her gaze with Marcus's and stared into his eyes' blackness, their intensity bored back into hers. He was right. The gods would need to understand this time. Unless they could spread word and warning to those who could repel the Saxons, there would be no one left to wield Macsen's sword, even if it could be found.

Claerwen straightened. "I can ride," she said and turned for her horse.

The wind speared in cold, relentless, unforgiving howls from the sea. Kneeling, the boy leaned his aching head against a rough, angular stone protruding from the sand. Rain and blown seawater soaked his hair; sand pummeled his face. He closed his eyes against the fury.

Mercenaries, they were called. Hired soldiers. He shook his head slowly against the wind's force. Hired murderers, in truth, ordered to kill, no questions of who or why. Mercenaries, a word and creature that should be expelled from the conscious world ever and forever.

The dawn's light would be coming soon. He was done with vomiting and let the rain wash his face. If only he had been able to do something, anything, but after the useless attempt to find the guards, he had been struck down and had fallen to the beach below, left as if dead himself.

He wiped his mouth on his sleeve and with a groan of self-loathing, the boy aged from youth to adulthood within moments.

Mercenaries. Men of Vortigern, the man of black robes of death. A Briton born. Risen to high king. Sunk to traitor. If only the wind could scrub free the memories of the faces and the smell, foul enough to melt steel. If only there would be no more killing, no more dead, like the young Saxon lying on the farmstead's turf…

Marcus couldn't breathe. He choked for air, opened his eyes, but the dead face stayed in his mind. He raked his gaze from one side to the other. He found only darkness, except next to him a pale face showed in the earliest of dawnlight, a body that rested along his side, so still, so white against the black.

With a harsh grunt, he wrenched free of the cloak and sat straight up.

"Marcus?"

He did not hear Claerwen. He gulped air to ease the tightness in his chest and ran his gaze across the darkness in search of something familiar, something to distract him.

Nothing was there, but neither was the rain. No stormy beach-head, no rotting flesh. No Saxon mercenaries. Vortigern the traitor was long dead. The two fresh horses traded for the old ones at the outpost three days before, dozed on their tethers. The first morning birds called.

And Claerwen, rousted from sleep, watched him. He realized she had been lying next to him in the dark. "Damn," he choked out and fumbled for the wineskin he had put down the evening before. He had been too tired then to pull out its stopper.

"Marcus?" Her voice was warm, comforting.

"Aye," he exhaled softly and leaned against the wall. His head thumped lightly against it. "Another nightmare." He stared up into the ceiling of the abandoned house in which they had taken shelter from the rain in the night. The wall's daub and wattle surface, cracked from years of neglect, was rough against his back through the deerskin tunic.

Claerwen moved closer and pressed her palm to his chest. "Tell me."

Her hand was warm, her voice full of compassion, yet he felt himself unable to respond, not even able to lift a hand to touch her. How could he tell her of the nightmares? He shook his head.

He drank, long and deep from the wineskin. It was strong, sweet mead, a gift from the outpost's officer, and it went down easily. Warmth spread through his belly.

"Tell me," she breathed again when his face lifted a tiny fraction. "Was it of the imprisonment?"

He closed his eyes and rested his face against her brow. If only it were. From that kind of torture he had healed. But from this, how could there ever be healing? No, it was enough that he should bear the abhorrence. Alone. He could not lay it on her and abuse her compassion.

He drank long again. "It was not the imprisonment," he said. The drink buzzed in his head. Taken in quantity on an empty stomach, he welcomed its numbing presence. He set aside the skin, rose and walked outside.

Claerwen followed.

He regarded her. She was so beautiful. Even smudged with dust, even in the rough, boyish clothing, her gracefulness was as ethereal as her gift of second sight. How had he ever convinced himself that he could drag her into his work? No choice this time. He shook his head, partly at his own folly, mostly to tell her could not speak of the nightmare, not this time, not ever.

He caught her hand and pulled her close. Face tilted to hers, he indulged in a heated kiss. Gods of the light, he could not help himself. He needed her distraction, an ease to the torture of his mind, no different than the use of drink. How many times had he given in, unwittingly or otherwise, and used her to appease his memories? He didn't know, but, damn, she felt so good in his hands.

Leaves riffled. Marcus pushed back his hair, clumped over his face, and peered over Claerwen's shoulder. All was still, silent, except for the birds' singing.

The leaves rustled again, out of place in the quiet. His skin prickled. No animals. Instead, one shadow moved, vague, disconcerting, a good twenty paces away. A man in dark robes, as unmoving as a standing stone, watched. His hood shadowed his face, the features indistinguishable. How long had he been there?

Or was it Handor? Marcus readied to move Claerwen aside and to safety, but the robes struck him as strange, bulky and made of layers of some unidentifiable material. The longer he stared, the more he thought the man wore feathers.

"By the gods…" he said and gently pushed Claerwen aside. "Tell me I'm not still dreaming." His sword and the belt with his biggest dagger were still in the house. He bent for a smaller knife kept in one of his boots.

Claerwen turned. Her mouth dropped open and she clamped a hand around his arm to stop him from pulling the knife. "You're not dreaming," she said and bounded away.

Marcus lunged to catch her, but she was already out of his reach. He cursed under his breath and yanked the dagger out of his boot. Yet he held. Claerwen had sensed no danger. He watched her skim through the bracken as lightly as a bluebird. Was his prickling skin telling him to trust her instincts?

The man dropped his hood as Claerwen neared him.

"Myrddin Emrys," Marcus said through his teeth. His eyes lifted to the sky. Relieved in part, he hoped for news, but he was also annoyed. The Enchanter might interfere.

Marcus tramped across in Claerwen's tracks. Halfway there, he noted that she hesitated before she took up Myrddin's hand in greeting. Strange. He had never seen her falter regarding the Enchanter. Finally she welcomed Myrddin with warm words and received a kiss on the cheek.

Approaching, Marcus nearly halted in astonishment. A mantle of large black feathers truly did cover Myrddin's shoulders. Beneath, he wore thick dark robes, and he carried a tall walking staff with a small ram's skull on top. He looked older, greyer, as if he had taken on a dozen years just in the few weeks since leaving Winchester.

A body like a raven, Marcus remembered Claerwen's description. When she turned at his arrival, he was certain fear lay in her eyes beneath a mask of calm. He flicked a fingertip at one of the feathers. "Why are you here? And what in the gods' names are you wearing?"

Myrddin gave a slight but stately shift of his shoulders. In return, his starker than usual eyes narrowed and first examined Marcus's rough hunting clothes, including the bloodstains, then moved on to Claerwen's identical garments.

The silence extended. "You have news, don't you?" Claerwen prompted. It was a statement more than a question.

A bitter twist squinted the outer corners of Myrddin's eyes and his gaze traveled between them again.

"Myrddin?" Claerwen reached out but held back from touching him.

Again hesitation, Marcus noted. What was she afraid of?

"Aye, there is news," Myrddin finally said. "After you left Winchester, Octa escaped prison."

"We know this," Marcus said. "And of the landing. They march to Hadrian's Wall. If what I've heard is true, most of the fighting will be to the east. Gododdin and Brynaich are prepared. But some of it will come this way, and I don't know how much. I've warned Strathclyde and Rheged and sent word to Uther as well. Now, what is the *real* news?"

"Uther knows, he gathers his war bands now."

"He knows already?" Marcus's jaw ached with tension. "How much does he know? Octa will be at the Wall within days. Where is he? Still in Cornwall?"

Myrddin stalled.

"He hasn't reconciled with Gorlois, has he?" Claerwen asked.

A hint of regret crept into Myrddin's bitterness. "You will hear the rumors soon enough. You may as well hear the truth now." He shook his head. "He challenged Gorlois—like a fool—after the last demand to return to Winchester failed. Gorlois virtually immured Ygerna at Tintagel, then made a war camp in a small fort a few miles up the coast. Uther besieged it for several days."

Myrddin glanced at the sky, still overcast and threatening rain. "During the wait," he went on, "my uncle acted on the remarkable notion of going to Tintagel and seducing Ygerna. While he was gone, a command was 'misunderstood,' so it seems, which caused a series of predetermined actions to be carried out. The wrong ones. The camp was attacked, breached, looted, and Gorlois killed. Uther returned, and found all this done. And what does he do? Go back to Tintagel to express his regrets to the newly widowed Ygerna."

Marcus snorted. "Regrets, my arse."

Myrddin glared acridly at the flash of humor. "Now," he spit, "while Uther goes off to fight Saxons, the Lady hides alone in her fortress. She sent her daughter from her marriage with Gorlois away, to other kin. She's even changed the spelling of her name to the Irish form, Igraine, an attempt to deflect some of the shame."

Claerwen edged closer to Marcus, touched his arm. "You were there, weren't you?" she said to Myrddin. "Uther forced you to help him enter Tintagel."

Marcus's lips twisted halfway into a smile. Her first remark had matched his own first thought, but the second one did not. "Myrddin is never forced to do anything," he said.

"I have need to be on my way now." Myrddin pulled up his hood.

"Are you being followed?" Claerwen asked.

"No."

"Then…please—"

He shook his head with too much conviction, too much stubbornness. He turned away.

"You know I'm going to ask this." Marcus caught the Enchanter's arm before he could take a step. "How did you get into Tintagel? Enough guards must have been there that a mouse couldn't squeak without getting beheaded."

Once more Myrddin stalled, his eyes unreadable, as always.

Anger rose in Marcus, born of frustration. "You dressed Uther in Gorlois's clothes, didn't you? He must have had a helmet with a face guard, or a hooded cloak. At night it would be easy to hide a face in the shadows."

"There was no helmet or hood," Myrddin shot back. "Only a carefully prepared face and a well-rehearsed voice to fool the guards in his rush to the Lady of Tintagel." Again he eyed their clothing in a stinging appraisal. "And from where do you suppose I learned disguise-making so well?" He turned on his heel and strode away.

"Wait!" Claerwen shouted after him. "It's too dangerous. You must turn back and go south. Myrddin?"

He paid no heed. His presence drained from the hollow like a dissipating cloud.

"It's no use," Marcus said. He returned the knife to his boot. "But I'd give a pot of silver to know where he's going right now. And why he hasn't tried to learn what we're doing." He gave Claerwen a mischievous look. "And why he wears feathers. Is he intending to fly?"

Her face, crestfallen, turned away.

His cynicism fled. "Forgive me, Claeri."

She shrugged it off. "He must have already known Gorlois would die, even before he left Winchester. He saw it in the fire. And of course Ygerna would say nothing that Uther came to her. Even with the best of disguises, she had to know the difference. Uther has blue eyes. Gorlois's were brown. He was short and husky. Uther is tall. She wanted the king in her bed, regardless of the consequences. Shame? Nonsense."

"And all the while," Marcus said, "the world will believe Myrddin's magic changed Uther into Gorlois for that one night."

He watched Claerwen walk a few paces in the direction Myrddin had gone. There, she picked up a feather that had dropped from the mantle and twirled it between her fingers. Myrddin's strange acrimony had unnerved her, even frightened her, Marcus realized, and she was trying to hide it. He leaned on a tree to rub his aching knee and decided anything else he might say about the Enchanter would prove unflattering and only hurt Claerwen further. He would keep the rest of his thoughts to himself.

"How does Tintagel look?" she gasped out.

Marcus stared at her. She stumbled towards him, her face suddenly ashen, and he caught her, sure she was about to faint.

"How does it look?" she asked again.

"It's a timber fortress that sits on a huge rounded rock off the Cornish coast. A narrow causeway is the only way to reach it."

Her fingers tightened on his arms. "Then it's all connected. All of it." Her gaze jolted up and drilled into his face. "I saw Tintagel in the vision, just as you described it. It *is* the prophecy, Marcus. It's no coincidence Myrddin found us here. No more than he was unwittingly drawn into helping Uther. No more than we have unwittingly been drawn to look for Macsen's sword. Ygerna…Igraine conceived on the night Uther went into Tintagel. The child will be born at Midwinter."

"And her child will be in the line to the king Myrddin prophesied?" Marcus's voice dropped into a whisper so strained it was barely audible even to himself. "Or will this child *be* that king?"

He held her gaze for a long, silent minute. Macsen's sword, she had said, must be found before it was too late. She had seen it in the fire as surely as Myrddin had seen Gorlois's death and all that was related to it. It was why they were in Rheged; somewhere there the sword lay hidden. They *would* have to find it, in spite of Octa, in spite of Meirchion, in spite of Handor.

Claerwen stepped back from him and shivered. She dropped the feather. "It's all coming true." Her hand rose to her chest and pressed against her heart as if she were in pain. "We should go on...to Caer Luguvalos." She broke away and strode back into the house.

Gods, Marcus thought, she was as imprisoned inside her visions as much as he was inside his nightmares. She was fighting to understand their meaning, and something in them terrified her. What horrible things had she been shown?

And here he had been using her to assuage his own pain. How selfish he could be sometimes. The image of her eyes, her wondrous green-blue eyes, tugged on him. How many times had he looked into them and been unable to pull away, unwilling to do anything but let her sweep over and through him, at once a rushing gale and a placid sky? Even with the house wall between them, the power of the bond they shared tightened. But why did it feel as if the gale was about to break?

Marcus followed her into the house. She stood next to the cloak on the floor where they had slept and was packing their gear. When he walked up to her, she handed him the first of the traveling pouches. Her eyes were filled with tears.

Marcus dropped the pouch.

"But we must go," she said. "There's no time. You said so." Fear cracked her words.

"Take me," he whispered. "Take me any way you want." He touched his lips to hers.

Her mouth shook. The tears spilled. Her arms went round him, tight, fierce, and every string of constraint was abandoned. Pressed into him, she leaned back and pulled until they fell together onto the cloak. Discarded clothing soon scattered over the hard-packed earthen floor; stray leaves floated up and away when each piece dropped.

Marcus emptied his mind of all but the intoxication of Claerwen's hair across his face, her breath against his shoulder, the familiar, heady passion of her kisses. By the gods, how he cherished this woman. Questions and gales be damned, his last thought came and went. All that mattered was the joining of their souls.

CHAPTER 9

Caer Luguvalos
Early Summer, AD 471

AT midmorning three days later, Marcus walked through the fort's gates at Caer Luguvalos.

Dressed once more in the grey Roman wig and the clothing of the old storyteller, he was quickly admitted by the gatemaster, but instead of being escorted to the king's seneschal, he was merely told where the man probably was. In addition he received an admonition for having arrived at a poor time. Word of the Saxon landing had already arrived.

Several paces beyond the gates, on the long, straight street that led to the great hall, Marcus leaned on his walking stick and observed. As he reoriented himself, he began to recognize the pattern of streets and buildings. Quiet compared to the town outside, the fort had not been altered much in the five years since his earlier infiltration. The baths and most of the barracks had never been rebuilt since the last razing on the Roman garrison's final departure. The commanding officer's great hall and residence, located directly in the center, had been refurbished to suit the British kings who had wrested control fifty years before.

Satisfied he knew where to go, Marcus started for the great hall. Along the street he noted only the spare, permanent contingent that guarded the fort was preparing for war. No signs of Meirchion's regular war bands were evident; neither there nor outside when he had approached the town that morning with Claerwen. Nervous but calm townspeople, their belongings carried on their backs or wheeled in carts, were gathering within the town walls and staking out places to camp in wait for the onslaught of Saxon terror. A few had recognized him as the *chwedleuwr* from the inn and greeted him.

His thoughts turned back to Claerwen. Against her protests and with his own misgivings, he had left her hidden in a grove near the town's west side with both horses and all their gear. With the likelihood that Octa's assassin was searching for them inside the town or even within the fort itself, Marcus had made the reluctant decision to hide her. He also did not want her trapped inside the walls should the Saxons arrive before he was done.

Marcus spotted the seneschal in the courtyard outside the great hall's front doors. The man appeared well occupied with his duties. Rather than wait, Marcus detoured along the cross street and on to the path that would lead him to the buildings behind.

He was glad he had no need to enter the hall. If it was the same as he remembered, and it likely was, its long and narrow interior hovered with darkness, dismal and as sullen as its people. The Roman-built hypocaust for heating beneath the floor had been long out of use, partially caved in, and like the barracks and baths, left unrepaired. The Celtic kings of Rheged had preferred the simplicity of a traditional hearth. The huge central fire pit they had built poured out smoke that blackened the high ceiling of curved beams with the permanent odor of burnt wood and peat.

In spite of the gatemaster's warning, Marcus believed the time he had come was the best he could have chosen. The house guards were too busy to pay attention to one more refugee. He passed the end of the great hall and the street that separated it from the commander's house.

Continuing on, he located a door midway along the house's wall. Face downcast, he leaned heavily on the walking stick and shuffled inside. Gently, he closed the door. No guards. All was quiet.

Stairs led him to a second floor. At the top, Marcus turned into a corridor lined with many rooms. All the doors were closed, and a few small oil lamps set at intervals shed the only light. Even in their dim cast he could see the walls had not been kept well; the plaster surface puckered from rainwater that had leaked in. A pair of wide doors, also shut and with two dozing guards on stools next to them, closed off the corridor's end. He knew the doors hid the king's chambers.

One of the guards stood. "Are you lost, old man?"

Marcus recognized him from the inn, and when he shambled up to the man, the curt manner dissolved.

"Forgive me, my lord." The guard bowed his head.

Marcus brushed aside the apology with a shaking hand. "I was told Lord Gwrast wished to see me if I returned to Caer Luguvalos. Would he have time now?"

The guard hesitated.

"Lord Meirchion told me to come here," Marcus added.

The guard inclined his head again. "I will inquire if the king is well enough to receive a guest. Please wait there." He indicated a bench along the wall.

Marcus carefully gathered his cloak together and sat. He was too warm, and he knew he would be once inside. He had worn the deerskins beneath the cloak instead of the storyteller's loose robes—the robes would be too much of a hindrance if he should need to run or fight.

He sat back against the wall and closed his eyes. The *galerus* itched. How did Romans ever bear them, especially in the Mediterranean heat? He breathed in a labored rhythm, one hand still on the walking stick's head, and he wondered if he would reach his own old age. How fine it would be to sit with Claerwen in front of their house and take in the cool, refreshing air of Dinas Beris.

Claerwen. He allowed his mind to drift back to her and the ruined house they had borrowed a few days before. A thin smile crossed his lips, half hidden beneath his greyed moustache. Behind his closed eyes the images unfolded as they had ever since, over and over.

Though curtailed by exhaustion, interruptions and lack of privacy during their travels, he and Claerwen had not forgone affection and often took it in quiet passion at night. But that morning, the extraordinary sensuality of their lovemaking had reached a depth he had never quite imagined. Swept away, he would not have cared if they had been in the middle of Winchester palace's crowded courtyard. Since then, the memories haunted relentlessly. Out of joy? Pure need? Or something else? It felt like somewhere deep in his mind he was afraid.

"*Chwedleuwr*?" the guard called softly.

Marcus's smile widened. The memory, so mesmerizing… How he was still wrapped together with her in the cloak an hour later, lusciously naked…

"*Chwedleuwr*? Are you asleep?"

Marcus opened his eyes. Both guards stared at him.

"Lord Gwrast will see you. Are you ill?"

"Ah, merely an old man's habit to nap at will, you know," he said and pushed up onto his feet. "Thank you."

He choked down laughter while they led him to the doors.

The chambers were dark, the windows shuttered and covered with thick woven drapes. The room smelled of smoke-blackened wood from years of hearth fires and an uncountable number of pungent herbal remedies. Gwrast, king of Rheged, sat propped up on a massive bed and what seemed like a hundred pillows. Frazzled strands of white hair strayed from the top of his head, but his eyes peered with bright alertness out of the sagging folds of his face. The last time Marcus had seen him, he had appeared at death's portal. Little had changed.

Marcus bowed. He started across the room, his normal limp from his damaged knee more pronounced. He passed two waiting house slaves. At the foot of the bed, he bowed again.

Gwrast waved Marcus to a chair next to the bed then snapped his fingers at the slaves. They scurried out.

"'Tis rather grim out there, so I'm hearing," Gwrast said. He cleared his throat several times before going on. "Not the way old men like us care to spend our last days."

Marcus rocked his head up and down in agreement. "I have come from the north. They will be here within another day at most."

"And my sons give so little attention," the king sighed. "How many times have I warned them?"

Marcus watched the frail framework of Gwrast's hand make a fist, the discolored, veiny skin stretched thin like gauze from wrist to knuckles. He hid his own hands, thick, scarred, powerful enough to break bones, in the folds of his cloak.

The king's gesture gave the impression that he had accepted the warning of the coming attack. The comment about his sons told Marcus that Rheged's war bands would probably not arrive in time to stop, deter or deflect the Saxons, if the warriors had been summoned at all. Worst of all, Gwrast had the sound of defeat. Disappointed, Marcus could only hope Uther's army was on the march and swift enough to step in.

"Are you looking to take refuge here?" the king asked. "You won't be able to outrun the Saxon—I'm sure you know this." He struggled against the pillows to find a more comfortable position. "In truth, I'd like to be selfish now. When they said a storyteller had come to visit, I couldn't believe it. It's been such a long time since we've had one here. I want you to stay, at least for a bit."

Marcus lifted one greyed eyebrow. "I heard talk that a bard once resided here."

The king's baggy face drooped even more. He drew breath to speak, a long, tired inhalation. But before the words came out, one of the slaves reappeared with a pair of drinking horns. The second man followed with a wide wooden platter of food. He placed it on a table next to the bed.

"Ah, fine enough," Gwrast said as one of the horns was placed in his hands. "Be comfortable, *chwedleuwr*. Accept my hospitality, poor as it is. Grant an old man a last pleasure and I will grant you a place of refuge, poor as that may be as well. Perhaps the Saxon will go east and we'll be lucky, eh?"

Without offering an answer, Marcus saluted the king with the drinking horn he had been given. He watched the slaves as he drank. They showed no signs of leaving. "And what story would you most like to hear?" he asked Gwrast.

The king picked up a small piece of bread from the platter and pondered among his pillows while he nibbled.

"My bard was Hywel of the Flowing Verse," he murmured, his eyes on the ceiling. "His favorite story was 'Macsen's Dream.' Ah, Hywel...in whichever world you walk now, I hope you're still telling that story." He tossed the half-eaten bread back onto the platter.

Hywel Gwodryd's favorite tale. Marcus knew the story well.

Though no sword was mentioned in it, both the sacred weapon and the tale were named for Macsen Wledig, a man who had taken up leadership of Britain through his resounding defeat of Saxons nearly a century before. The connection could not be mere coincidence.

Alert again, the king slowly dropped his gaze from the ceiling. He waved away the slaves and shoved the platter aside, its scrape on the table loud.

Marcus looked up at the king, then glanced after the two attendants. They had gone through the same door but left it open this time. He listened whether they remained within earshot, or if others were in the room beyond. All was silent except for the king's raspy breathing.

"They will have returned to the kitchens if you're worried about unwanted ears," Gwrast said with a faint smile. "But usually bards appreciate an attentive audience."

Marcus lifted the drinking horn in another salute. Perhaps so, he thought, but more than house slaves occupied the fort. "Ah…I was thinking," he said aloud, "how fine it would be to stay in one place for a while. Your bard must have savored his status."

"Aye, Hywel was a good friend as well as my court bard. Such a waste it was when he was killed."

"Killed? Raiders?"

Gwrast shook his head. "Fell. Broke his neck."

Marcus studied the king's face. Did Gwrast believe his own statement? Or was it rehearsed, a mask over the truth? "An accident?" he asked.

"He especially liked the river…said it was his muse. He would go down there and practice his verses—even in the pouring rain. His booming voice could be heard above the worst downpour. Magnificent. That day he stood too close to the edge and slipped on the slick turf."

"He fell into the water?"

"No. He was found on the embankment, his head snapped back over a rock."

Marcus grunted in sympathy and wished he did not know better that Hywel's neck had been twisted, broken by human hands, not crushed by falling on a stone. He had seen the results too many times in battles. "His family must have been very distraught," he said.

"The only kin anyone knew of was a son. We haven't seen him since he was, oh, probably about twenty winters. Rumors had it that Saxons took him as a slave. We thought perhaps Hywel's wife died when the boy was very young. No one knows the truth. Hywel wouldn't talk about it." The king picked up the bread again and bit off a small piece.

A son. A son who might know of the sword? Marcus wondered if Meirchion knew of this son as well, and if so, knew where he was. "Did anyone try to locate this—?"

The guards' voices rose in the corridor and the doors slapped open. Meirchion charged in. When he came to a halt in the middle of the room, his flowing hair and robes settled like sails on a suddenly becalmed boat. "Father, they are—"

"Mind your manners, boy," Gwrast cut him off. "Do you not see I have a guest?"

Meirchion glanced at Marcus, nodded his recognition of the storyteller. "The scouts have come in," he plunged on to Gwrast. "They say they'll be here within the hour. Far more than there should have been."

Far more than planned? Marcus thought. He glared at Meirchion's panic-stricken face. Not the single war band meant to filter in and quietly grab lands that belonged to Ceredig of Strathclyde?

"Are you surprised?" the king asked. "And where are *your* men? No, don't answer. We all know. The whole of Britain knows. Probably even the emperor in Rome knows."

"But the Saxon should have gone east—"

"Gone east? What are you blathering about? I don't want to hear more, Meirchion. Again I have had need to take matters into my own hands." The king's bright eyes gleamed from under his drooping eyelids.

Meirchion scowled. "What have you done?"

Marcus rose from his chair, a slight smile on his lips and in his eyes. Gwrast, though old and frail, still held the true reins of Rheged through his capable, calculating mind. The words of defeat were merely meant to lure a bard into staying. "You've taken control of them, haven't you?" His smile broadened.

The king's grin matched Marcus's. "I would never have offered you refuge unless I knew my kingdom's warriors would be here to fight for my own wrinkled arse. You've realized that. Smart man."

"How dare you!" Meirchion said.

Marcus shuffled the few steps to Meirchion and caught the prince's arm. He bored his glare into his face. "Your father was right to do so."

Meirchion fumed, but held his tongue.

"The war bands belong to all of Rheged," Marcus continued. "Not you, not your brother. *All* of Rheged. The high king is coming as well. Whether in time before the Saxon reaches here, I cannot say, but he *is* coming. And by now…Ceredig of Strathclyde prepares."

Meirchion blanched. "How do you know all this? You're only a storyteller."

Marcus ignored the slight. This was too important to stop now. "You must learn one thing if you ever learn anything in this life. Most of our own people, including you, look no farther than the next hill and see it as a grand prize. That won, you turn to the next hill and take it as well. But all the while your back is turned, those from the last hill come and steal back their land *and* yours. And how many dead each time? The Saxons instead see Britain as *one* kingdom to conquer. *All* of it. Not dozens of tiny kingdoms to take one at a time at their leisure. Don't you see, while we are busy thieving and slitting each other's throats, the Saxon is stealing our freedom?"

"But I know of treachery in Gododdin that—"

A clap and a loud laugh from the bed interrupted Meirchion's response. Marcus turned. The king actually looked gleeful and struggled to stand against the side of the bed. Afraid Gwrast might fall, Marcus rushed across to lend an arm for support.

"You shall listen to this man," Gwrast said to his son. "He knows, more than anyone in these lands, the meaning of freedom. And no one has fought harder for it. Not even Uther or Ambrosius before him."

The king touched Marcus's neatly trimmed beard and felt the ash coloring. "I thought so. Wash that out, if you like, you won't need it any longer." He pointed at a small basin filled with water then grinned. "I recognize not only your voice after all these years, but your words as well. No one has ever spoken of freedom in the way you do."

To deny Gwrast's recognition was pointless. Marcus leaned the stick against the chair and reluctantly pulled off the grey wig. His black hair cascaded onto his shoulders.

Meirchion frowned, confused, and drew a hasty conclusion. "You must be the Pict that didn't—" He bit off his words before he said too much.

"A Pict?" Gwrast laughed. "Where did you come across such a notion, boy? This is Marcus ap Iorwerth. You've heard of him, I'm sure? You see, a courier arrived not long ago with some news." He turned to Marcus. "Your warning was well heeded."

"Marcus ap Iorwerth," Meirchion started. "You're the—" He clamped his mouth shut again.

Marcus gave him a sarcastic, all-knowing smile. Aye, the spy, he silently completed the thought for Meirchion. The man Gwrast hired to stop the uprising years ago. The man Hywel had needed to talk with at the time of his murder. And the man who had just sabotaged another plot and an alliance with Octa that never truly existed. The prince's face reflected all of it.

Gwrast sat again on the edge of his bed, his legs too weak to hold his meager weight for long. His eyes tracked from Marcus to his son and back, a sly pleasure at how the divulgence of Marcus's identity made Meirchion look foolish.

Gods, Marcus swore silently. He strode to the basin to wash the ash from his face. His chronic bluntness had often gained him much respect, but it sometimes, like now, became his undoing as well. This time he could not even blame Uther's homage ceremony for exposing his identity. Even if he recreated the disguise, the king's outburst had probably been overheard. Guards and slaves spread news faster than disease. Now, to leave the fort without Octa's assassin discovering him would be difficult at best. He wiped his face dry.

"Father?" Meirchion's tone had abruptly shifted and was now

laced with true concern.

Marcus turned. Gwrast sat on the bed facing the slaves' doorway and stared in amazed silence, his mouth slightly open, his pale face the consistency of bread dough.

Marcus sloughed off the cloak and exposed his deerskins and sword. "My lord?" He looked through the doorway.

"'Tis the son of Hywel Gwodryd," the king murmured.

A man stood in the shadows, a familiar snarl on his face. An instant later he was gone.

Marcus whipped around. "*Handor* is Hywel's son? Are you sure?"

"Aye, it was him," Meirchion answered for his father. "But why, after all this time?"

Marcus shot him a cold eye for the ludicrous question. How could Octa's hateful assassin be the only one in the world who might know where Macsen's sword was hidden? And how could he be in league with the conniving, lying man who had murdered Hywel, his father?

"Damn," Marcus hissed under his breath. How much had Handor overheard? Then he realized from the cruel, ironic twist of the assassin's face that Claerwen was not safe. Not in the woods, not anywhere. Leaving behind the wig and cloak, Marcus sprinted through the slaves' doorway.

Almost to another door at the opposite end of the slaves' room, Meirchion caught Marcus and grabbed his arm. Marcus skidded, veering, and rammed into the wall. The prince slid into him.

"How dare you—" Meirchion started.

Marcus shook loose, the big knife from the back of his belt now in his hand. "Do not waste my time," he spit. "You have a kingdom to defend. Go to it now, and remember, quite a few would like to know exactly how Hywel Gwodryd died. And if you dare give consideration to sending me to the same fate, that would raise a bloody fair lot of questions. Wouldn't it?"

He turned and raced away.

Rain began to fall. Claerwen pulled up her hood and drew

breath, long and deep, in an attempt to ease her tension. For the third time since Marcus had departed for the fort, she inspected the horses and gear. All the leather pouches were secure—still—and she patted the animals' necks, spoke a few comforting words and sighed with the hope that she and Marcus would not be there when Octa's forces arrived. He had not been gone so long, but by the light, she hated waiting.

The effigy was inside the last leather pouch she'd look into. So gruesome, she thought, but from curiosity she pulled it partially out anyway. If only she could read Latin. Excalibur, the last word, still puzzled her. A place, a tribal name, a person's name? No new ideas came to mind. "Beware…Excalibur," she muttered aloud. "What *is* it?"

"Excalibur?" A woman's voice cut through the quiet.

Startled, Claerwen crammed the effigy back into the pouch. She had heard no footsteps, no rustle besides the light, hushed rain.

A frail woman stood before her. About fifty summers of age, she wore the cream-colored robes of a women's religious order. Her hair was completely covered by kerchiefs and she wore no adornments except one pendant of dull, unpolished pewter on a leather thong. It twisted and turned as she moved, and Claerwen recognized it as one from an order of the old religion. The white robes were spotted with raindrops and smelled of wet wool.

"How do you know of Excalibur?" The question, though spoken with challenge, held an element of fear in the tone. Her gaze raked over Claerwen's boyish clothing.

Claerwen ignored the critical assessment. Who was this? Taller than the stranger, she took a step closer.

The woman had to lift her face just a bit to meet Claerwen's gaze. A faintly brighter shaft of light caught her eyes—brilliant, wide-set green eyes, staring, calm, sad, solemn—the same eyes from the vision.

Claerwen shuddered. *Beware*, the effigy's warning struck her. Beware of more than the sons of the north? Beware of this woman?

The green eyes tightened.

No, it was not the effigy's warning. Fire in the head was cautioning her. In the same instant, she recognized it also lay behind the green eyes—the same sense she'd had at the farmstead. Had this woman followed from the north? Had she seen Marcus kill the young Saxon? Or was she connected to Octa's assassin?

The fire was not to be feared and composure returned to Claerwen. "You have fire in the head," she said and folded her hands. "Like I do. And you know this."

The eyes grew hard. "Who are you?"

Claerwen offered no answer. Compelled to hold the green eyes' gaze, she could not help but think the woman had been drawn there through the fire rather a more logical reason. "What have you seen?" she asked. "Why have you come here?"

The rain increased its patter on the leaves around them. Shouts echoed in the distance. Claerwen glanced past the woman and caught a glimpse of two men galloping towards the fort. The Pendragon standard flapped on staffs above them. Scouts. Uther would not be far behind.

The woman gripped Claerwen's arm. "What do you know of Excalibur?"

The horses snorted discontent at the outburst. Claerwen held still and continued to gaze into her face. Sadness deepened there. Loss. Fear as well. Why? Who was this woman?

Tangwen. The name whispered within Claerwen, the female name Marcus said the Saxons had spoken. He had sloughed it off as insignificant, believing it was a Saxon word that merely sounded like a name in his own language. But connections sparked through her mind. A woman. Handor and Meirchion sought a woman, and it appeared the three Saxons had as well. Claerwen squinted at her. "Are you called Tangwen?"

Fear rippled in the green eyes.

Claerwen pried the fingers from her arm. "Are you Tangwen?" she asked again.

Panic flashed in the woman's face. She backed, one step, three more, then she whirled around in a swish of her white robes.

"Wait!" Claerwen shouted.

The woman fled from the trees. Claerwen raced after her, across a small stream and into the field that lay between the woods and the west side of the town. Much younger and unencumbered by long skirts, she easily began to catch up.

Horns blared from the fort's ramparts. Their mournful howl careened over the field, and Claerwen pulled up short as if caught in a spider web. It was the raw sound of war horns, the call to arms, and they chilled her down to her bones. She whirled. Those who had not yet gone within the safety of the walls ran for the gates at the lower end of the town. She turned back but could no longer see the woman.

No use to follow any farther. With the call to war, Marcus's ruse would abruptly end. He would be coming soon.

Movement whiffed behind Claerwen, the sound like a bird's wings. Rainwater sprayed against the back of her shoulders, then pain seized her neck and ran up through her skull. Numbness flooded her and she lost balance, unwillingly, her legs no longer able to hold her. Her hands groped but found nothing within reach, and she started to fall forward. Greyness clogged her eyes, then cold, slimy green wetness struck her hard on the left side, from her face to her feet. She slid limply on the grass.

Claerwen knew her eyes were still open, but only blank space spread in front of them and the vague impression of a riffling hem of mud-stained white skirts. The greyness grew heavier, too thick to breathe, too confining, too painful.

The grey turned black, and she fainted.

CHAPTER 10

Rheged
Early Summer, AD 471

RAIN. Soaking, cold. Claerwen's only wish was to go back to sleep.

But she had not been asleep. She knew that, and she knew she was lying on soggy ground with rain pummeling her. She tried to overcome the sickening, wooly grey pain in the back of her head and neck that clogged her thinking. It refused to clear.

Her eyes slit open, but she saw nothing. Her hair had loosened from its braid and fallen over her face. With effort, she slid one hand over the grass and dragged it back.

Claerwen lay in the center of the meadow more than fifty paces from the horses. Tilted away from the town wall, the field rolled in waves down to meet the stream at the woods' edge. With the townspeople and those from outlying farmsteads racing for refuge or to take up arms, no one had seen her or what had happened. Or no one cared to risk a few moments to help. She pushed herself up.

The rain began to lessen into misty drizzle. At the north end of the field, shadowy figures moved. Claerwen wiped her eyes and blinked several times to focus. She first saw two men walking away, then realized they supported a third man between them. Unable to walk, his feet dragged, toes pointed together, head down. A fourth man, running, was catching up to the others.

A small broken tree limb lay in front of her. Claerwen touched the tender bump at the base of her skull. Had the unconscious man had been struck the same way? She snagged hold of the broken branch and used it to get her feet under herself.

She stood. Though wobbly, she gazed again at the figures. The drizzle lightened a little more. She could not see the unconscious man's head, but his clothing and the sword across his back were as familiar as her own skin.

Clarity came fully upon her. "No… Marcus."

The men dragging him away were Saxons; *seaxes* hung from their belts identified them. Both were tall and filthy, one lean, the other husky—the descriptions Marcus had given of those who had tried to capture him only days before. She shivered. Why they had not taken his weapon, she could not guess.

The last man, now within twenty paces, picked up speed, his sword drawn. Claerwen staggered forward several steps; her heart started to pound. Reddish-brown hair and a tan cloak—Handor was closing in, his path straight for Marcus.

The husky Saxon let go of his burden and spun around, his *seax* in his hands. He screamed at his companion in words that sounded like orders, and with brute strength rather than skill, he blocked Handor's sword as it came down. Undeterred, the assassin hacked again. The Saxon's longer reach compensated for his shorter weapon and though perhaps unwilling, he valiantly drove back his assailant.

The thin Saxon hung onto Marcus and shifted course towards the trees. As long as his attention was fixed on the fight, Claerwen hoped he would not notice her. She started running. The softness of the ground hushed her footsteps and she closed in on him, her unwavering gaze fastened on his hands. The worn, scarred gauntlets he wore were stained with fresh blood.

Like talons, her fingers gripped the broken stick. Close enough, she lifted and swung, whacked the Saxon in the arm. He dropped Marcus with yelp. Claerwen whipped completely around, the full force of the turn behind her next blow. The limb thunked and jarred her arms and shoulders. The Saxon went down on his knees.

She had not aimed well, and her feet had slid on the wet turf, taking away some of her power. She had wanted to imitate one of Marcus's best moves in a fight, but her blow had in truth glanced off the man's upraised shoulder, lifted to protect his head. Panic gripped her in the belly as he slowly got to his feet, far from losing consciousness.

His fingers wrapped around his *seax*'s handle.

Claerwen backed and raised the limb to strike again, but she already knew it was useless against the nasty blade he was pulling from its sheath. Her eyes flicked from his face, to Marcus, to the other Saxon, then back to him. She could try to elude him in the woods, but she doubted she could reach them or the hidden horses fast enough. Marcus had said he was no warrior, and though the man was rangy rather than muscular, he was long-legged and could easily outrun her.

She watched his eyes. For a moment, a hint of confusion crossed them and they diverted faintly in the direction where Marcus lay. His brows knotted together. Then he smiled halfway. "Tangwen?" he said.

He thought she was Tangwen? Claerwen frowned. His smile was neither of familiarity nor congeniality. Nor did it reek of lust. Instead, it spoke of greed.

He said the name again.

Claerwen shook her head vigorously and backed farther towards the trees. He advanced. She glanced at Marcus again. If she could reach his weapons… If he would suddenly wake and be coherent…

The Saxon made a grab for her arm. Claerwen twisted and he missed. She stumbled across the stream and thrashed her way through the underwood. She did not get far. A fist struck sharply between her shoulder blades, and she fell against the nearest tree. Impatient, the man forced her around and pinned her by the neck.

Claerwen held onto the broken branch as if it were a lifeline. She fully expected the *seax* to come up against her throat, but oddly the man sheathed it instead, then fumbled with a short length of rope hung from his belt. Her eyes widened. He was going to take her prisoner.

Instinct took over. Her will steeled, she stared up into his face, eyes wide, hypnotic lucidity a mask for her fear. She rammed the stick upward into the man's wrist to force the fingers on her throat to open, and before he could realize his mistake and recover, Claerwen pushed him away with as much strength as she could call upon. She rammed the stick again, this time between his legs. The Saxon gagged, crimson-faced and outraged, and clutched himself as he fell on his backside.

All his previous considerations were now abandoned and he gave in to anger. He kicked at her feet and she went down; the branch sprang from her hands. Unnerved, she watched him lurch onto his feet, fists balled. His eyes clearly showed that though he might not cut her, he was not going to let a woman unman him so easily.

Her mind focused in the instant she glanced at the Saxon's belt sheath. The *seax* had fallen out unnoticed and lay off to the side. With her gaze locked on his face, she waited, crouched. He took a step. Her stomach twisted sourly, but he was one more step away from the long knife, and she held her ground. He advanced another step. One fist tightened and drew back. One more pace…

Claerwen dropped and rolled. In the same motion, she grabbed the *seax* and came up on her knees, both hands around the hilt. She raked the weapon upward, her intent to hold the Saxon at bay, but its sharp edge met resistance. Horrified, she froze. The man had plunged down on his knees after her, an attempt to stop her from reaching the knife.

He stared, first at her, then at the sweeping red line that had opened across his belly. Instinctively he pressed his hands there to stanch the flow, but blood rushed unhindered between his fingers. He looked up again, the spark of life already faded in his eyes, and he fell forward.

Claerwen scrambled back out of the way. He flopped down limply, blood in spatters. All went quiet. She shook, and heard her own uneven breath draw in and out as if it belonged to someone else. She averted her eyes from him, but they involuntarily went to the blade still in her hands. Blood dripped from it. Terrified at herself, she tried to drop the weapon, but her fingers were so tightly wound around the hilt, she could not let go.

"Is this what you feel, each time you are forced to kill?" she asked Marcus in a hoarse whisper. But he wasn't there. He was injured and unconscious in the meadow. "I'm such a cow-wit," she said. She dropped the *seax* and ran.

At the edge of the meadow she halted. Marcus still lay facedown on the ground, still unmoving. Just beyond him, Handor and the bigger Saxon continued to fight. The slowing of their movements showed they were tiring. Handor's skill would give him the victory in time, and without a grain of doubt, Marcus would die once that victory was won. If only they would move away… If she could just reach him without being seen…

"Please wake up, Marcus," she pleaded softly as if he could hear her. "Please, before they finish." She swiped at stray tears.

The horses. That was her only choice now. Somehow, she would have to find someone who could help. She turned for the horses and ran.

The clash of blades echoed. They grew louder, the ring of their strikes familiar in the audible intention of death. Marcus tried to follow their pattern, but his head reverberated painfully with each hit.

He raked one hand over the grass to his temple and poked his fingertips at the source of pain. Warm and sticky. He winced. It was more blood than rain. He rolled onto his side and slowly pushed himself up, all the while muttering curses at his spinning head. Finally he opened his eyes.

He blinked once, twice, and again, and stared in the direction in which he heard the swordplay, but his eyes only focused halfway. It was enough though, to see that Handor and the huskier of the two Saxons fought. He didn't remember the attack, but logic told him the Saxon had caused the cut on his temple. Handor would have killed.

A scream shattered the otherwise stillness of the meadow, an eerie, shattering shriek that could have blown the soil from the nearest barrow and rattled the bones in the burial chambers beneath. Marcus jerked his head to the right.

Another figure raced at a dead run on a dark horse straight for Handor and the Saxon. Dressed all in black and a masked helmet that hid the face, the rider defiantly thrust a huge two-handed sword to the sky.

"Bloody *shit*…" Marcus swore aloud. Someone had found the Iron Hawk gear. And if Claerwen— Claerwen? Where was she? Dizziness swept through his head, and he dropped back again onto the grass.

He turned onto his side once more. Sickness rolled in waves from his head to his stomach. Unable to sit up, he waited for the roiling to ease, both in his belly and in his mind. Gradually, his eyes cleared enough to see again.

Handor swung his sword, caught the *seax*'s edge and ripped it out of the Saxon's grip. An instant later, the usurping Iron Hawk rode between them and yanked the horse around in a tight circle to separate them farther. The Saxon bolted.

Handor, obviously tired from fighting the brawny Saxon, took a defensive stance. Would he challenge the warrior? Marcus held his breath. The Iron Hawk circled, but Handor hesitated. That was a mistake. The warrior suddenly swung in, and the brilliant steel blade clanged against the assassin's sword. The finely balanced weight of the weapon easily swept Handor's smaller sword out of his hands. Like the Saxon, he ran.

Marcus sat up again. The rider turned the horse to face him and held still. New waves of dizziness plagued Marcus. He had to get up—the imposter, whomever he was, would attempt to imitate the Iron Hawk's brutality. Marcus eased onto his right knee, left foot forward and flat on the ground. He pulled his sword, but gods, how was he going to be able to fight, even an imposter?

With a slight motion of the heels, the rider urged the horse forward. But instead of challenging, the imposter pulled up several paces away, dismounted and walked up to Marcus, dropped the sword and knelt. For the course of several moments, they stared at each other.

Then the helmeted head moved just a bit and Marcus caught a glimpse of green-blue through the eye slits. He sat down again, placed his sword on the grass, and held his aching head. "By the gods, Claerwen," he sputtered and lay back again. Laughter born of relief claimed him.

"Marcus, are you—?" She reached for the cut on his temple.

He caught her wrist. "We have to get away from here. And put that gear away. Where are your clothes?"

"Underneath," she said. "But—"

"You've got to get out of that gear," he insisted and dragged in a long, labored breath. "Hand me the swords. Can you get me on my feet?"

She pulled him upright and supported him, his arm across her shoulders. He grasped the two hilts in his other hand. Together, they rose. "Can you walk?" she asked.

He shook back his wet hair and tried to get his bearings. "I'll be fine enough," he said.

"You always say that."

Marcus peered through the eye slits when her head turned to him. Even on her, the Iron Hawk's gear was ominous, enough to have driven off Octa's relentless assassin with fear more than force. It was profoundly incongruent with her comforting voice. "I do say that, don't I?"

In silence, they hurried to the woods.

Within the privacy of the trees, Marcus watched her strip off the gear and pack it away in the oilcloth, ready to load. Still a bit disoriented, he rested his face against her horse's neck. He realized then that she had moved all their gear to the other animal and freed the horse she had used of its burden.

"What happened?" he asked. "The last I remember… I was coming for you, from the western gate."

Claerwen took the other sword he was still holding and slid it into its sheath. "Let me see this." She pushed his hair away from the cut on his temple. With a kerchief from around her neck, she cleaned the blood from the side of his face. "It's not deep. It should heal quickly."

The eerie wail of war horns blasted from Caer Luguvalos again.

"Damn." He took the kerchief and held it to the wound. Wincing, he bowed his face close to her cheek. "The bulk of the Saxons will be here within minutes. Gwrast has sent for Rheged's war bands. Which way did Handor go?"

"North, I think. Towards the auxiliary fort. Uther should be here soon as well. Two of his scouts rode in not long ago."

Marcus pushed away from the horse. He swayed and mumbled

another oath. "If Handor finds a way into that fort, he can get through Hadrian's Wall. I've got to get him, before he can reach Octa and disappear into his war bands."

"But you're hurt."

He grabbed a wineskin, pulled the stopper, and soaked the kerchief. "Makes no difference," he said and pressed the cloth to his temple, winced again then drank several full swallows. He plugged the skin and handed it to Claerwen.

"The other Saxon went that way as well, before Handor," she said.

"I think he's the one who hit me." Marcus draped the kerchief over his shoulder. He angled the oilcloth bundle beneath the other gear along the burdened horse's flank.

"Oddly, he saved your life," Claerwen said. She helped him to arrange it. "Probably not with intention, but he stopped Handor from beheading you."

"Well, I shall thank him, if I should come across him. And the other?"

"He's dead."

"Dead?" Marcus stared at her.

She nodded, her face bowed.

"Damn," he mumbled again. "If only there would be more time." A stream of bitter images escaped from his memory: a piece of stripped flesh, the sense of helplessness, the stench of death. He muttered more oaths. Control, control. Don't give in now.

"Handor is Hywel Gwodryd's son," he said.

"His son?" Claerwen's eyes jerked up. Her hand pressed against her heart. "His son?"

Marcus squeezed his eyes shut. All the questions that had flooded his mind would boil up in hers, but there was no time for answers. He straightened and forced his eyes to bore into her face. "I'm going after him now, to try to bring him back—alive."

The war horns cried again.

Marcus untethered the horse with the gear and handed the reins to Claerwen. "Take everything with you. Go to Uther as soon as he arrives. You'll be safest there."

"Marcus, no. Not with the battle about to engage. You'll be

trapped between three armies."

The distress in her rocked him. He pulled her close, as much to hide it from himself as to comfort her. He tilted his head and pressed his mouth to hers. It was not the brief, fervent kiss of goodbyes and returns, or the rough affection born of impending terror, but a long, bone-melting lover's kiss.

"Don't you dare follow me this time, Claerwen," he warned after. "Go to Uther when he comes." He hardened his mind against the ache in his heart and withdrew.

She clung to his arm. "No. You're not thinking clearly. Not when it comes to Handor."

By the light, how he hated to hurt her like this, hated to send her into Uther's care, hated Handor all the more for it. He pulled away and vaulted onto the unburdened horse.

"Handor's the only one who could know where Macsen's sword is," he said. "This may be the only chance to find it. I must do this now." He turned the horse towards the field.

"Marcus, wait!"

He kicked the animal into motion. Her shouts followed him and he sensed her gaze on his back, but he broke free of it when he left the trees. The horse splashed through the stream, and he pressed on into a gallop.

"Marcus! There is someone else who could know!"

Her voice was lost against the drumming hooves, and he raced away.

CHAPTER II

Uxelodunum, Rheged
Early Summer, AD 471

MARCUS galloped across the fields towards the auxiliary fort. Smoke spiraled from inside the large, square and crumbling stone structure. He had expected fire. Advance Saxon bowmen in the steep, brush-filled ditch north of Hadrian's Wall had already been shooting into the abutting fort with arrows dipped in pitch and set afire. War cries rose from farther north.

On the southwest side of the enclosure once called Uxelodunum, Marcus swerved around groups of armed Britons running to fill gaps in the defensive lines. Those willing to fight refused to be trapped inside the smoking fort and chose to man the ramparts on the Wall. Though mostly local men, some of Meirchion's soldiers were among them, their shouted orders to organize mingled with shouts of panic. To the southeast, the bulk of Rheged's war bands could be seen. Surprisingly, standards from both Meirchion and his brother Masguid flew in the forefront. At least for now, Marcus hoped, the two princes had set aside their pettiness.

Marcus pulled up within a stone's throw of a small postern gate that had been left open, the last and only place he had glimpsed Handor's flight. He slid off the horse and bounded up the incline on which the fort sat. Near it, he slowed and veered in on one side of the small gate, then strode several paces along the wall. At the opening he stopped and leaned enough to see the interior.

Now abandoned like the settlement that spilled below it down to the river, Uxelodunum had once housed a thousand Roman cavalry soldiers and horse, but when he gazed through the swirling smoke, Marcus was stunned at how decayed the fort had become, especially compared to Caer Luguvalos. He counted several small, dilapidated timber buildings, their shabby thatched roofs full of mold. Some smoldered. Ramparts built onto part of the outer wall of stone were broken in many places, blackened from previous fires and never repaired. Beyond the timber buildings, the courtyard was churned mud and dung from the years animals had been kept there.

Several small round braziers in metal racks, normally set in the courtyard for light and warming hands, burned from the incoming arrows. Several had tipped over, the coals in them spilled. One had lit an isolated pile of straw. Billowing smoke dragged up the mud's stink with it and filled the entire enclosure with a dismal pall.

Marcus wondered if the damp timber and thatch would ever truly catch fire. The gates that led through the Wall, however, were fully engulfed, probably set by the Saxons to break their way in, but until it burned through, escape that way was impossible, for Handor or anyone else.

From the courtyard, unintelligible speech pulsed in argument. Marcus recognized Handor's bitter, rough voice. He spoke in Saxon. The voice that answered was weak, strained.

Marcus slipped inside the gate and ran into the nearest building. Dark inside, it smelled intensely of the rotting thatch. Through a crack in the wall, he saw the tall, husky, cleft-chinned Saxon who had inadvertently saved his life. He was kneeling in the mud, his face swollen with bloody bruises.

Handor stood over his prey, his hands clasped together, his back towards the building. He shouted, sharp and full of anger. His hands drew back and he swung them like a hammer into the Saxon's face.

The big man took the hit, swayed, then slowly righted. Bloody bastard, Marcus wanted to spit out loud. The Saxon offered no response. Face downcast, disarmed and exhausted, he could no longer defend himself.

Handor shouted the same words again and followed with another flesh-curdling smack. He showed no sign of stopping. To satisfy his cruelty in a display of brutality had become more important than to escape the oncoming battle.

The burn in Marcus's stomach rose up inside his chest. If only he could understand the words. Control. Never lose control. He stepped out of the building, sword drawn, and strode into the courtyard.

"That's enough," he said and pricked the back of the assassin's neck.

Handor tensed.

The Saxon tried to lift his eyes. One was already swollen halfway shut; the other ran with blood and tears. Recognition flashed in his face and Marcus jerked his head at the gate, but the Saxon's eyes shut.

Handor struck again.

"I said that is enough!" Marcus shoved his foot into the assassin's hip to turn him around. The blade's tip came to rest against the man's neck.

"Get out of here," Marcus shouted at the Saxon. He heard the man struggle up and trudge away.

"You," Marcus ordered Handor, "are going to cooperate. You will like it not, I am sure, but you *will*." He stared, cold, hard.

Handor backed up against another of the buildings. He spit on the ground.

"Your father would be ashamed," Marcus said. He dug the tip against the softer skin under Handor's chin.

The man's face buckled into the wolfish snarl.

Marcus ignored it. "Aye, I know who you are, who your father was." He forced Handor's head back farther and pressed him along the wall towards the postern. "Move out. Now."

Handor's eyes twitched when the tip scratched, but he stalled, and one hand lifted to clutch a small rock hung on a thong around his neck.

"What have you done with Lady Tangwen?" he shouted.

Tangwen? Then it *was* a name the Saxons had said. Marcus maintained the cold-eyed stare to hide his relief the woman they sought was not Claerwen. But who was Tangwen and why was she so important? A lover? Kin? Of Handor's? Meirchion's? What of the three unsoldierly Saxons, now down to one. And who, in truth, actually held Tangwen?

"We're leaving. Now," he ordered.

"I'm not going anywhere with you." Handor's grip tightened on the rock.

Rum-bumm. A double strike on a deep-voiced drum rumbled in the distance to the southwest. Uther's war drums.

"You don't have a choice." Marcus stung the side of the assassin's neck with the flat of his blade.

Handor flinched but still refused to move. He glared back. "Well, go on. Slit my throat. You want to."

Aye, Marcus thought, he would have liked to carve Handor into some ghastly monument if it would serve a purpose. He kicked the man in the leg to pry him loose.

Handor replanted himself against the wall. His snarl descended into sarcasm. "Ah…you can't do it, because you want something, just as I do. You would have killed by now, but you can't. Not yet."

An arrow trailing flames skimmed through the overhanging thatch above Handor. He jerked and was nearly snagged on the sword. Marcus twisted, the rush of the arrow and its heat close enough to singe his hair before its head struck into the mud. Undeterred, he swung the tip in again.

"I'll give you back the woman," he bluffed. "For a price."

Handor snorted. "And what is it you think I can give you? You already hold the only thing of value I ever had."

A new notion dropped into Marcus's head, and a near-smile crossed his mouth. It had to have been Octa who'd lied to Handor about the mysterious Tangwen's whereabouts. Revenge for prison, Nehton mac Aedan had said. Marcus had seen other times when Octa's revenge came with a deeply skewed humor, if it could even be called humor. If it had produced the effigy and the strange warning, it could certainly produce a lie meant to send a hotheaded, hateful fool like Handor to hound an old enemy. Sooner or later, though, Handor would have to be convinced there was no hostage to rescue. Harder still would be to convince him to give up any knowledge of Macsen's sword. If he could get the man out of this fort alive…

Handor's face reddened with deepening rage. He tried to push forward but the sword tip pressed in. "Go on. Kill me now," he taunted. "If you don't, I'll keep coming after you. And one day I'll peel your flesh, strip by strip, until you give her up."

The ground vibrated. As much as Marcus wanted to give in to a retort, he calculated the Saxon war bands were within the last arrow-shot to the Wall. "I know you can feel them coming," he drawled coldly. "In the earth. In the wall you lean on. If Rheged's warriors can't hold, the Saxons will swarm all through this fort. They won't care if you belong to Octa. They'll cut your balls off as good as mine."

Rum-bumm. Uther's drums boomed again, closer. The smoke thickened across the courtyard. In spite of the damp rot, most of the structures had finally caught fire. Beyond, the roar of the army from the north rose like a thunderhead. The burning timbers in the rear gates shifted, and Marcus saw them push forward, little by little. The Saxons were ramrodding their way in.

"Death?" Marcus swept a hand in the direction of the Saxons. "Or freedom?" The rattle of weapons and screams of men told him the battle was about to be engaged.

Fire spread quickly along the fort's ramparts. Pitch crackled inside the supporting beams then exploded, one after the next. The assassin eyed them. Finally he glared into Marcus's face.

"Freedom? From you? You're the cause of all that's gone wrong! You and your interference. My father would have lived it weren't for you!"

An instant later flames broke through the rickety wall behind Handor. Screaming, he crashed into Marcus like a runaway horse to avoid the searing heat. Both men sprawled in the mud. Thick smoke poured over them.

Rum-bumm. The drums drew in fast.

Stunned and choking, Marcus dragged himself onto his feet. He took a few steps, but he had lost his bearings, the pain and dizziness swirled once more in his head. His sword had slipped from his hand and was sunk somewhere in the mud; he could not see it.

"Handor!" he yelled. Only the drums answered. He turned in the hope he was facing the postern gate and could reach it. "Handor!" he shouted again. The man had disappeared. A few more strides, he told himself, and the gate should appear.

The breeze lifted some of the smoke. He was facing the wrong direction. The gash on his temple pounded and was bleeding again. His gut ached. On the far side of the yard, a few paces inside the Wall's gates, stood more than a dozen soldiers; elite warriors, he knew, from their chain-link armor and their weapons. They were unusually well armed for Saxons. The man in the center, obviously the ranking warrior, gestured as he spoke, an indication of a precise list of orders.

The warrior's helmet was familiar, too familiar. Marcus swore under his breath. That helmet was Octa's, and the man next to him was his kinsman, Eosa. Both of them, there, in Rheged, not to the east. Two sons of the White Dragon. And death.

The Saxon leader's head turned, stopped.

Rum-bumm. Uther's war drums pounded, ever closer.

The hill from which Claerwen watched was not high enough to truly be called anything other than a rise; its crest was barely level with the top of the fort's enclosure. The lands surrounding Caer Luguvalos, from Hadrian's Wall to the south, spread flat for miles. The only hills tall enough for observation were too far away to be of use.

She had ridden a little more than a half-mile to the south, around the end of the town. From the rise she had hoped to glimpse Uxelodunum's interior. The drizzle had stopped and the view cleared, but she could only see thick black smoke rising from inside, flames beneath the pall.

From her vantage, Claerwen could see that advance contingents of both Saxon and Rhegedian soldiers skirmished along the Wall to each side of Uxelodunum. But she knew this was only a precursor to a much larger battle. The bulk of Rheged's army approached from the southeast. The Wall prevented her from observing Octa's war bands, but from the rising noise, she knew they were many and strong and close. Her heart sank. Perhaps it was just as well she could not see them.

Then she heard the drums.

The high king. To the southwest, Uther's war bands marched, their ranks in orderly groups. Standards bearing the Pendragon symbol fluttered across the front lines as well as above a small group of mounted guards, the king himself in their midst.

For a brief moment, chills of hope ran over Claerwen's skin. Then she flushed, hot and dizzy, and dread crept across her scalp as if someone had taken up her hair and yanked. She gazed from the Saxons at the Wall to Rheged's army then back to Uther, and calculated the time she believed it would take them to converge. It could not be more than a few minutes. They would engage, the burning fort in the middle.

She stared again at the enclosure. "Where are you?" She wrung her horse's reins, knotted them, pulled them taut, knotted them again, over and over.

Movement stirred in the open postern, and she held her breath. From his clothing, she recognized Handor. He raced away into the deserted settlement. No one followed.

Cold chills replaced Claerwen's hot flush of dread. The drums vibrated the earth. So did the marching feet. Her horse stamped and sidled. She wished the drums would stop, except that would mean the beginning of the battle.

Another figure appeared in the postern. Though the man had dark coloring, at that distance she could not be sure it was Marcus. She knotted the reins again. Then he made the familiar gesture of raking his fingers through his hair.

Hope swelled. He was alive. But instead of following Handor, he ran south—away from the town. And he lacked his sword.

Claerwen strangled the reins. More men emerged from the gate. One selected several of the others, a finger pointed with precision at each he chose. "By the gods," she murmured. "Octa's elite warriors. And Eosa is leading them."

The drums continued the ominous double thud.

Octa's handpicked men, loaded down with spears, began the chase. Marcus ran unencumbered before them. His lead increased slightly. Again Claerwen calculated. If he stayed on a straight course…

She dismounted and began to unbind the ties that held the gear to her horse. She could not leave behind the Iron Hawk's gear, but everything else could be replaced. If she could lighten the animal's load, perhaps, just perhaps, she could pull Marcus out of the path of war in time…

She looked down on the field once more. A spear streaked close to him. He glanced over his shoulder and veered to his left. A second missed him. At a full tilt run, he moved eastward, away from her. Another spear soared. Again he swerved, then disappeared among the lines of soldiers. Uther's thudding drums changed into a low, steady beat. The leading line of offense was nearly organized.

Claerwen muttered an oath and abandoned her task. She mounted, swung her horse around and drove her heels into the animal's flanks. Her only hope was to go to Uther.

The anxious horse balked. Seconds later, a small contingent of heavily armed men rode up the rise and surrounded her.

"Leave this field at once!" the ranking man shouted. The harshness in his voice belied his surprise and irritation at a woman on horseback—in male clothing no less—in the middle of a battlefield. "We'll be building our command tower on this hill. Whichever man you want has no time for you now. Go home!"

"I have no man in your war band," Claerwen shot back, annoyed at the assumption. "Take me to the high king. I have information he must know."

"He cannot be bothered with trivialities."

"This is no nonsense! I have information about the battle. He must know this!"

"And how do we know you are not a spy sent to give false information?"

"Because I am Claerwen of Dinas Beris. Tell him so. Now!"

The man muttered the name to himself and his companions. They shrugged.

"Do you know who Lord Marcus ap Iorwerth of Dinas Beris is?" she asked.

The soldier sucked in air and snapped an order to a younger man beside him. The rider galloped across to the clump of men guarding Uther, pushed his way through and spoke briefly to the king, who in turn looked up in surprise. Uther signaled at his second-in-command to take over, and quickly rode up the rise.

Claerwen slid off her horse and dropped to her knees. "Please, my lord, forgive my intrusion, but I must speak with you privately."

Uther dismounted and waved away the other men. He took her by the elbow, raised her. "Where is he?" he asked, his voice quiet, focused. "What is happening? Why are you here?"

She told him. "Please, my lord, you must wait just long enough for him to escape."

Uther removed his helmet. His vivid blue eyes gleamed coolly out of the dirt and sweat on his face. They reflected both tiredness and determination. "I can't delay, Lady Claerwen. This may be the best chance—the only chance—to take down Octa. We must be decisive here, now."

Claerwen gazed into the distance where she had last seen Marcus. Only soldiers covered the field now. She turned back to the king and met his blue eyes. "Please. Please hold, for just a few minutes. It is all I ask, my lord…please."

Uther's mouth opened, his expression already a denial.

"He holds information that will prove of value to you," she said before he could speak. "Don't lose it, my lord." Whether her bluff was true, she was unsure, but Marcus always had a wealth of knowledge stored away in his memory. Anything was worth a try.

The king hesitated.

"Save his life, my lord, as he has saved yours." Claerwen gripped the king's arm with both hands. Chain-link armor was beneath his sleeve. She squeezed harder to make certain he felt the desperation in her hands as much as in her voice. She watched her words sink in—his memory still had to be fresh of how she and Marcus had saved his life only months before.

"Please," she said, her voice low and clear and full of aching need. "I beg of you, my lord. If you will not save his life, then I must try."

Uther exhaled softly, his eyes cast down on her face. "You would walk straight through a fully engaged battlefield to find that man, wouldn't you?"

She nodded and remembered Marcus had told her of a conversation on love, loyalty and women he'd had with Uther while still in

Winchester. Marcus's opinion of the king had greatly altered with that talk, drawn on the belief that Uther's philandering had abruptly ended upon finding his life's bond in Igraine. She hoped the king remembered the conversation as well and would find enough respect in that ideal to grant her request.

Under his breath, the king swore a mild curse of resignation. "He would do the same for you. But I cannot wait long. So be it."

They were coming from all sides. Some moved with determination and calculated precision, in the way rows and columns of ants converged on a honey-smeared oatcake. Others ran like wild bulls and roared strange, raging shrieks. And the worst, like phantoms among all the rest, were the tall, broad-shouldered, brass-helmeted men who carried long-range spears and screamed in their indecipherable guttural language.

Marcus turned once in a complete circle. Most of what swept through his vision was a blur, partially from the pain in his skull, the rest from the need to be gone. He sought open spaces between the advancing warriors and ran through with no thought to direction, only freedom and a way back to Claerwen.

The path before him narrowed and more soldiers from Uther closed in. If they maintained the same speed, he believed he could slip through, reach their farthermost limit and be free of them. If only they would catch Octa's elite warriors. He pumped harder, each stride pushing him faster.

Six spearmen appeared across the narrowing breach, different from the ones that had followed from Uxelodunum. Marcus skidded to a halt. Nearly unbalanced, he swore aloud and reversed.

One spear shummed past him and chucked into the turf directly in his path. He swerved but could not avoid tripping over the shaft. He rolled, flipped back onto his feet. Another spear skittered over the grass straight at him, but its head caught in a hummock. A third thunked into one of Uther's warriors. It pinned the man's dying body to the earth. Fury loosened, a portion of the advancing army abandoned its orderly march and began to slaughter the Saxons.

Marcus pulled two daggers, the biggest one from the back of his belt, the next biggest from one boot. The original group of spearmen raced in howling behind him. Half-crouched, teeth gritted, he allowed them to come dangerously close. They spread around him, their spears like a barrier.

They never counted on his agility and experience. Marcus dropped at the last instant and rolled under the spear shafts. He came up with one knife imbedded in a man's gut and pulled it out again. He swung around and slashed the throat of the next. Deep in concentration, he heard none of the Britons' shouts cheering him on as they raced in to help. Five lay dead or mortally wounded by the time Uther's men joined in, intent on annihilating Saxons.

Marcus wiped the blood and sweat from his face and tried to catch his breath. He felt the glare of eyes. One more spearman stood grimly watching him. Eosa. Another appeared just beyond him. Another two with *seaxes*. A fifth man. Doom pitted Marcus's stomach. More of Octa's elite would be coming, but the king's soldiers were well occupied and moving northward.

Cold fear broke in chills on his face as Eosa gave orders. Marcus knew what the command was for though the words were useless to him. Think, he berated himself, think. Woods were not far away. If he could reach the cover of trees, perhaps he had a chance to elude the warriors. There was no use to try to outrun them. He was too exhausted, in too much pain.

The decision came. Marcus moved so fast, the Saxons saw no hint. He threw both daggers, each blade a missile that struck the throats of the two nearest warriors. Both dropped.

And he ran as never before; each pumping stride carried him a little closer to deliverance. His breath came hard and rough like a winded animal, and he cleared away any thought or care except to reach the woods.

He whipped past the first of the trees. A rider appeared to his right. Another Saxon—this one on a stolen British horse.

The man swerved to block his path. Marcus dodged. The Saxon tried again and kicked out, but Marcus eluded each strike and grappled both the bridle and the rider's belt. Using his weight for leverage, he pulled down hard.

The animal began to topple. Marcus leapt aside. The rider ejected and fell, and the horse rolled onto him. Glad to be unburdened, the animal immediately righted, shook itself and neighed loudly.

Pounding footsteps and shouts neared from behind. Marcus caught the reins and vaulted on, kicked hard. Like a cocklebur he clung, and silently thanked the gods that he and horses had always gotten on well.

"Hyaaah!" he urged the animal faster and plunged on through the trees. The ground sloped downward, and the horse's gait jarred with each step until he felt as if his bones were knocking together from head to hip.

"Yaaah!" he goaded again. The wind in his hair felt like the breath of freedom to his soul. Instinct told him he was drawing away from his followers, and if luck held, if the woods remained open enough, he could outrun Octa's men, circle around and go back for Claerwen.

Claerwen. There was his hope. He pounded on down the slope. The footing grew more precarious with rocks protruding through slick mud and tufts of grass. A little farther and perhaps he could slow. A stream gurgled somewhere close by. There he could lose his trail in the water. Just a little farther, a little lower.

The woods suddenly thickened, the already dim light unable to penetrate the dense canopy of leaves. The horse's right front hoof struck a small, curved rock. The hoof slid and hooked under a grass-covered root. Its leg cracked, bone thrust through hide, and the animal screamed

Marcus released his knees' grip and let go of the reins. The ground below disappeared. The horse crashed down the slope like a squealing, fleshy boulder.

Pitched forward, Marcus sailed through branch after whipping branch. The last one, thicker than the others, rammed through his shoulder and broke, the impact hard enough to halt his momentum.

He heard nothing more, and saw nothing except blurred green and brown and grey shadow flash past as he dropped. Too shocked to think, he fell, scraping down, down, down so far there seemed to be no bottom.

Then he was lying on a thousand rocks and soaked from streamwater. Agony raged all through his body. He could not move his right arm, pinned beneath his back. He tried to right himself, but the pain grew too strong, and he gagged for air. His eyes squeezed shut against the swirling world. The only sound he gave was a single, truncated "ah."

By the mercy of the gods, he fainted.

CHAPTER 12

Rheged
Early Summer, Beltaine, AD 471

"THE first of the scouts is coming in now."

Claerwen felt Uther's glance when he said the words, but she couldn't look away from the battle. She wound her horse's reins around her hand so tightly her fingers lost all their color.

Uther turned to his second-in-command and detailed a long list of orders. His personal guardsmen, handpicked for their war skills and loyalty, ringed the rise where she waited. On the crest behind, the king's support camp was beginning to take shape. Craftsmen worked furiously to raise the observation tower that would give Uther and his war commanders a proper view of the field. Even if the battle ended before the tower could be completed, the structure would continue to serve as part of the Wall's security afterward.

Finished with the orders, he turned back to Claerwen. "Lady? Are you well? You're white as fresh snow."

She gave no response and continued to stare across the field at the battle. Uther's foremost lines of offense, approximately a third of his forces, as well as Rheged's war bands, had reached the land below Hadrian's Wall just as the Saxons began to pour over the broad stone barricade. The remainder of his soldiers split into several flanking units, ready to join in as needed.

Earlier, Uther had begun to send out scouting parties in search of Marcus and to hunt down Octa's elite soldiers. Now, the ranking officer from the first party to return rode into the circle of guardsmen and dismounted.

"Report?" Uther said.

The officer saluted. "Four-and-thirty dead of the elite, my lord. Nine-and-twenty on the field itself. We caught four more in the woods to the south, there." He pointed to a broad expanse of trees beyond the field. "A fifth was found injured in the woods. From the marks on the ground, he was probably mounted and thrown. Didn't speak our language at all."

Alarmed, Claerwen gazed in the direction pointed out by the officer, then lifted her eyes to Uther's face. Her skin crawled. Only six she had counted at Uxelodunum's postern gate, including Eosa. How many more were there? How many had Octa sent after Marcus?

"You took care of that one?" the king asked.

"Aye, my lord. Following procedure."

"And Lord Marcus?"

The officer faltered, his eye on Claerwen, and he produced a large, blood-covered dagger. "We found this in one of the dead. In the throat."

The Dinas Beris symbol was carved into the handle. Claerwen shuddered. It was the knife Marcus carried in the back of his belt.

"We've seen no other sign of him, Lady," the man said. "But we're still looking."

She turned away and gripped her horse's saddle.

The king laid a hand on her arm. "What are you doing?"

"I must find him." Her jaw was so stiff she could hardly speak.

"This battle has barely begun," he said. "Let the scouting parties do their work. They'll find him."

Claerwen stared into the afternoon sky and shook her head in faint, quick movements. "No, I must go myself. Something is wrong."

Uther tightened his fingers on her wrist. "Not now. It's too dangerous. Let the war bands work their way farther towards the Wall first. We'll find him for you."

"No," she repeated, her voice thin and scratchy, like she was choking. She pressed a fist to her chest. "Too much time has passed. Octa has sent too many—"

Claerwen could not finish. She slipped free of the king's hand

and sprang, gained her seat in the saddle and wrenched the animal's head away before he could catch the bridle.

"How can you possibly know where he is?" Uther questioned.

Claerwen kicked hard. The horse surged forward, and she heard Uther curse. Orders followed.

"You'll lead those warriors right to him!" he shouted.

How could she pay heed to caution when Marcus could be dying out there? Claerwen dashed across the field behind the last lines of soldiers. It was not the length of time that had passed since he had disappeared. Nor was it the astonishing number of Octa's warriors that had been counted—and those were only the dead ones. Something was wrong. She could feel it, the same gut-nagging ache she had felt when he'd been betrayed and imprisoned years before, the same sinking sense that her insides were half torn away, the ragged edges left to whip in the wind.

Uther was right to question how she could find Marcus; she had no notion exactly where he was, but if Octa's warriors had left the field for the woods, they had a reason. She kicked the horse again.

Once into the woods, she guided the animal up a pathless, gradual slope. Broadly spaced, the trees seemed to go on for miles. She moved swiftly through them. Then the slope crested. Beyond, the trees grew close together. Forced to slow, she continued on more cautiously, and quiet closed in.

The forlorn sense of misfortune grew steadily worse. Not a vision or a sense of the future, the foreboding felt as if Marcus called out to her from the core of his soul. Nearly overwhelmed, she reined to a halt. Breathe, she told herself. If only the tightness in her chest would ease. It did not.

Neither did the watchful eyes waiting in silence mere paces away.

She moved on. Instinct drew her farther down into terrain even thicker with overgrowth, and she found recently torn leaves and small branches. She stopped again. Nothing stirred except a light breeze and water rippling somewhere below. The gloom made her shiver. With her hand clenched again over her heart, she smelled blood.

Claerwen dismounted. A few steps farther and she came upon a sharp drop. Below, a shallow stream trickled through a narrow channel—the water she had heard. The banks were ragged; chunky boulders, moss, grass, roots and rotting leaves covered both sides.

Then she saw the horse, dark against the dark, limp in an impossible position along the far bank—clearly dead, the neck and a leg broken, its blood in the stream. It was not the animal Marcus had taken, and the gruesome way it had died filled her with uncanny dread.

A soft moan hummed to the right of it. Claerwen could not see him in the shadows, but she sensed Marcus was there. She left her horse tied to a tree and began the descent into the streambed, bare roots her ladder, each ginger step unstable. Even on the narrow streambank footing was hazardous, the moss-covered rocks slick as ice. She nearly fell several times.

A young willow leaned from the opposite side, its lowest branches misshapen and dragging in the water. The moan came again. Then she saw a mud-streaked boot.

Claerwen stumbled through the bloodied, ankle-deep stream. Breath held, she bent aside the willow. He was there, at the edge of consciousness and trying to regain his senses. His face, hair and beard were covered with filth and streaked from splashed water. Sluggish, he writhed in pain, as if trying to find his balance though he was flat on his back on a bed of half-submerged rocks. His right arm was pinned beneath him.

"Can you hear me?" She knelt on the uncomfortable stones and took his face between her hands. His skin was cold, his eyes closed. "It's me…Marcus? Can you hear me? Where—oh, no."

She saw the broken branch imbedded in his shoulder, the end of the wood freshly torn. Little blood had escaped, and the wound was in a place where it had probably caused little internal damage, but bloody raw flesh streaked a rock just above his shoulder. The branch had gone all the way through, and the wound would need to be cauterized once the wood was removed.

"Lady Claerwen!"

She started at the call of her name from above—the king's voice. "Uther is coming," she said but could not tell if Marcus had understood her. "By the light, I hope he brought a healer."

Shouts echoed through the woodlands, more distant than Uther's call. She peered up at the embankment but saw no one. The clatter of weapons followed the voices, then as quickly as the noise began, it stopped.

Marcus's left hand, cold and wet, slid up along her neck and clung.

Startled again, she leaned closely. He was regaining consciousness. "Thank the gods," she said. "Don't move, Marcus, help is coming."

"You found me," he murmured, his voice thick and hoarse. "You always find me." Though his eyes were still squeezed shut, his lips made a faint smile. His hand tugged her closer, and he rested his cheek against hers. "What did you hear?"

"Uther's guards. They may be fighting some of Octa's warriors."

Thirsty, he swallowed with difficulty. "The spearmen…so many…all through up there. Claeri, can you help me sit up?"

"Wait for—"

"Claeri, please…my arm, no matter…how much…get me up, now, please. Some of the ribs…are broken…this time." His eyes were open now, more alert, tense with pain.

She bit her lip and hoped his insistence meant his injuries were not as dire as they appeared. From his left side, she slid her arm around him, her hand behind his neck to avoid the wound. Braced against a large rock for leverage, she pulled gently, a bit at a time, and paused when air hissed through his teeth.

"Go on," he said and drew up his knees to balance himself. Sitting, he breathed more easily though still in brief, uneven gulps with each spasm of pain.

"What happened?" She tried to see the shoulder wound through the hole in his tunic.

He reached for his right wrist with his left hand. Watching him, Claerwen winced in empathy. His body shuddered and from the way his soaking and muddy hair quivered, she knew a wave of incoherency was threatening to flatten him again. He lifted the hand, drew it around, and rested it in his lap. His wrist was swollen and badly bruised, and he could not flex his fingers. Regardless, he never grunted.

Nausea gripped Claerwen's stomach. His arm, even shrouded in his tunic's sleeve, had an awkward twist to it, and when she ran her fingertips with the lightest touch along the bone above his elbow, her eyes came up and leveled with his.

"Broken?" he asked.

She nodded.

"Damn." He tilted his head back and squinted at the opposite embankment. "It wasn't even so far down...the willow must have broken my fall." He turned his face to her. "You came alone?"

She nodded again.

"So dangerous. You should have waited. You probably led—"

"I couldn't wait. I knew—"

"Are you here, Lady Claerwen?" the high king called again.

She saw him now on the embankment where she had climbed down. Waving, she caught his attention.

Uther took in the dismal scene, his mouth halfway open, then commanded a portion of his guards to encircle the entire area. He ordered the remainder to patrol in a ring farther out, the intent to warn of approaching Saxons. To a group of escorts, he gave instructions to remain with the horses and await further orders. Finally, he gestured to another man, a physician, to follow. They descended into the streambed.

Claerwen relinquished her place to the healer. Before he even looked at the wounds, he declared that such pain should never need to be endured. He withdrew a heavy wineskin slung from his shoulder, pulled out the stopper and held it for Marcus to drink as much as he wanted. Grateful, Marcus indulged. Within minutes the healer reported the bone was broken through but cleanly. He also confirmed that cauterization of the shoulder wound was necessary. They would first need to move Marcus to a better location and as soon as possible.

While the physician worked, the king watched in grim silence. After a time he squatted on the rocks.

"Octa will not relent," he said to Marcus. "Not against you anymore than me. Not until he lies in his grave."

Marcus listened.

"I've heard he's been hounding you with an assassin as well."

A nod for an answer.

Claerwen watched Uther's blue eyes glance up and return to Marcus. She took a step towards them.

"I believe," the king said, "I have no other choice but to exile you for a time."

"Exile," Marcus echoed.

Speechless, Claerwen met his eyes.

"Your woman begged me to delay the battle," Uther went on, "to save your life. I hope I succeeded." Again he eyed the wounded shoulder and arm.

Marcus drank again. Claerwen knew he was trying to concentrate on Uther's face while he mulled the king's words. By now, she hoped, the mead had begun to dull his agony.

Minutes passed in silence and the physician finished his ministrations. When he withdrew, Claerwen eased down next to Uther.

"Where will you send us?" she asked.

"Claerwen—" Marcus interrupted before the king could answer. Pain caught him and he stalled, tried again. "Can you…bring the cap with the red horsehair…to me? Now?"

"Of course." A disguise to shield their departure, she understood. "Should I bring the other one…for myself?"

He shook his head. "No, no need." The slight motion brought on more pain, and he hunched over.

"Marcus?" She touched his knee.

His head came up. "Go on, Claeri. Now, please."

She rose. Midway across the stream, she heard him begin to talk, his voice too low to understand. She glanced back. He was gripping a thick wad of the king's tunic, but his face was unreadable, unclear if he was angry, urgent, or merely giving news. Uther listened with equal intensity, a slight bend to his brows, a nod on occasion. The ache of dread had never left her, Claerwen realized.

She ascended the embankment. Quickly, she located the cap and turned to go back, but a member of the king's guards signaled at her. She halted. More of his warriors, rigid with tension, tightened their formation, weapons poised. Footsteps crunched beyond their line of defense—Octa's brutal spearmen, on the hunt for Marcus. Claerwen crouched next to her horse.

Minutes passed. Then rustling erupted, brief, violent. Silence again. More minutes drifted. Another clash, grunts. Dark figures, half-seen through the trees, moved swiftly, decisively, stopped again. More deaths, Claerwen thought. She smelled them.

The guard remained motionless on the other side of her horse, listening, watching. At last a signal was called. The man sighed in relief. He gestured for her to continue on her way.

At the top of the embankment, Claerwen readied to climb down the roots, but she was shaking so hard her grip felt unsure. Had the proximity of Octa's fierce warriors unnerved her so much? In spite of having Uther's equally fierce personal guards for protection?

She gazed down at Marcus. He still spoke intently with the king though now with more animation. Uther held a small rolled parchment in one hand. He passed it to a man from the escort, apparently one with ranking authority, who bound and sealed it, then tucked it inside his tunic.

Uther's face reflected a faint slyness. Deepening concern needled Claerwen. What was happening? She descended, but before she could cross the water, the king met her halfway. Beyond him, the healer and one of the escorts prepared to lift Marcus onto his feet. Uther took her elbow and turned her away, took the cap from her. His eyes were serious now, and guileless.

"I'm providing you with six men," he said. "One is a decoy. Take the horse you have with you. You're to leave immediately."

Claerwen frowned and twisted around to see Marcus. "A decoy? Where are we going?"

Uther gazed at her, steady-eyed. "You will know when you are there, Lady Claerwen. He is going elsewhere."

She stared at the king, too shocked to find her voice. His eyes showed grim stiffness but they were not unkind. Finally the words rushed all at once. "Elsewhere? Where? What do you mean?"

Shouts rang out, a series of commands ricocheted along the embankment above. "Octa's warriors are closing in. Lady Claerwen, you must go now—"

"No—"

"When Octa is removed from power, you will both come home. It will only be that long and no more."

"No, please, my lord. Send us together, wherever it may be. Please don't separate us."

He tightened his hold on her arm. "There is no time, we have to move him out now."

"But you can't separate us! I refuse."

"You have no choice, Lady Claerwen."

One of the men appeared next to Uther. "Forgive me, Lord Marcus is asking to speak with his wife."

Claerwen bolted between the men. Still sitting, Marcus waved aside the physician and escort. When she reached him, he grabbed her wrist and pulled her down.

"Listen to me." His voice was soft and intense. "Do as the king says—"

"You agree to this?"

"Do it—"

"Where is he sending you—?"

"I don't know…Claerwen… listen. I can't fight. This is my sword arm. It will take a long time to heal, a year at the very least. Even then…I may not be able to fight again if it doesn't heal properly."

Tears began to rise in her eyes.

Heartache gilded his face. "I can't defend myself…how can I protect you? It's summer, the fighting will not subside for months…Claerwen…please understand…it's to keep you safe, until Octa is gone from power. This battle may achieve that…"

"If Octa dies in this battle, why can't we wait until it's done? Perhaps—"

"No, Claerwen. Handor. Handor has more reasons than Octa to kill me."

His words stopped and he choked for air as the agony swelled once more.

A tear strayed down Claerwen's cheek. She felt sick, sick down to the innermost part of her being. Her Marcus, her invincible Marcus, who could wriggle out of any trap and face death without a flinch, sat before her with the same stoicism that had kept him alive and sane through unspeakable torture. But with every breath he took, every minute gesture, inconceivable pain raged through him. His life was threatened with wounds that could fester and kill as swiftly as Octa's spearmen or Handor's sword. He could die—that night, on the morrow, in a fortnight, a year. Somewhere distant. Somewhere she did not know, somewhere alone. And she would not be allowed to do anything to help him. Another tear dropped.

Marcus struggled to lean forward and pulled her close with his good arm. He pressed his face to hers. "Be safe…for me," he whispered. "And be careful of what you carry on that horse. Hide it, any way you can."

At that moment she cared nothing about the Iron Hawk's hidden gear, but she nodded just enough to acknowledge his warning.

"I will be with you soon. I promise." Then not caring who watched, he kissed her as if no one else were there.

Tremors shook his mouth. Another tear fell and trickled between their faces. Hers? Or his?

Marcus eased back. He reached out for the cap in Uther's hand. "Can you do this for me?" he asked Claerwen.

More shouts echoed from the woods above, the ring of swordplay followed.

Claerwen gazed upward. What choice was left? She took the cap from the king. Another tear fell. She gathered Marcus's hair together, slid the cap on over it, and tucked stray black locks underneath. She arranged the red hair until it hung properly. Her fingers still shook.

Cries pierced the air from beyond the embankment, cries of attack, cries of death, closer than the last time. Commands and messages relayed among the king's men.

Uther pulled his sword. "Take her. Now!" he commanded. Two men from the escort gripped her arms. When she refused to stand, they dragged her away.

"Get him out of here!" Uther yelled to the remaining men. Two others moved in and lifted Marcus onto his feet. "Turn him around so his face can't be seen."

The violence edged closer, loud, disturbing, as if a portion of the main battle had shifted away from the Wall and moved all the way into the woods.

The escorts rushed Claerwen along the stream. She struggled to turn back for a final glimpse, but they held on too tightly and never gave her a chance.

"Get him out of here!" she heard the king repeat behind her. The sound of splashing feet followed, headed in the opposite direction.

At a shallow place along the embankment, the two men guided her up to a group of horses. Hers had been brought there. Three other men waited with a horse-drawn cart. The sixth man, dark-haired and wrapped in bloodstained bandages, lay inside the cart's rear space.

Claerwen mounted and drew alongside the cart. Rain, cold and misty, closed in again. It muffled the sound of slaughter and intensified the numbing sense of aloneness. She wrapped her cloak around herself and pulled up the hood, all to hide her face, the boyish clothing and the heartache that bit like thorns.

Without further delay, they began the long march to nowhere.

CHAPTER 13

Into Exile
Summer, AD 471

WHY did this happen? How could it be? Claerwen asked herself the same questions day after day. No answer came, not from herself, not from the gods. Five-and-ten days had gone, lost in numbing shock. Night fell once more and here she was, camped with six silent armed guards and not a word of where they were going, not a word of Marcus. Why had this happened, why to *him*?

The ride into exile had been tedious and strangely circuitous, not a wild flight through the night to a distinctive location as she had expected. After leaving the broad flatlands below Caer Luguvalos, Uther's men had first taken her southwest into the lush, pine-forested highlands that skirted Rheged's western coast. They had pulled the cart with the decoy along endless rugged mountain tracks at a dismally slow pace.

Claerwen had avoided the man in the cart. Other than his dark hair, he did not resemble Marcus, and she could not begin to pretend he was her husband. Instead, she kept her cloak wrapped about herself, hood up, continued to wear her deerskins and hoped she looked like one more male rider. Once well into the mountains and certain no one had followed, the guards abandoned the decoy ruse. They sank the cart to the bottom of a long, narrow and very deep lake. Claerwen never needed to ask why—the journey south was meant to look as if they were going to Dinas Beris.

Unencumbered, they circled west, then back north, and stayed off the roads most of the time. Claerwen had no notion of where they were, only direction. She sensed they had expected her to complain about the long, tiresome days, but, accustomed to travel, both by horse and by foot, she remained just as silent as they were.

On the six-and-tenth morning of exile, dawn lightened the low sky from black to grey once more. Claerwen packed her own horse as she did every morning. She wanted no questions regarding the oilskin-covered bundle.

Another long, useless day ahead, she thought. The farther they traveled the more she suspected their destination was in the far north. She could not help but wonder if she would be placed in some remote and forbidding fortress in the way Ygerna had been immured in Tintagel—Igraine, now, she had to remind herself. Alba—she had been there before long ago, in the lands of the fierce and wild Picts and where small, lonely fortified hilltop enclosures and crannogs were widely scattered, often hidden in nearly inaccessible places.

She rested her brow on her horse's neck and prayed, more to Marcus than the gods. If only he were there instead of the guards and this journey had a purpose. Wherever she ended up, she hoped it was not so isolated that word couldn't reach her when the exile did end. With a sigh, she mounted.

The trek continued. By evening, a steady breeze from the west blew in, the tang of salt in it. The sky suddenly cleared.

Unexpectedly, a wide estuary appeared, the water a dazzling gold below the lowering sun. Straight up from the northern banks rose a massive, doubled humped rock. Silhouetted against the dusky sky, a fortress loomed on the eastern hump.

"Dun Breatann," Claerwen murmured. She looked to her escorts, one by one. Would they stop there to replenish their dwindling supplies? None of the men even glanced at her.

With her in the middle of their formation, they continued on in dogged silence, but soon they turned due west. Claerwen reckoned they would run into the single Roman road that crossed fens on the north side of the rock. From the one other time she had been there she knew the only other way in or out of the place was by obscure tracks or by boat on the river. Within an hour they reached the Roman road and turned towards the rock.

Relieved they were going to the fortress, Claerwen hoped Ceredig was in residence, but she was aware he could still be off with his son fighting Irish raiders. Even if he were there, would he bother with her? Moreover, would they even stay for the night, not merely stop for supplies and move on to make camp elsewhere?

Or was this her destination? Apprehension crept inside her. She gazed up at the rock. This was Ceredig of Strathclyde's stronghold. The rock was so steep that bank and ditch defenses were unnecessary. The river, given to the sea's fitful tides, protected its south side; treacherous fens guarded its remaining flanks. The narrow path to the gates was cut into the rock face with several switchbacks and was easily defendable by only a few guards. Not only was Dun Breatann unbreachable, it was as inescapable as Tintagel.

Just after darkness fell, they rode through the gates.

Exhausted, Claerwen waited in the flagstone courtyard, her escort in a ring around her. They declined to dismount, but their leader pushed his tired horse to the forefront. Dun Breatann's ranking guardsman met him. They spoke and the officer sent a messenger boy running to the great hall.

Within a few minutes, Ceredig appeared. His faded red hair flowed with each robust stride into the yard. He looked miffed, Claerwen thought. Perhaps his supper had been interrupted by a routine arrival to which his seneschal should have attended.

The escort's leader dismounted and held out a sealed roll of parchment, the same one Uther had handed him in the stream near Caer Luguvalos. Ceredig took it and broke the seal, unrolled two sheets. The first page received a cursory scan. The second won a look of shock. His gaze raked up past the escorts.

Claerwen met his eyes. His grey brows dipped downward, then he carefully read the rest of the writing. Finished, he rolled the parchments together and slid them inside his tunic just as his tardy seneschal trotted into the courtyard. The king gave him a stream of orders then pushed his way between the mounted men.

Claerwen dropped off her horse.

Wordless, Ceredig caught her hand in greeting.

"What is happening?" she asked.

His eyes extended concern. "Come with me, lass."

A slave ran up and waited for the command to unload her horse. Claerwen tightened her grip on the animal's bridle. "Am I—?"

Ceredig nodded.

She assented to having the slave unload her unessential pouches, but she released the oilcloth bundle herself.

Ceredig eyed it then glanced at her marriage ring. "Something that belongs to…?"

"You could say so," she hedged and hugged the bundle tighter. He would have an apoplexy if he knew what was inside. Even Macsen's sword, however it might look, had to be less obtrusive than the Iron Hawk's. When he smiled faintly, seemingly satisfied for the moment, Claerwen hoped she would not have need to lie further.

They walked across to the palace. Years before, she had stayed in a small guesthouse somewhere behind the great hall. She couldn't remember where now, but this time she was assigned a small, private chamber a short distance from Ceredig's own rooms. Compared to Winchester's Roman trappings, this residence was primitive, dark from low ceilings and small windows, smoky from the torches and oil lamps that fought the dark. Her chamber was no different. Fitted with simple furnishings, it was spare but comfortable enough. A broad wooden platter laden with a hot supper already awaited her along with a small ewer of chilled mead. Her other belongings had been delivered and stacked together on the floor.

Claerwen dropped her bundle on the bed and sank onto the mattress's edge next to it.

Ceredig sat on a stool opposite her. "Smells good." He tipped his head towards the platter, then eyed the oilskin again. "I won't ask what you and he have been doing—I know better—but can you tell me how bad he is?"

As familiar and as trusted as Ceredig was, she did not want to be there. Eyes downcast, she could not look at him. The image of Marcus lying on rocks in bloody, cold water, his arm twisted like scrapped iron, filled her mind. The smell of the food made her sick. But she told Ceredig everything from the point of finding Marcus in the streambed to when Uther's guards took him away.

"And he never gave a sound in discomfort, did he?" Ceredig said, a knowing smile on his lips.

Claerwen shook her head. "He even refused a litter, insisted on walking out. If only I knew where they took him."

The warmth in Ceredig's brown eyes dimmed. He looked as if he were listening to one of his military commanders report. After a long silence, he reached for the ewer of mead, filled a cup with the cool, golden liquid.

"You need to know the terms of your exile." He placed the cup in Claerwen's hands. "I know they told you nothing."

She held the cup but didn't drink.

"The orders say you are to remain in Dun Breatann until Octa the Saxon is confirmed dead."

"Dead? Not imprisoned *or* dead?" Claerwen tried to set down the cup and nearly missed the table's edge. It clacked against the wood and she tried again. This was wrong. *Removed from power,* Uther had said. So had Marcus.

"The orders say 'dead'," Ceredig verified. "Only dead. They are specific, very adamant."

Shock crackled inside Claerwen. Uther had imprisoned Octa before, instead of executing him. That choice could be made again. But for how long? Permanently? Or until an execution sometime in the distant future—at Uther's whim?

"You are not to be allowed beyond the walls of Dun Breatann whatsoever until the exile is lifted," Ceredig continued. "There will be no contact with anyone outside the fortress—no letters, no couriers, nothing. If anyone should enter Dun Breatann whom you know, you will not be allowed to speak to them or to let them know you are here. Except within your chambers, you will simply be known as "the Lady." Your name, origins, family members and titles will be unknown by anyone here other than myself and Uther's guards."

"I can't send a message to Dinas Beris? Not even to my father? Or to Marcus's cousin, Owein? So they at least know Marcus is alive?"

"And that *you* are alive as well," he reminded her.

"Aye, and me." She flipped a hand in self-deprecation. "Why?"

Ceredig shook his head. "I am sorry. The terms are specific."

"Does he face the same terms, wherever he was sent?"

"I don't know, but it is likely so."

Alarm tightened Claerwen's throat and she stood. "Octa could have been killed in the battle at Caer Luguvalos—"

"That battle was indecisive," Ceredig cut her off. "Uther's war bands pushed the Saxons back over the Wall. They continue to skirmish and move east, but slowly. You will know if Octa dies. A courier from the crown passes through here daily."

Claerwen glared into Ceredig's face. "And if I choose to disobey the terms?" Her voice was husky, exact, a shade of threat in it.

The king stood, his face stony. He towered over her. "Do not try. The escort that accompanied you? They will be indefinitely garrisoned here for the purpose of making certain you do not try to escape. More will come. And I will assign a contingent of my own guards for the same purpose."

Claerwen's mouth dropped open. "But you defied—"

"Aye, I have defied high kings in the past, including Uther for Marcus's benefit. But I cannot, not this time."

"Then I'm a prisoner."

"An exile," he corrected her. "An exile in grave danger, as is he. The terms are for your well-being, as well as his. It is so you will live long enough for him to come back to you once the exile is lifted."

He paced to the doorway, stopped and turned to her again. His face softened. "Would that I could welcome you in a proper fashion, lass. You deserve better than this." He retreated into the corridor and softly closed the door after himself.

She stared at the empty space where the king of Strathclyde had stood. "So does Marcus."

Claerwen opened her eyes. Her back ached. She had no sense of how long she had been sitting there, rigid and still, winding her marriage ring around and around her finger.

Marcus had said that Handor had more reasons to kill him than Octa's orders. What else had he to tell but had been unable to? She could not even guess. And she'd had no chance to tell him what she'd learned of the mysterious woman called Tangwen.

"If only..." she began and shook her head. No use to wish he'd stayed away from Uxelodunum. No use to wish anything now.

She stared into the smoking, red-orange coals of her brazier. They had burned brightly earlier, newly stoked by the slaves who had brought her supper and the pouches. The coals still burned but with little life now. The food was cold. A lamp on the table hissed and stank of sheep's oil. She closed her eyes again. "Where are you?" she whispered. Her words drifted with the smoke to the ceiling and disappeared in silence.

The weight of the Iron Hawk's sword and armor pressed against her leg. By the light, where was she going to hide that? A plain wooden chest below the window was not large enough to hold the length of the sword, and though the oak-framed bed had space beneath it, both locations were too accessible should someone—slaves, spies or anybody else—become nosy. Until she found something better, the bed would have to be good enough and she stashed the gear between its frame and the feather mattress.

Lamp held high, she examined the small chamber. The walls were solid stonework, mortared together, and looked recently re-chinked. Decorative coverings, usually hung to keep out draughts and dampness, had not been placed in the room, not even over the single shuttered window. Disappointed and sluggish with exhaustion, Claerwen dropped to her knees to test the flagstone floor. She crawled from one side to the next, even moved the bed to look for loose stones. They were as solid as the walls.

Tools. Maybe there was a tool that would help. She turned one of the pouches over the mattress and dumped out the contents. Horseshoeing tools, feed for the animals, a small brush, two spare horseshoes.

"I should be in the stables," she muttered and emptied another pouch. Dried meat, dried fruit, comfrey roots she had gathered near the farmstead in Rheged, a half-dozen tiny ceramic vials of medicinals. The third and last pack contained the few spare clothes she and Marcus had brought, along with a comb, Hywel Gwodryd's two brooches, the other cap with dark brown horsehair, the effigy and the pouch Handor had lost.

She knelt again and tried to pry one flagstone loose with a hoof pick. No luck. To dig out the mortar would take a long time—then the earth beneath would have to be excavated as well, and secretly. She sat on the floor and tossed the pick into the open chest. The bang and rattle felt good for the raw satisfaction of her anger.

Claerwen leaned back against the bed. She could lie to Ceredig, tell him the gear was stolen and ask him to hold it for her. She grimaced. His astonishment she could imagine, but would he believe the lie?

Frustrated, she gazed up at the ceiling. Though low enough she could reach its large rafters with her fingertips when she was standing, it was invisible in the deep shadows. She had seen that the beams pitched slightly up from the outer wall to a peak at the building's center, over the corridor outside her door. Smaller beams crossed the larger ones at right angles and supported the roof thatching.

She rose and stood on the stool, squeezed her fingers between one of the beams and the thatch. Her hand was about the same thickness as a sword at its deepest point.

It was not an ideal hiding place for a weapon. Moisture could eventually pit a blade, even inside a solid scabbard. Yet she had often seen swords and daggers hidden in thatched roofs. A common enough practice, one that could make the roof as vulnerable to snooping people as the underside of a bed. Except for the proposed lie to Ceredig, she decided she had no other options and the beams would have to suffice. Hopefully, no one would find a reason to believe she was hiding anything.

The thatch was tightly lashed down. With a horseshoe, she pried up the reeds enough to slip the sword lengthwise along a heavy beam. The cross-guard came to rest almost in position over one of the smaller supports. She crept the weapon along until the cross-guard was hidden.

Now, for the rest of the Iron Hawk's possessions. The black leather tunic and breeches, belts, boots and gauntlets were not uncommon in their looks and construction, but the helmet was. Claerwen picked it up. It was devised to fold nearly flat when an iron ring inside was removed, the ring meant to hold the helmet's shape as well as protect the skull from serious blows. It had been collapsed for storage, the ring loose inside.

Claerwen's gaze ran to the mattress and came to a halt. Yellow feathers escaped one worn corner. Here was opportunity. She could mention the broken seam and request a needle and thread, then rip the covering open and sew the helmet inside. Until then, it would occupy the bottom of the chest with the leather armor. The horsehair cap, effigy and Hywel's brooches would come next, then the oilcloth and everything else on top. She was glad the chain-link Marcus sometimes wore had not been in the bundle—too heavy for long travel.

She shut the lid and blew out the lamp. In the dark, she stared once more into the brazier. If only she could look into the coals and conjure an image of Marcus, where he was, how he fared, but she knew none would come. Her tired, scratchy eyes registered only the dying red glow. If the gods wanted her to know anything more, they would show her on their own terms.

She made a fist and rammed it down on the chest's lid. "Why did this happen?"

None of the gods answered.

Cold drizzle resumed the next day, a perfect mirror for Claerwen's mood. She opened the door of her chambers and looked both ways along the corridor. Three men stood together in quiet discussion in front of Ceredig's doors but no one else. No guards? Strange, especially with the stringency of the exile's terms.

She walked slowly down the hallway away from them. Near a door that led outside, she glanced over her shoulder. One man had separated from the others. Though his face was averted, his eyes watched. Air hissed between Claerwen's teeth. She would be followed everywhere. Expected. So annoying.

Claerwen exited into the courtyard. She remembered little of Dun Breatann from years before, but the descriptive name of "stronghold" fit perfectly. Like the rock it sat upon, its buildings were all of stone, thick-walled, forbidding. The outer wall of spiked timbers embedded in a stone foundation was lined with ramparts. Disciplined warriors patrolled them.

The great hall and palace sat side by side on the yard's inner edge. Dressed in women's tunics again, Claerwen folded her arms against the cold and walked towards the hall. Drizzle quickly settled into her hair and clothing, and she hugged two large kerchiefs draped around her shoulders more tightly. Though damp and chilled, she halted near the steps instead of going inside.

A small garden sat within a low wall of dry stone behind the great hall. That was the one place she could never forget in Dun Breatann. In the coolness of an autumn night eight years before, she had met Marcus in that garden. Though she had seen little of it in the darkness then, she hoped it had not changed much, if it was even still there.

She turned towards the alley that led to it. Her watcher followed and when she hesitated, he loitered in wait. No, she could not revisit this place with a stranger intruding on her memories. Exasperated, she started for the hall's steps.

The hall itself had not changed at all except it was more laden with soot. The huge fire pit in the center burned hot and stifling as ever, even at the early hour. Claerwen approached a row of food-laden tables against the back wall. She needed to eat, but the dense, stinking smoke that streamed from the torches and the fire pit made her stomach queasy. Or was it that she just did not feel safe?

Her eyes strayed to the rear doors, the same she had escaped through on that long-ago night to find momentary refuge from the suffocating hall and a contract to marry a man she despised. More than refuge, she had found Marcus and the beginning of a journey she never could have imagined. But now, another man, this one in Uther's livery and a member of her escort, edged closer to the doors. She snatched up an apple from the table and retreated out the front.

Claerwen bit hard into the fruit and put a mask of resignation on her face to hide her growing anger. This had to change. She began a circuit of the grounds and noted the number and position of the guards on the ramparts, at the gates, at their barracks. The patterns of their patrols would indicate if they were regular guards or the auxiliary men assigned to report her movements. She quickly discovered each supplementary man had been delegated a plot of ground from which to observe her. If she moved from one plot, the man in the next one took over the watch.

She continued to explore the stronghold's grounds. Houses and storage sheds spread out behind the main buildings. Another garden, this one full of healing herbs, spread over a long swath of earth behind the palace. She knew most of the plants by sight.

The steady clank-clank of a blacksmith's hammer on an anvil started up. Claerwen jerked around, startled. A smithy stood next to the stables. So familiar a sound at Dinas Beris when Marcus was home—he did most of the smithing for their clan. Now, she wondered, how would he be able to work the forge any more than he could wield his sword, unless he could use his left hand?

Claerwen turned away and faced the great hall and the palace. From the rear, they appeared especially massive, grey, dismal. The thatched roofs dripped miserably in the rain. Not much different from their front sides. Only the welcoming torches were missing, but in truth she didn't think they were very welcoming at all. Even the pennants on the ramparts looked disheartened. They clung to their staffs, colors muted.

Voices chattered from behind. A long line of women hurried along the rear wall towards a small open gate. Slaves, Claerwen surmised from their poor dress. Most wore a kerchief over their hair, meager protection from the weather. All carried baskets full of goods.

Trade, she guessed. Through the gate she saw steps that led down between the rock's two humps. Below, a small shore fronted the river where merchants brought in fish on boats.

Her eyes sought the window of her chambers. The drizzle was quickly thickening into rain and reducing visibility. Teeth gritted, she considered the contents of her room. Did she dare? She shouldn't, but... She sidled into the women's path. Without a pause, they parted around her.

The minding guard assigned to the plot near the gate perked up at her movement. His eyes tracked back and forth from her to the gate. Watching him, Claerwen took another bite and gave him a deliberate, sly smile. She drew up her own kerchiefs over her hair and matched the pace of another woman whose head covering was the same color.

The guard tramped over the soggy turf towards the gate, a splash of water with each step. He shouted at the slaves to halt, but several had already gone through the opening. The river's rush and the sea beyond drowned out his orders. The other women stopped short, surprised, annoyed that they had to wait in the rain. None dared ask why he kept them from their work.

From a tiny space between two beams on the fortress wall, inside and a short way to the right of the gate, Claerwen watched. The guard inspected the women's faces and found she was no longer among them. With a curse, he shoved his way through the line, then the gate. He looked down to the place her partially eaten apple had lodged in the rocks beside the steps. Another curse, then he lifted a ram's horn that hung from his belt and blew a screeching alarm.

The call was strange, one Claerwen had never heard before, and she reckoned it was newly devised just for her should she attempt to escape. Several men ran from between the buildings. They shouted orders to close the docks and search the boats. The narrow causeway that led around the rock's face to the marshland would be blocked as well.

Claerwen slipped off one kerchief to expose the second—a different color. She glided along the wall beneath the ramparts from one beam to the next. Nearly all the way around to the front of the fortress, she aimed for the main gates and picked up speed.

"You! Stop there!" a shout came from close behind.

Claerwen's stomach pitted. She recognized the voice—another of Uther's men, burly, strong, but slow. Rough hands grasped her arms. An instant later, the gates crashed shut. The boom vibrated through the walls, down into the bedrock. She shut her eyes against the sudden stares of the fortress's occupants. Why had she tried?

Whipped around by the guards, she nearly fell. Without a word they bound her wrists behind her. She wanted to cry, to scream, to be savage, to simply disappear in a puff of mist, but all of that was useless, as useless as trying to escape. She bowed her head and let the guards march her to the palace.

"If you weren't Marcus's wife..." Ceredig's fist lightly thumped the table in a slow, steady rhythm. "And if you weren't my kinswoman..."

Shivering, Claerwen knelt before Ceredig in his chambers. Still handbound, she had been locked in her room ever since that morning and unable to free her hands. No coal for the brazier or food had been delivered. Her clothes were still damp from the rain.

"I told you not to try this, lass. And only last night." On his feet, he walked around behind her and cut her bonds with his belt dagger. "Rise."

She stood and turned towards the doors. He stopped her, his thick hand on her shoulder. "Claerwen. For all the gods' sakes, be patient. You've brought a lot of attention to yourself now. It can get you killed."

She regarded him with a blistering glare. "Do you think I don't know that? How close death can be? Let me go. Let me find Marcus."

"You don't know where he is, lass." The tolerant glint in his eyes showed he understood he was not the target of her frustration.

"Uther's guards must know."

"They don't—"

"I think they do. Where was he taken?"

"Claerwen, stop this."

"I can't. Everything he has worked for will be for naught. It could cause a disaster. At least let me send a message to Uther."

"It's not allowed."

"Then to Myrddin. I cannot stay here."

"No one has seen or heard from Myrddin since—"

Claerwen's glare deepened. "What happened to Myrddin?"

He shook her arm. "You will follow the terms as stated. Do not do this again. There will be consequences."

His voice had gone cold in the way Marcus's did when speaking with absolute finality. Claerwen recognized it. Here was the source Marcus had learned it from. "Are consequences named in the terms?" she asked.

"If need be, you will be chained to your bed inside your locked chambers. And I *will* see it's done." His face softened just a bit. "When I read the terms, I would not have said such measures would be necessary, not from how we have met in the past—including the very recent past. Now I know why they were."

Ceredig's mouth turned halfway into a grin. "I also know why he chose you for a wife. You match him bloody well in stubbornness."

His smile was infectious. Claerwen dropped her gaze. The sheer nerve that had buoyed her evaporated. "I was foolish. I am sorry. May I go now, please?"

Ceredig eyed her downcast face. "Aye. You may. But, lass, give Uther a chance to fight Octa. Perhaps this won't be for so long, eh?"

She nodded sullenly. Uther and Ambrosius had been exiled when quite young and had not returned to Britain until well into their adulthood. Exactly how many years, she didn't know. How long would she and Marcus need to wait?

"Go now," Ceredig said. "Get some rest. But remember, I will be watching."

Claerwen straightened, her shoulders squared. She walked through the doors, leaving them open so he might observe her all the way to her room. Though slack-kneed and unsteady, she forced herself to keep moving. Her pride hid the effort it took to complete the twenty paces. Once inside her chambers, she slammed the door, her last act of defiance that day.

She halted in the middle of the room, eyes closed, face to the ceiling. If only she could cry. Anger tangled inside her like a spider's web, but the tears would not come. None had since the day exile had been imposed.

Was it anger? Or was it nagging fear left from the vision? In the night—every night—she reexamined the distorted, jumbled stream of images but could not decipher their meaning. While the need to search for Macsen's sword continued to pull at her, the last image, the impression of drowning, of being swamped in endless water and horrendous pain, haunted her more than all the rest together. And the more she tried to remember, the more the sense in her gut told her Octa's assassin would have something to do with it. Where was *he* now?

Claerwen pressed her hand to her heart. So many guards, a stronghold that was unbreachable, and she could not feel safe.

Warmth. The smell of roasted meat. The hiss of burning oil.

Claerwen opened her eyes. A tray of steaming food—barley broth, a thick chunk of roasted venison, a baked apple with honey dripped over it, and a small ewer of mead—waited on the table, lit by the warm glow of her oil lamp. The brazier, full of red-hot coals, heated the room. A stack of neatly folded dresses and undershifts of finely woven wool lay on her bed. Though not fancy, they smelled warm and comfortable. Her fingertips brushed their dry, soft cleanliness, so inviting after shivering for hours in cold, damp clothes. All gifts from Ceredig.

"Marcus said you were kind," she whispered. "Why can't I be kind to you?"

CHAPTER 14

Into Exile—off the coast of Breizh
Late Autumn, AD 471

THE sea never quieted. Its monotonous rush ashore, only to turn back, seemed so pointless. Marcus watched the water break and spray from the entrance of his cell. It must have been a hundred thousand times by now. The noise clogged his ears, his mind, and grew in annoyance like the slow onset of madness. And always the smell of salt, seaweed, fish, nothing but fish to eat. The only change came during gales, when the tiny battered island, one of a multitude of others like it, was over-washed with relentless howling winds and waves. He had always hated the sea.

The tiny cell he occupied was one of several built into the rock hillsides of the islands off the northern shore of Armorica, or Breizh as the increasing influx of Celtic Britons called it. Lined with dry stone and topped with a corbelled roof, its only opening was supported by a thick lintel that was not quite shoulder high and was covered with a thin leather drape. Some called the group of cells a monastery, but upon his arrival nearly six months before, Marcus realized the island colony was a hermitage founded by Christians who had fled Britain's unrest in search of solitude and the fulfillment of religious austerity. The monks kept to themselves and expected him to do so as well.

Hunched, Marcus stepped out from beneath the low lintel. Dressed in the same monk's garb and cloak as the island's other occupants, he straightened and squinted against the glare of daylight, breathed deeply of the fresh air. At least this side of the island was green like the mountains of home, he thought, and surveyed the steeply pitched slope than ran from his cell down to the rocky shore. And it was greener than all the dozens of other tiny islands huddled off the coast. He raised his face to the sky.

"By all the gods that bring hope, may they…" he began softly in his Cymraeg dialect from Gwynedd.

His thoughts scattered, and he smoothed his beard, grown out full and long from its short, neat trimming for the storyteller's disguise. His arm ached. Indeed his arm, like his long-time damaged knee, had never stopped aching in all the time he had been there. Though the shoulder wound had healed well, the cold, damp wind never gave his bones or joints a chance to find a moment of warmth, even over the small fire pit inside the cell.

"Your gods don't appear to be helping," a familiar voice said behind him.

Marcus did not bother to turn around. The grizzled monk who was walking up to him countered with the same remark everyday. It didn't matter if it was in response to a prayer, a comment on the weather or mere silence. Usually Marcus ignored the intrusion—he accepted the man's presence only because he had been entrusted with completing the treatment Uther's physician had begun.

He switched to Brezhoneg, the only tongue the monk understood. "You don't even know what I said."

"You pray standing, with your hands and face to the sky instead of kneeling in supplication."

"And why should anyone have need to fear their god? Is yours always so testy?" Marcus hitched his cloak tighter and turned to walk away. "You leave my gods alone and I won't bother yours."

The monk laid a hand on Marcus's left arm. "Not today."

Marcus glared at him. Most days, the sun emerged for a brief time between bouts of heavy mist, and since his broken ribs had healed enough to allow more comfortable movement, he had climbed daily atop the scruffy, peaked hill into which his cell was dug. Strength was slowly returning to his arm—not enough to place much strain on it—but he could flex his elbow and use his right hand again. He had no wish to miss those few moments of warmth that helped to ease the ache that was as constant as the sea's maddening din.

Marcus heard the rhythmic slap of oars. Below, a small boat slid onto a tiny sliver of shoreline.

"You are to meet someone today." The monk shivered in the cold, penetrating wind and tucked his hands inside his sleeves. He bowed his head at the boat.

"Who?"

Contempt and relief filled the monk's face, but he offered no answer. Marcus was accustomed to the contempt, displayed ever since he had told the man he was not Christian and stubbornly refused to be converted. The relief was new. Dared he hope that news was coming from Uther, that the exile was over? The monk retreated and Marcus picked his way down the slope.

A tall man stepped out of the boat. He wore normal clothing, not the trappings of the island's religious men. Brown-haired with generous grey streaks, grey-bearded and grey-eyed, he had a likeable enough face that showed at least fifty winters. Refreshingly, he had none of the strained self-repugnance that was embedded in the eyes of the hermitage's permanent residents.

"You are to come with me," the stranger said. His voice was authoritative yet humble. He also had spoken in Brezhoneg, but with a slight accent.

"Where?" Marcus asked.

"You will know." The man swept a hand at the boat.

Marcus held. "Who are you?"

"It is not important. If you please." The stranger again waved a hand at the vessel.

Marcus gripped his shoulder and glanced at the boat. "Not until you tell me who you are and where you are to take me. And don't bother if it's not the truth."

The man winced. From inside his tunic he pulled a leather thong that hung around his neck. A heavy gold ring dangled from it. "This man has sent me to take you from here."

Marcus's left eyebrow lifted in recognition. The ring belonged to Budic, the king of Breizh, Uther's cousin. "And where is he sending me?"

"You will know, soon enough."

"Uther Pendragon still fights the Saxon?"

The stranger gave a single nod.

How much longer? Marcus released the man. Six months had already passed. Winter approached. Everything he and Claerwen had done would soon be lost if he could not return to Britain and continue. And what had happened to Handor—had the assassin survived the battle at Caer Luguvalos? If so, what had he done since and where was he now? All the harrowing hardships, all the nerve-wracking ruses...all for naught, Marcus scowled. And Claerwen. Damn, he missed her. He raked his fingers through his hair. "I need to get my belongings," he said.

The tall man followed him to the cell and watched like a bird of prey.

Marcus emerged with only the ragged, stained tunic and breeches of deerskin, rolled together and tied with a leather belt.

"That's all?" the man asked.

"I came with nothing but the clothes I wore."

They spoke no further on the brief journey down to the cove or during the crossing to the mainland. There, on the quay, a mounted escort waited with a two-wheeled cart. They were the same men who had taken him out of the streambed and guarded him until Uther's physician had finished his tasks, then spirited him across the sea.

"You will wear these," the tall man said. He reached into the cart's bed and lifted a handful of chains, shackles at their ends.

Once his health had recovered enough to give him fair mobility, Marcus knew he would be suspected of flight, especially the closer the year advanced towards winter when the seas closed to crossings. Of course they were right, he did want to break free. Most prisoners and hostages fled when they were transported from one location to another. But irons in a cart?

He took a step closer to inspect the load of chains. The links were thick, heavy, and had enough length and shackles not only for both wrists, but both ankles and his neck as well. Another length ran from the neck ring to a bolt in the cart's floor. The guards closed in around him, spears partially lowered, the crunch of their boots on the sand like the crush of a thousand eggshells.

"Careful. We cannot damage Uther's goods," the ranking officer said under his breath to the man next to him.

The guard that the officer admonished had a hand on his sword hilt. It returned to his spear shaft. Marcus silently damned Uther. With a vicious glare, he held out his wrists to accept the cold weight of the irons.

For three days he was jostled in the back of the cart. They drove him south first, then west, over mist-shrouded, nearly flat ground. The sea, though many miles away, continued to pour dampness and chill into the wind's eastbound sweep. His relentless guards offered no respite except for a few hours of sleep at night and necessary latrine stops. Meals were eaten on the march. Near the end of the third day, Marcus was sure his spine had drilled a hole into the cart's floor.

A fortified enclosure appeared on a barely noticeable rise. They soon turned into the lane that led to its gates. The tall stranger rode closer to the cart.

"What is that place?" Marcus asked.

The man's mouth curled into a wry expression that was neither a smile nor a grimace. "This will be your residence for a bit."

"No more gloom-faced monks, I hope." Marcus knew a monastery would never have been selected—Uther and Budic would choose more hardy and warrior-worthy guardians than monks to control him.

At dusk, they passed through the gates into a sprawling complex of buildings, the largest of which had been a Roman farmhouse at one time. Similar to villas still found in southern Britain, it appeared to have been rebuilt, expanded and strengthened, a response to the ongoing shift of powers across Gaul. Only a handful of people were present, slaves Marcus judged from their clothing and duties.

Three young male slaves hurried forward. From their similar features and coloring, Marcus guessed they were brothers. The stranger gave them instructions in a tongue other than Brezhoneg. While authoritative, his tone was not that of a master. The boys gathered the reins of the guards' horses and led the animals off to the stables.

One of the guards unbolted the chains from the cart. Exhausted from the jarring ride, Marcus found his legs nearly numb when he stood. The chains seemed heavier than before. Straightening, he glared at the tall man. "You didn't answer my question. What is this place?"

"Come," the stranger said and he led Marcus deeper into the complex. The guards followed, spears halfway down.

"You spoke Saxon to those boys," Marcus said. The accent suddenly made sense.

"I am called Blaez." The man spoke in a quiet, even tone. "I'm sure you know that means 'wolf' in Brezhoneg. They gave that name to me because so many Germanic men's names end in 'wulf.' But I am Frankish, not Saxon. The languages are quite similar. For now I will tell you no more of myself."

"Or of this place?"

They stopped before a long barrack-like building with thick, solid doors. Blaez met Marcus's eyes. "Let me ask you—in your lands, your kings usually have a capital, no?"

"For most, they do. Usually a place of birth."

"The king of these lands does not enjoy that. His court travels from one nobleman's lands to the next. He is at once home everywhere he goes, yet he is without a home. In a few days, the king of Breizh will arrive here."

Blaez swept a hand at an open door in the building.

Inside was a small, square room. The only window was fitted with shutters that were permanently sealed. The tile floor was long ruined, the plaster walls plain, chipped and smelled musty. The only furnishing was a chamber pot.

Court. In a nobleman's borrowed estate. Court was the one thing Marcus disliked as much as monks and the sea and the smell of fish. He gazed with a hint of ironic amusement at the chains hanging from his wrists. At least he would not be wasting his time playing a court fop.

He stepped into the blank hole of the cell. The door thumped shut behind him, the latch engaged, the thick iron bar on the outside driven home. In the center of the cold, damp room, Marcus raised his face towards the ceiling and stared into the black nothingness. Silence drew in like the walls of a grave.

"May the spirits of the ancestors keep you safe, *cariad,*" he prayed softly while he envisioned Claerwen's face. "I may be a while coming."

He wondered if winter in Breizh brought snow like it did in Britain.

CHAPTER 15

Breizh
Late Autumn, AD 471

"SO—you are the man my cousin has me keeping for him, eh?"

On his knees, tired and mud-stained, Marcus blinked at the flagstone floor. After two days in complete darkness, he needed time for his eyes to adjust. The guards had hustled him from the prison cell into daylight and then into this brightly lit set of chambers in the villa's main hall. His mouth flattened then twisted, but he held back from answering.

"Do you understand why you've been brought here in chains?" the king asked.

How many times had he been chained in his life? Marcus lifted his smoldering eyes, met the king of Breizh's gaze. "Uther must have warned you about me."

Budic studied him. "He did."

Marcus's left eyebrow flicked upward, a gesture more in disrespect than amusement.

Budic folded his arms across his broad chest and began to pace. "You are angry, obviously. So would I be, if I had been dragged across the countryside like a criminal. I know who you are, what you are, and why you are here, Marcus ap Iorwerth of Dinas Beris."

At least they were alone in the king's chambers before details began to be discussed, Marcus thought.

"You will not be allowed to return to Britain for any reason," Budic continued. "Not until Octa the Saxon is dead, his head on Uther's pike. No exceptions will be made."

He paused to let the words sink in and matched the grim glare Marcus gave him. "*No* exceptions. If you try to leave before the exile ends, or even hint at it, I am to send word immediately to Uther. If you intercept the courier, there will be several alternates to replace him. He must reach designated checkpoints within a certain amount of time. If not, there will be consequences."

"What consequences?" Marcus squared his shoulders to relieve the fatigue in his arms and neck and back.

"You will like this not," the king said. He scrutinized the effect of his warning.

"Get on with it," Marcus spit.

"Uther will see to it that your wife is handed over to Octa the Saxon."

Searing astonishment struck Marcus. Paralyzed, heartsick, he felt his resolve bend, stretch to its fullest capacity, then shatter into a thousand dusty scraps.

"I am only a messenger here." Budic avoided Marcus's eyes. "But I can tell you that these words are no jest. Not from Uther. You may read his letter yourself if you wish." He held out a curled sheet of parchment.

Marcus's scalp crawled as he glared up into Budic's face. Short, stout and balding, Uther's cousin bore little resemblance to the tall, fine-looking high king of Britain, but the trace of self-satisfaction in his face told him they shared a sly streak. Budic liked delivering bad news.

Marcus took the dried sheepskin between his shackled hands. As he read, words he had spoken months earlier smacked back at him like the relentless sea, words of advice he had given Uther about manipulating both the martial and political sides of Britain's intricate factions. The advice had indeed been taken. He had known he would not be able to go home until Octa was dead. The other was unexpected.

He lifted his glare again, and felt cold and startlingly cruel. "I am a prisoner," he said, "not an exile. And my wife is collateral."

Budic nodded.

The remark made on the quay now made absolute sense to Marcus. He was Uther's property, a prisoner of political intrigue.

His life could be the seal on a high-stakes bargain should negotiations with Octa become more useful than elimination.

"Will there be a need to keep you in chains any longer?" the king of Breizh asked.

Numbing indignity filled Marcus. Uther possessed the one way to control him completely. He stared at the shackles. "No," he answered. "There is no need."

The night sky, for once clear and star-filled, rotated on its curving path from sunset towards sunrise. Marcus gazed up into it and ached with the coming of winter. Except for the drinking horn still in his hands, the remnants of his long-finished evening meal sat neglected on the bench next to him. He wished the light, cool breeze that stirred his hair could whisk him away home.

Two days had passed since his release from the prison cell. The guesthouse he had been assigned was small but private, and after the hermitage he savored the solitude more than any amount of space. He had been allowed to shave his beard and trim his hair a bit. He had also been given normal clothing, hardy and warm woolen tunics and breeches, the kind of garments a simple man would wear every day, so welcome after the clumsy monk's robes.

The midnight call rounded the compound from guard to guard. Marcus bowed his face. Six months—too bloody long a time—and that could lengthen far longer. He had tried to sleep earlier, though he had not expected to be able to rest. Still fully dressed, he had lain on the bed, eyes unable to shut. He had paced after that, but it held no satisfaction. Then he had taken to sitting outside. He felt like a fox worn down by hounds.

The horn's contents finished, he set it on the bench and retreated into the house. At the fire pit, the only light inside, he stared numbly, its orange-red glow cast onto his face. He could not even think. Instead he prayed that Claerwen would not try to find him. As much as he missed her, he knew that was her only way to survive—she had to wait out the exile, however long it became.

"Are you still awake?" someone called through the doorway, a light knock at the side.

Marcus had left the door open, though not for visitors. He recognized Blaez's calm voice and crossed to the doorway. "Couldn't sleep either?"

The Frank shrugged. "Take a walk?"

Marcus stared across the villa's grounds. Uther's guards moved forward. Watchers. Since Budic's arrival, he had also noted a quarter war band—five-and-seventy men—had arrived and set up armed patrols. The resident nobleman's slaves, joined by others from nearby lands, constantly cleaned, organized and prepared food and drink. Now, with the quiet of midnight, most of the houses were dark, the occupants asleep. The main house was still brightly lit, a mark of Budic's residency.

"So be it," Marcus replied and smoothed his moustache.

Blaez paid no heed to the guards and began to walk. "This is how you're supposed to look?"

"More or less. Better?"

The Frank smiled. "I thought you might like to have a brief tour without the eyes of daylight following."

"Except for them?" Marcus thumbed over his shoulder. Two men watched, one for himself, and apparently another for Blaez. Why would a slave, he wondered, have a special guard assigned to him when the others worked under a slavemaster?

Blaez smiled again. "Aye. Them. Always them."

They circuited the compound and the Frank quietly pointed out each building and noted its use. The watchers followed all the way around. Then, nearly back to Marcus's house, Blaez approached another dwelling, slightly larger and dark inside. He glanced into an open window.

Following, Marcus saw three boys asleep on pallets. Blaez guided him several steps away. "My nephews," he said and waited for the significance to sink in. "Aye, the same you saw when you first arrived."

Marcus eyed the guards. "Why were *you* sent to bring me here?"

Blaez gave a smile full of irony and started to walk again. "I have told you I am a Frank. What do you know of my people?" He spoke in an educated manner, as if he were a tutor.

"Well," Marcus said. "It's my understanding the Franks were settled on lands in northeastern Gaul—east of Breizh—in return for military support of the Roman rule, much in the same way Vortigern settled Saxons in southeastern Britain in return for fighting Irish and Picts. Except the Saxons grew out of hand."

"You realize that by now Rome holds very little influence in much of Gaul?" Blaez asked.

Marcus laughed. "Rome sways under its changing emperors like a drunken man. Anyone with good sense knows it cannot go on as it has. Kingdoms have sprouted in spite of still being under Roman rule. I believe your king is called Childeric? However, I have heard, he has been at times rather…unstable?"

"Ah, I am impressed. You've been taught well." Blaez flourished a hand in a gesture of acquiescence. "There was a great amount of concern about his character before he became a king. Quite a bit of debauchery, enough to earn him eight years of exile, presumably to cool his…well you understand."

"Indeed," Marcus responded with a grin. They arrived at his house and sat on the bench in front. "Yet, he must have learned some capability since taking kingship—how to use alliances with the Roman leadership, such as it is. Isn't it so that now he pushes westward into these lands? And at the same time, Budic tries to advance eastward into Childeric's kingdom?"

"That is true. Many refugees have come from Britain. As the west grows crowded, people move east. The Saxons push from the other side into Frankish lands because theirs have become flooded by the sea."

"Flooded?" Marcus was genuinely surprised.

"The sea has been rising over many years now. Very strange."

"Aye," Marcus agreed. "That would make another reason they're so intent on land in Britain. They push us west and north."

He leaned his elbows on his knees. Though he enjoyed the intelligent conversation, a rarity since the exile had begun, he suspected the discussion of Frankish and Breizhad politics held more significance than the mere passing of time. He straightened; his eyes narrowed at Blaez. "Who *are* you?"

The right side of Blaez's mouth curved up the same way as when he had told Marcus the fortified villa would be his current residence—neither smile nor sarcasm. His voice dropped to a level just above a whisper, and he tilted his head towards their guards. "Too many ears listen here. You may have noticed I have watchers as you do. But I *will* tell you, should I attempt to leave this place or do anything against the will of…certain people in authority…my family will be executed."

The revelation, though not a surprise, struck Marcus as disheartening. Blaez was as much a prisoner of a powerful man's politics as he was. But whose?

"You either know too much," he said, "you are related to the wrong person, or you have an enemy you cannot escape."

This time Blaez smiled. "Let's just say for now, I know too much. There is another point I think you might like to know."

Marcus lifted an eyebrow.

"A bit to the east," Blaez went on, "lies a region in Breizh that Budic has never been able to control. Because of the dispute, Childeric attempts to infiltrate it, to find a foothold there. These people have lived there since time out of mind."

"True Gauls?"

Blaez nodded.

"And they resist?"

Another nod. "Fiercely. The Romans call them *bacaudae.* They have fought to overthrow the Roman yoke for hundreds of years. It's one reason why this farmstead was fortified and why Budic chooses to stay here, not in nearby Plouguer."

"Plouguer? That was a tribal capital, before the Romans took it, no?"

Once more, the nod.

Marcus studied him. Did Blaez know he was a spy? "Why do you tell me this?" he asked. "*Should* you be telling me this?"

"It's a fine treat to have someone with intelligence to talk to at last, but I thought you should be warned. It is dangerous here. For many reasons."

Many reasons. Which ones? Why would Budic hold court there if it were so dangerous? With an eye to the watchers, then to the patrolling guards, Marcus kept those questions to himself. "How long have you been banished to Budic's court?" he asked instead.

"Five years. I have come to accept it as permanent."

Five years. Permanent? Marcus opened his mouth to speak again. Instead he stood and turned away. He had thought six months was too long. And Uther, damn him, could deliberately allow Octa to live out his years if it would serve a purpose.

Years of languishing as a political prisoner. He might never see Claerwen again.

Marcus stared into the blackness of the sky. His head became crowded, stained with the rush of memories, tainted with the images from his nightmares. The horrendous stench in the shadows rose again and filled him with sickness, the sounds of the scurry of rats with each step and the sea behind the words he could not understand. Sweat broke out on his skin. His throat choked. If only the sea could have washed away the stains, those of the dead, those of his mind. Instead it made him want to vomit. How he hated the sea. His mouth clamped shut.

"Are you not well?"

The words pried at his thoughts. A hand shook his arm, but the images refused to release their grip.

"What's wrong?" Blaez's voice intruded again, a little louder.

Marcus blinked, once, twice. The tightness in his throat eased, and Blaez stood before him. His presence scattered the images.

Marcus's eyes focused on him. "You speak several languages, don't you?"

Blaez nodded.

"Saxon is one of them?"

The Frank frowned with confusion in his grey eyes.

"Will you teach me?"

"Teach you? Why?"

Marcus dropped his gaze to the ground and considered how to answer. "I need to know the words," he said in a quiet, strained voice. "I've needed to know for a long time. I've hurt a lot of people."

"Because you didn't know the language? But, why now, if… It's guilt, isn't it? Guilt is a powerful force."

Guilt, Marcus echoed silently. That seemed too simple. He regarded the Frank closely, and for an instant he thought the man looked familiar, like someone he had known a long time before and had forgotten. The impression passed. Then a second revelation racked his mind. Perhaps it was only that he now realized Blaez's enigmatic expression hid more than political secrets, that it was the same dark barrier he had seen reflected in his own face for many years, the same force that held back the memories.

"When you came for me," Marcus said, "if I had fled, those boys would have died just as surely as if you had escaped yourself, wouldn't they? Guilt's been wedged into you, for that thing which you know too much of?"

The lines in the Frank's face drooped like overheated metal. He drew breath, slow, labored, then let it go, the sound like that of a dying man. He nodded faintly, once. "It appears we have something in common," he said. "So be it, then. I will teach you."

CHAPTER 16

Dun Breatann
Winter, AD 471

"YOU look at that patch of ground like it's a grave, lass," Ceredig said, a tired smile on his lips.

Claerwen glanced up but quickly returned to staring at the thin crust of snow that covered the garden. The planting, nurturing and harvesting of herbs throughout the summer for Dun Breatann's healer had kept her sanity from fleeing, and the garden had been a place to feel useful. Now, grey in the evening's twilight, the small plot of land behind the palace indeed looked like a long, narrow grave. How would she survive the lethargy of winter? She bundled herself tighter into her cloak.

"Lass?" Ceredig laid a hand on her shoulder. "Come inside. It's too cold to be standing here."

She could not respond. She knew he had come from his chambers and had left the daily courier's report from the high king on his table, spread out the way he always read it, its edges pinned down with a cup, a gauntlet and a dagger. No need to ask if there was news. She only had to look into Ceredig's warm brown eyes. He would say the same thing he did every day; that the message scrawled on the parchment and signed by Uther himself had not differed.

Voices exchanged in the courtyard, loud enough to be heard behind the palace. Ceredig looked up at the disturbance.

"What is it?" she asked.

"Come. We'll find out."

He led her around to the yard. A man, so filthy he looked as if he had lived in bogs, had come to the gates. His hair, covered in mud, could have been any color and hung halfway down his back. He seemed exhausted, his spirit defeated, and was only able to answer the guards with a face full of distress and confusion, and a few unintelligible words.

"Ah," Ceredig sighed. "He is Saxon."

"You understand his language?"

"No, no. I only recognize its sound."

The questioning continued, and the man gradually calmed. The communication between him and the guards improved. In time, they understood he was begging to be taken in.

"They will put him with the slaves," Ceredig said. "One will have to translate and teach him our language."

"So many are like him. Lost, alone."

"Aye," he agreed. "Some have criticized me for keeping slaves. But they do serve a purpose. That man may not be grateful, but it's better than dying in a cold ditch."

His remark evoked silence. After the guards had disappeared among the buildings with the newcomer, Claerwen gazed up again at Ceredig. The news, or lack of it, had been his purpose in finding her. Might as well let it be confirmed.

He met her eyes and acknowledged the daily routine. "More than seven months, nearly eight, isn't it? How many more days will I have need to disappoint you, lass? How many days to watch the light of hope in your eyes extinguish with the shake of my head?"

"I hate the waiting."

"I know you do."

"You sound troubled," she said.

"Just an old man's ruminations, no more than that." He cupped one hand in the other and rubbed his knuckles.

"We're making a new salve for your hands on the morrow," Claerwen told him. "As soon as it's ready, I'll bring it to you. How are they?"

"Same." He flexed his fingers and showed her how they bent only halfway then corrected himself. "Worse. I appreciate your helping the healer."

Claerwen shrugged. "Raising the herbs gave me something to do in the warm time. Helping to make the remedies will fill the cold time. I hope I won't have to be here for the next…"

She turned away. After her frivolous attempt to escape, she had tried to stop counting the passage of time as the exile extended from fortnights into months, but she could not seem to help herself. Her minders had tightened their scrutiny since then—any more attempts would be nothing but hopeless musing. She gazed sadly in the direction the Saxon had been taken. "I wonder who he is, where he's from."

"He'll likely be here the rest of his life, lass," Ceredig said. "Who he is matters little. Go on back to your chambers. It's late and cold."

Days passed and Claerwen thought no more on the Saxon, although while she worked in the healer's hut she took to pondering the lives of Dun Breatann's slaves. Over the months, she had listened to the hum of their dialects blend together when they passed by in their chores. About half the men were Irish or Saxon, along with several Norsemen as well—injured warriors left behind in raids on Britain's shores. A few had been there for years and expected to die paupers' deaths in foreign lands, separated forever from home, family, custom. Another group, a mixture of men and women, had been brought from Ireland, captured in Ceredig's retaliation of the Irish raids the previous spring. Others had arrived over the years. Starving and homeless, they had been gathered throughout the summer and autumn months from across Strathclyde and given shelter and food in return for work. Of these, many were native Britons forced from their homes in the same raids that had produced foreign slaves. Not considered charity, the sweeps were an attempt to reduce the presence of beggars within the kingdom.

Footsteps crunched in the snow near the open door of the hut. Alone since the healer left for her house, Claerwen cleaned off the worktables. Another day's work almost done. The steps passed. Must be someone going home from the smithy. She glanced, but the person was already gone.

Claerwen tossed her rag into a basket with others that needed washing. She considered how the isolation and ostracism of exile was similar to the deprivation of hearth and home the slaves had to endure. Of course, how many homelands had been lost to invaders and could never be home again? She brushed the remaining bits of dried plants into a small pail and wondered, would she ever see Dinas Beris again?

Ah well, Claerwen sighed to herself. Nothing could be done until Uther caught Octa on the battlefield. She hung bundles of unused herbs on a wall rack, her final task of the day. The sun would set soon. She donned her cloak, picked up her small pail to empty outside, and turned into the doorway.

A slave, tall, husky, with wavy blond hair strewn over his shoulders, blocked her path. He loomed over her. His jaw dropped in astonishment.

Claerwen's stomach plunged, and her bucket chunked down into the crusty snow.

The deep cleft in his chin and his ice-blue eyes confirmed to her that he was the Saxon who had fought Handor and had tried to take Marcus captive. His nose had obviously been broken and probably his jaw as well. Neither had healed quite right and ruined his features. She felt the blood drain from her face.

His pale blue eyes bored into hers and he spoke, but she understood nothing he said.

"What do you want?" she asked then immediately thought how ridiculous she was to even try to talk to him. He could not understand her any more than she could him.

He spoke again, a hand raised and reaching out.

In spite of the cold, sweat broke on Claerwen's temples. She sidestepped then bolted, but with just a few long-legged strides he caught her arm.

"I know nothing. Let me go," she hissed and wrenched free.

He caught her wrist this time. His words continued, insistence in their tone.

"No, stop!" Claerwen pleaded.

His fingers tightened on her wrist. With his other hand he pointed at himself, spoke a word, then pointed at her. "Tangwen," he said.

Speechless, Claerwen could only stare. And then she realized this man was the filthy Saxon who had arrived only days earlier. Ceredig had been wrong, it did matter who he was. He could be as dangerous as Handor.

Questions raced through her mind: had Dun Breatann been his choice for a refuge or was it coincidence? And if he and his two dead companions had misunderstood she was Tangwen, as he appeared to still believe, was his slavery a ploy, a new opportunity to take her captive? Or did he want revenge for his companions' deaths?

"Tangwen," he repeated, then another word she could not understand, "*Cynn*." His finger kept pointing back and forth between them. "*Cynn*."

"I don't understand!" Where were her minders when she needed them? She wriggled, struggling to free her arm, but his hold was like a shackle.

"You, there!" One of the guards finally appeared, his spear's tip in line with the slave's belly. "Leave the Lady alone and get back to work. Move!"

The Saxon understood the weapon better than words. He released her.

Claerwen sprinted out of range. Run, she told herself. Escape him. She pulled up her cloak's hood and slipped into the gathering shadows of dusk, angled between the buildings, and out into the crowded courtyard. She scurried through the thickest swell of people and shifted course as needed to avoid guards and minders. Near the gates, wide open to accommodate the bustle, she wished she could shrink and become as obscure as a common mouse.

The gateway was jammed with traders on their way out of Dun Breatann and slaves returning from tending cattle in the fields beyond the northern fens. Claerwen plunged through the middle of them. No alarms had been called yet, but she was sure the first would come momentarily. She didn't care. They couldn't protect her.

Once past the gates, she ran down the terrace-like steps cut into Dun Breatann's rock. North-facing, they were coated with ice that could not melt for lack of sun. In the fading light, she could barely see their contours and nearly slipped twice.

The first alarm rang out from the ramparts, the same strange call of horns heard the last time she had evaded her minders. Claerwen spit an oath. She was almost to the bottom of the rock where the Roman road began. A shout cracked directly behind her. One of Uther's guards—and she swore it was the same who had caught her the last time.

She whipped around. In the instant her knee crashed into the guard's groin, she saw his outstretched hand had almost reached her. It flung upward then jerked down again as he grabbed at himself in pain. With her fists clasped together, she swung hard and rammed them into his throat. Unable to cry out, he doubled over and went down on his knees.

Claerwen ran on into the twilight. Instead of taking the road, she turned into the first place she could hide, a long line of thickets next to a shallow stream. She plowed through them, crossed the water and came out onto a narrow track that wound past a thickly treed woodbank. Facing east, she knew the track would take her safely through the fens. She had no sense of where she should go, but once past the marshlands, she crossed through the woodbank. Watching to all sides, she hoped the darkening skies would keep her safe.

She continued east. Her thin shoes were not suited for travel, but she ignored the rocks that jabbed the soles of her feet. Not only on watch for guards, she scanned the cloudless sky as well. Darkness was welcome, but the cold would be another problem. Without food or a horse, her strength would soon wane. But she had survived before. She would do it again. And she would find Marcus.

Night fell as she completed a second mile. She cut northward. In the distance she had seen a steep, heavily treed hill and decided that would be her refuge for the night. Only another mile to go.

The click of iron and flint. A hiss. The sharp smell of pine pitch. Torchlight flared.

To her right, fresh flames shot up and guttered wildly. They rushed towards her like a spectre out of the blackness. Instinctively she veered. The flash of light spilled like liquid fire over a group of rocks as it bounced then settled among them. An instant later, hands grabbed her ankles. Tripped, she smacked the ground with a grunt.

"You run well, mistress," a harsh male voice mocked. The assailant rolled her over, pinned her down by sitting on her hips.

One hand clamped around her neck.

"If you're who I think you are..." The man reached for the torch, an arm's length away. He struck its pointed butt end into the turf, deliberately placed so she could not see his face.

"Aye...those eyes for certain. Lady Claerwen." He drawled her name in contempt and the fingers on her neck tightened. His nails dug into her skin. A large knife appeared in his other hand.

Frozen between fear and rage, Claerwen recognized Handor's voice. She groaned. He must have followed the Saxon. How else could he possibly have found her? Such a fool, she was. Fool to leave the fortress, fool to panic.

The man leaned down. The straggly ends of his hair, caught in the light, were filthy. "You're going to tell me where that spy is," he mocked again, his breath on her face.

Rage drove out her fear. Claerwen wrenched her right hand free of the cloak and rammed her fist up. She caught Handor in the temple. Stunned, he jolted upright, but her strike was not hard enough. His fingers never left her neck, and she could not free her other hand.

He leaned over her again. Claerwen heard none of the taunts hurled at her. The pressure on her neck increased, the fingernails ever deeper. Deprived of breath, her head felt like a brick that had been thrown against a stone wall. Only bursting apart into a thousand pieces could relieve the agony. The black night sky swirled in a sea of dots. She tried to gag, but no air could enter her starving, burning lungs. Rage helped little now. Fading, her head drummed so hard she thought the ground vibrated.

At the edge of consciousness, she vaguely heard Handor's bitter voice scream expletives somewhere above her in a loud howl. Then it all grew softer, floated away. Moments later the shackling hand withdrew, then the weight lifted from her body. She barely felt the difference.

Her throat abruptly opened. Air, cold and searing, rushed in and raked icily into her lungs. She gulped it in and rolled over, her chest in convulsions, her fists clutched to herself. The pain gradually eased. Coherence began to return, and her eyes opened.

Handor was kneeling beside her, close enough to touch. His

knife gleamed in the torchlight, gripped in his closer hand, and he glared at two heavily armed soldiers, men from Dun Breatann. They shouted at him to stand and drop the knife. Two more horsemen pulled up, a pair of torchbearers with them. The new soldiers slid from their mounts, swords drawn.

Her eyes shifted to the assassin. With the additional light from the soldiers' torches, she saw the cruelty in Handor's face matched that in his words. From his position, he had only to make one sideways slash to slit her throat. He would never obey the orders, she knew, and should he meet force, he would wreak as much destruction as possible before being taken.

The soldiers advanced. Handor's head began to turn.

Now! She squeezed her eyes shut and punched out. The heel of her hand struck his wrist. The dagger shot free and disappeared beyond the torchlight.

Claerwen had no chance to realize her success. Furious, Handor cracked his knuckles against her skull in retaliation. Her last impression was a blur when he leapt up into the dark. The soldiers lunged after him, their shouted orders lost in the churning confusion that filled her head. She sank away into unconsciousness.

CHAPTER 17

Dun Breatann
Midwinter, AD 471

"CLAERWEN, wake up."

The voice soothed. A man's voice, familiar, deep. A face floated above her in waves like a reflection in a pool. Dark eyes, long black hair. His lips moved. Though she could not understand what he said, she felt the words as if they dropped like rain on her face, cool, comforting words of remembrance, words of hope, words of affection.

"Marcus..." she breathed into the pillow and wriggled down deeper into its comfort.

"Wake up, lass."

Lass? That sounded wrong.

"Marcus," she repeated, but the image of his face slowly twisted then shattered into tiny bits. From behind, a pool of black water appeared. A new face rose from it—cruel brown eyes, a harsh mouth...

The sense of drowning overwhelmed Claerwen. Her chest felt like it was collapsing inward with pain. Was she alive? Or was this already the path to the Otherworld?

"Wake up, lass."

The pool disappeared. Claerwen jolted upright, her hand pressed to her pounding heart, and she forced her eyes to open. Ceredig sat next to her. The voice had been his, not Marcus's, and she had been returned to the small room within the palace. Though she was not in Handor's clutches, disappointment flooded her. She dropped down again on the pillow.

Ceredig picked up a cloth that lay next to her head and dabbed at her temple. Warm and moist, it smelled of marigold. When he laid it down again, fresh blood showed in a small patch.

"You've a nasty cut and a bruise to match, but it should heal well enough," he said. "You've also a ring of bruises around your throat. You can see where every fingernail cut. When you feel better, I will give you a very stern lecture."

Claerwen tried to respond, but her voice rasped. Her neck, from jaw to shoulder, hurt. She pushed herself up again and cleared her throat several times.

"Give it to me now," she squeaked.

"Don't, lass. You will faint."

A muffled clink followed the movement of her ankle, and she recognized the cold hard feel of a shackle clamped around it. Chains. The terms had been invoked. Her senses reeled and she lay flat again. "What happened?"

"I think you already know, if you would like to tell me about it."

She was too tired, too groggy.

Ceredig smiled. The hour was late and he looked tired as well. "When you are feeling stronger, I will return. We'll have a fine talk then."

Eleven days passed before Ceredig returned.

When he reappeared at her door, Claerwen had no desire to look up. She sat on the bed and counted the links in the chain for the nineteenth time that evening. Three-and-ninety, from where it was embedded in the stone floor to the shackle on her ankle. The length was enough that she could reach anything in the room, from brazier to chamber pot. No, she did not care to look at him.

"I'll remove that if you take a walk with me," the king offered.

She shrugged.

Ceredig pulled the stool next to her and sat. He slid a key into the shackle's cylindrical lock and opened it, laid the iron aside.

Claerwen eyed it. He would leave it there as long as he suspected she might bolt once more. She shoved back her hair, loose and uncombed for eleven days. "I know what you're going to tell me."

His brown eyes, stern, gripping, leveled with hers. "Perhaps so, but I will say it, regardless. Even if it's only for my own satisfaction. Even if it's the least I owe Marcus."

She flinched.

The king sighed. "There's a lot of anger in you right now. I can't blame you for that. But you were sent here for good reason that cannot be repeated enough."

Rage rumbled just below the surface. Claerwen could barely contain it. She stared directly into his eyes, unblinking, unmoving.

"I investigated what happened," he went on. "How you ran from that slave. I can understand that he frightened you. But why didn't you just come back to the palace? The guards would have protected you."

He waited for her reaction, received none.

"You didn't consider how persistent Octa's men are. We have always watched for them, long before you arrived here, and always will, out of necessity. That's why the soldiers got to you so quickly."

Claerwen continued to stare at him. He rose and reached for her cloak.

"Come walk with me, lass. Some fresh air might remedy a bit of the ill feelings you have right now. Perhaps you'll feel more like talking."

Her brows rumpled together. Tears threatened but never came. Eight months and she still could not cry. "No," she said.

"If it's the Saxon," Ceredig said, "he's been moved to another location outside the compound where you won't come in contact with him."

"Outside?" Her breath quickened. By the gods, if Handor were still out there… The Saxon did frighten her, but she didn't want him killed. No one should die at the hand of a ghoul like Handor.

"Claerwen, what's wrong? Do you know who that slave is?"

She stood with her hands balled into fists and knocked her knuckles together. She couldn't tell him, not without opening the gate to everything else she and Marcus had been doing.

"Let me send a letter to Uther," she said. "No, please, don't just say 'no' again. Let me negotiate the terms. He must listen to me."

Ceredig's face remained unchanged. "The terms are not for negotiation."

"Then let me send word to Myrddin. He can influence the high king." She took a step towards Ceredig, but he stopped her, a hand on her arm.

"I can't, even if I knew where to send a message."

"What are you talking about?"

Ceredig sighed again, frustrated. "Myrddin has not been seen or heard from for months."

"You said that before. How do you know this? Is this rumor or fact?"

"I know nothing more than exactly what I just said. And no one else does either."

Claerwen's stomach convulsed. Perhaps Myrddin would not help anyway, not after the anger he displayed the last time she and Marcus had seen him. She clamped her fingers around Ceredig's arm. "You must let me go. You have the power. Send an escort with me. Send decoys, do whatever is necessary, just let me leave this place. Let me find Marcus."

"No."

She flinched again and expected his ruddy face to redden even more. It remained the same, his eyes calm.

"You cannot leave here. Not until Uther lifts the exile. You've seen for yourself why. If Octa and his henchman capture you, they will torture you the way Vortigern's Saxons tortured Marcus years ago, to try to make you tell them where he is or lead them to him, except you don't know anything."

"No—"

"The man who attacked you? The way he left marks from his fingernails in your neck tells me he did not intend to kill you. Not yet. He meant to hurt you enough to make you think you would die. If he was going to kill you, he would not have used his nails—he would have used his fingers and hands flat against your neck so their full force could easily crush your throat. He wanted you to fear him. Then he would use you to get to Marcus."

"But—"

Ceredig was relentless. "And if, just if, you should be lucky enough to get past that man and any others from Octa, and then somehow against enormous odds reckon out where Marcus is, you would lead them to him. Then he would die. Is that what you want? To kill Marcus?"

"But, I wouldn't be—"

"Aye, but you would. The terms must stand if you want to live, if you ever want a chance to be with him again. There is no negotiation. If you go to Marcus, you *will* kill him. Men like the one who left those marks on your neck will follow you and take his head to prove his death to Octa. Is that how you want him to die? Think of how it would look: Marcus's head picked up by the hair, his face blue-white in death, eyes staring, mouth open, blood dripping from his neck, and some Saxon dog to carry it back to Octa?"

Claerwen let go of his arm and stumbled back as if she had been struck.

"You must realize they have been watching Dinas Beris as well," Ceredig went on. "And any other place they suspect you might have been hidden. Now they will likely withdraw from all the other places."

"And come here in force?"

Ceredig nodded.

"Will they attack?"

"I don't know. Octa may send a war band, but Uther probably has them too well occupied. It's more likely they will attempt infiltration."

Claerwen fingered her neck. "Your soldiers didn't catch him, did they?"

Ceredig started to shake his head before she finished the question. He offered the cloak again. "Come."

Her breath moved in and out of her throat with difficulty. She shook her head and sank onto the bed again. "You've been so kind…in spite of my stupidity. No, I will not cause you more trouble. If I show my face…your people will resent what I have done. They might blame you as well."

The king smiled. "I am both blessed and blamed for everything that happens in this kingdom, simply because I was either lucky or cursed enough to be born the son of high-ranking nobility. I learned long ago to never take unfounded criticism to heart. Like this."

He pulled a roll of parchment from his tunic and opened it. "This is from the bishop called 'Patrick of Ireland.' Do you know of him?"

Claerwen glanced at the writing, all in Latin. She shook her head.

"Patrick was kidnapped when he was young," Ceredig said. "Sold into slavery in Ireland, then escaped. Years later, he returned there as a priest and missionary of the new religion. Apparently, my war bands carried off some of his disciples as slaves when they completed their task in Ireland last spring. This letter was intended to be read to my men, but they brought it to me. He calls me a tyrant. Can you imagine? Of course, by now, perhaps you agree with him."

Claerwen stared at her hands in her lap.

Ceredig grinned. "The raid was necessary to deter the Irish from harassing us. We were swift and very harsh; we made our point. The slaves are a spoil of war. Patrick, of all people, should know that—having been carried off himself. It's a common enough occurrence. The exile is a necessary part of war as well."

Ceredig quietly rolled the letter together again. He sat on the stool, laid a hand on her shoulder. "I know you're lonely, lass. It will be so until the exile ends. And I know how disheartening that can be. My wife died giving birth to my only son."

Her eyes lifted. "Marcus said you never married again."

He went to the window and opened the shutters. Cold air rushed in. "I had no heart for it, not any longer. I find my comfort in friendships and in my son and his two young boys. Children can be such a pleasure—"

Claerwen looked up when he stopped. "What's wrong?"

A hint of embarrassment clouded his face. "I'd forgotten. Marcus told me there would be no children. Forgive me, I should—"

"Pay it no mind," Claerwen said to brush away the uncomfortable moment. She had been long resigned to a life of barrenness and though children might have been nice, both she and Marcus had accepted it with no regrets. A spy's life made children, like a wife, ready targets.

"On nights when I am too troubled, I like to go up there." Ceredig pointed to the ramparts that overlooked the river. "It's no consolation to you, but it's all I can offer right now, if you'd like to come with me."

She joined him at the window. The night was clear, moonless, starlit. Frost had already formed on the timbers' sharp, upright points. In spite of the stern upbraiding, Claerwen liked Ceredig's plain good sense, a trait she was certain Marcus had been infused with during his fosterage. She considered his offer, but finally shook her head.

They watched the night sky in silence. From the direction of the courtyard, music and voices gradually rose along with the shuffle of activity. Then one voice emerged from the rest, a voice trained to speak before crowds.

"I have been the dragon star, I have been the golden light that fires across the sky, I have been the Holly King who steals the light away, I am in the secret of the unhewn stone..."

"What day is it?" Claerwen suddenly asked.

"Midwinter Eve."

Her mouth made a wordless "oh," then, "I had forgotten."

"I am in the voice of Myrddin the Enchanter! And I welcome you tonight!" the voice boomed from the courtyard.

Claerwen froze, chills on her skin. Unable to see the speaker because the window faced away from the yard, she turned for the door.

"No, lass." Ceredig caught up and gripped her arm. "It's only my court bard, not Myrddin. He will perform the Winter King ceremony."

Unconvinced, she stared hard enough to burn holes through the walls and see the courtyard beyond. The crowd quieted in wait for the bard to continue.

Ceredig smiled. "It will be a simple celebration. The bard, and the usual singing, dancing. Would you like to attend?"

Music began again. A lone man played the pipes, but instead of the sound of celebration, strains of sorrow flowed.

"I am in the voice of Myrddin the Enchanter," the bard repeated.

Disappointed, Claerwen ignored Ceredig's offer. The invocation of the Enchanter's name was meant to attract a stronger spiritual power to the ritual than the bard could muster himself. It was probably meant to boost his credibility as well. She remembered the ceremony's path well enough, though she had only seen it performed a handful of times.

The bard began to chant, his voice carried on the cold night air with clear, sparkling resonance. In verse, he told the story of the Wheel of Time, how since *Nos Galan Gaeaf*, the eve of the first day of winter by the ancient calendar, the festival the Christians now called All Hallow's Eve, that the year had gone to rest. The earth had shed its leaves and color and warmth to become encased in frost-burnt grass, ice and snow. The sun had withdrawn into its winter burrow just as people withdrew to the warmth of their hearths. The Holly King, clad in his green, waxy leaves and red berries, bright against the dismal, colorless land, stole away the last of the light.

The music spoke with equal poignancy to the bard's words and emulated the loneliness of icy winds blowing off the sea. Claerwen's stomach knotted. "Please go," she said softly.

Ceredig lightly squeezed her elbow and bowed his head to her. If he spoke when he withdrew, she never heard him.

The bard paused. The music drifted away. Claerwen turned back to the window. She watched the lights dim across the fortress, then go out altogether. Likewise, in reverence, she snuffed her oil lamp.

Claerwen lay down on the bed and listened for the second half of the ceremony to begin. She knew the bard would call forth the Oak King, played by a man dressed in oak leaves and who carried a basket of acorns. In response to the bard's verse, he would declare that he had defeated the light-thieving Holly King in battle. Sometimes a mock fight between the two kings was staged. In the end the victorious Oak King would raise a torch representing the recaptured light. He would then ignite a bonfire in the courtyard and scatter acorns, a symbol of the coming springtime. The music would begin again in cheerful reels and jigs and the people would celebrate the rebirth of the sun and the turning of the Wheel of Time.

The earth waited, Claerwen waited. But for the stars, all light had gone, all was silent except for the crackling of ice on the river below. No music, no people in celebration. How long had it been since she had lain down? She must have fallen asleep, still dressed. Shivering, she reached for the bed covers.

An eerie sense of pause gripped her. Her hair stirred. A breeze, ever so light, bore a faint impression of warmth. It filled the room. Was it the turning of the year? The window was still open. She shivered again and turned her head.

On the face of her brass oil lamp, a tiny ball of golden light arced across the rounded surface, a tapering golden trail behind it.

Claerwen sat up. A similar glow filled her window, but it did not come from torches on the buildings or ramparts. All was dark below.

"By the gods..." She launched up and leaned on the window's casement. The light, mirrored on the lamp, came from the sky, a brilliant white light that streaked from one side to the other. A trail of sparkling dust followed it. Seconds later, it disappeared beyond the horizon.

"Dragonstar..." She closed her eyes. Within the hollow of her soul she could hear Igraine, the high king's woman, scream with the pain of childbirth. The woman was exhausted, but the midwives called to her, over and over, to keep trying. Claerwen smelled the musky odors of the birthing room. Then, in her mind, the image of the red-gold dragon fluttering above Tintagel appeared, identical to her vision months before. This time, it raced upward into the heavens. The screams and women's voices disappeared with it.

Igraine's son was born. The name he would be given rolled through Claerwen's mind, again and again. Arthur. Arthur was born.

Miracle.

Now, he had only to stay alive.

Myrddin...Tintagel. Of course, Claerwen thought. Myrddin had been the key instrument of conspiracy to bring about Arthur's conception. If the Enchanter was missing now, it was because he must assure that Arthur's birth came about as well.

Miracle-maker.

Hot stinging welled in Claerwen's eyes. She dropped to her knees and gazed up through the window into the sky again, black now. Would Marcus, wherever he was, know of the birth? She wished she could see his reaction. Certainly, if he did know, he would wonder at all the years of danger and frustration and hardship he had spent in search of this day, that this miracle should finally happen and begin the long-awaited fulfillment of Myrddin's prophecy. Would relief fill him?

At odds with herself, Claerwen found no comfort in knowing the child was born. So much could happen in the years yet to come. So many years had to pass until the boy could learn all he needed to know, gain the strength to hold Britain together against the Saxons, and accept the courage to wield that strength and knowledge. Certainly Marcus would be as frustrated as she was, that until the exile ended they could do nothing to help keep the child safe. Would all that they had done be for naught? Or would Octa defeat Uther first, and they would all die having gained nothing—no freedom, no peace, not even each other?

"Ah, Marcus…where are you?" she asked of the sky.

The anger she had harbored for months suddenly drained away in a rush, as if a hole had been punched into the barrier of bitterness she had so carefully built. It left her with no more nerve to combat the creeping loneliness that closed in. Eyes shut again, she conjured Marcus's face in her mind, every detail, every expression in his intense eyes, his smile, his voice. She leaned her face into the bed's feather mattress to stifle the first sob.

CHAPTER 18

Breizh
Spring, AD 473

"THE court may be going to— What are you doing?"

Marcus turned around. Blaez stood in the open doorway of the house and frowned. He had not bothered to knock.

"Practice," Marcus said. Clad only in breeches and boots, he held two long sticks at their centers, one in each hand, and twirled them in a graceful, coordinated pattern.

The creases in Blaez's forehead deepened. "For what?"

"If I'm ever allowed to have a sword again."

"Strange swords."

On the opposite side of the fire pit, Marcus moved back and forth as he worked the sticks. "Strange even for wasters. These are for coordination and strength. The weight of each stick is about the same as the swords I usually carry." He handed one to Blaez.

The tall Frank hefted it. "Only a swordmaster carries a weapon of this weight."

Marcus spun around, the other stick in his hands as if he held a real weapon. With painstaking concentration, he swung at one of the roof's support beams. The stick hissed with speed and halted within a finger's width from the timber. If it had struck, both the stick and the beam would have cracked.

He straightened. "If I had enough space, I could demonstrate more aptly."

"That arm has not only completed its healing, I see," the Frank noted. "You've regained strength as well. I can also see your temperament is that of a warrior, not merely a soldier."

"And what makes the difference?"

"A soldier does what he is told. A warrior—a true warrior—is the man who faces and accepts a challenge that could end in his death. He is not disconcerted by it. Of what I have seen, you fit that profile. Except it seems to be a bit clouded—anger, frustration, a little too much of the drink."

"Hmm..." Marcus grunted. He, a warrior facing his own death? Many times, and he had done so without question. But how many had died because of him? In time, how many more would? Yet in lands so encased in violence meant to stranglehold its people, how could he not have been a warrior? Freedom was all that mattered.

"I am correct, aren't I?" Blaez smiled. "Don't worry, I'll not ask who you are, but if it would be allowed, I'd ask you to teach my boys. They're past the age when they should begin to learn this."

"Budic's denied them any training? They're not slaves."

Blaez nodded.

Marcus took back the second stick and leaned both against the wall. "I would expect as much from him. Nothing is *allowed,* is it? I'm surprised we're even *allowed* to use the bloody latrine pits. Is he about yet this morning?"

"Probably. He's to meet with the leader of the *bacaudae* Gauls, a man they call Judikael, around mid-morning. Ah, that's what I came to tell you. Rumors are circulating—the court may be moving soon, and I think this meeting has to do with it. I thought you'd want to know."

"I've heard. Aye, don't look so surprised. It's my nature to be rather...meddlesome."

Blaez's curiosity showed starkly, and Marcus knew the man craved an explanation. But after nearly two years of exile, Marcus refused to utter a word about his identity or the kind of dealings that would have filled his days had he been on Britain's soil, not even to Blaez, with whom he had become good friends. It was for the same reason he never asked Blaez his true name—safekeeping. The Frank had honored the mutual secrecy.

Marcus grabbed up a tunic and belt from a chair. "I'll see if I can persuade Budic to *allow* your boys a chance to learn. He probably won't listen, but it's worth trying."

"Don't make trouble for yourself by intervening on my behalf."

Marcus dragged the tunic over his head. "It's worth it just to vent a bit of spite on him," he said and tied the belt. He strode for the doorway. "I'll tell you what he says."

As soon as he appeared outside the house, one of his watchers took up after him. Privacy would be such a fine thing to have, he mused and ignored the guard that followed like an aura. They had to be as bored of their duties as he was tired of their ubiquitous presence.

The meeting between the king and the Gallic leader had already begun by the time Marcus arrived at the villa's main house. Bluntly told to come back later, he chose instead to wait and insisted with equal bluntness that he could waste time there just as efficiently as he could in his house. Reluctantly, the guards led him into the private courtyard. Though in two years he had given them no reason to think he would attempt an escape, he had seen to it his stubbornness became a long-standing bramble for them to endure.

He waited two hours. Seated on a marble bench in the shadows of an ancient and morose-looking apple tree, he memorized how many pillars held up the roof that covered the walkway around the courtyard, studied the remains of the flagstone floor and determined how many different kinds of plants drooped in the old and stained marble urns. The place might have bordered on elegance at one time, but the nobleman who resided there took little care of the decaying house and grounds. And Budic had never offered to improve it in return for its use.

Heat from the midday sun warmed the courtyard, so welcome between cold spring rainstorms. Marcus noted how family members of the villa's owner prowled sullenly in spite of the fine weather. Resentment of the long-term intrusion gloomed their faces and posture. Few spoke except to give orders to the house slaves or quietly confer with each other. All ignored him. Most had probably not even noticed his presence. He was certain they would relish the king's departure if it came.

Shortly after the end of the second hour, the house slaves, loaded down with platters of fruit and sweets and many ewers of wine, rushed in a brief flurry across the courtyard. They arranged it all on tall, narrow tables on the far portico. Moments after they disappeared, a door opened and the guards stiffened. Several men emerged into the open corridor.

Marcus turned on the bench, slowly enough that none would notice him. Through the branches of a wild gorse bush growing below the apple tree, he observed not only Budic and a man dressed in traditional Gallic clothes, but five others. Of the five, Marcus recognized one as the king's court interpreter. The others were dressed similarly, their clothing finely made but not in the style he had seen in Breizh.

He peered closer. A distinctive shape and pattern of decorative metalwork on their belts gleamed, square-shaped on one end and typical of Saxon finery. Saxons? Or some other Germanic tribal leaders? What was Budic doing? Testing the waters for an alliance? Or had he already made an alliance meant to disguise some form of treachery?

The men walked along the promenade behind Marcus towards the food. They spoke in low tones, polite but wary. The interpreter shuttled translations among them.

From their dialects, Marcus counted two Saxons, one Frank, and a Frisian. Their speech was similar enough that they could understand each other. In listening, he found his year and a half of learning new languages fully opened the talk to him. It was like light flooding a cave, and he wondered why he had never made the effort before. No time, he answered himself. Never enough time, yet long ago, knowing would have made so much difference. He rested his face in his palms.

Now he had more time than he knew what to do with. He lifted his face and stared at his hands—big, thick-fingered, strong. Hands meant to work but now disused, the hard calluses faded away. Hands that had acted in terrible, bloody violence yet could play a harp with alacrity. Two years had passed since he had even touched a sword—two years since he had touched Claerwen. He gazed at his fingertips and could almost sense them drawing across her skin in the way he loved to stir the warmth within her. With a deep breath, he pretended the apple blossoms on the tree behind him smelled instead like lavender, the herbs she put in her bath water at home. Her hair always smelled so fine. His fingers slowly curled inward, but they only felt air.

Marcus closed his eyes against the glare and laid his face in his hands again. His breath expelled slowly between his fingers. If only he could know she was safe, if only he could touch her. The voices behind him droned on.

Another hour passed before inklings of the meeting's end were spoken. Finally, when the food and drink ran out, the conversation fizzled.

"As discussed," Budic said to one of the Saxons, "we will meet at the doors of stone, on the high mountain. Ten days from now."

The interpreter translated, first in Saxon to the Germanic men, then in the common Latin spoken by Judikael.

Marcus's brows lowered. To the Saxons, the interpreter said *heahburg,* the high city or town. He should have said *heahbeorg,* the high mountain. A mistake, certainly. Accidental? Or planned? The translation to Judikael had been correct.

Marcus twisted around. All had the same expression, wary yet pleased for a step forward in their quest, whatever it might be. None had the look of deception. The interpreter appeared neutral, not a hint that he had made a mistake. The Frank, Saxons and Frisian saluted their host and strode away along the promenade towards the villa's front entrance. The Gaul followed shortly afterward and left on his own. Dismissed, the interpreter disappeared into a corridor that led towards the rear of the house. Budic retreated inside the way he had come out.

On his feet, Marcus started across the courtyard for the front of the house.

"I thought you wanted to talk to the king," a guard said as he marched past.

"Not now."

"But he has time—"

"No." He pushed on through the entryway.

"Then why did you wait so long?"

Marcus ignored the comment. He rounded the outer wall and tramped back through the compound, his watcher trailing after.

Within minutes, he stood before Blaez, the concern on his face enough to rouse the Frank into following him to his house without question. There, he shut the door on their guards and quietly confirmed if his own translation was correct.

"Budic thinks he'll be meeting them all somewhere called the 'high mountain,' but they're going to a 'high town.' Except Judikael. I'd reckon the high town is Plouguer because it once was a capital and it's nearby. What are the 'doors of stone?' Do you know?"

Blaez shrugged. "Could be—and this is only a guess—some part of the Roman buildings in Plouguer. Perhaps the temple, or the forum?"

"That could make sense. What of this 'high mountain'?"

"This is another guess," the Frank said. "Have you seen the hills to the west when you were brought here?"

Marcus nodded.

"Hidden in that thick forest is an old hillfort. The Romans burnt it long ago when they took these lands. It's never been used since. The remains, if you can find them, are surrounded by huge stone boulders. They could be called 'stone doors'."

"How far away?"

"Half-day's march, I'd say."

Marcus thumped a fist in a slow beat against the beam on which he had practiced swordplay, the rhythm meant to bring calm and order to his thoughts. His eyes narrowed. "Who has more control over the *bacaudae* right now? Budic or Childeric?"

"Budic," Blaez answered without hesitation.

Marcus's jaw worked, his teeth clicked together. His eyes shifted to Blaez and pierced into his face. "It's a bloody ambush."

"Are you sure?"

"Absolutely. Budic understands enough of the Gaul's Latin. The Saxons know none of it. It's just too convenient that Budic and Judikael are to go one place, the Saxons another. I think the Gaul plans to trap Budic in those hills. Once the king is eliminated, the Gaul will have more control of his lands, and perhaps even gain new territory."

"Why didn't you just stay there and tell Budic?" Blaez asked. "You had the perfect chance."

Marcus squinted at him to keep his voice low. "He has no reason to trust me. He'll think I'm the one trying to outwit him, not them."

"Then you must give him a reason to trust you," Blaez said.

"Gah! He doesn't even trust Uther, his own cousin. And I don't trust either of them. No, Blaez. Budic has to know of this, but it can't come from me. Not directly. He won't trust you either—he'll know I'm the source."

Blaez folded his arms. "What you will do?"

Marcus shook his head and thumped the beam with his fist again. "I'm so bloody tired of being useless here. If it weren't—" He clamped his mouth shut.

Blaez nodded in understanding. "If it weren't for someone whose life you must save at all costs, even if other lives are lost because you must remain idle?"

"But if my idleness costs lives here, that could *also* doom—" Marcus stopped again.

"I know… I know you can't tell me, though perhaps you might like to," Blaez said quietly. "You cannot tell me who or what you are, anymore than I can ever tell you my true name. But is there anything I can do that will help?"

Marcus shook his head again, adamant. "Don't ask. You don't want to be associated with me right now. For the next few days, watch those boys of yours with great care."

The guards came in the middle of night, three days later.

Marcus woke as if slapped when the door to his house crashed open and torchlight rampaged through the dark. Muddled with sleep and the remnants of too much drink that evening, he felt their cold hands clamp around his wrists and ankles. He wrenched an arm free and landed a fist in a jaw but received a stunning kick in the head in return. They dragged him off the bed, across the floor, pinned him down. Shackles, even colder, replaced the hands.

The guards half-marched, half-carried him to the villa's main house, across the private courtyard and into Budic's chambers. Fiercely shoved, he toppled and skidded over the tile floor. The king, seated in his favorite place behind a long table, ordered the guards outside. When the door closed, he threw a thin piece of bark onto the tiles.

"You wrote that."

Marcus pushed upright onto his knees. Dressed only in breeches, he shoved his hair back from his face. The chains clinked. He already knew two lines of lettering carved on the bark in the Brezhoneg language were a warning to Budic of ambush. It mentioned nothing of the interpreter's role.

Marcus glowered. "What makes you think I wrote that?"

Budic rose and came around the table. "There are only so many here who can write. And those who do can write only in Latin, not a native tongue. That leaves you, spy."

Marcus shrugged. He had known Budic would reckon out the truth. It had been a poor ploy at best.

"You were going to try to escape, weren't you? And this was the distraction." He kicked the bark. It skittered across the floor, hit a chair leg, and cracked apart in the middle.

Marcus nearly laughed. If Budic truly believed that, he would have already sent word to Uther to release Claerwen into Octa's control. The king of Breizh was bluffing, but to simply deny the deceit would be useless.

"How could that be a distraction? If I planned an escape, the ambush would be the distraction." Marcus gave him a sarcastic grimace.

The king's face froze.

Budic couldn't think of a properly resentful reply, Marcus thought. "Have you had your spies out asking questions about this ambush? Enough to know if it's true?"

"How do *you* know of all this?" the king blurted.

Marcus got to his feet. Unembarrassed at being half-naked and chained, Marcus glared into Budic's face. Barely taller than the king, he loomed like a wild, dark cloud.

"You haven't, have you?" he said. "Even though you suspect I'm right? Ask your interpreter."

Budic's round fleshy face flushed all the way into his thin-haired scalp.

The temptation to goad Budic even more stuck in Marcus's

throat. He wanted to say that Uther—though certainly not always a fair man himself—would have at least investigated the incident before shackling the wrong man. Marcus had learned that although Budic had taken in Uther and his brother Ambrosius during their exile, and had even helped them raise an army to take Britain from Vortigern, he now deeply resented having to house his cousin's political prisoner. Why so much resentment, Marcus couldn't guess, but he suspected Budic was jealous for having won little or no reward in helping Britain regain its rightful leadership.

"Guard!" Budic shouted.

The door whipped open. The four men filed in, hands on their sword hilts.

"Bring Tanet here. Now," he ordered, then cocked a thumb at Marcus. "And take him back to his house. See that he stays there. The chains stay on for now."

After sunrise, the guards returned to the house. This time they knocked. They quietly removed the shackles and allowed Marcus to dress before they led him back to the king's chambers.

Alone in his rooms, Budic was again seated behind the table, studying a map. As soon as the guards left, Marcus chose a Roman-style chair next to a brazier and slid into the seat. Minutes passed and Budic didn't look up. Might as well be comfortable, Marcus thought. He slouched with one leg draped over the chair's arm and spotted a jug of mead within reach. He lifted it. Full. Good. He poured himself a large cup, settled back, and generously swigged it down.

"Feeling quite at home?" Budic's voice finally cut the quiet.

"Absolutely."

The king looked up from the map. "You're an arrogant one, aren't you?"

Marcus saluted with his cup. "No more than you."

Budic grunted in disgust and leaned back. "The interpreter was offered land in return for the 'mistake' he made. To him, it was a way out of servitude."

Marcus swallowed another mouthful. He gazed up at the ceiling and yawned loudly. "Of course, he never would have received anything but a knife in his back some cold night."

"Aye. He'd been in the court three years and served well. So I thought."

That was as close to an admission of error, an apology, or thanks as Budic would ever get, Marcus knew. He was surprised the king had even bothered to tell him personally. A message from the guards when the shackles had been removed would have sufficed.

"And the alliance?" Marcus asked.

"False."

"Ah... Nice of you to notice."

"Do you know what that means?"

"You don't?" Marcus drank again.

"Always sarcasm with you, isn't it?"

"You're such an inspiration." Marcus scrunched up his brows in the middle as if he smelled something foul.

"I'll tell you what it means. The *bacaudae* were going to use the Saxons as mercenaries, similar to what happened in Britain. If I had been killed, and they had taken control of Breizh, they would have then turned around and fought Childeric with those mercenaries."

Marcus laughed. "I thought as much."

"What do you mean, you thought as much?"

"The *bacaudae* don't want mercenaries. And besides, the Saxons are smarter than that by now. They want land, not employment. If the *bacaudae* had killed you, the Saxons would have come in behind them and cleaned out every last one of them, then taken Briezh, then turned around and fought Childeric."

"And how do you know this?"

Marcus grinned. "I've been at this game a bloody long time. So have you, but you've apparently learned nothing. Hmm, keep the Saxons busy here...perhaps that's one way to keep them out of Britain..."

Budic leaned forward. His eyes, an indescribable combination of grey, gold and deep blue, squinted at Marcus. "*You* will be my new interpreter."

Marcus lifted the cup halfway to his mouth, stopped, then proceeded up. He drained it and banged it down on the chair's arm.

"No."

"You have no choice."

Marcus pushed himself up straight, his eyes calm, steady. "I refuse."

Budic stood, his fists pressed onto the table. "You will not refuse."

"And why is that?" Marcus rose and crossed the room. He knew Budic wanted to exploit his talents as a spy more than a new interpreter. That was merely an excuse. "Are you going to offer me lands? Or my freedom?"

The same sly self-satisfaction crossed Budic's face as when he had told Marcus he was a political prisoner. "You will act as my interpreter. If you don't, I will trigger the report to my cousin that you have escaped and we cannot find you." He let the words sink in a moment. "And if you should deliberately make a 'mistake,' such as the one you discovered, the result will be the same as refusal. Do you understand?"

"You must realize my open presence in your court is more dangerous than that Gaul's duplicity." Marcus poked a thumb over his shoulder. "Too many high-ranking noblemen know me and what I am."

"And you've made enemies of most of them. Oh, I know this. You won't be needed for them—"

"I'm talking about danger to you. If anyone should, even by accident, let slip that I'm here, Octa's assassins would come like midges in summer." Not to mention, Marcus kept to himself, they could start rumors in Britain that Claerwen might hear, and with her stubborn penchant for following him…

"Haven't you seen how very few visitors come to court? It's because of you and the terms of your exile that Uther laid out. You read them. It's why I chose this obscure place instead of Plouguer or any of the other capitals. It's not just to keep you in, but to keep your enemies out. You *will* do this, man—"

Marcus pounded a fist on the table. "I will not be your begging dog—"

"You will be my interpreter, or your wife will be fed to Octa the Saxon. Which will it be?"

Marcus glared. Now was the time to be a soldier, not the warrior Blaez had described. May the gods suck Budic's soul out through his arse, he cursed in silence. And Uther's as well.

"So be it," he hissed at last. With his mouth clamped in a flat line, he spun around and strode out. He made sure the door slammed hard enough to startle the house guards, the slaves, the nobleman's family, his watchers, and perhaps even the emperor of Rome as well.

CHAPTER 19

Breizh
Late Autumn, AD 475

MORE than four years. How had it become so long? More than four years and no sign, not a hint that Uther had made any headway against Octa. Years of moving with Budic's court from one side of Breizh to the other, from flatlands to ocean, scrappy gorse-filled fields to cold, damp promontory strongholds. How much longer? The unanswerable questions mounted.

Damp, salty wind struck Marcus in the face and drove his hair back over his shoulders. He ignored the discomfort. His thoughts were too locked in both the past and the uncertain course of the future. He drank deeply of the strong dark ale in his cup, his third since turning his gaze to the blackness of night and the sea within it.

Having been extorted into acting as Budic's interpreter had been mixed with both blessings and curses. Because Breizh was tied to Britain through its people and leadership, Marcus was able to again view his homeland's political and military maneuverings, though like peering through a keyhole, it came only through Budic's narrow standpoint. It was better than no view at all, but he had been able to learn little of true significance. Among the worst news, Saxon pirating had escalated on both coasts of the Narrow Sea. They grew ever bolder, a fearsome sign that Uther's campaigns were not going well.

In addition, tension was rising among the *bacaudae*, the Franks, and the growing population of Breizh. In response, the court had moved every few months since the thwarted ambush. Tired of this,

Budic finally made the decision to gather much of his family and occupy one of the promontory fortresses on the western coast, a stronghold not unlike Tintagel but disused since the Romans had conquered Gaul hundreds of years before.

Marcus rubbed his tired eyes and listened to the sea's furious spite. Did anyone else in the world despise it as much as he did? The wind and crashing of waves on the rocks below had increased all day. Another late autumn gale, another winter approached.

Wind blasted through the window. This time rain showered him. He closed the battered, deteriorating wooden shutters and drew a leather drape across them to keep out the draughts. He drained the cup, refilled it. He wished the drink could take away the hollowness that had carved itself into his being throughout the years, but the ale only made him tired now, he could not even get drunk anymore.

He returned to the table he used for writing and glared dispassionately at the parchment lying on it—a long letter he had translated into proper Latin and was due to be sent to Rome. The hour candle had shown it was nearly midnight when he had finished and after breathing in the smells of ink, goatskin parchment and lamp oil, he had been glad to be done. Even the scratch of the quill's tip had begun to annoy him. Another hour had passed since.

A degree of quiet settled in the room with the shutters closed. Voices murmured nearby. He glanced up. The leather curtain that served as a door was pushed slightly aside. One of his watchers was seated just outside. Alone, the man yawned broadly.

Marcus picked up the quill he had used and twirled it between his fingers. How could his gift for languages be at once so useful yet so wasted? He placed the quill in its holder then tested if the ink had dried enough for the parchment to be rolled together. It wasn't. The damp air, worse with the rain, made the ink slow to dry.

His mouth twisted into a sardonic smile. In the letter Budic suggested that certain sectors of the Roman army be repositioned, mostly in the disputed area between Breizh and the Franks, to keep the Franks at bay. But with one emperor falling to the next like rocks crushing each other in a landslide, Marcus wondered why Budic hoped to receive any kind of cooperation. No use to worry—no courier would be going out in one of those horrendous gales. No message could be so urgent, especially to Rome where it would be ignored.

The voices murmured again. Two men, Marcus noted. The talk was quiet and spoke of travel eastward. Then he frowned. Northern British accents? One voice seemed familiar, but he could think of no one in the court who sounded like that. The guard yawned again.

If it was true that Budic only allowed high-ranking noblemen in the court and only for highly important reasons, Marcus wondered who these men were. He edged closer to the entrance, careful to keep the lamplight behind him and his shadow from falling beyond the curtain. The small room, also connected to Budic's chambers by a short corridor, opened onto a large, rectangular great hall that was used as a meeting room, living quarters for court attendants, and a place to take meals. Centered on a large hearth, it was the only well-heated space within the stronghold.

He peered through the narrow slit. The men stood near the hearth, but one of the hall's massive support timbers blocked Marcus's view. He angled closer, and in the same instant the man with the familiar voice moved.

Surprise rippled through Marcus and he stifled a curse. Thin to the point of emaciation, Meirchion of Rheged stood next to the fire pit looking as if he had just arrived, his clothes wet and mud-stained. What in the gods' names was he doing in Breizh? He and the other man must have just come from Budic's chambers and had stopped to warm themselves before going on to the guesthouse, a separate dwelling for high-ranking visitors. And who was the other man?

A private joke passed between the men, their soft laughter faintly reverberated in the hall. Moments later, Budic's seneschal, apparently roused from sleep, joined them, spoke a few words then led them towards the front doors. Marcus caught a glimpse of the second man before they left. From the profile and build, he thought he recognized Masguid.

Nearly ten years had passed since the only time he had seen Meirchion's younger brother, and that had been from a distance, but there was a good resemblance. This man limped heavily, and Masguid had not at that time. Could be he'd been injured recently,

Marcus speculated, perhaps even at Caer Luguvalos, and he wondered if their feud had truly ended. The congeniality appeared genuine, but that could simply be a mask.

With his face blank as if he had seen nothing, Marcus stepped into his doorway, his hand lifted to signal his yawning, stretching watcher that he was done for the day and going to bed.

"Stop," an order came from behind.

Budic's voice. Marcus halted, grimaced and turned. Budic stood in the entrance of the corridor that led from his chambers. A soldier waited behind him.

"Come away from there," Budic ordered. He entered, his eyes on the drying letter. "This is done?"

Marcus pulled the other curtain and crossed to the table. "It's done." He picked up the full cup of ale. "But it needs more time to dry."

Budic cocked his head towards the hall. "You saw them?"

Marcus nodded.

"You'll be staying here tonight, perhaps for several nights, until they leave."

"So be it." Marcus was too tired to care. If he slept there or in the meager stone hut he had been given as another temporary home made little difference. He drank down half the cup in one gulp.

Budic's eyes narrowed and his gaze swept from the parchment to the large pitcher of ale, well on its way to being empty. "I hope that letter is accurate."

"It's correct. It's also useless."

"Your duty is to translate, not judge."

Marcus emptied the cup and filled it again. "What do they want here?"

"I could ask you that. Surely you know them."

As if Budic did not? Marcus smirked and sat again at the table. "Merely good will, I'm sure. Do they speak of their father?"

"They say old Gwrast the Ragged is dead. How much of this have you drunk?"

"Does it matter?" Marcus set to ignoring Budic. He drank again, but behind his unfocused eyes, he fought the fatigue. Gwrast was dead. It had been bound to happen for such a long time, but, damn, a shame to lose a good man. That both brothers had traveled so far was certainly not for good will. Meirchion especially had never done anything for that. What were they up to? Or had they come at Budic's request? He regarded the king's round face. No bargain was ever struck without gain on both sides.

"Sleep it off," Budic grumbled. He ordered the soldier to guard his ward well and retreated to his quarters.

Eyes shut, head leaned back, Marcus heard the corridor's drape swish across and the man shuffle into place on its other side. In the hall, he heard a fresh watcher replace the yawning guard.

He should have kept Budic talking, Marcus knew, but he was relieved to be alone and free to think for himself. Cup in hand, he eased off the chair and dropped a pallet down that had been leaning against the wall. The ale had finally begun to buzz in his head. He lay down, wanting to sleep in peace, yet he knew the nightmares would come again. They did nearly every night now. If only the ale could take away the awful images, the smell, the swell of sickness in his gut. If only it could rectify the years of waiting. By the gods, he missed how Claerwen could evoke peace in him.

And now Gwrast was dead at long last, his sons unleashed to spill the cauldron of trouble, a cauldron in which he was certain he would soon find himself swirling. If only he could open a truer, clearer, broader window on Britain's crazed world. The two sons of the north allied with Budic of Breizh? His black eyes brooded at the entrance to the king's chambers.

"What part do *you* have in this?" he asked softly. "Are you *with* your cousin, or against him?"

Relentless rain-filled wind wracked the old building of stone. It lifted loose tiles on the roof and dropped them again with a continuous clacking. The sea's endless crash and swell hissed through the crevices and stirred the darkness, the tortured staring-eyed faces, the stench of loosened bowels and rot, the dozens of bat-like shadows, the rippling of pooled blood on the floor.

Marcus writhed on the pallet. Why could he never outrun them? Would they never leave him be? His stomach threatened to heave up through his suffocating chest.

Control. Think of Claerwen. Think of her walking out of the mist into sunlight in the high meadow above Dinas Beris. Think of her smile. Concentrate—her face, her sparkling, beautiful aquamarine eyes, like the sea on a calm day.

Damn. How could he compare her eyes to the sea? The *sea*? How could he be so cruel to her? He recoiled and slung himself back into the night, hurled into the cold smell of death, but he dragged her image with him. She became like the rest, a bloodless phantom, no more than a strung up, gutted hunting kill.

Marcus moaned. Cold sweat dripped down his face. His throat closed, his breath stuck in it like a wineskin's wooden stopper. He ached for the images to subside but they clung to his mind, icons to be worshipped in a temple of evil.

Slowly, he opened his eyes. There was the room, the shuttered window, the half-full cup of ale on the floor next to him, the lamps that still burned but were running low on oil and sputtering. Lost in the drink's influence the night before, he vaguely remembered the gale striking onshore, the rain furious on the shutters like thousands of fists pounding, but he had quickly fallen asleep.

Marcus mouthed Claerwen's name; if only he could say it aloud. Gods of the earth, more than four years, and he had not dared to say even her name. His chest began to ease and he sat up, looked inside the cup out of habit and the need to fulfill his craving for the alcohol. Sick of the taste, he knew he drank too much, but with every nightmare, every day of idleness, every minute separated from Claerwen, he could not help himself. He glared at the liquid swirling in the cup and contemplated the desire to smash it against the wall out of spite. With a grimace at his folly, he shook his head—drawing attention would negate the satisfaction of vented anger. He returned it to the floor and lay down again.

The effigy. After the arrival of the two sons of the north the night before, the warning played in his mind as clearly as the first time he had translated the words from Latin. *Death to you. Two sons of the north or two of the White Dragon. Your choice. Beware…Excalibur.*

Excalibur. He had still discovered no clue of what it meant. To what language did that strange word belong? It almost sounded

Latin, yet not at all. The prefix, "ex," if it was Latin, meant "from." But the word ended in "ur," the same as many words and names in his native tongue. Calibur… "Calib" sounded vaguely like someone slurring "calad," the word for "hard." From hard? Hard what? So many languages he had learned, but here was a word only Octa seemed to know. He wondered if Claerwen still had the effigy with her.

Pale light seeped through the crack between the shutters. The storm was already dissipating. Marcus realized the great hall's occupants were awake and beginning their duties. Daybreak had passed along with his thoughts and wishings. How long ago, he could not guess. Perhaps he had even fallen asleep again.

Sluggish, he rubbed his face with his palms. His eyes itched more than when he had finished the translation. He picked up the cup, rose, and set it on the table next to the letter. The ink had dried. He was rolling the parchment together when the leather curtain swished aside and his watcher let Budic's seneschal into the room. A small, dark-haired man, he exuded efficiency and a controlled disdain for those of less ambition.

"You must be looking for this." Marcus held out the letter.

The seneschal took the parchment.

"Courier leaving with it today?" Marcus glanced past him into the great hall. Blaez, taller than most of the court's attendants, was wrapped in a long cloak, hood up. His grey eyes pierced steadily towards the far end of the hall.

"On the morrow," the seneschal said.

Marcus moved his gaze back to him. "The roads will be barely passable, even by then, don't you think?"

The seneschal shrugged. "'Tis my understanding one of the lords from Britain has urgent business near the letter's destination. The courier will accompany him." The man walked away with economic strides. He left the leather curtain pushed fully aside in the entrance.

"Ah…" One side of Marcus's mouth curved up. A lord from Britain going to Rome? Whatever for? And only one of them? What nonsense had they fed Budic?

He scanned in search of Blaez. The Frank had advanced towards the front of the hall. Marcus lifted a hand to catch his attention. For an instant, their eyes met, but Blaez's quickly shifted away, and he retreated through the front doors. His watcher followed.

Marcus's brows lowered—strange reaction from the normally unflappable Frank. And he sensed fear. In the entrance of his room, he leaned out enough to see where Blaez had stared. In one of the alcoves at the less-congested far end, Meirchion and Masguid spoke with Budic. The king's seneschal waited a short distance away, letter in hand.

The watcher tapped the butt end of his spear on the floor in warning. Though done lightly, the sound reverberated in the high-roofed hall, enough that several heads turned. Marcus withdrew.

Exasperated, he leaned against the wall. Could Blaez know the sons of Rheged? Of course it was possible, he answered himself—he knew nothing of the Frank's life beyond exile, not even his true name. But if the mere presence of Meirchion and Masguid caused such discomfort, perhaps to learn Blaez's identity was becoming needed.

Marcus crossed to the window and pulled open the shutters. Wind rushed in. It raked back his hair and filled the stale room with fresh air. The clouds were beginning to break and sunrays appeared one by one over the grey sea. On the hunt for tiny crabs and sea snails, brilliant white gulls glided in the dull sky.

"If I could just..." He left the wish unfinished, his envy of the birds' freedom too much to bear.

"I understand you speak several languages and can translate well." The words shot through the entrance of the tiny stone hut with quiet intensity. No preamble, no warning accompanied them.

Seated cross-legged on the packed-dirt floor in front of the makeshift fire pit he had built, Marcus rested his elbows on his knees. A large wineskin of mead leaned against his leg. His eyes lifted to the entrance.

Masguid's face glowed faintly there, illuminated by the firelight. He entered the hut. The leather curtain fell to behind him.

"It is so," Marcus said. Tempted to blurt the question of why the visit, he kept his bluntness to himself and instead studied the prince for the first time at close quarters. Or, should he presume, this was now the king of Elmet? Like his brother Meirchion, Masguid had plain, dark brown coloring, but he was a bit taller and of normal weight. His features were plain as well—his shapeless, clean-shaven face resembled that of many other men. He leaned in favor of one leg. The best difference between the brothers though, Marcus thought, was in Masguid's calculated and direct expression, a sharp contrast to Meirchion's snobbery.

Masguid's gaze ran from the hut's ceiling to the dirt floor, then on to the shabby pallet, dented chamber pot, and complete lack of other furnishings. Marcus watched the man's eyes take it in, and he caught himself smiling. Must be surprised that a king's interpreter should live in such squalid conditions.

Of more concern, why had Masguid not accompanied his brother? Marcus had wondered this since Meirchion had departed a fortnight earlier after only two nights at the promontory fortress. The courier had accompanied him along with two assigned escorts and no one else. Shortly after, Budic's seneschal had told Marcus he could return to his hut. Why, when Masguid was still there, he had questioned ever since.

The tiny structure, made of stone to withstand the unyielding coastal gales, was built into an obscure curve of the stronghold's granite rock wall and was barely noticeable to a stranger's eye. Yet Masguid had found it in the depth of night and had somehow evaded the watchers.

"Is it true you can speak the native Latin of the Gauls?" Masguid asked. He seated himself on the floor in the same cross-legged fashion.

Marcus raked back his hair and regarded him with caution. Masguid, who spoke tolerable Brezhoneg, had to have been educated in Latin, though in the highborn style spoken by royalty, not the common Latin. "Aye, 'tis true."

Masguid eyed the wineskin. "I need your assistance, if you are…capable."

"I'm sober enough," Marcus shot back and wondered—did Masguid expect to be recognized as a prince or king? From the imperious attitude, probably as a king. Suspicion prickled. "Budic knows nothing of this…visit. Does he?"

Masguid's brows pinched together. "No."

"Then I cannot help you." Marcus rose from the floor and moved into the entrance. He saw no sign of his watchers and turned his glare on Masguid.

"They won't remember anything." He stood and displayed a small ceramic vial in his palm. "I don't want Budic to know of this…visit."

"What do you want from me?"

"Simply, some assistance. Nothing more."

"I cannot leave this place—"

"There will be no need. As long as you reveal nothing of what is exchanged, as long as you speak nothing of this meeting—not to anyone—you will be safe. Do you understand?"

Marcus licked his dry lips. How could he pass this by? But he could jeopardize both his life and Claerwen's if he consented and Budic later discovered the meeting. He could also unwittingly upset a delicate balance in the politics between Britain and Breizh. Worse, if Masguid knew his identity, either refusal or acceptance could be a trap. That notion chilled Marcus. To exploit opportunity was often a dangerous option. Sometimes it was no option at all. Tanet, the previous interpreter, had been executed for his duplicity.

"Are you willing, man?" Masguid prompted, a hint of impatience in his voice.

"Why trust me?" Marcus tested. "You don't know me. How do you know I won't—"

"Tell Budic?" Masguid cut him off. "Because he trusts you."

Hardly, Marcus thought, but he let surprise cross his face. "He said so?"

Masguid shook his head. "No king keeps a man he distrusts in his court for long. Or if he does keep him for the purpose of watching him, he will not assign duties that require trust. Such as those of an interpreter."

Marcus grunted and moved back to the fire pit. If Masguid knew he was recruiting a spy instead of a simple translator, his answer implied otherwise. And if he did know, could he be so naïve as to not recognize extortion was behind the interpreter position? Unless he was excellent at bluffing…

"So be it," Marcus said. "When?"

"Now."

That was a signal. Moments later, a man slipped into the hut so swiftly and quietly the curtain barely moved. His face was as rough-seamed as a granite escarpment long tortured by lightning. Marcus recognized him from his grizzled iron-grey hair and beard and the many weapons he carried. Blaez had identified him as a warlord of the *bacaudae*, a military counterpart to the Gallic leader, Judikael.

The man nodded at Marcus, his dark eyes nearly invisible between the squinted, angular folds of his eyelids. Marcus swept a hand towards the fire pit, an offer of a seat near the warmth. He held out the wineskin to the Gaul first, then Masguid, an expected hospitality regardless of how makeshift the household. Both men held up a hand to decline.

"We have little time," Masguid said. "Tell him I have information he needs to know. Tell him the leader of his people, Judikael, has pledged an alliance with the Franks."

Seated opposite them, Marcus unobtrusively moved his gaze from one man to the other. He translated.

The Gaul's eyes drilled into Masguid's face on hearing the news. They shifted to Marcus, found no reaction, then returned. "For what purpose?" he asked.

Masguid kept his tone low, even, to evoke confidence. "Your people have long sought to throw aside Roman rule," he said. "The Franks now want this as well. Judikael and Childeric have pledged to stand together to fight them." He waited for Marcus to complete the words in Latin.

The Gaul's already hard eyes grew as cold as the granite stones of the hut. Masguid drew breath to continue.

"Stop." The warlord held up a hand for emphasis. "How do you know this?"

How indeed? Marcus wondered if Meirchion had already returned and had something to do with this alliance. If so, what would be the excuse for not reaching Rome? He repeated the words in Brezhoneg.

A faint smile touched Masguid's eyes. "Judikael intercepted a letter written by the king of Breizh, addressed to Rome. In it, Budic asks for Roman military help to defend his lands against *bacaudae* rebels. When he understood its message, Judikael took insult with Budic, then went to Childeric seeking an alliance. Childeric agreed."

A long pause. "You've seen this letter?"

"Aye. And this man," Masguid tilted his head towards Marcus, "has seen it as well."

The Gaul turned cold eyes on Marcus. "Not only seen it, you transcribed it, no?"

With his face blank under the warlord's scrutiny, Marcus added up how many lies Masguid had already told in the course of a few minutes' talk. No such alliance could have been made on the basis of that letter. While the expulsion of Roman control could be a plausible and common desire, a request for Roman help was laughable as a threat. If an alliance did exist, in all likelihood Childeric and Judikael had already formed it, perhaps as long ago as the failed ambush on Budic. It stung Marcus to be an unwilling witness, but he held his tongue, not only to keep from giving himself away but to allow the talk to run its full course as well. Then he could decide the best way to react, if he could react at all without endangering himself. Or Claerwen. He nodded to the warlord.

The Gaul's frazzled brows cocked downward, an evaluating glint in his eyes. His head swiveled back to Masguid.

"Budic is a fool," Masguid said. "What he has done is create his own doom and yours. The Franks do have the strength and power to remove Roman control. But once accomplished, they will turn back to fight Budic. And I've heard talk…Childeric intends to take not only your lands, but to take southern Breizh, Morbihan, as well, because of its sea power. They plan to weaken the strongest part of Breizh first."

The Gaul's head lifted sharply. "Morbihan. My wife's people…"

"You must break this alliance," Masguid continued. "And you must break it now. They will attack early in the spring. If you break it now, Childeric will have winter to cool his temper. He will go back to fighting Saxons on his eastern border."

One brow lifted, barely visible against the Gaul's seamed face. "Why do you tell me this? What is your gain?"

"If Breizh is lost, it will deeply affect Britain. We have enough problems with Saxons without having to face the Franks as well."

All very high-minded, Marcus thought. The warlord would not believe that either. There was something much more valuable, more personal for Masguid and his brother to gain from this. But what?

The Gaul sighed heavily; his piercing gaze showed disgust. "We have fought, generation after generation, to be free of Rome. Even with all their failings, they still hold, we still fight. Now this fool gives away the last of our strength to the Franks?"

Masguid leaned forward, his face intense. "Before spring," he reiterated. "Before their plans are placed into action, you need to break Judikael. You need to drive him out and those who follow him—"

"Drive him out? To where? With this alliance the Franks already swallow him in the course of their laughter. And they will swallow the rest of us after that."

"No. Drive him north, across the Narrow Sea. To Britain."

Marcus's gaze snapped up. Was the man mad? He forced himself to say the words in Latin.

"To Britain?" The Gaul stared at Masguid, his craggy brows knotted.

Urgent, Masguid spoke directly to the warlord in halting Roman Latin laced with phrases of the common language. "If you remove the man you have called leader for so long, you will have the chance to hold onto your lands. Drive him out now, force him to take the war bands and weapons he promised to the Franks to Britain's high king instead. Uther needs warriors against the Saxons. He will reward them with a new homeland once the Saxons are ousted. But you must do this now."

The hair on Marcus's scalp rose as he realized Masguid's intentions. He and Meirchion were driving a wedge into an existing rift between the two Gallic leaders in the hope that one would be sprung out of Breizh. With perseverance, it could even work and could be the answer Uther needed, but inwardly, Marcus cringed. They were offering land to the rival of this man in return for soldiering—a bargain Vortigern had struck years before when he brought Saxon mercenaries into Britain to fight Picts and Irish, a bargain that had proven to be a horrible mistake.

The Gaul cocked his head slightly, not sure he had understood Masguid's plea. Masguid could not even speak the Latin of the Romans well. Marcus interpreted the words properly.

He wondered how Masguid had come to know the warlord and how many times the Briton had woven his lies to the man. He had no power to offer land in Uther's name. But Marcus also suspected Budic was the keystone in this conspiracy and was using Masguid's mysterious influence with the warlord. What better way to weaken the *bacaudae* than to drive out a good portion of it?

Lips pressed in a flat line, Marcus studied the Gaul's face. He speculated the brothers were gambling that the warlord was the easier man to manipulate after the depletion of the *bacaudae*. But Judikael had been to the court several times, and Marcus found him arrogant and given to mistakes. The man seated across the fire pit was tired, disappointed and had been frustrated many times. But he was not weak-willed.

Masguid and the Gaul both rose, their exchange at an end. "Think on this," Masguid said. "If Judikael flees, you will at last be able to take full control of your own lands."

Another lie. Marcus translated and rose with them.

"If Uther gets the men he needs," Masguid continued, "Britain will stabilize, trade will improve, all will prosper."

"I must go," the Gaul said. "I will consult with my council and return."

"When?"

"You will know." He moved into the hut's entrance. He turned slightly, and between his squinted lids a sparkle of firelight caught his dark eyes. They bored into Marcus's face. Then he slipped between the leather and the doorframe, his presence no more than a whisper.

Masguid nodded at Marcus, his smiling eyes full of warning. He left the hut.

Beneath the smile, Marcus had caught a glimpse of calculation. A resemblance to Meirchion struck him then, and the pit of his stomach cramped. The sons of Rheged were raising an army. Fine enough, not unusual, but the thought lodged instinctively in his mind that the war band was meant for their own purpose.

He pushed aside the leather drape and stared across the compound. What if they were going to fight *against* Uther in the hope of gaining the high kingship? Rheged was strong, with more wealth than most of Britain's small kingdoms. With help from warriors given to rebellion they might even succeed, but to take down Uther would not earn them any loyalty from the island's other kings. It would only serve to empower the Saxons.

Two sons of the north. Why had Octa—of all the people in the world—cautioned him against the sons of Rheged? Inadvertently or with deliberate purpose, Marcus could not fathom, but it was incredibly apt. "Two sons of the north," he muttered. "By the gods, how can you be such fools?"

CHAPTER 20

Breizh
Late Autumn, AD 475

"YOU don't belong here."

No, I don't, Marcus agreed.

Had he spoken aloud? His eyes opened. The dark-enshrouded stone roof of the hut loomed above, silent, empty, the glow from the banked fire pit too dim to reach that high. The voice had seemed directly present, and his response too easy in coming. Had he dreamed? Had he even been asleep? Or had the mead thickened his mind…?

A figure moved, black against the charcoal shadows. "You don't belong here," the voice repeated.

Marcus sat up on the pallet. The Gallic warlord squatted two paces away. His muffled, gruff voice identified him more than his features, indistinguishable in the dark. He had spoken in the language of Breizh, not the common Latin. Patient, curious, Marcus waited for him to continue.

He did. He crept closer, his voice barely a whisper. "The way you speak…no, not the languages…you are something else than an interpreter. Someone with more than the education of tutors. Perhaps you are even of high rank. And you have guards who watch you all the time. I say…you are in truth a prisoner, like the Frank who is called Blaez. Perhaps you were sent here for a similar reason?"

"Perhaps," Marcus hedged. "He and I have respected each other's secrets."

"That is good. For now."

What did that mean? Marcus reached for his wineskin and offered it to the Gaul. "You speak Brezhoneg. And very well it seems. That means you held your tongue last night to wait for the truth. And you understood every word said without my help. Are you to meet again with…?"

The Gaul accepted the wineskin and relieved his thirst. "No," he said and licked his lips. "No more meetings with the one who limps. Last night, you played the unwitting fool as well, to learn the truth, and I read in your face what I already suspected—he lies."

A grin crawled across Marcus's face. He recognized intelligence, astuteness, and a bit of the sly, so rare a combination in most of those he had met in the tedious years of exile. "And now you want to know if I have the truth of how that letter got to Judikael."

The warlord grunted softly and handed back the skin. "No need. The chieftain of the *bacaudae* does not read. He will only hear the words of the one who is too thin, who takes the letter to show, but not tell what is in it. You should know as well—Judikael is chieftain in name alone. He has no authority to offer men and weapons to any creature, especially not the Franks. *I* control the war bands. He controls only words, and they have had little truth in them for many years."

Marcus heard a knowing, wry smile in the Gaul's voice. "You know who the two men from Britain are, don't you? You've known them a long time."

A low rumble came from the warlord's throat that vaguely resembled a chuckle. "They are the piss of pigs," he said and adjusted his crouched stance more comfortably. "You are from Britain as well, though from a different place. You hide your accent well, but it betrays you."

Still wary, Marcus confirmed it.

"The Frank you know as Blaez fears them," the Gaul went on. "You have seen this."

Marcus murmured an agreement and swallowed a mouthful of mead.

"I believe it is personal," the warlord said, "and connected to the reason for his exile."

Marcus leaned to stoke the peat bricks in his fire pit. With the mild increase of light, he took in the Gaul's deeply seamed face. Instead of the tired, disappointed man he had seen the night before, this night he saw an old warrior with the wisdom of life in his eyes. "And you want to know if I know anything, and if I do, would I tell you."

"Not necessarily. You have an interest in them as well. But unlike the Frank, you have no fear. Why is this?"

"Perhaps…I understand them. Doesn't mean I always know what they will do, but they are rather predictable."

The warlord grinned this time. "Your eyes said otherwise when you realized they attempt to raise a war band. I believe Blaez understands them as well, perhaps differently. Aye, you belong to another world, a world connected to something more than personal intrigue." He rose and stepped to the hut's entrance, glanced beyond the leather curtain. "Your guard will be waking soon. We will talk again."

On his feet, Marcus crossed the floor. "You have spies in the court, don't you?"

At the question, the Gaul produced a ceramic vial identical to the one Masguid had shown the night before. "For good reason," he said. "The blond kitchen slave is my nephew. He is very good at potions. If you have need to send a message to me, tell him."

Marcus lifted an eyebrow at the vial before it disappeared inside the warlord's belt pouch. Several suggestions lay in the presentation. "Did you get what you came for?"

The older man nodded. "I merely wanted to know what kind of man you are. It is as I suspected."

"And…? What else?"

Again the rumbling chuckle. "Very good. Think on what I have said about connections." He put his hand on the leather drape, and his eyes again drilled into Marcus's face. "Beware that secrets sometimes need to be broken. Ask the Frank about a woman called Tangwen."

The warlord disappeared from the hut.

Another day passed. A spate of cold rain started, and shortly after sunset Marcus walked into the great hall. He loosened his wet cloak but left the hood up and moved along the rear wall on long, slow strides. A watcher tailed him.

Years of discipline had taught Marcus to show no evidence, neither in his face nor in his bearing, that his mind worked in the opposite manner of his calm demeanor. Clamped around the warlord's talk, his thoughts churned—question after question followed by a broad number of speculations in answer of each. Only Blaez could provide some of them.

He wove his way among those who had gathered for the evening meal and assessed who was present and who was not. By the time he approached the row of tables spread with food and drink, he had confirmed neither Budic nor Masguid were in attendance. He still could not determine whether Meirchion had returned.

Blaez stood at the end of the row of tables, his back turned, his hood pulled far over his head to hide his face. He was packing a bread trencher with stewed meat and vegetables as full as possible and trying not to tear the crust.

Marcus watched from the opposite end of the display. The night before, after the warlord's departure, he had turned back into his hut with disbelief firing all through him. The name had struck like a well-aimed rock and he asked himself again and again if the man had truly said the name "Tangwen." Was this the same woman whose release Handor had demanded and who was sought by both Meirchion and a scruffy trio of Saxons? Added to Blaez's reaction to the brothers' presence, a connection very likely existed. But why in the gods' names would an exiled Frank and a hardened Gallic *bacaudae* warlord have anything to do with either the woman or the sons of Rheged?

Advancing along the tables, Marcus collected his meal. He stopped beside Blaez. The Frank glanced up then averted his grey eyes.

"I cannot talk to you," he whispered.

"You must."

Blaez turned away, took a step.

Marcus blocked his path.

"No," Blaez protested.

"People here are accustomed to us talking," Marcus said, his voice low and arresting. "In avoiding me you will draw attention. We will be watched even more closely."

"You cannot allow yourself to be seen with me. It's dangerous."

"I'm already in danger." Marcus gave a mock wince. "Aye, from the same two you've been careful to avoid." He watched the anguish he had seen days earlier reclaim Blaez's face. Softening, he tipped his head towards the hall's doors. "Come. We'll find a place to eat outside."

Blaez drew breath then exhaled, short and strained, as if his chest were knotted inside. Then he gave in and followed Marcus through the doors.

The rain had subsided into a light drizzle. Marcus tramped through the courtyard's mud and located a niche in the fortress's wall that had once framed a small gate. Stones now filled the opening, and a wide indentation was left above a few steps. Far from torchlight, the niche provided privacy yet was open enough that no one could approach without being seen.

Seated on the damp stone, Marcus observed the watchers take up their usual positions, ten Roman paces away.

"They will hear us," Blaez said. "We cannot risk talking."

"This hole is not deep enough for sound to carry well." Marcus licked his fingers, sticky with juice that leaked through his trencher's hard crust. "Keep your voice low. Act as if nothing unusual is happening."

Blaez concentrated on picking out chunks of meat from his trencher. He calmed; his movements slowed with each bite. "Why are they here?" he finally asked.

"To raise an army." Marcus bit off a piece of the bread along with the meat and chewed slowly. He wanted to allow time for Blaez to think.

"For themselves?" the response came.

"Very likely."

Minutes passed in silence while they continued to eat. Marcus studied the compound. Few people were out in the evening's dismal weather. The watchers—sullen—paid minimal heed. Over the years, their attentiveness had diminished though they continued their duties faithfully. "I want to know why you hide from the brothers," he said.

Blaez shook his head, a refusal to answer.

Marcus had not expected Blaez to talk readily, and in truth he disliked having to pry into what appeared to be the private anguish of someone he respected. But if the Frank held a secret that provided a firm connection between the sons of Rheged and the mysterious Tangwen, perhaps even a clue leading to Handor and the location of Macsen's sword would surface with it. For this, he was willing to risk a degree of offending his friend.

Marcus swallowed the last bite of his supper. He held out his fingers and let the light rain wash them, then he licked them dry. "Have you seen the *bacaudae* warlord has been here as well?" he asked.

The Frank stared at a small piece of his bread's crust still cupped in his hands. His eyes widened. He shook his head.

"I have spoken with him," Marcus said. He felt the tension thicken in Blaez, almost like a hard flinch even though the space of several hands' lengths separated them on the step. Another interesting reaction. "Why do you avoid them? What hold do they have over you?"

Still no answer.

Marcus's voice dropped more. "You've been exiled a long time. Are they part of the reason for that?"

Again the anguished face.

"I need to know. Now."

Blaez met Marcus's eyes. "Why? Who are you?"

The crimping role of interpreter temporarily shed from Marcus like a cloak that melted to reveal armor beneath. Though fully aware he was still a prisoner and could be for a long time to come, his familiar, instinctive function as a spy emerged in all of its skin-prickling challenge and quest. He had not felt such a sense of purpose in a long time.

"Who I am is not important," he said. "They are trying to raise an army, and not for the good. But if I can locate the right information and pass it on to the right people, I may be able to avert a disaster."

Blaez's brows knotted. "What can you remedy of this…this disaster? You are just as much a prisoner as I am. And what has this to do with me?"

"Who is Tangwen?"

The last of the bread trencher slipped between Blaez's fingers and dropped onto the lowest step. Juice-laden bits splattered in all directions. In disbelief, he stared at Marcus. "He told you of her?"

"Only her name."

The Frank's gaze drifted as if he sat alone. He stared into a puddle below and watched hundreds of circles expand and overlap with each tiny raindrop that struck.

The silence extended too long for Marcus. "A woman by the same name has connections to Rheged," he said. "People there seek her whereabouts. I need to know why."

"She still lives?" Blaez's surprise turned into a hard frown of objection.

"You're protecting her. I understand, but—"

"I trust you, but I betrayed her once. I'll not do so again."

"Your silence could betray her as well," Marcus told him. "Meirchion is looking for her. So is an assassin loyal to Octa. There are others. And I don't think any of them are of the friendliest demeanor. Who is she?"

The Frank clamped his mouth together and turned away.

Marcus waited.

The pause lengthened. Then a soft sigh indicated a subtle change. A faint smile followed then a glance at the main hall. Blaez turned on the step.

"It's true," he said. "She was from Rheged. I had known her there, long ago, when we were quite young. We…parted ways. Then about nine years ago…well, ten by now, I guess. I went back. I couldn't help myself; I wanted to know if she was still there. But before I could find her…" His gaze moved up again towards the main hall. "I witnessed a murder."

The silence drew in once more. Marcus studied him. "You saw the older of those two brothers?"

Blaez's mouth dropped open. "You know of this?"

Marcus nodded. "He knows you saw him?"

"Aye," the Frank said. "But…there is more. There was a woman."

"Her?"

"I only caught a glimpse before she ran."

"And she saw this killing as well?"

"I believe so. He must have seen her and assumed she and I were together, though we were not. I don't know if she ever saw me."

"And that's why he looks for her? Then you escaped?"

Blaez shook his head. "He caught me. I was certain he was going to kill me like the other man he murdered. Obviously he didn't. Instead, he gave me the choice of exile or being handed over to Octa. Like a coward, I chose exile instead of going back to find her and try to take her far away. As long as Octa lives, I remain in Budic's court and silent. So you see, by taking the choice of exile, I betrayed her."

Marcus wiped a hand over his face. He remembered the thoughtful conversation they'd once had on guilt and its overwhelming power. He wondered if the Frank was haunted by nightmares as well.

"As long as Octa lives," he echoed with a frown. "Why Octa? And how does the warlord know—" He cut himself off. Their watchers had moved. Two more appeared. He stiffened, his sudden stillness an alert to Blaez.

"Change of guards," the Frank whispered.

Marcus sat back in the alcove and silently observed the men settle into the watch. His thoughts ran on. Why had Meirchion gone to such measures to hide the killing? Murder was not uncommon among high-ranking princes or even kings. How often had one brother poisoned another to gain control over the pieces of a kingdom split on their father's death? More times than could ever be named.

And Blaez. Why had Meirchion not simply killed him—and the woman—to hide his secret? Was Blaez, whomever he was, too important to risk killing? And Tangwen as well—what made her special?

Many more questions plagued Marcus, but he hesitated to ask. He watched the relieved guards saunter towards the main hall. The new guards took up positions closer than the others had been.

Head tilted back, Blaez looked as if he were deep within his memories. "If she still lives as you say," he murmured, "she must still be hidden away in that women's colony. She was beautiful. You should have seen her. Her name means 'white fire' in your language, doesn't it?"

Marcus regarded him. "It seems you cared very much for her, didn't you?"

Blaez's eyes grew wistful at the night sky. "Still do," he said. "Tangwen was my wife."

Marcus stared, speechless.

"Both of you," a figure called lightly from out of the gloom.

Marcus pried his attention away from Blaez. Budic's seneschal walked towards them.

"To your quarters. Now. You're to remain there until told otherwise—king's orders."

Marcus glanced at Blaez. The thought that Meirchion must have returned flew between them. Parting, they slinked away through the compound's shadows, hoods pulled low.

Several days passed.

Sharp breezes replaced the rain. They seemed to stir Marcus's incessant speculations. Late in the evening, he leaned on one of the wooden practice sticks to catch his breath after a long, fake swordfight with his hut's beams. The exertion, done daily for nearly three years now, felt good, not only to relieve the idleness but to alleviate frustration as well.

"As long as Octa lives," he muttered, unable to shake his thoughts from Blaez's story. Octa's death would free them both. He wished they could have completed the conversation. Without learning more, he could not reckon out the logic of how Octa controlled Blaez, but a lie from Meirchion to Octa made the best sense. If so, how ironic. Though still an assumption, Marcus believed the lie that Tangwen was his hostage had come from Octa to Handor and passed on to Meirchion. That made both Octa and Meirchion fools for having believed the lies. It also made fodder of him and Blaez.

He straightened and took up the stick to continue his ritual of practice. Then a new thought flashed in his mind. The warlord had led him to Blaez's tale. "What if," he said and tapped the stick's end on the earthen floor. "What if…"

He clamped his mouth shut and reasoned: ever since Uther created the fiasco that had ended in Gorlois's death, disunity in Britain had increased and the high king's support diminished. Uther desperately needed to regain that support to accomplish what had become the seemingly impossible: to at last take Octa in battle. In five years no one had successfully taken Gorlois's place as military commander. What if another man with capability to inspire soldiers to loyalty and courage would step forward? Marcus smiled wryly.

Murmuring voices intruded on his thoughts. Masguid's, he recognized first, then Meirchion's. At the entrance to his hut, he leaned on the wall and pushed the leather drape just enough to see outside. The brothers stood several paces away, silhouetted against torchlight from the main hall. His lone nightwatcher, seated on a stool and dozing, jerked each time the voices' pitch changed, but he was not truly listening.

The talk stalled. The brothers glanced from one side to the other, peered past the hut and the snoozing guard, then moved several steps over. Stopped again, they gave a few more furtive looks. Marcus could not see their faces.

"It's safe here?" Meirchion asked.

"Safe enough."

"Good. It's gone well…all of it."

"He is convinced?" Masguid asked.

Meirchion nodded. "That man is of no great mind. He was all too eager to believe the worst, that his rival warlord is allied with the Franks against *him*. You should have seen his outrage. And that fed his fear well. He will be a fly ready to flick aside once the warlord comes after him—ready for us to catch."

A fly? Marcus leaned back his head and slowly shook it. If, in their minds, Judikael were no more than a fly to be swatted away, how could they expect him to stand with Uther against Saxons, or, in truth, with them against Uther? Arrogance, like a fly, could be persistent, but it could also be easily made into worthless mash.

"And the letter?" Masguid asked.

"Burned. Budic's courier carries a piece of blank parchment to

Rome. He and the escort think I returned due to illness."

"Good."

Marcus's lips curled into a cynical half-smile. Just as he thought—no alliance and a deepening rift between Judikael and the warlord to the brothers' advantage. The letter was for Budic's benefit, to keep him thinking he had a hand in the deceit.

"And you?" Meirchion prompted.

Masguid surveyed their surroundings again. "I need one more meeting with the warlord to set the time for him to attack. What does Judikael say about his war bands?"

"They'll be ready." Then Meirchion's tone suddenly shifted and took on menace. "But you had best be sure that warlord performs. All the time we've spent planning this will be for naught if you fail."

Masguid sneered at his older brother. "Have faith, just once. Now go."

Marcus grinned. The brotherly reconciliation was a sham. If they did succeed in raising an army against Uther, he wondered, which brother would be in control?

Moments later, Meirchion disappeared between the buildings. Masguid started towards the hut.

Marcus cursed and retreated. His watcher had been drugged again. He stretched out on his pallet next to the fire pit, laid the practice stick on the floor and grabbed up his wineskin. He poured mead into his mouth, spilled more on his tunic.

The leather drape whipped aside. Marcus swallowed. He lifted his head slowly, his eyes deliberately not quite in focus. "What do you want?" he mumbled.

Masguid snatched up the wineskin and thunked it down against the wall. "I need you sober. Now."

Marcus lay flat on the pallet. After days of thinking like a man with true purpose again, to revert into the sullen interpreter felt like annoying gravel in a shoe. "Who cares?" he said.

"You do." Masguid booted him in the leg and squatted down. "If you don't want Budic to know what you've been doing…"

Marcus grinned sarcastically and blew his stale breath into Masguid's face. "Then he will know what you've been doing as well, won't he? What do you want?"

Masguid dropped a pouch on the pallet. "Open it."

Sighing, Marcus sat up and dragged the pouch into his lap. He dumped the contents. A small sheet of parchment, a stoppered ceramic bottle of ink and a quill fell out.

"I want a letter to the high king of Britain," Masguid ordered. "Written in the common Latin, as if spoken by the *bacaudae* chieftain. I will tell you what to say, you will translate."

Marcus rubbed a hand across his face. How many lies he would be sending to Uther in Judikael's name? He sighed again and readied himself. "So be it," he muttered in disgust. "Begin."

Marcus studied the compound from his hut's doorway. First light was still an hour away. Masguid's diminishing figure, completed letter in hand, strode away through the darkness towards the main hall. Certain this missive, unlike the other, would reach its destination, Marcus had hoped to steal across to the kitchen house and arrange a meeting with the warlord through his nephew. The guard, however, had already wakened, and though still groggy, was too alert to elude with success.

Marcus swore and let the drape fall into place.

"You have need to speak with me," a now familiar voice said softly behind him.

Marcus spun around. He stared beyond the fire pit's light, unable to see clearly. A dark shape moved in the rear of the hut. A seamed face appeared, grim but resolute, also familiar.

"I was following him," the Gaul said.

One side of Marcus's mouth curved up. The warlord's stealth reminded him of his own and how much he missed the freedom of moving like a shadow. He reckoned the Gaul had slipped in during a moment of preoccupation with Masguid and the letter.

They sat at the fire pit. Questions crowded Marcus's mind, everything from how the man knew of Blaez and Tangwen to news regarding the sons of Rheged.

The Gaul raised a hand, a decline of Marcus's offer of the wineskin. "Do you believe an alliance exists between Judikael and Childeric?"

"No," Marcus answered. "Do you?"

The warlord was silent as if he would not answer, but his dark eyes studied with care. Then in his gruff whisper of a voice, "Not at all."

Marcus pulled on his moustache. "What will you do?"

"You have a suggestion, it appears."

Marcus detected an allusion of a smile in the squinted eyes. "I have taken a risk."

The folded eyelids tightened. "That means you changed the wording in that letter."

Marcus felt his own eyes perk in the beginnings of a smile. He picked up the wineskin for a drink, looked at it questioningly, and set it down again.

"A hint. Just a hint. That the Pendragon shall look to the Small Sea for those who help. And to beware of sly dogs who slink from the north."

"Sly dogs…of Rheged?" The warlord gave his rumbling chuckle. "And the Small Sea… Morbihan?" He frowned. "What have you done?"

Marcus bowed his head. His fingertips picked at the curly sheep's wool cover of the wineskin. Then he looked up. "How many of those loyal to you are Breizhad?"

"Many. More than are Gallic."

"Because of relations? Your wife's family? Others?"

Cautious, the warlord nodded. "Why?"

Marcus's eyes grew intense. "How many are refugees from the kingdom of Cornwall? From Dyfed? From other of the British kingdoms? How many are sons and daughters of refugees?"

Again caution. "More than I can say."

"How many wish to reclaim their homeland?"

A glare and a grunt in return.

Marcus leaned forward. "How many wish to *fight* for their homeland?"

The warlord's brows jammed together.

"Think on it," Marcus said. "The Frankish and Breizhad kingdoms *will* overrun the lands of your ancestors, even if you and the man you call chieftain should suddenly set aside your differences and strengthen your tenuous hold together. Your homeland's doom was written in the sky many years ago. You don't need anyone to remind you. And no ploy will ever change this. It *will* come. In that letter, I did not write a commitment to the high king. Only a warning—and a possibility."

The warlord's eyes hardened. "Are you mad? Do you realize what you've just done? What you've proposed?"

Marcus's lips pressed together tightly, and his head slowly rocked up and down. "Absolutely," he said, his voice low, concentrated.

The Gaul exhaled roughly, and he rose to leave. "Tell me," he said at the doorway, his hands wound around the handles of his belt dagger and his sword. "If *your* homeland were utterly doomed, would you abandon it? Or would you give anything, even your life, to keep it?"

Marcus stood and squared his shoulders. He let the firelight touch his black eyes. His gaze beamed steadily into the warlord's face. "I think you already know," he said. "Wherever you are, and wherever are those belonging of your heart, is where your soul resides. For yourself, for them, freedom is *all* that matters."

He watched the Gaul's rough face take on a faint smile. A moment later the man retreated into the night.

CHAPTER 21

Dun Breatann
Late Spring, AD 476

NOS *Galan Haf*, or the Eve of Beltaine as it was becoming more commonly called, was less than a month away. Claerwen dreaded it. The festival usually meant a time of happiness and betrothals, of hand-fastings and marriages celebrated, a time of gatherings among clans. Coinciding with the earth's entry into summer, it represented rebirth and the renewal of hope. To Claerwen, Beltaine meant a large influx of people into Dun Breatann and reinforcement of the terms of exile. She would be forced to remain in her chambers for the festival's duration.

Unable to clear her mind of the coming chaos, she wandered into the great hall. Her day's duties with the healer were finished but she was not ready to face the boredom of her room. Instead, she wove between the women slaves who were clearing away the remains of the evening meal. She had no notion of what she sought. Rather she was filling up time with aimless meandering.

Near the front doors, someone caught her by elbow.

"You walked right past me, lass, without a word," Ceredig chided gently.

She could not muster a return smile.

"I know you're not happy about the spring rites," he said, "but if I set aside tradition, it would raise more questions than your presence here."

She looked up into his warm brown eyes. Every third year, according to tradition, a high celebration occurred. This time Dun

Breatann had been selected as the center of gatherings.

"I know," Claerwen said. "I would never expect you to. If it's another escape that worries you, I won't try. But I can avoid the strangers. It's so…so useless to lock me away."

Ceredig slowly shook his head. His eyes changed from fatherliness to a stern bearing. "It is *not* useless, lass."

Claerwen sighed in frustration.

"Come with me," he said. He led her outside into the courtyard. "You have a right to know something I've not told you." He surveyed the preparations for the festival in the yard. Contests, disguised as sport but in truth practice for warriors, would take place there. Displays of swordsmanship, handling of horses, knife throwing, and running races were expected. Other competitions in singing, storytelling, poetry, and dancing would be held as well. For these, several wooden platforms had begun to be built around the yard's perimeter. A large crew worked on the construction.

"We needed as many strong workers for this as we could find to have it completed in time," Ceredig said. "My seneschal chose several of the slaves from those who work out in the fields." He pointed at a tall blond man helping to saw planks near the far end of the great hall.

Claerwen drew a sharp intake of breath.

"He'll be watched carefully, as are all the slaves. I didn't want you to suddenly see he was there and panic. Like last time. He's never given any trouble in the years he's been here. Never tried to come back into the fortress to look for you. I'd be cautious, but I don't truly think you need to worry much."

If Ceredig knew why she had run away, Claerwen thought, he would not say that.

A ram's horn rang out at the front gates—the call that announced the high king's daily courier.

"He's late today," Ceredig said. "He'll be wanting to stay overnight. Want to come and listen?"

She shook her head. Nothing new about Uther's war would be in the dispatch.

Ceredig nodded and left her alone in the courtyard.

While she watched him walk towards the palace, a faint swoosh passed her, close enough to feel air stir against her cheek. A flash of deep, glossy blue careened upward and angled towards the hall's roof. Startled, Claerwen watched a swallow hover for a few moments while it inspected a mud nest under the eave, give her a curious look that could only be taken as a greeting, then race off again.

She gazed into the dusky sky. High up, hundreds of swallows swooped in circles above the fortress and the river. How lovely, she thought. In another fortnight, the bird that had just reclaimed her home would begin to repair one of the nests or build another, then start a new season of raising young with her mate. The pair had returned each summer as long as she had been there, and Ceredig believed the birds had already nested there several years.

Voices and the clattering of tools brought her attention back down to the courtyard. The sun was setting and the slaves were putting their tools in a barrow to be locked away. The big Saxon was among them. In a way he seemed out of place. Though he was dressed the same and acted no differently, and though he looked similar to several of the other tall, light-haired Saxons or Northmen, she thought he held his resignation to slavery more easily than the rest, that he carried the filth of slave work well. She caught herself shaking her head.

The slaves began to file away for their quarters. Claerwen started towards the palace. The tall Saxon watched her pass, a steadfast but sad interest in his ice-blue eyes rather than the bitterness she would have expected. Uncomfortably caught in his gaze, she held it, her stomach in knots. Strangely, fear did not rise up to choke as it had the other time. Only a sense of loneliness.

It occurred to her then that here was someone she knew from the past, someone who had experienced an event in common with her. Except for Ceredig, he was the first person in nearly five long, pointless years of isolation who knew something of her life, and she of his, even though he had been misinformed of her identity. The urge to talk with this stranger wrenched inside her.

But why? How could she even contemplate trusting him? It was absurd. In Rheged, he and his companions had tried to take both her and Marcus captive. But she rarely acted on logic in the way Marcus did. Instead, a sense of fate often surrounded her like a transparent force and drew her in, sometimes with subtlety, sometimes with harsh intensity. Now, as always, logic stalked her, but instinct claimed her.

He moved to turn away, hesitated, then took several steps nearer. He approached with caution, humility. He was so tall, even taller than Ceredig, she had to tilt her head far back to see his face. If he chose, he could have swatted her away like a midge.

Her minder moved forward. Claerwen held up a hand to stop him. A second guard took up another position within several paces. Where they so unsure of this slave, unlike Ceredig?

The terms. She was not allowed to speak with strangers. But he was a slave, not an outsider. She advanced a step towards him. His mis-healed face, though thinner than she remembered, had a slight puffiness that emphasized the cleft in his chin. She wondered what other hardships he had seen in the intervening years. He remained calm, sad. She took another step, this one to test her guards.

"It is not allowed, Lady," her minder said. He strode forward, caught her elbow.

"I only wish to speak a few words to him."

"It is not allowed."

Deflated, Claerwen backed. She stared while the other guard herded the Saxon off to the slaves' quarters.

"Not allowed," she muttered and pulled free of her minder's fingers. She marched across to the palace.

Ten days, Claerwen counted. Ten days to get through the preparations and then the festival—until sunset, three days after Beltaine Eve. Mostly everyone would go home then. A few might linger, but not many. She sighed and came down the palace steps, wishing, wishing it was all over and she could continue with her simple, dull routine…

In light of the Saxon's temporary return to the fortress, perhaps it was a blessing to be isolated, she told herself. Yet she could not help but sense that was wrong. The more she thought on it, the more she believed he had not truly threatened her when he'd tried to speak with her all those years before. Rather, he had appeared insistent, needful, not at all like Handor. And she had panicked like a sheep.

Claerwen passed between two unfinished platforms to reach the alley between the palace and the great hall. She wanted to work in the herb garden while the day was early and still cool. The late spring had been excessively warm, or so it seemed to her. Perhaps it was only her frazzled nerves. Then, as if summoned out of her thoughts, the Saxon loomed from behind one stage.

"Lady Tangwen," he called softly.

Claerwen halted. By the light, he still believed she was Tangwen. And why was he was there alone, before the day's work had begun? She glanced back into the courtyard, aware her minder watched.

"If you sit there," he whispered, "on the steps, and pretend you wait for someone, they may leave you alone." He crouched down behind the steps, just out of the watcher's sight.

She hesitated. He had spoken in the dialect of Strathclyde. Though accented and he mispronounced some of the words, he spoke it well enough. "You've learned our language," she said.

"I was given no choice," he countered matter-of-factly. No guile lay in his tone, only fatigue and a willingness to talk. "Please. No other chance, perhaps?"

She regarded him with caution but sat on the steps leading up the side of the stage. He would soon reckon out the truth of her identity, that was inevitable, but as long as he believed she was Tangwen, she could not pass the opportunity to play into the misunderstanding.

"I am called Beornwulf," he said. "I am your kinsman."

Kinsman? Claerwen leaned her elbows on her knees and shielded her face from the courtyard with her hand. She waited for him to go on.

"I want to know," he said. "Why are you a hostage so long? Why so many years?"

A hostage? True, the difference between an exile, a prisoner and a hostage was often a very thin line. Perhaps he confused the words in his new language. And with most of his time spent outside the fortress, he would have missed that half of her guards wore insignia belonging to the high king. Then, whose hostage *was* he thinking?

The answer jumped at her and she bit her lip. He meant Marcus. Beornwulf and his companions, as well as Meirchion, Handor—they had all hunted Marcus, sure he was hiding a woman.

"You would think he should have forgotten about me by now," she bluffed.

He frowned up at her. "You must know, or have, something he wants."

"In truth," she said, "I don't know why I'm being held."

Beornwulf stiffened. "You don't know? How could you *not* know? He must have—"

"Why?" Claerwen cut him off before his questions became too pointed. "Why did you come here? To try to take me away again?"

He gave a harsh laugh, more like a grunt. "You forget, I'm a slave. How can I?" A pause, then, "Your mother told you nothing? Who your father's people were?"

"Father's people?" she echoed. Genuine confusion filled her.

"Nothing?"

She slowly shook her head. "You tried to take me captive. Why? Why do others? Why do they want *me*?"

He stalled. "Not my place to tell, Lady Tangwen."

"Tell me what you can. I want to know."

Troubled, Beornwulf glanced from behind the steps. The guard, too distant to hear, watched Claerwen but still took no notice that she spoke to anyone. The Saxon winced and his voice grew soft, ominous. "I don't know why Handor did. But you…you are the only heir to a high-ranking sea-warrior loyal to Hengist, Octa's father. He was important in a cult that worshipped a sea-god, Eoger. I don't know how they learned of you, but they wanted you for a…" He winced again. "Ritual."

The color drained from Claerwen's face. Had she been mistakenly captured or the true Tangwen taken instead, the implications were clear. Some cultures conducted sacrificial rituals involving humans. It had even been rumored of the druids of her own ancestors, but during the Roman conquest the truth had been twisted into grotesque falsehoods, a method to discredit the druids' powerful influence and wrest control of the people from them. The only human sacrifices she had heard of in Britain were those of particularly heinous lawbreakers. But in other places…

She searched his face. "How did my mother…?"

"When your mother was a priestess in that old religious colony somewhere in the kingdom you call Rheged," Beornwulf continued swiftly, "she had visited someone on the eastern coast, a friend, relation—I don't know. There was a raid. Your mother…was raped. She went home, later found she was with child. She kept you in hiding, raised you in the colony as a priestess to keep you secret."

Tangwen, a priestess of the old ways? That made sense, Claerwen thought. The pewter symbol she had seen hanging from the woman's neck confirmed that—as well as the gift of fire in the head.

"And the two men with you?" she asked.

"My cousins. The older one? He knew the cult wanted you for the sacrifice. He promised he could bring you back. We sailed with Octa's fleets and broke away when the chance came." He shook his head at himself. "The sacrifices to Eoger never sat well with me. Don't fear me, Lady Tangwen. Ever again. I have no use for that kind of cruelty."

The sadness in his face deepened, but his gaze lifted and raked over her more closely than before. His mind was turning. Soon the truth would strike him. Claerwen's heart started to hammer and she held her breath.

"Eyh…" he started, then cursed in Saxon. "The sea-warrior belonged to Hengist's generation…in the time of Vortigern. Your mother would be… Eyh, you're not old enough to be Lady Tangwen. You lied."

Claerwen gazed straight into his anger-wracked eyes without a hint of shame. "You assumed."

Beornwulf nearly rose but caught himself before he was seen. He thumped a fist on one of the platform's supports. "You lied. Why?"

"I need to know all I can about her. You wouldn't have said anything to a stranger."

"Who are you?"

"I think they have fed you much nonsense." She lowered her voice with the hope of inducing calm in him. "Who told you I was Tangwen?"

He sat on the ground and leaned against the platform's supports, hands over his face. He was too stunned, too confused, and while Claerwen waited for him to gather his thoughts, she allowed herself the pretense of a yawn, a stretch and a glance at her minder. Still no more than the usual cursory attention. She leaned her elbows on her knees again.

Beornwulf finally looked up. "Octa knew Handor badly wanted to locate her," he said softly. "He told Handor that the spy held her hostage. He said he knew where she was hidden and he would trade that knowledge for the spy's head. I don't think Octa knew anything. It was only a way to get the spy's death."

"And because I was with him, you thought I was Tangwen?"

He shrugged. "Why would a spy have a woman with him? None of us knew anything but her name and a story like a fable."

"Octa doesn't care what happens to Tangwen, does he?" Claerwen breathed. "But what is she to Handor?"

"Egh. Handor." Beornwulf grunted and pointed at his face. "He did this. Always so bitter, so miserable. Always made everyone angry. I don't know why he wanted her so much. Not for the same reason we had, I don't think. Wherever she is, she'd likely wish he'd turn to dust and blow away."

If Handor had succeeded in assassinating Marcus, Claerwen wondered, was the man fool enough to think Octa would honor such a trade and reveal the woman's whereabouts—if he knew—and then that she would willingly lead him to the sword? Not likely. Claerwen wished Marcus could have heard all this. If only…

Beornwulf reached up and lightly brushed her wrist with his fingers. "Who are you? Why do you always look sad?"

She flinched at the brief touch then calmed. "I can't tell you who I am," she said. "But you have every right to hate us."

"Hate us…? Who? You? And…you mean the spy?"

She nodded.

"Why? Because he killed my younger cousin?"

She nodded again. "And…and I was forced to kill the other." She cringed, sure Beornwulf knew nothing of this. After her ploy as the Iron Hawk had broken the fight between him and Handor, he had run towards Uxelodunum. With the battle of Caer Luguvalos quickly spreading across a great expanse of land, he could not have gone looking for his cousin.

"He's dead." Beornwulf turned away. "Figured as much, but *you* killed him?"

"Aye. It is most regretted."

Beornwulf's head turned again and he looked squarely at her. "Regretted?" His face split into a laugh. "Don't be sorry. We wanted the silver and land we thought we would get. We were stupid."

He pushed out from the platform and glanced into the courtyard. The minder had finally caught notice. "Beware, Lady," he said. "Your curiosity may bring light to more than you wish to know." He stalked away, still laughing.

Sunset again. Nine days left.

Beornwulf's reaction to the killing of his cousins plagued Claerwen. Anger, silence, disappointment, even disregard she would have expected. But laughter? Strange. Eerie.

She had wanted to ask if he had ever seen Handor outside the fortress, but the chance had been lost when he walked away. Likely, he would have spoken of it on his own. He clearly harbored no respect for Handor and in spite of learning she was not Lady Tangwen, he had not turned against her.

On her way from the garden to her chambers, she passed through the courtyard. More guards were on duty there than usual, both from Uther and Ceredig and they were more heavily armed. Had they seen her speak with the slave the day before? No, she reasoned, not until the end of the exchange—they would have separated her from him if they had seen. But so many armed soldiers? Just for her? Why? And how long had their presence been increased without her notice?

By the light, she was tired. She had no care to put more thought to minders, guards, or Beornwulf, or anything else. Sluggish all day, she only wished to relinquish an hour's worth of time to some rest before the evening meal. She trudged inside and into her room. Why so tired? Long days of work? The heat and strain of the coming festival? Perhaps it was confusion over Beornwulf's reaction. Or was it the endless waiting? By the gods, she hated waiting. She sat on her bed and leaned against the wall.

Just sit and listen to the gradual quieting of the evening… So tired…

She fell asleep…

Dragged at, then tilting, farther and farther. A thousand hands grabbing hold, pulling, the pressure gathering. Falling, so slowly, from a high place down, far down, to the damp earth. No pain, no shock, only the absence of air, no more light, the din fading away. The weight unbearable. To crawl out from beneath impossible. The earth smelled good, so fine indeed, but it filled the nose, the mouth, the eyes with darkness…

Claerwen woke. She lay on the cold flagstones of her chamber's floor. When had she climbed down there? She was gulping for air, but she breathed with no difficulty. Her stomach was knotted so hard she thought it must be bruised. Had she dreamed? She raked her mind and remembered nothing. No visions, no dreams, nothing.

Except the cramped sense of death lingered. Why death? Whose? She immediately questioned if the increase in armed men outside was related, but that connection was not obvious. Unlike forebodings in the past that clung with a tenacious sense of doom, this time the notion that someone had died merely faded into a memory. She crawled to the table and grasped its edge, pulled herself half-upright to stare into the hour candle's flame.

"Who was it?" she begged of the gods. No name was whispered in her soul. No face in her mind. Nothing. The gods had been silent for so long.

She slapped the candle. It fell and rolled to a stop against a cup. "Who was it?" she asked again, but the flame died, the wax spilled.

"Lass?" Ceredig's voice called at the door. He knocked quietly and with insistence. "Lass, what's wrong?"

How long he had been there? Claerwen couldn't guess, and she couldn't tell if she had made any noise he might have overheard. Perhaps one of her watchers had sent for him. No more rested than earlier, she rose and groped for the door.

"Are you ill? My seneschal says you missed supper in the hall."

To distract him, Claerwen stepped out into the corridor. More soldiers had been added there. She leaned on the wall and shook her head with vigor to counter his concern.

"You are so pale." His gaze slipped past her to the upset candle. "What happened?"

"Merely…startled, I suppose. I had fallen asleep." When his hand pressed her arm and his eyes filled with questions, she knew her bluff was pointless.

He smiled. "Will you share my supper with me? They'll be delivering it to my chambers in a bit…and they always bring too much."

Food held no interest for her. Though she welcomed his company, this time she preferred to stay in her room. If she could concentrate on the strange dream, or whatever it was, perhaps her memory of it would clarify.

An officer of the guards approached and politely cleared his throat. Claerwen recognized him—he patrolled the outlying lands of the fortress. He was holding a small square of parchment, folded twice.

A report? News? Her gaze followed the parchment as it passed from his hand into the king's. Ceredig thanked and dismissed him with a nod.

"Supper would be fine enough," she murmured, her eyes still on the note.

"Ah, I am pleased." Ceredig walked her the short distance to his chambers. Shortly, two kitchen slaves arrived with the meal, arranged it on a small sideboard just inside and left.

Claerwen had seen his chambers only a few times in the early months of exile and had paid little notice then. Now, cautiously curious, she found the spacious room took up the full end of the palace and was centered on a large fire pit with a stone rim high enough to sit on. Comfortable Roman-style chairs were placed next to the pit. Thick woven draperies hung over alcoves along the walls and discreetly hid storage, sleeping, and lavatory areas. From an open window at the south end of the room, an evening breeze stirred the drapes. Nearby, a large table was covered with dozens of parchments, some rolled and sealed, others stacked with their ends curled together. A ceramic ink crock sat in the middle, several quills piled next to it.

Ceredig walked to the table. He opened the folded parchment the officer had given him and scanned it for a few seconds, then placed it with a roll that had been set aside. He straightened the other stacks and prepared to move them out of the way. Claerwen followed his movements.

Death. The word came at her out of the air. Was it her own doom, as she had seen in her vision years before? It was only a word—death—but she could not leave it be.

"Are you sure you feel well enough?" Ceredig asked. "You're so pale."

She was staring into space. "Why are so many soldiers out there?"

Ceredig straightened and met her pinched gaze with quiet directness. "I didn't want you to worry, but you must be aware Octa still has spies or scouts watching—they are always there, but new men have arrived recently, and I like it not."

"Warriors?" Claerwen's eyes grew round. "Elite warriors? The guards have seen them?"

He nodded. "And keep count of their numbers, their positions, their duties. I've ordered my men to not take any of them. Octa will be less likely to suspect how much we know."

Claerwen flushed at the thought of elite warriors like those who had chased down Marcus. "Surely…surely he must realize by now I know nothing of—" She caught herself from saying Marcus's name aloud.

"They probably still believe you could know where he is, even after all this time. Octa must have a reward promised they can't resist."

"Or punishment," Claerwen said. She touched the tiny scars that encircled her neck. "What of the man who did this? Is he here?"

"Leave it be, lass." He scooped together the rolled parchments. "Let the guards do their duty and you'll be safe enough."

Claerwen turned away. Safe? With the possibility that Handor could be among Octa's elite warriors? She wished the increased presence of guards would ease her discomfort. If anything, it made it worse.

Death. The notion grabbed at her mind again. And the useless waiting. If only Marcus would just walk through the door. She closed her eyes and fought tears and the scattered nature of her thoughts. Marcus. Where in the gods' names could he be? She raised her face and tried to compose herself, but apprehension tingled relentlessly. She turned back to Ceredig.

"What drove him to his work?"

The king's eyes lifted sharply. His brows rumpled down. Then they retreated just a bit. "He never told you?" Ceredig walked to one of the drapes and elbowed it aside. Behind, a narrow door stood ajar, a small room beyond. He carefully placed the rolls in a basket inside.

She shook her head. "He refused. Always. Do *you* know?"

Ceredig's lips twisted. He returned to the table and collected the rest of the sheets. In the alcove he placed them in another basket, this time with less care, and drew the drape back into place. He pointed at the waiting meal, a request for help to move it to the larger table.

"In truth?" he said. "I don't know. I don't know if one incident caused it, or an accumulation of all the raids and battles that've gone on since long before he was born."

Claerwen carried the platter of food across to the larger table. Her stomach cramped again. "He was having horrible nightmares before the exile. They were getting worse, and he wouldn't talk about them. But I think something happened to him long ago, and they come from that. If you know, please tell me."

"I only have suspicions, lass, and I'm not sure you want to hear this. It's very ugly, and I only know part of it. Why now?"

She could not understand herself why she had asked the question—she felt no connection between it and the odd sense of death. "I want to know. I must know…why he always has to be in danger. Myrddin once asked me why, and I had no answer to give him."

Ceredig poured two goblets full of mead and handed her one. He seated himself in a chair next to the fire pit.

"There was a raid on the coast not far from here," he said. "Saxon pirates, not the usual Irish. Marcus was about…one-and-ten winters, I think. In the middle of his fosterage here. He may have witnessed something those pirates did."

Ceredig took a sip of mead. "Sit, please, lass. And try not to break that."

She was squeezing the goblet. Queasy, she sank onto the hearth-stones.

"People, mostly families," Ceredig went on, "were rounded up across the countryside and taken to an old, ruined Roman fort on the coast. They were hostages…or so the Saxons claimed."

Her eyes widened. "They killed them?"

"Murdered them—every last one. Then they were burned."

Claerwen winced and set down her goblet.

"It's worse than that, lass. When the bodies were found…" His voice grew labored and he took a long swallow. "When the bodies were found, even though they were burned badly, it looked like they had been…"

Her eyes drew up again when he did not go on. He was staring into the fire pit. Finally he drew breath. "They looked like they'd been flayed."

Claerwen needed no more than her imagination to fill in the missing parts. If Marcus had seen the atrocity, she could not blame him for his silence. She found herself unable to speak, her hand at her mouth to control her shaking jaw.

"He could have been there, but no one knows," Ceredig said. "We were all so stunned. But he was very, very quiet for a long time, like he was ashamed in my opinion. I questioned the lad, but he never would talk, just glare into space with those black eyes of his. Then, about a half-year later, he started doing some of the most maddening, daring acts that made some of us think he was rather weak in the head. Turned into a bit of courage, though, as you've seen."

"Or a wish to end his own life," she mouthed.

Ceredig's eyes drilled into her. "Don't ask him again. If he wouldn't talk to an old war dog like me, he won't talk at all. Not to you, not anyone. Some things are best left alone."

They shared the silence that followed. After a time, Ceredig shifted in his seat. "Have I made you old?"

Lost in her thoughts, Claerwen listened to the peat hiss its warmth throughout the room, its rich smell, like burnt mud, a small, comforting reminder of home, or homes anywhere. Tears welled in her eyes. He had spoken, she realized and looked up at him.

The platter now sat on the hearthstones, and he waved a hand at the food to remind her it was getting cold. "Whenever I sit with you," he said, "I talk old men's talk, and you are either too polite to object or walk away. Or have I made you think like an old man by now?"

In her nearly five years in Dun Breatann, Claerwen had watched both his health and ambition slowly decline like the fading of red from his hair. She sometimes felt guilt in looking at her own reflection, still young, though her face and body had settled into a bit more angularity and the beginnings of lines fanned out from the corners of her eyes. She often prayed the exile would end in time for Marcus to see Ceredig once more. She slowly shook her head. The tears fell. She wiped them away. More came.

"This waiting," she said. "It would make anyone old."

"I am sorry, lass. I know how much you miss him. Perhaps some good news will come soon."

"Ah, we both know better, don't we?" She picked up a piece of bread but put it down again. "Do you miss being able to go with the war bands?"

He hummed a soft moan of remembrance. "I miss the wildlands. Riding across the moors with the wind in my face. Ah, and I miss the young girl I married so, so long ago."

His palms swished together lightly, as if he recalled how his wife's skin felt. Claerwen watched and smiled. No, he was not old. He had none of an old man's forgetfulness or making light of all that surrounded him.

In companionable silence they drank generously of the mead—the mood had diminished any desire for food. Ceredig rested his feet on the hearthstones. Claerwen refilled his goblet. She watched him drift and grow sleepy. He continued to steadily sip. Finally, his head bowed. She caught the goblet before it fell from his fingers and set it next to the platter with hers.

"Forgive me," she whispered, "but you never answered my question." She padded back to the table. The folded record from the guard and the single roll still lay there. On the smaller record she found a date and a list of men, each with a brief description and locations. She was drawn straight to one: a man with red-brown hair, brown eyes, medium height and build. Mean face. Not Saxon.

Though she had expected to find Handor on the list, her breath still caught in her throat. Next, she spread out the roll. It was a tally of the guards' observations over the fortnight since Beornwulf's return to the fortress. Handor was listed repeatedly.

"He is not waiting," she whispered, then spit a curse. Chills crawled on her skin. "He is coming for me."

She rolled the tally, careful to leave it looking undisturbed, then, backing, she turned to go, but a basket on a sideboard caught her attention. Several small tokens of brass that bore the insignia of Dun Breatann lay inside—safe conduct tokens that allowed entrance and exit through the fortress gates. Her eyes shifted between them and Ceredig. Should she?

She gazed at him. He slept soundly. She had employed the most common of spy tactics ever invented—ply a person with drink until they were asleep, then search their quarters. After years of no ruses at all, it had come so easily, so naturally that it scared her.

She remembered Ceredig had said how little it mattered who Beornwulf was. But it had mattered. At least to her it had. Now she was sure it mattered far more that Handor had returned to stalk her.

"Forgive me," she repeated and took one of the tokens. "I must find a way to save myself." She strode to the door and let herself out.

CHAPTER 22

Dun Breatann
Late Spring, AD 476

"YOU must help me."

Beornwulf nearly toppled backward. "And you should not come here." He jerked a thumb at the latrine pits' entrance behind him. "Have you a wish for death?" With his nose scrunched up, he only half-jested about the place's pungency.

"I am serious," Claerwen said.

"I cannot help. Remember? I'm a slave." He backed from her.

"Listen to me." She lunged after him and caught his sleeve. She was unsure what reaction to expect, but she had to try. A full night and a day had passed since she had learned Handor lurked somewhere beyond the gates. This was her first opportunity to speak with Beornwulf.

He shook his arm free and started away from her again. "It's getting dark and I must go before I'm missed."

"Handor is here," she said.

Beornwulf halted. He turned and stared at her with a deadly stillness. "Where?"

"At the edge of the fens, about a half-mile west of the road. He's been seen watching the fortress for the past fortnight or so. He's coming after me, but if he learns you are here as well, then so are you in danger."

The Saxon frowned. "You've seen him yourself?"

"There is proof. More than enough."

"You're bluffing."

"I am not. I've seen the soldiers' tallies. Octa's elite warriors are watching this fortress. Have you noticed how many additional soldiers have been posted in here?"

Beornwulf folded his arms. "What do you want of me?"

Claerwen glanced around for her minders. "Come, before they realize where I've gone." She beckoned him to follow her into the shadows of a broad oak tree near the fortress wall. "Once this festival starts, the guards will not be able to watch everyone. People will be moving in and out of the gates at all hours."

"Many have already begun to arrive," he broke in.

"Aye, and I think Handor will try to get in when the most people are at the gates. During the same time, from the day of Beltaine Eve through the next three days and nights, I will be required to remain in my chambers."

"Because of who you are?"

She nodded.

"Death trap, if he comes."

Claerwen's jaw tensed. "I need to trust you. I need you to help me."

He cocked his head to one side.

"Choose a slave who works outside the walls everyday—one you can trust. I need to arrange a meeting with Handor."

Beornwulf's eyes widened beneath his lowering brows. "Are you *mad*? He wants to kill you, and you offer him a perfect chance?"

"I'm going to offer him a trade for something he wants very badly. It will send him away from here."

"Something he wants? Lady Tangwen?"

"No, something else."

Beornwulf's head swiveled side to side. "He'll never take the bait. Not that man."

"I can't sit in there," she pointed at the palace, "and wait for him to come with a knife in the dark."

His breath rushed out in a rough stream. "Even if you succeed, how long do you think he'll be gone? Once he knows you lied, he'll come back, worse than a hornet. Why don't you go to your king?"

"What can he do? Surround me with more guards? Well, fine enough, but you know Handor. He's too clever, too persistent. It only takes a well-planned diversion."

"But they'll be prepared for that."

"It's not enough. Will you help?"

"Absolutely not."

"Then I will find another who is willing. In truth, I had no right to ask." She whipped around and strode from him.

Beornwulf caught her arm and pulled her back under the tree. "What in Odin's name could you have to trade with Handor? And what do you think he has to give you?"

"I can't tell you."

His eyes rolled. "Of course not. It's some of that spy's business. Isn't it? That's the truth of why you won't go to the king?"

Her eyes came up. "Whether it is or isn't makes no difference now. You are caught in this as much as I am. I want to survive."

Beornwulf gave her another look that confirmed his opinion of her madness. Beneath that was a second opinion that spoke of amazement. He leaned down and closely peered into her face. Thoughts spun behind his eyes. "How soon?"

"You've changed your mind?"

He half-smiled. "What have I to lose? I don't expect to be anything but a slave ever again. This," he tapped his crooked nose, "was only part of the damage Handor did." Then he rubbed a scar that cut down across the line of his jaw. "Handor nearly beat me to death. You have loyalty to that spy. Why—not my place to ask, but he stopped Handor and let me crawl away. He saved my life. For him, I will help you. How soon?"

Relief swept her. "Before Beltaine Eve. Before most of the guests arrive."

Beornwulf rested his hands on his hips, straightened, and stretched his tired back. "Ah, I must have lost my own mind. I will try. No guarantee."

Relief again swept Claerwen. "May the gods bless you."

He snorted. "They'll need to. Both your gods and mine. And if I cannot arrange a meeting? What will you do?"

Vulnerability stabbed at Claerwen's resolve. She still had the Iron Hawk's weapon hidden in her chambers, but she was no swordsman. And Marcus had told her Handor was excellent with weapons.

Beornwulf's hand reached halfway towards her shoulder then withdrew. He glanced past her. "Your minder is looking for you. What will you do?"

She honestly did not know, but she lifted her head proudly. "Kill him," she said.

He stared in amazement. "You must have the heart of a Valkyrie. I will find you when I have something to tell." He strode for the slave quarters.

"Where *are* you?" Claerwen watched the night sky. Her fist thumped lightly on the casement of her window.

Three days had gone by with no news from Beornwulf. She had seen him laboring to finish the Beltaine preparations throughout the daylight hours, the pace of the work frenetic with the approaching holiday. She had deliberately passed close enough that he would be sure to see her, but he kept at his work with diligence. The slave-master would likely punish him if he neglected his duties.

But time was running out. Her fist thumped one more time, harder, then she closed the shutters. Had he even tried? Had he been able to? Or could he not find anyone to cooperate? Or if he had found a slave who worked outside the gates, could that man not locate Handor?

Perhaps she should try to access the assassin through the guards who actually watched him. She shook her head. They would never allow her to contact any of Octa's elite warriors, especially Handor. And she had nothing with which to bribe them.

"Where *are* you?" She paced the floor. Worn down, she had slept little the last two nights and knew she should go to bed. Why bother? She'd never sleep now.

In the center of her chambers, she looked up at the ceiling. The Iron Hawk's sword still lay wedged between the beam and the thatching. If need be, she would use it. On tiptoe, she ran her fingertips along the top edge of the beam. They brushed against the sword's scabbard.

One of the shutters swung open behind her. Claerwen dropped

her hand and jerked around. Out of breath, Beornwulf clung to the window's casement and gestured at her to come. She set the lamp on the floor and knelt before him.

"The man will meet with you, only if he knows what you have to trade," he whispered. "If it suits him, and you have proof, he will make a time and place within the fortress." His eyes arced up to the ceiling then back down to her

Claerwen hesitated. "You found a messenger? Can he be trusted?"

He nodded. "The guards pass again soon. Tell me."

"Tell Handor I will give him the Iron Hawk's identity."

Beornwulf nearly lost his grip on the casement. "Are you—? How? Why would he want that?"

"Who broke up your fight with Handor before the battle at Caer Luguvalos? Have you not ever wondered why?" She stared into his face, her own fiercely masked, as if to shield her mind from his should he even faintly suspect she had masqueraded as the warrior.

His eyes could have lit the courtyard. "The Iron Hawk wants Lady Tangwen?"

"I believe he does," she said. "It was not the first time he fought Handor. I think the warrior either wants to take her himself, or he protects her from Handor. I don't know which it is or why, but Handor surely would want to know his identity."

Beornwulf swore. "You have proof?"

She crossed to her bed and swept aside the coverings. Kept in perpetual disarray, the rumpled bedding served as a disguise for the lump close to her sheepskin pillow. She tore open the corner of her mattress, scattering feathers, and pulled out the warrior's masked helmet. She expanded it into its full shape.

"Have your messenger give him a description of this."

His eyes widened in utter astonishment.

"I'm not bluffing," she said. "I am one of only three people who know who the Iron Hawk is. And where he is. Handor has something I want in return. Give him a complete description of this. It's one of the two helmets the warrior uses. I will trade *Y Gwalch Haearn's* identity for what I want."

Beornwulf watched her turn the helmet. This time he swore in

Saxon. "You would betray this warrior?"

"I'm gambling…" She swallowed hard. "I'm gambling the Iron Hawk will kill Handor first. Before Handor can tell him who his betrayer is."

"Ho…this is a deadly game you play, woman. What do you want in return?"

In truth, all she wanted was freedom from the threat of Handor's presence, to deflect him away from Dun Breatann, but that would give away her lie.

"I will tell him when he meets with me," she said.

Beornwulf's eyes narrowed at her hedge. "I'll give you the time and place by—" He glanced behind. "I must go—the guards are coming." He dropped away from the window. His light footsteps quickly faded.

She sank onto the bed and hugged the helmet. "Please," she prayed. "Let me survive this."

"Come, please, please, please. There is no more time." Fists clenched, Claerwen paced the length of her chambers, over and over. "This is the last night to do this."

Knocking lightly rattled the door. The evening meal. Be calm, she told herself and forced composure onto her face. At the door she was startled to find Beornwulf with a small platter of food. He had switched places with one of the kitchen slaves. Inside, he set the platter on her table.

Her gaze followed him in search of any nuance in his movements, his posture, his face that said he had news. He straightened without a word. Halfway to the door, he slowed. "Tonight," he whispered. "Midnight. The great hall."

Before he could leave, she half-closed the door and clutched his arm. "Disappear from the fortress. Now. If anything goes wrong, you will not be safe."

"Not until I know—"

"No, don't wait. Save yourself, Beornwulf. You have done enough, more than I can repay you."

"He's going to kill you. You know that, don't you? This is too dangerous."

She shook her head. "He will kill me for certain if I sit here and do nothing. But I want you to give yourself freedom." From under her mattress she retrieved the stolen safe conduct token and placed it in his palm. "Take this. It will get you through the gates."

"Where could I go?"

She bit her lip then the words came in a rush. "Go south, to the kingdom of Gwynedd. Look for the high road that goes into the mountains, past a place called *Yr Wyddfa.* When you can see it on your right as you head south, look to your left. High in the pass will be a small hillfort. You can barely see it. Go there. Describe how the spy looks, and me. They will take you in."

"What is this place?"

"Never mind that now. Just go. Save yourself."

He glanced at the token then studied her eyes. His head slowly swayed back and forth. "Lady…I hope, whoever you are, whatever you are, whatever this is you are involved in, it is all worth it to you." He slipped the token inside his tunic.

"May the power of Frea be with you," he said. "You *do* have the heart of a Valkyrie." For barely an instant, he touched her face, his ice-blue eyes full of admiration. Then he turned and strode out. The door softly closed behind him.

Claerwen felt like anything other than a Valkyrie. In truth, she was not even sure who or what Frea or a Valkyrie were. But she hoped Beornwulf would survive.

Seated at the table, elbows on its surface, Claerwen rested her face in her hands. By the gods, she thought, what had she done? Every word, every expression, even the way she moved, would have to be convincing. Well, she would just have to do it.

Eat now. Act normal. She hoped the food would settle her reeling nerves. She had convinced Uther in a ruse years before. She could do it again. Of course Marcus was with her that time. This time she was alone.

The hour candle crept downward. The wax formed a soft, warm pool around the bottom. Half an hour before midnight, Claerwen wrapped a large shawl around her head and shoulders, blew out the flame and picked up the tray Beornwulf had brought.

She opened her door. The corridor, even at that hour, was bustling and noisy. One minder stood at each end, two guards at Ceredig's doors, another two patrolled. Beornwulf had come before the last change of shifts, and she hoped they had not altered their schedule.

Three men and a woman talked loudly opposite her door. She pulled the shawl to shadow her face as much as possible, stepped into the corridor then turned back into the doorway. With the platter balanced on one hand, she held the latch, ready to pull the door shut.

"Will there be anything else, Lady?" she spoke into the empty room. She used a voice like the one in the ruse to leave Winchester. "Good night then, Lady." She dipped in a curtsey and pulled the door shut.

The walk from the palace to the great hall seemed longer than usual. Each step jarred. Face downcast, she followed the flow of people up the steps and hoped not to trip or drop the tray with a loud crash. Inside, late arriving nobles ate a late meal. Even Ceredig was still there and shared a drinking horn with each new arrival. Claerwen avoided him. She found an empty table in a corner, one that was rarely used—it was too far from the fire pit's warmth—but from where she could view most of the hall, most especially the front doors.

Shortly the king left. Slaves cleaned, added peat to the hearth, replaced spent torches. The sounds of tired, half-drunken voices and the clunk of eating knives on tabletops, though not loud, were constant.

Claerwen's eyes followed each newcomer. Several times she thought she recognized Handor, but she ruled out each. Sure that midnight was near, she began to lose faith that he would honor the arrangement. What if he had changed his mind or something had gone wrong? Panic stabbed at her resolve.

The doors opened again. A female kitchen-slave guided yet another man into the hall. This one wore a helmet of iron and brass. The woman splayed a hand towards the far side of the hall and tables laden with all kinds of food and stands with drinking horns. He nodded politely, and she retreated.

Claerwen's stare followed him as it had all the others. This man looked out of place. Alone instead of with family and retainers, he appeared to be on official duty rather than a festival guest. His clothes, dusty and mud-spattered from travel, were well made and of fine wool. Beneath a long cloak, a small pouch on a leather strap hung across his chest. He removed a pair of mud-stained gauntlets.

The man scanned the entire hall in a broad, smooth perusal, then he walked to the table of food and drink. Claerwen was drawn to the helmet. To her, it looked like a kind of Saxon headgear. And, anyone else would have taken it off inside the hall, partly for politeness, mostly for comfort.

Gauntlets off, helmet on. The significance struck Claerwen. She could see almost nothing of his face behind the helmet's low brow, nasal and hinged facial pieces. None of his hair showed. The blood started pounding in her head. He was about the same height as Handor, but his build was hidden in the thick cloak. Such fine clothing she would not have expected of the assassin, but it had been a long time since she had seen him, and she was sure he was not above stealing.

Claerwen rose. If she circled around, she might be able to see his face. Moving slowly, she watched him pick up a drinking horn and take a long swig. He appeared to enjoy how the mead ran down inside his throat and washed away the road dust.

She could not tell the color of his eyes at that distance, but they appeared dark. Another two paces and she saw he had a moustache and a short beard that skirted his jaw.

The flow of people passing between fluctuated. His gaze moved in another full scan of the hall. It crossed her, stopped, held. For an instant his lips parted, then clamped shut.

Claerwen's stomach tightened. The contact had been made. What she could see of his face held no expression, but he leaned his head faintly towards the hall's rear doors. He moved a step in that direction, a test if she understood to follow.

Rooted to the floor, she felt the sweat start in her palms. She gripped the shawl's edges together under her chin and made herself walk. Again each step jarred down to the core of her soul. She crossed the hall and slipped out the doors.

The night air chilled the sheen of perspiration on her flushed face. Though refreshing, it was not enough to cool her fear. "Dangerous" was a beginner's word to describe Handor.

She descended the steps and watched the man slowly walk through the gate of the tiny garden behind the hall—the other garden she had avoided for years, the garden of too sacred ground and too many memories to enter. Outrage flared in her—his presence would desecrate the place she had met Marcus, but it was too late to balk, too late to lure him to another location. He was already inside.

No torches lit the garden itself; the only light spilled from one tiny window above. Why did it look so much like *that* night, all those years ago? Knots thickened in her jaw, her neck, her heart, and she closed her eyes. A drip of sweat trickled down the center of her back. Go on, she told herself and passed through the narrow opening in the garden's low stone enclosure.

Escape routes—she noted the wall was low enough that she could leap over it easily if she hitched her skirts high and well in advance. The rear doors to the great hall were only a short distance away. There was no other exit from the garden. So familiar it all was. So much a trap.

A throat cleared. Handor waited near the opposite wall, turned away from her. A shadow himself, she thought, only a shade lighter than the night. Then she saw the lump of a sword underneath his cloak.

Claerwen stalled. A deadly shadow. How many other weapons were hidden on him? Even if she had access to a dagger, she was no match against his strength. She only had fists, a swift run, and her wits. Nothing more.

The sole of her shoe rasped lightly on the flagstones. He glanced over his shoulder and she caught a glimpse of his profile, barely visible and partially blocked by the helmet, before he turned away again. He folded his arms over his chest.

Resolve, born on a crackling spark of anger, shot through Claerwen. Handor would not make a fool of her. She must do this—she must convince him the Iron Hawk could give him Tangwen. Composure. Be calm. She jammed her hands under her elbows to keep them from shaking and strode into the center of the garden.

"I am here." She forced her voice to stay even.

The man turned halfway again. This time his eyes slid towards her and held. His left hand came up in a signal for silence.

Claerwen waited. He gazed up at the surrounding walls, as if in search of listening ears or intruding eyes. She followed his line of sight. Under the eaves, some of the swallows' nests clung. She hoped Handor would not disturb the birds—their counterparts in Winchester, years before, had dived at him out of distrust. But these birds merely watched with curiosity.

Another trickle of perspiration raced down her back. At the same time chills shook her in spite of the nervous heat that racked her. Where was the anger that had spurred her forward? It was gone. Instead, the memory of Handor's fingers digging into her neck on a cold night filled her. She was searing molten lead and the razor of glacial ice together, and both tore away all her hope.

Finally he turned fully around. The brass brow band of the unusual helmet caught in the dim light. Metalwork chasings decorated it, and because it protruded to hold the nasal in the correct position, it also created empty black pits that hid his eyes.

Slowly, he loosened the chinstrap. His hand lifted farther, and he hooked his thumb beneath the brow band. He moved a step, then another, until the light from the window struck him. The corner of his mouth perked into a near-smile. He pulled off the helmet.

Claerwen's eyes widened and her skin tightened as if someone were pulling on it. No straggly reddish-brown hair, no sneering mouth. Instead, a cascade of wild, thick black hair fell around the man's face and onto his shoulders. Feeling faint, she froze in profound disbelief.

His black eyes glittered.

Claerwen's breath scraped through her throat and caught before she could speak, but she abandoned any words. Nothing needed to be said, nothing more needed to be thought. He was coming towards her, his hands held out and rising. Like the fluid flight of the swallows, she crossed the distance between them, never felt the footsteps she made, never noticed the ground she covered. The shawl dropped to the earth unheeded. Nothing in the world mattered. The unbearable, endless years of waiting fled, and she cast herself into Marcus's embrace.

CHAPTER 23

Dun Breatann
Late Spring, AD 476

"How... When..." Claerwen could not make her words comprehensive. In the thick invisibility of the night, in the rare privacy of the tiny garden, clutched in Marcus's arms, she reeled. He felt good, so good, solid and warm and comfortable, like no other being could ever feel to her. He was exactly the way she remembered and had recreated in her mind every day they had been separated. All her conscious thoughts vaporized and left her filled with his presence.

"Aye, 'tis true, Claeri. I am here."

Though his words were spoken softly, his voice sent more tremors through her, its deep richness a sound she had ached to hear for so long. And he had said his favorite name of endearment for her. No one else ever used that name.

The birds watched from the nests under the eaves. Now she understood why they had remained simply curious. Tears flooded her eyes. She tangled her fingers in his hair and buried her face in it. It was cool like the night air. Mingled with road dust and crushed grass, the smell of horses and leather emanated from him, just as when she had first met him in that same place. She drew a long, deep breath as if in doing so would fill her with him even more. "Is this real?" she whispered in his ear.

He dropped the helmet and it thunked softly into the grass next to his feet. He took her face between his hands, drew it tightly against his then caught her lips in a long-craved kiss so full of naked heart and the freeing of soul that it bordered on pain.

Tears streamed down her cheeks by the time the kiss ended, yet a smile spread over her face so uncontrollably she could barely breathe. Her hands slid down along his neck, her fingers on his warm flesh. She felt blood pulse through him, alive. "By the gods," her voice shook. "Does this…does this mean…?"

He gently wiped her tears with his thumbs. "It is done." With one hand he lifted her braided hair and held it to his face, breathed in its scent. "Lavender," he said. He loosened the tie at the end and ran his fingers through it to set it free. His own smile widened.

She searched beneath his cloak for his right arm. "Are you well? Are you—?" Through his tunic's sleeve the muscle felt hard, sinewy, the bone whole.

He hushed her. "The break healed fine enough, so did the other wounds." His fingers took in every contour of her face as if she were a magical creature. "How I have missed you—"

She leaned into him, arms tightened, and stopped his words with another kiss so hard her lips burned afterward.

"Claeri…" He slowly broke the embrace and held her hands to his chest. "Will you do something for me, please?"

"Of course." The smile in his voice had lessened, become a bit more serious. "What's wrong?"

"Nothing, nothing is wrong. Ah, would that we could simply disappear into the night, right this moment, but…" He lifted the pouch. The Pendragon insignia sealed it.

"You're a courier? For the high king? In truth?"

He nodded. "Will you walk with me to Ceredig's chambers, like you were leading a stranger?"

"Stranger?" His tone meant he needed to remain anonymous. A hint of laughter touched her. "A stranger?" So close to him, she felt heat rise on her skin in defiance of the cool night air.

His smile spread again and he cupped a hand to her cheek. He kissed her once more, this time gently, with pure enjoyment.

"Come," he said. "We must go."

She watched him collect the helmet and pull it on. By the gods, she wanted to shriek and rejoice like a fanatic—he was there and whole and she could still feel everywhere his hands had touched her. How could she rein in the giddiness?

With her face down and away from the guards the whole distance, she led Marcus to the palace. Her minders, she thought, must not have realized yet she was gone from her chambers. No alarm had been called. But now, what did she care?

At Ceredig's doors, she hung the drab expression of loneliness on her face that she had worn for so long. She told the guard she had come across that day's royal courier in the great hall and he had urgent messages for the king.

The soldier knocked. A pause, then Ceredig called for the guard to enter. The announcement was made.

"So late?" she heard the king query from inside. "Ah, well, tell him to come."

Inside, Marcus stopped in the shadows beyond the fire pit's light. A single oil lamp by the window provided the only other illumination. Claerwen eased in behind him and closed the door after the departing guard.

Ceredig—tired, miffed, and in his old man's mood again—sat by the pit, his face in a frown like a rumpled cloak. "Well, where's the dispatch, man?" he demanded without looking up.

"Forgive my tardiness, Lord Ceredig." Marcus took a step and performed a deep bow. Straight again, he pulled off the helmet, tucked it under his arm, and held out the sealed pouch.

Ceredig's sigh gave away how annoyed he was. "Hmm, thicker than usual. Why so late?" He took the pouch.

Marcus backed into the shadows. "A matter of a lame horse, Lord Ceredig."

The king's eyes opened wide, suddenly alert. Claerwen knew he had recognized Marcus's voice. His face smoothed out; his eyes lifted. Over the course of mere seconds, they came alive and took back some of the enthusiasm they had gradually given up over the years. He rose and turned, took in Marcus from head to muddy boot.

"Octa the Saxon is dead?" Ceredig held up the pouch.

Marcus nodded. "Confirmed dead. Eosa, his kinsman as well. In a spectacular battle. Seven days ago."

Ceredig threw the pouch onto the seat he had vacated. "Why, you ugly old fart of a dog!" He took the helmet from Marcus and snorted. "If I know you, you probably stole this off that bloody Saxon's head himself." He handed it back, clamped his hands on Marcus's shoulders, and gave him a hearty shake. "This is so very fine indeed! Sit, sit here, both of you."

He strode across the room and filled three pewter cups to their rims with mead. The first he shoved into Marcus's hands.

"I can't stay long," Marcus warned and sat on the hearth. He dropped his cloak, gauntlets and the helmet on the floor.

Ceredig ignored the comment. "Well I would say so. I've never seen such a smile on you, lass. King's courier, indeed." He winked and eyed her loose hair.

Face reddened, Claerwen accepted her cup and took a chair next to Marcus.

Ceredig downed a long drink. "And how have you come to know of the Saxon's death so quickly?"

Marcus stared into the golden honey wine swirling in his cup, a half-amused tilt to his mouth. His gaze lifted to Claerwen. "I was there."

"There? Where?" she asked.

"Verulam, or I should say, St. Albans, as it's called now. Octa's war bands had been harassing the town for some time. When Uther arrived, he besieged the place and nearly won it. The walls were breached. Octa seemed unprepared. Some say he and Eosa had grown complacent from having thrown off Uther's army so many times."

Ceredig leaned forward in his chair. "Then the Saxon got smart?"

"Aye. Smart. Angry. It's my understanding that by daybreak the next morning, they had pushed Uther's men out of the town and into the open fields around it. Uther split his bands in an attempt to surround the Saxon."

"Your understanding?" Claerwen asked and glanced at Ceredig. Confusion on his face matched her own. "You said you were there."

Marcus curved his hand around her fingers, and his eyes grew intense, distant. "I was, shortly after midday. The fighting was very fierce. A lot of dead on both sides. But Uther had some fine luck. New warriors arrived to fill the holes in the Britons' dwindling ranks. I saw Octa dragged off his horse. He was crushed in the melee. Eosa was hacked to death shortly after."

Claerwen's throat constricted. Dragged from his horse? Her gaze ran from Marcus to Ceredig and back. Crushed? Seven days ago. The dream and the foreboding of death had been of Octa's demise, and she had sensed Marcus's reaction to it. He must have left immediately to reach Dun Breatann with the news so quickly. She swallowed a mouthful of mead. Had the gods at last opened up to her again? Or were they merely allowing the bond between her and Marcus to flow freely once more?

"Is Verulam where you spent the exile?" she asked.

"No. I was in Breizh—Armorica—across the Narrow Sea. Until about a month ago."

"So far away?" Claerwen sputtered. "That's where Uther sent you?"

Ceredig's grey eyebrows lifted. "Budic's lands?"

"In his court, no less."

"But if Octa was still alive and fighting in Verulam, how were you able to leave Budic's court in time to see the Saxon die? If your terms of exile were as strict as mine…" Claerwen lifted a hand in question.

This time a smile cocked Marcus's lips. "An army was raised in Breizh to fight in Britain—no I didn't raise it myself," he said to Ceredig's conspiratorial look. "I merely…redirected…a few people, just a bit." The smile turned sheepish.

"Ah…hah-hah!" Ceredig threw his head back in laughter. "I can imagine. You and your classic chaos, and in the wake of it, you slipped away with this army. Just one more lowly foot soldier? And when Uther discovered this, it was too late for him to object? Because Octa was dead by then."

Marcus tapped the helmet with the toe of his mud-spattered boot. "He was rather…should I say…ready to cram my arse down a rathole, to be mild?" He grinned, but his smile faded quickly.

Claerwen set down her empty cup and picked up one of the gauntlets. Beneath the mud, flecks of dark reddish-brown were dried into the leather's creases. A strip of thin cloth, its end showing, was wound up inside. The cloth, she knew, was a protection against blisters during heavy swordwork. Her lips flinched. He had fought with Uther.

She felt him watching and looked up. Was he still plagued with the horrible nightmares? His eyes were as haunted as ever. She thought of Ceredig's advice to leave certain questions unasked, but to ignore the war within him was not what she wanted. More than anything, she wished to take that burden from him. If only she could. She dropped the glove.

"I have news, Ceredig." Marcus drained his drink in a few quick swallows. "You need to be prepared."

Ceredig refilled cup. "Your news is always better than any courier's. What do you know?"

Marcus explained Meirchion and Masguid's elaborate plan to raise the war band in Breizh, then how he had manipulated the change in the army's command from the inept *bacaudae* chieftain to the warlord. The warlord, clearly pleased to slash holes in the brothers' plot and Budic's ambitions, had recruited plenty of capable men, especially from Morbihan, even more than expected. They had needed little persuasion to leave the impending Frankish incursions and go home to reclaim their own land. Surprisingly easy, the maneuver carried a price. The brothers, stripped of their soldiers once they struck shore in Britain, were likely to be revenge-bound and with Uther currently strong in the southern regions, Marcus calculated that revenge would strike northward.

"It was a choice of losing Uther to the sons of Rheged then fall to the Saxons under the brothers' disunity," he said. "Or to do anything plausible to keep Uther on the throne and prepare for the backlash we hopefully can control."

Ceredig nodded at the logic.

Marcus set his unfinished cup on the hearthstones. "I have a request of you."

"Name it."

He gazed into Claerwen's face while he spoke to Ceredig. "I need a place for us to be a while." He intertwined his fingers with hers. "But I also need to continue acting as the king's courier. I must leave tonight. Alone."

Claerwen stiffened.

"I can understand why you don't want it known you're out of

exile," Ceredig said.

"It should stay secret as long as possible." Marcus squeezed Claerwen's hand then rose. "At least until I know more of what's happening. I need an escort. Five men. Armed and mounted. An indirect route. Use some of her watchers—you won't need to explain much to them. Once they're done, they can go back to Uther."

"Five?" Ceredig questioned. "Not the usual six?"

"Claerwen will be the sixth instead of a woman under guard. No need for an extra horse or a litter. They can move fast." Marcus grinned at Ceredig's surprised face.

"Ah, always the unexpected. When do you want them, lad? And where?"

"Her chambers. One hour. To leave immediately. I will find a spare uniform for her."

Ceredig nodded. "I know the place for you. A half-day west from here. Very private, very much under my control."

Marcus's eyes narrowed faintly in recognition. "The loch? One of the islands?"

"Ynys Murrin. A small house stands in the middle that can't be seen from the mainland or from the water. Suitable?"

"I know the place."

Ceredig stood and clamped a hand on Marcus's shoulder again. "Consider it done."

Marcus picked up the pouch and crossed to the table. Staying out of the lamplight, he glanced out the window then dumped the pouch's contents. He poked a fingertip at the small rolls. "You will need to dismiss the remainder of Uther's men, according to these orders."

Ceredig examined one of the rolls. "I will wait as long as I dare."

Marcus smiled his thanks and glanced again out the window. "What is it out there? Beltaine?"

"Aye, the high festival that occurs every third year. *Everyone* is coming in."

"Well, a bit of confusion makes for a sleeker departure."

"Ah, can you not visit just a wee bit longer, lad?"

Marcus shook his head and grasped the older man's arms, shook them. "The gods be with you, Ceredig. I wish I could, but…you know the game as well as I."

Claerwen rose when he turned back to her. He took up his cup and quaffed down the last of it then slid his arm around her shoulders, pressed his face to her cheek. "Say goodbye to Ceredig, then return to your chambers. Be ready." He kissed her. "I will see you very soon."

Seconds later, he whisked on the cloak, gauntlets and the helmet, and strode out.

Claerwen grasped the latch on her door with both hands. It was the last time she had to pass the glare of her minders. She bounced into the dark room with steps like a skipping child's. Inside, she twirled in a circle, arms outstretched. After so long, the sense of freedom was shocking, alien and very seductive.

Then the door closed. Claerwen froze. It had never shut on its own before. The window's shutters were wide open. Soft rustling came at her and she sensed the need to flee, but a hand lit on her arm, the sound a light tap. Fingers curved around her wrist, strong, unyielding. Another hand came around from behind and clamped over her mouth.

"It's me," a whisper came, and the scent of leather and horses stirred next to her. The hand on her mouth lifted.

"Marcus?"

The fingers squeezed lightly.

She prodded with her free hand and recognized the feel of the wool tunic, the belt, then his hair, his moustache. The cloak and helmet were missing, but the sword, hidden before, rested in a scabbard across his back. She released her breath. Relieved. Thrilled.

He kept his grip on her arm. "Forgive me, if I've frightened you. I need to know—"

"I have it…here."

"All of it?"

She nodded, the movement in the dark enough to make him understand. His hand released. At the bed, she reached for the torn corner of the mattress. Her fingers brushed strange wool and leather. "What is this?"

"Your disguise."

"Ah…" She collected the gear from all its hiding places. The last piece, the sword on the beam, was the hardest to remove.

"You did well," he said and finished packing it all securely in the oilskin. "Change quickly, they will come for you soon. Bring only what you must. I'll be waiting."

With the gear under his arm, he turned for the window.

She caught his sleeve. "Marcus—"

"I must go—"

"Please, just for a little."

His face almost touched hers. "If I give in now," he murmured, "I'll never be able to stop. I wish, Claeri—"

The ache in his voice perfectly echoed her own wish, a maelstrom to be unleashed from the dark. She locked her mouth onto his, slid her arms around him, dug her fingers into him.

He moaned softly and dropped the bundle onto the bed.

She felt his chest heave, and he indulged in the kiss, his breath in a rush over her face, his hands a cradle for her head and neck. Then he pulled away.

"I must go before it's too late," he whispered. Gear under one arm, he slid onto the window's casement and gave a brief scan outside. He held his free hand out to her, and when she came to him, he touched her cheek once more.

"I will be waiting," he said. Then he drew his legs and the gear through the opening, and dropped away into the darkness.

Alone again, Claerwen felt as if she had been filled to bursting then half of herself torn away. Tears threatened again—if only she could have gone with him right then. She swiped at the wetness under her eyes and pushed aside the moment of selfishness, then doubt crept into her mind. After so long, was he real? Or just another dream to die away? She needed light, needed to see something she could touch to keep the doubt at bay. She groped for her supply of straw, lit a piece in the brazier's coals, and pressed the burning end to her oil lamp's wick.

The escort's uniform lay in a neat pile on the bed. Beneath, a sword, small and light enough for her to carry easily. A dagger and a helmet. Then her gaze was drawn aside.

"Ah, Marcus," she breathed. Tiny flowers of yellow, violet, and white lay on her pillow. Cheerful in the drab room, they were held together with a slender leather tie—the one he had pulled from her hair.

A smile returned to her eyes and she wondered how a man who had faced so much brutality in his life and had to sometimes strike back with equal ferocity to survive could still show such kindness. She picked up the flowers and traced the delicate petals with a fingertip. Heartsease, she recalled the name. Healers made a tisane from it to ease the pain of a broken heart. The uniform and weapons gave her proof of the end to exile. The flowers gave her Marcus.

CHAPTER 24

Ynys Murrin, Strathclyde
Beltaine Eve, AD 476

IN spite of the days of hard, fatiguing travel that had him led to Dun Breatann, Marcus felt good, solid and as strong as ever, perhaps even more so with the years that had added maturity to his body. But the rush of newborn freedom gave him more—the ease and fluidity of movement he had not felt in so long. He cared little that the lines in his face had deepened and grey laced his hair now. Nor did he care that his voice was still rich and deep, though he knew Claerwen would be delighted if he were to sing for her.

That notion brought a brief trace of a smile. He was past thirty, halfway or more through this lifetime. So many years he had defied the odds of survival. How much longer would he have to complete the requirements he had set for himself to accomplish? Or of those the gods required? Push it aside for now, he told himself. Soon enough he and Claerwen would have need to return to reality.

He peered into the darkness beyond the island's shoreline, and the gentle dip of an oar met his ears. It paused as it swung across and dipped again. Ripples of dim light on the water's surface reflected the first hint of dawn. Mist, barely visible, wisped in thin furls just above the water. He backed into a thick patch of ferns and crouched down to wait.

The dip and pause repeated, drew closer. The only other sound was the soft lap of water on the narrow beach. He saw a dim lump that wobbled against the blackness, then a tiny, round, hide-covered coracle surged forward a little with each stroke. Soon, the boat scraped onto the shore.

Regardless of the uniform and helmet that matched the oarsman's, Marcus recognized Claerwen's lithe, graceful figure when she climbed out of the boat. The man with her, one of the escorts from Dun Breatann, passed several leather pouches to her. Without a word or even a salute, he re-launched the coracle and disappeared into the dark.

Silence drew in. Marcus stood. Claerwen waited until the man was well away from the shore. Then she loosened the helmet and removed it with care, as if quick movement would disturb the quiet. Her tawny-brown hair, braided and coiled around her head under the helmet, unwound and fell to her hips.

Every move she made stirred fascination inside Marcus. He stepped out of the ferns, strode a few paces towards her. What could he say after so many years that would sound appropriate? A jest? Some speech meant to be eloquent? Just her name?

She turned around. Her face glowed softly under the dawning sky. Her eyes found him, traced over him, and he knew she was taking in that he had changed into simple clothing, shaved the thin beard and left his thick moustache. She had sensed his presence. She saw everything, felt everything—always.

Caught in his fascination, Marcus barely heard the helmet drop from her hand. She was running, but he never heard her steps. She was there, her arms around him, her hands in a fierce grip on his tunic. Gods, she felt so fine, so alive in his arms.

Many minutes passed.

Dawn speared pale purple over the mountains to the east. Marcus lifted Claerwen's chin. "The house should be back that way," he said and tipped his head towards the length of the island. A track led from the shore and wound into shallow treeless hills. A section of woodland rose beyond.

Her eyes flicked in the direction he indicated. "You're exhausted," she said. Her fingers brushed the dusty circles beneath his eyes. "How long has it been since you slept?"

He smiled. "I don't remember." From how she was bundled in his embrace, Marcus knew she needed rest as much as he did. The fatigue in her voice, in spite of the reunion's thrill, was plain.

They retrieved their gear and started up the track. From the first rise, they saw the small dry stone house with its sod roof leaning into the wooded hill behind it. Their silence deepened and Marcus matched her stride down into a hollow between the rise and the house. Halfway across, he slowed then came to a halt.

"Claeri. Wait."

She came round. "What's wrong?"

He dropped his gear. "Nothing." He took her pouches, tossed them aside as well. "Nothing at all." He laid a hand along her cheek, and his thumb lightly stroked her skin, a gesture he had first indulged in on the night they had met all those years ago. It came so easily, as if of its own accord, as if his hand itself remembered.

"I don't know how you knew to meet me in the great hall," he said, "but it was a blessing."

She shivered and he edged closer. Her arms slid up around his neck. She moved against him in a gentle sway, and he turned with her, slowly, in a circle. Not quite a dance, it felt more like an ethereal ritual set to music, the melody so sacred the human ear could not hear it. Spellbound, he could not break from her green-blue eyes.

Claerwen took the hand he held to her cheek and kissed his palm. "I didn't know," she said. Her swaying steps slowed, and she tugged at the buckles on his baldric and belt and loosened them, shrugged the weapons and gear from him.

Her face, so close, seemed trancelike, and her answer slipped past him. It was the morning of Beltaine Eve, and the thought crossed his mind that the hollow, wide and shallow, was shaped like a grail, the supreme symbol of renewal. Was it offering them the renewal of their lifetimes? The holiday's timing was pure coincidence. Or, was it? Any more than her knowing when and where to find him? Fire in the head, he was sure.

His breath quickened. For now, nothing else in the world mattered. He could no longer help himself, and when her lips met his in kisses so uncontrollable he thought he would burst, he knew Claerwen cared nothing if they ever reached the house.

Clothing followed the gear, pulled from each other and scattered with no thought. Marcus collapsed onto his knees and took her down with him onto the grass. Hands to flesh, at first reverential, skin more precious than silk or silver, luscious was the word that came to him as his fingers roved over her, cupped her breasts, traced gentle lines to those most intimate places he had craved to touch for so long. He loved the feel of her skin pressed against his nakedness, her hands everywhere on him. Thank the gods she had been kept safe all this time, he prayed silently. The heat rose within him and he surrendered to a force they were both incapable of and utterly unwilling to stop. He sank into her and loved her with all of his soul.

Curled together with Claerwen in the warmth of their cloaks, Marcus woke hours later, late in the afternoon. He stroked her hair, loose from its braid in the tumble of their lovemaking. She wriggled and settled once more with her head on his arm. Her hand smoothed the hair on his chest and he watched her fingers move across him, from one side to the other and back, then creep towards a red and black indentation in his right shoulder.

"That's where the tree hit me," he said. "Or rather, I hit the tree."

Her eyes flicked from the scar to his face.

He grinned. His wish was to spend at least a fortnight alone with her, and he had no desire to ruin the mood with a long exchange of news. But with his comment, the latch on the past was already lifted. Now he had to step up to the threshold.

"Uther's physician forced the broken limb on through, in the same direction it went in," he said and sat up. He showed her the matching scar on his back. "Less bleeding that way, of course. He ran a red-hot iron in behind to seal the wound all the way through."

Claerwen grimaced. "Did you faint?"

"I don't remember much. After, they told me that I gritted my teeth, grinned, and toasted the physician with a bloody lot of mead."

Her breath expelled, not truly in laughter, but her eyes brightened. "That does sound like you."

He shrugged. "The mead likely sent my senses beyond the stars as much as the wounds." He twisted one way then the other, grabbing for pieces of his clothing within reach. "We'd best get on to the house. Rain's coming. And I'm hungry. And I need to go for a piss.

Do you see my loincloth?"

"You mean to say you've taken up modesty after all these years?" The smile spread over her face, sudden mischief in it.

He burst out in laughter, long and hearty, a laugh free and alive. By the gods it felt so fine. "Well, I suppose not," he said and slipped out of the cloak's folds. He strolled for the hill behind them where a bank of ferns grew and retrieved his garments on the way. The sound of her giggles followed his naked backside.

Dressed, he returned to find Claerwen nearly finished donning her own shifts and tunic instead of the escort's clothing. He collected the pouches for the walk to the house. Arms loaded, he straightened. "Can you—"

A swift change in Claerwen's eyes from happy mischief to shock stopped him. She was staring at him then took up a heavy lock of his hair. The shock dissolved into tears.

Marcus dropped the gear and grasped her arms. "Why do you cry?"

"Grey… There's grey in your hair. And it's not ash, it's not a disguise."

He smiled and smudged away a tear. "It's been that way a while now. No matter. No?" Less than two years younger than he was, she was exactly as he remembered—no dullness in her hair, no thickening of her waist. He imagined she would be just the same in another twenty years. Even longer.

She drew her fingers through the full length of his hair. It was as thick as ever, from temple to shoulders. "I…oh, you'll think I'm foolish, but…I wanted to see that first grey hair. Like…like a child's first step. I wanted so much to spend every day growing old with you."

Her words caught him off-guard. He had known emotion would run high and rampant for both of them, but he was astonished at how easily tears filled his own eyes. He had missed her, but now the swing from euphoric laughter to sorrow over a lost cherished milestone struck him hard. He embraced her, his face buried in her neck.

Time drifted. The clouds thickened and marched in from the west, shoulder-to-shoulder from the distant sea, and though sunset was still hours away, a premature darkness spread over the sky.

The island reminded Marcus of a lush, green blanket dumped in disarray on the floor. The half where he stood with Claerwen was devoid of even a single tree. In contrast, the opposite side was thickly wooded.

The first raindrops struck. "Come," he said, reluctant to let loose of her, but the rising wind told him the sky would disgorge torrents of rain within minutes. With the pouches and gear shouldered, they quickly crossed the meadow and reached the house as the storm began in earnest.

The tiny, disused house was little more than a *hafod*, a summer house normally used by herders. Made of dry stone and a sod roof, its only furnishing was a fire pit. Dead windblown grass and bits of twigs were scattered over the dirt floor and thrust into every crevice. By nightfall they had cleared the debris, settled in with a fire burning evenly and had shared their first meal together.

In the narrow, box-like entrance, Marcus sat against one side, comfortable in only breeches and a loose tunic. He watched firelit raindrops fall just past the edge of the roof, darkness beyond.

A wineskin to his lips, he drank. He held the mead on his tongue and rolled the cool, sweet honey wine from front to back to front again. Thank the gods, he prayed, the island's contours shielded the sound of the loch's rippling waters. Though nothing like the relentless roar of the sea, he still had no desire to hear the movement of water. Damn, he hated the sea. He trickled the wine down his throat, lifted the skin and drank again.

His thoughts swayed at will. Uther had finally accomplished his goal: Octa the Saxon was dead at last. So was Eosa. But now, would another man come to the forefront and lead the Saxon goal of expansion across British soil? Or would chaos ensue with the leaderless foreigners desperate to keep their conquests and settlements? And what of Uther? Would he find it easier to control them now? Would he gain more support from his own people? Or would the fighting grow worse?

Marcus closed his eyes. The moodiness had reasserted itself over the last hours. He was not drunk, not in the least, only dull and tired, the same as he'd been in Breizh, where he had felt like leaden boots were pulling him down, step by step, into the dankest of places. He was free now, he told himself. Claerwen was with him. But his mind kept winding back through the convoluted journey of his life. The euphoria that had swept him earlier was gone.

On a gust of wind, streamers of hair slapped lightly at his face. Claerwen's hair, flowing in the breeze. "Do you know what a Valkyrie is?" her voice asked.

How long had he sat there drifting, he wondered? He opened his eyes. With scarcely enough room for one to sit, she had taken the opposite side of the doorway and had settled between his bare feet. Knees up, eyes closed, she breathed in the rain-fresh air.

"A Valkyrie? Why?"

"Someone told me I had the heart of a Valkyrie. I don't know what it means, if it was an insult or a compliment."

A near-smile perked one side of Marcus's mouth but his mood was too heavy to lift. "A compliment, I suppose. Valkyries are female battle spirits who conduct dead warriors from the field to a place called Valhalla, a kind of Otherworld, where the dead are honored. Unlike us, Northmen, Franks, Saxons, all of them, invoke their gods' names in prayers and curses."

"They're not forbidden to speak their gods' names? How strange."

His gaze moved back to the dark and the raindrops. His smile faded. "Why are you asking this?"

"Curious. You've barely spoken since this morning."

"I was thinking of Uther." He grimaced and drank again. "I was his political prisoner."

Claerwen's face squinted up and loosened again. Her mouth moved to echo the word "prisoner," but she could not quite push out the sound.

"Exile was merely a beneficent name," Marcus said. "In truth, I was his property. If I had been bait to lure Octa into a trap, I would not have been sent to Breizh. Rather, I was Uther's goods, a thing of value he could use in a bargain. For peace, a trade for a hostage, or for some other reason, I would have been handed over to the Saxon."

Claerwen sat upright. "How could he do that to you? After all you've done to save his life and keep him in power?"

"It's not unusual. I'm sure he has others hidden away like I was." He raised a finger and waggled it sarcastically. "At hand to be cast into the fire of his political needs."

"And now?" she asked. "Doesn't he recognize you helped bring him the soldiers he needed? He must have acknowledged the end of exile if he allowed you act as his courier."

Marcus stared up at the roof's dripping edge. "I'm a spy, Claerwen. I know too much. I hold secrets that Uther must control."

"But...shouldn't Uther want to protect you at all cost—" Her face lost its sparkle. "By the gods, instead of protecting you, could he go so far as to have you killed to keep those secrets from falling to the wrong people?"

Marcus nodded slowly. "How much he may or may not believe in my loyalty makes no difference. That is exactly what could happen. He has to protect himself first."

"Then, in truth," she said, "you're still a prisoner. Only there are no walls."

"In truth, we are both prisoners." He leaned to her, touched his lips to her mouth. "At least, if I must be a prisoner of sorts, I've much finer company now."

Her eyes softened, but her expression changed little. She reached a hand to his left knee.

Marcus watched her fingers move in familiar patterns to ease the constant ache in his knee. How easily she slipped into the old habit. He began to count in his mind how many other gestures they had taken up again without thinking—favorite words of affection, a simple touch, a long-forgotten jest, the depth of intimacy between them. A wistful smile broke into his brooding.

"In spite of all the commotion in Dun Breatann," Claerwen said, "you brought flowers, just to let me know I wasn't dreaming. No one else would have taken time for such kindness."

His toes teased against her leg and slid up under the hem of her skirts. "I don't want to think on Dun Breatann, or Breizh, or any of that right now."

"Neither do I." Claerwen moved closer. "Thank the gods you switched places. That's enough to know for now." She kissed him.

Long and slow, sumptuous, the kiss gradually ended. His eyes lifted. The renewed contentment in them dimmed. "Switch places?"

"Aye…to be in the great hall at midnight. In that disguise."

He frowned. "How do you mean 'disguise'? I *was* Uther's courier." He watched confusion claim her face.

"But it *was* a disguise." She stared into his eyes, her fingers suspended from their task. "Wasn't it? It had to be. So no one would recognize you, and so I would think you were—"

He watched the confusion gain ground. Her other hand went to her chest and pressed there. When had he seen her do that before?

"Think I was who, Claeri? You're not making sense."

"You said seven days, from Verulam?"

"Seven with good mounts, which I had, courtesy of Uther."

"Then, you couldn't possibly— While the arrangement was—"

The distress in her face set off warnings in Marcus. Then he recalled her words from the night before—she had *not* known to meet him in the great hall. He had ignored the response. Now it clanged in his mind. He took hold of her hand that rested on his knee. "Claerwen? You were expecting someone else. Who?"

He watched her eyes dart back and forth. Fear was in them, deep and profound. Fear of his reaction? Or fear of the man she was supposed to meet? And that her other hand remained tucked over her heart, disturbed him. When, when he had he seen that?

"Who, Claerwen?"

Finally she let go of her breath. "Handor."

Steel-like coldness gripped Marcus in the gut. Anger, long simmering throughout the exile, flashed into rage. He contained it as quickly as it had come and returned it to a rumbling boil. "Tell me."

The words of explanation rushed from her, of how she had discovered the assassin was among Octa's elite warriors watching the fortress, that she had used one of the slaves to arrange the meeting, and the trade she had hoped the assassin could not refuse.

Marcus stared into her face after she had finished, speechless for longer than he expected of himself. "You were actually going confront him?"

She nodded.

"Damn," he said softly. "You realize he would have come back once he found the trail was false."

"I know. There was no time to think of anything better."

Relentlessly, he studied her. In the past he had seen her confront other dangerous people rather than run. But her logic did make sense. Running, in this instance, could have been even more dangerous if Handor had isolated her outside the fortress. Hiding might have sufficed, but not necessarily. And to have Ceredig provide additional guards might have served to concentrate them in one place, only to have them diverted away.

Then he saw a tiny red mark on her neck, shaped like a shallow crescent. He touched her skin. It was a scar. "What is this?" he asked. More were next to it. "Who did this?"

"When I ran away I—or tried to—"

"Ran away? How could you—? Go on."

"Around the time of the first Midwinter. It was Handor—he was outside the fortress. Ceredig's soldiers came in time, but he eluded them. It wasn't until just before Beltaine, this year, that he came back."

Another shock of rage shot through Marcus.

"You can tell me how stupid I was," she said.

"Would it help?"

"Ceredig made certain I understood. He left me chained in my room for days. I never tried again."

"Ceredig chained you?"

She nodded.

He turned his face away. "I never thought it would come to that," he muttered.

Her eyes came up. "What did you say?"

He shook his head. Control, he told himself and tried to imagine what she could possibly offer Handor that the man would seriously consider. "The only thing Handor ever seemed to want—besides my head—was a woman called Tangwen. Did she have something to do with this trade?"

Claerwen met his gaze. "Not directly. I was going to give away a secret, give him the identity of someone else who knew where she was, to make him look for that person."

The stall in her words made him wary. "Who?"

"You won't like it."

"Tell me."

She hesitated then plunged on. "I was going to offer him the Iron Hawk's identity."

Marcus's left eyebrow lifted. His posture shifted, halfway between the slumping of shoulders and the stiffening of disbelief. He sat back against the doorway.

"Of course I was going to lie," she quickly added.

"Of course you were," Marcus echoed. To suggest the Iron Hawk's taking of a captive was almost as ludicrous as Claerwen being the Iron Hawk, he thought. But given the circumstances, the false Iron Hawk's brief involvement near Caer Luguvalos made her reasoning sound. Slyness narrowed his eyes. "And who might be the one you would have told him is the Iron Hawk?"

"Meirchion Gul."

He sputtered in short bursts of laughter. Then euphoria returned with an all-out guffaw.

"Oh, that's good! Too good! Can you imagine Meirchion Gul as the Iron Hawk?" More laughter overtook him and he slid backward off the doorframe until he lay flat on the floor.

"Not plausible to have chosen him, I suppose," Claerwen mumbled when Marcus began to calm.

"Plausible enough," he said. He sat up and grinned into her face. "What a nice bit of irony. Wouldn't he like to be thought of as such a warrior?"

"But what of Handor? I reneged on the meeting. By now he must know I'm gone and the exile is over. Then he'll know you're here somewhere. He'll be furious."

"Let him be furious," Marcus said. He pulled Claerwen close and savored the return of humor, of happiness, even if it were only fleetingly. He needed her to help him hold onto it as long as he could. She was his sanity. With his mouth pressed to hers, he unhooked the doorway's leather drape covering and let it fall into place.

The Iron Hawk's sword gleamed sullenly in the sunrise as Marcus examined it and tested its balance. It was still perfectly serviceable though it needed a good polish and the edges sharpened. A full two-handed sword, it was a fine weapon indeed, the best of all he had ever forged. He tossed aside the scabbard and positioned his hands properly around the hilt.

Handor. The image of the assassin with his hands around Claerwen's neck had plagued him throughout the night, over and over, along with the sneering face, the effigy, the words spoken in Saxon, the shadows that hung from the old roof, the smell of—

He swore and took the stance of a warrior. In silence he began to trace the steps of swordplay. The practice with wooden sticks in Breizh had proven invaluable and had provided him with the strength and honing of skill needed for Verulam, but he had felt stale in those few hours of battle. He needed to regain his full skills—and soon.

The storm had cleared in the night and left the turf wet and slippery, though the air promised warmth for the day. Dressed only in breeches, Marcus ran through the long routine with smooth agility. He relished the weight of the weapon in his thick hands. After more than an hour, he worked one of his favorite variations. With the blade upright, he whipped it back and forth so fast it could both mesmerize and taunt an opponent. Which way would it fall? Which way would it slash? He plunged the tip deep into the earth.

"Damn you, Handor," he spit. He stared with vehemence at the pierced ground. Sweat trickled down his temples and glistened on his skin, and while he caught his breath, he bowed his head, but not in prayer. Gods, it was all still there, as much as ever.

The sense that someone watched nagged at him and he looked up. Barefoot, Claerwen stood in front of the *hafod*, astonishment in her gaze. He had never noticed she'd come outside. His teeth were clenched so tightly he had to consciously loosen his jaw.

"It's never so accurate in battle," he said and walked to the wall of the house. A tunic, belt, wineskin and a small gourd-shaped flask lay below the overhanging roof. The other sword he had carried since leaving Breizh, a hand-and-a-half weapon, leaned against the wall.

"Take this," he said and held the smaller sword by the blade just under the cross-guard. He extended the hilt towards her.

Her hand reached but stalled midway.

"Here. Hold it like this." He positioned her hands, the right behind the cross-guard, the left tucked in behind. He turned the handle until the blade was perpendicular to the earth.

"This hand and arm," he touched her right wrist, "is stronger and is used to guide and to provide the main strength. This hand," he moved his fingers to her left wrist, "gives balance and additional strength. If you need to let go with one, let it be the left if possible, so you still have your main strength with the right arm. Then, move up smoothly, like so, to block." With his hand on her arm, he guided her motion.

He swung around and snatched up the Iron Hawk's sword. In the warrior's stance again, he held the weapon at an angle midway between horizontal and vertical. "Try it," he said. "Use the flat of the blade to stop me."

In imitation, she clicked her weapon against his in a brief salute. Slowly, carefully, she matched his moves as he demonstrated each. The blades arced up and crashed together, then retreated, right to left, then left to right. The rhythmic speed gradually increased.

"Harder!" Marcus shouted. The weapons clanged. "Harder! As hard as you can!" He guided the swordplay across the grass, but he could feel Claerwen's strength wane under the strain of each hit. She grimaced and swung again. Her eyes closed with the shock and the blades rang harshly. Marcus gave a last sweep and knocked the sword out of her hands. It thudded onto the grass.

"That's enough," he said and retrieved the smaller weapon. "Not bad."

Claerwen rubbed her stinging fingers. "You'll never make a swordsman of me." She held her slender hand to one of his, palm to palm. His was nearly twice the size.

He wiped his face with his arm. "They're big from smithing rather than swordwork, though I haven't done smithing in years." He leaned both swords against the wall.

"You're worried," she said, "else you would not be practicing at dawn. And you would not want to teach me this." She went to him again, and pushed back the hair that fell into his eyes. "You had another nightmare this morning."

His lips flattened. "As bad as ever."

"Because of my foolishness, I've disturbed your memories."

He frowned.

She touched the scars on her neck. "Whenever Handor is mentioned, the anger rises in you like high tide."

He shut his eyes for a moment and swore. He had wanted to spend days and nights with her with no interruptions, no worries, no thoughts of exile or war or anything else. But he knew himself well enough—he would never let go of the anger until all was resolved. If he could even let go of it then…

He donned the tunic and belt then tried to empty his mind to relieve the anger, the bitterness, the anguish of the memories that refused to leave his dreams alone. Automatically, he reached for the wineskin but passed it over for the smaller flask. The sharp scent of distilled grain rose from it when he pulled out the stopper. He drank, the vapors like thunder inside his head, the golden liquid a line of flames from his throat all down into his belly.

"I didn't mean to— Marcus—"

He turned back to her. "No, Claerwen." He pressed two fingers against her lips. By the light, how he had missed her compassion. He ran a hand in one long stroke from her shoulder to her hip. The smooth curve of her shape was warm through her thin overtunic and shift.

She sniffed at the flask. "*Uisge beatha*? From Ceredig?"

He held it out in offering.

Her nose wrinkled and she shook her head. "There is so much anger in you."

"If I could only rectify…" He walked a few steps away and stared across the lumpy green of the island.

"Rectify what?" Claerwen said after a long pause. She stood beside him again.

Once more he had missed her approach. "Everything. Hywel Gwodryd's death. All the wasted time. And Handor. Most of all, Handor."

"Guilt? Why guilt for any of this?"

Her green-blue eyes bored into him. Now he had to talk. She would never let it rest. Neither would he.

"In the last weeks before I left Breizh," he said, "I learned two people witnessed the murder Meirchion committed. One was the woman called Tangwen."

Then the words began to spill in earnest. In truth, he thought he would explode if he kept quiet any longer. He explained his friendship with the man he knew only as Blaez, the premise of the Frank's exile, and the warlord's advice to ask about the woman.

"Blaez was the other witness," Marcus said. "He had gone to Rheged to find Tangwen. She was his wife."

"His wife? Did he come back with you?"

"No. After Octa was found dead I sent a message to Blaez, so he'd know he's been freed. I expect him to come—soon. From the way he spoke, he must have cared very much for her." He took another swig from the flask, plugged it, and tucked it inside his tunic.

"Why Meirchion didn't just kill them both to hide the murder, I don't understand." Marcus strode back to retrieve the Iron Hawk's weapon. "I think they must be too important. At least now we know why Meirchion's been hunting her. And why everyone else as well. I'd wager those Saxons wanted to ransom her to Meirchion."

Marcus lifted the sword and he traced the simple, graceful lines of the long blade once more, along the tapered edges, up the fuller in its center to the steel cross-guard and the black iron hawk on the pommel. *Y Gwalch Haearn* will need to flush out Handor, he thought. Then—

Claerwen's hand clamped around his arm. "No. That's not it. Not all of it."

"What do you mean?"

Her eyes dug into him again. Marcus knew she was testing his mood, if he were ready to listen, or if he were still too sullen, grim, preoccupied.

"There is more you need to know," she said. "The three Saxons did not want her for ransom. And Meirchion—he has another reason to find her."

He struck the sword into the ground again. "How do you know this?"

"The man's life you saved in Uxelodunum—he told me."

Marcus folded his hands over the pommel. "Go on."

Claerwen told him of how Beornwulf had come to Dun Breatann, her fear of him that had caused her to run, and the subsequent discovery that he was not dangerous at all. She detailed what he had told her of Tangwen's parentage, her training as a priestess, the sea-warrior's cult, and how the doomed quest Beornwulf and his cousins had embarked upon had been based solely on a lie they had overheard Octa tell Handor.

"And this lie—it prompted Handor to act as Octa's assassin?" Marcus questioned. "Then that was true. I had guessed there was some way Octa had manipulated Handor. When I caught Handor he wouldn't talk, except to blame me for Hywel's death."

"Blame you? Whatever for, when he knows Meirchion killed his father? Or doesn't he know this?"

"Oh, he does. By his reasoning, if I hadn't been brought to Caer Luguvalos to foil Meirchion's uprising, Hywel wouldn't have tried to talk to me and Meirchion wouldn't have needed to kill Hywel to stop him."

"Does it even make sense? If Meirchion murdered Handor's father, how could they be allies?"

"Allies by mutual extortion, not trust," Marcus said. "Handor could turn Meirchion over to Uther for the murder. But Meirchion could turn Handor in for having broken Octa out of prison. What's the other reason why you think Meirchion hunts Tangwen?"

"I can't prove it—yet—but I think that woman knows where Macsen's sword is. Everything points that way, ever since the vision years ago."

"You never said anything then."

"I didn't understand until it was too late. On the day you went back into Caer Luguvalos alone, while I waited with the horses, she was there, Marcus. She must have been at the farmstead and followed us—or me—because of the fire. She has it, like I do, and I think she was the source of it that I felt there."

Claerwen detailed the confrontation.

"And she ran when you guessed her identity?" Marcus asked when she finished. "And then she came back and hit you?"

Claerwen sloughed it off as inconsequential. "She was frightened, but I'm sure she knows where Macsen's sword is. It was *her* eyes in the vision, *her* eyes staring at the sword. *And* she knows what or who Excalibur is."

Marcus scraped his fingers through his hair. Claerwen's characterization of a harsh, unkind woman did not match that of Blaez's wife in the least. But many years had passed. Much could have changed. "Why didn't you tell me?" he asked.

"I tried to, but you were so intent on following Handor, I couldn't stop you."

"Damn Handor. If I would have listened—" He lifted his face to the sky. "Damn my own bloody stubbornness," he shouted in defiance at the gods. He tore the Iron Hawk's sword from the earth and started for the house.

Claerwen ran after him. "Marcus, not the Iron Hawk. Not that way." Halfway to the house, she caught up.

He halted. To him, she looked like her throat was clogged with more that needed to be said. He trusted Claerwen's judgment. And he needed her. Gods of the earth, he needed her. But Handor had hurt her. That man could not be stopped with fine words or subtle stealth. "With him, I don't know any other way," Marcus spit.

"No," she whispered. "A lake. In the north. A standing stone like an anvil. Fire in the head."

She was gripping his arm with fingers that quivered, like they were so full of power and spirit that she could not quite control them. Watching her, Marcus felt as if he could almost see the parts she named fall into place, one after the other.

"Beornwulf said Tangwen was hidden in a women's colony," she said. Her fingers tightened. "Those that teach the old ways are usually near lakes or stones that are sacred. Like Ynys Witrin—the Isle of Avalon. Marcus, Tangwen must still be in Rheged. I can feel it."

He gazed steadily into her eyes. The fire was not showing itself, but he sensed it lurked just below the surface of her soul. Then the bond between them reached out and encircled him. His mind suddenly disengaged from the anger, and he dropped the sword on the grass.

"Just as I was leaving with the war band," he said, "Blaez told me where the colony was—in a thick grove next to a lake. Near the border between Strathclyde and Rheged."

Claerwen let go and covered her face with her hands. "We're leaving already, aren't we?" she asked between her fingers. "For Rheged?"

Marcus gave no answer. Instead, he drew her into a fierce embrace. In the way her body molded to his, he sensed a degree of relief in her, but fear as well. Over her shoulder, he glared at the warrior's sword.

CHAPTER 25

On the Strathclyde-Rheged Border
Summer, AD 476

CLAERWEN watched the morning mist drift. The first daylight illuminated it in pale shades of yellow and lavender. Wispy one moment, thick the next, the vapor rose and fell in the capricious breeze. A swath was creeping down into the wooded hollow she and Marcus had chosen for a camp the night before and was filling it with an oppressive, sticky dampness.

Since leaving the island, they had retrieved a pair of horses from one of Ceredig's outposts and traveled south, almost to the border with Rheged. Days had passed—she had lost count—but with each that went by, Marcus became more taciturn, more dark in his moodiness. She had hoped he would shake it off once they started on the quest again. Instead, it worsened.

She held out a deadwood stick with a sizzling trout spitted on it and watched his eyes narrow. Their camp lay above a stream rich in fish. Tired of dried meat, she had relished the opportunity of catching fresh trout.

He took the stick, then the first bite. A mild scowl followed.

"I know. You hate fish," she said. Now she wished she had chosen differently. "At least it's cooked." She lifted a second trout from over the fire.

Minutes of silence followed.

"Do you think Myrddin could have been sent into exile as well?" Claerwen hoped again for a change in mood.

Marcus chewed, swallowed and drowned his mouth with mead.

"Myrddin? Why?"

"Because no one has seen or heard from him for so long."

He shrugged. "Possibly." He looked up, his right eye squinted. "What of the child you said Uther and his woman would have by that first Midwinter we were gone? Did this ever come true?"

"Nothing…official."

He finished the last bite of fish and hurled the spit into the fire. "Rumors?"

She nodded. "Dim like shadows on an overcast day. The only word in Dun Breatann—this came from one of Ceredig's spies—was that a courier had been seen delivering a tiny scroll to the high king a day after Midwinter that year. He was off chasing Saxons as usual. Except for a faint smile when he read it, he shared it with no one. Uther's been phenomenally tight-lipped."

"He didn't return to Winchester, or Tintagel?"

"Not that anyone knows. When the message arrived, it was believed Ygerna—oh, remember? She's calling herself Igraine now, I always forget. Igraine was still in Tintagel. A month later she was in Winchester. She seemed exhausted and deeply distressed, but she had no child with her."

"Distressed the child had died?"

"Or was taken from her," Claerwen suggested, "for safe-keeping?"

"Did Uther ever marry her?"

"It's assumed—mere hours after Gorlois's death."

"Hours? Hmm. He was absolutely convinced he and the woman were…destined, if you will…to be together. And no word of Myrddin?"

"Nothing. Silence. That's why I wonder if Uther exiled him. Perhaps for his role in helping him get into Tintagel? If he forced you to be a political prisoner after all you've done, he might have done the same to Myrddin."

"The Enchanter in chains." A sardonic smile twisted Marcus's lips. "Indeed."

"You'd like to see that, wouldn't you?" Claerwen knew she would never change his mind about Myrddin. Regardless of how alike their goals were, each man bristled at the mention of the other.

Always. They simply disliked each other.

She watched Marcus reach for a piece of bannock that warmed on one of the campfire's rocks. Dark red scars from the shackles with which Vortigern had bound him showed below the hems of his sleeves. Shackles and chains. Shackles on his wrists, his legs and neck; shackles on his mind.

"When I told you Ceredig had chained me," she said, "you mumbled something about not thinking it would come to that. What did you mean?"

His smile disappeared.

The change was so abrupt, uncertainty set off pangs in her gut. She probably should not have asked, considering his foul mood, but it was too late to take it back.

"Marcus? What do you know about the chains?"

He threw a dropped fish bone into the campfire. His nose flared at the smell.

She caught his hand when he reached for another bone. "You've become so difficult to talk to these last days. Did you know Uther was going to send me to Dun Breatann? *Before* he sent you away?"

He sighed harshly. "I did."

"He told you?"

"Claerwen." He swung his head back and forth, eyes downcast. "Uther dictated the terms of my 'exile.' You know the true circumstances of that now. But he allowed me to choose where you would be sent—"

"You knew? All that time? You knew where I was? Why couldn't I know where you were? Did Ceredig know?"

"No. He only followed instructions."

"Instructions?" She remembered the parchments handed to Ceredig. "How could Uther be so unfair? Why—"

"Stop, Claerwen. It's not his fault." He squeezed her wrist lightly then let go. "I wrote the terms of your exile."

Claerwen stared at him. Cramps snaked up inside her all the way to her throat. Unable to catch her breath, she dropped her gaze from him. She remembered the shock on Ceredig's face when he read the sheets of parchment, then he had quickly hidden them inside his tunic. Not an inkling had come from him. Even in her rebellion against the terms, she had never questioned who had written them.

"I placed you under Ceredig's guardianship," he said softly, "because Uther couldn't possibly give you the refuge you needed. All I ever wanted to do was protect you. To make you feel safe."

Claerwen barely heard him. Only the word "safe" stuck. She had never felt safe.

"I knew you might try to escape," he went on. "Because of that, Ceredig was the only one I could trust to keep you alive."

"Not even letters?" She hated the sound of her own words, weak and scratchy with hurt.

"Not even letters. There could be no trail, no notion that anyone could follow. I could not let you come with me or let you go home, it was too dangerous. Because of Handor."

She heard him get to his feet.

"I never expected it to last so bloody long," he finished.

"You changed the course of an army, but you could not have changed anything else?" Claerwen immediately regretted her sharpness. Her face reddened. "I'm sorry…that wasn't fair."

She rose and started to climb the hill in search of clearer air. She needed to walk, to go somewhere, to be alone. Near the top, she broke free of both trees and mist. At the hill's crest, she breathed deeply of the soft sky.

Morning birds sang in the grass. To the southwest, the mist gradually dissipated and revealed more fells like the one she stood atop, one neatly tucked after the other. Patches of trees grew amongst them like deep green paint that had run down into cracks. In the distance, the patches expanded into true forestland. An animal, too far away to identify, was the only creature that moved. It traversed the face of one fell.

Or was it not an animal? Claerwen stared. Dark, its motion seemed to flow like a bird in flight, except it was too slow.

"Claerwen?" Marcus called from below.

The mist swirled towards the figure. Likewise, the birds' singing lightened, the sound seeming to drift in the same manner. A second figure, smaller and in white, chased after the first. A child? Claerwen blinked for more clarity, but the distance was too great.

"Claerwen?" Marcus called again, closer.

The strange creature disappeared in newly gathering mist. The childlike figure followed. Numbing quiet filled Claerwen. Her senses had clogged, the relief gone again. Dull pain ached between her eyes and she rubbed her forehead. Had the fire flashed through her and left nothing but discomfort in its wake?

"Claeri? What is it?"

Marcus stood a few short steps from her, a hand held out and concern on his face. She opened her mouth but turned back in the direction she had been staring, unable to voice what she had seen. Had it been real? Or was it another vision? And why did it bother her so much?

"By the light," Marcus said quietly. "Look at that." He grabbed her arm and turned her to the left. "Look…there. Quickly, before the mist moves again."

She stepped forward then to the side for a better view. Her skin tingled and the ache in her face grew. He had not noticed the two creatures she had seen. Instead, he was pointing to a dip between the hills. A long, narrow stretch of woodland filled it for several miles. Water sparkled through gaps in the trees.

Familiarity overwhelmed her. She had seen that lake, the trees on its banks especially thick on the opposite side. Oak, rowan, birch, hawthorn, alder—all of their scents mingled with the earth's pungency. She could see, feel, smell it all in her memory better than she could across the distance before her. The water's spirit, in the form of a woman thrusting Macsen's sword into brilliant sunlight, was close enough in her mind to touch.

Claerwen felt the blood drain from her face, yet she continued to stare, her eyes wide, stark, memories of the vision alive inside her.

"This is it, isn't it?" Marcus said. "I knew we were close—"

"I will go now," she interrupted. "Before the mist lifts again."

He came round, his eyes cold and hard. "I'm going with you."

"They won't let you enter the grove. They'll turn us away if you come with me and we'll never have another chance. I must do this alone."

"It's not safe. Not from how you described Tangwen's reaction about this…thing, this Excalibur. She's dangerous. You can't trust her."

"I know, but she and I share the bond of the fire. If the gods want Macsen's sword to be found, and if she knows anything, she must reveal it. Perhaps not now, perhaps not to me, but perhaps in a way she won't even realize. The notion will grow in her until she can bear it no longer."

"I trust you," he said. "I trust the fire. But I do not like what it does to you."

"We had already decided this, Marcus. If I'm to pose as a woman who wants to join the colony, you cannot come with me."

"Think of a different way."

"You said you wanted to listen to the local gossip at the inn Blaez told you about. If it's only a ways up from the lake like he said, that's not so far. Take my horse with you and do that while I look for Tangwen. Then we'll meet here, an hour before sunset."

He sighed and rubbed his eyes with the heels of his hands. "Better would be closer down, between the inn and the grove. There." He pointed down the slope. "Looks like a lot of reeds there on the other side of the river, where that stream meets it. Would be a good place to hide."

"Then you agree to this?"

"No. I don't. I like it not at all."

Claerwen turned away. He was being overprotective. Fine enough, she thought, but if she wasted this opportunity, another one might never come. She marched back to the camp. He followed.

"I'm taking this to look like I'm traveling," she said and seized up one of their small pouches.

"Claerwen, wait." He caught her hand.

"Now is the best time, while the mist is still heavy."

"You can't go now, you're distracted. I've upset you—I can see that. You could make a mistake, say something wrong. You could be walking into a trap."

"I understand why you made the terms as you did," she shot back. "And I appreciate that you try hard to protect me. I do. But sometimes, Marcus, the trap is when you keep me from knowing what danger's coming at me. Like Handor—especially Handor. I must go."

She broke free of his grip.

"No, Claerwen!" He caught her arm again. "Not now. Calm down first."

She glared up into his face. His black eyes were tortured with anger and hatred. By the gods, she thought, his dark side, usually only exposed as the Iron Hawk, was seeping out from that place deep within him where he kept it under control. She had seen it start before the exile, and now, after five years of festering, it had become like a horrible sickness. If only she could find Tangwen and the clue to the sword, then they could finish this and go home before he got himself killed…

"You want to kill Handor, but that will not free you from this." She laid a hand to his beard-roughened cheek then raised up to press a light kiss to his lips. "I will meet you an hour before sunset." She withdrew into the mist.

Claerwen's steps across the fells accepted no falter, her face no expression. She forced herself to concentrate on finding the correct path into the grove, and to ignore the words she had heard Marcus whisper when she walked away from him.

"I would sell myself into slavery, if it would keep you safe," he had said, and he'd meant it, without hesitation, without thought of his relentless need for freedom that permeated every moment of his life. But it seemed he had already sold himself into slavery, the slavery of anger, and this guilt he had spoken of. What had he meant—if only he could rectify "everything"? Was it guilt that produced his horrible nightmares? By the light, is that why he wrote the terms in the way he had? Guilt?

Concentrate, Claerwen told herself. She had forded the river on stepping stones. Now she was nearing the grove and needed to begin to memorize landmarks so she could find her way back. Clear the mind and concentrate. She chose low-lying objects, peculiar rocks or easily identifiable foliage that would not be obscured in the mist. But after another hour had passed, she realized she had not paid enough attention. She had already come through the outermost trees that preceded the grove.

Her pace slowed. Why had she lost track of the landmarks? She turned one way then the other. The confusing mist had darkened more than usual in full daylight, a clue that heavy cloud had moved in above it.

"You were right, I am distracted." Claerwen wished Marcus could have heard her admission, and she wondered if she had enough concentration to do this. If only she could slip into another persona with the seamless ease that he could. In a matter of minutes he could change his appearance, take on different mannerisms, even alter his voice, with no rehearsal, no hesitation, then insert himself in the midst of a hostile scenario as if he had belonged there all along. She had never been able to come close to that kind of performance even when swept into the course of a ruse. Now, alone, not lost but not quite sure of her location, she needed to not only regain her bearings, but the confidence to execute the ploy as well.

Yet Claerwen sensed she was exactly where she needed to be. Dressed in tans and browns, she blended well into the woods, and the vicinity's familiar feel remained with her from the long-ago vision. She slowly turned in a circle. "What are you trying to tell me?" she asked the gods.

The first soft drops of rain fell on her upturned face. The mist was giving way to the heavier cloud above. Trees swayed, their branches filled with a breeze that promised thick, iron-fisted gusts to come.

A woman in flowing white robes and cowl-like kerchiefs picked her way through the trees, a little more than a stone's throw away. Claerwen withdrew behind an ancient oak, and saw that she carried a wide, shallow basket of willow that overflowed with cuttings—the kinds of flowers and roots used in treating ailments. This woman was a healer from the colony, and the closer she came, Claerwen recognized the extended variety of plants suggested a master healer. Her own knowledge of healing, though long disused, could make the link that led her into the colony.

Claerwen stepped from behind the oak. "Mistress?"

The rain thickened. The woman, not hearing, picked up her pace.

"Mistress?" Claerwen called louder.

This time the woman stopped and turned. Claerwen rushed forward but left several long paces between them. Without knowing rank within the colony, she took a stance of reverence, head bowed, hands folded.

"Forgive me," she said. "I am seeking one who could guide me to the women of the lake."

The woman kept her face downcast against the wind. "What is it you wish here?"

"I wish to be accepted as a novice."

A pause of both surprise and suspicion. "That is not possible," the woman said. "One does not merely join. You must be nominated by the high council of the elders."

"May I speak to them?" Claerwen persisted.

Another pause. Thunder rumbled in the distance.

"It is not allowed," the answer finally came.

Claerwen could have spit one of Marcus's oaths. She had only one more tactic to use and it was not good. "I know one of your priestesses," she said. "May I speak with her?"

"What is her name?"

"She is called Lady Tangwen."

The woman's footsteps swished swiftly over the humus-covered earth. Claerwen lifted her face. In the same instant her kerchief was grabbed and pulled back. She took in Tangwen's hard, green-eyed glare. Dull-witted cow, Claerwen told herself, she should have come in the night instead and gained entrance by stealth.

"What nonsense is this?" Tangwen demanded.

Claerwen straightened and smoothed back loose strands of hair, now wet with rain. "I think you know why I have come." She forced her tone to be even and clear.

"You do not belong here. You must leave."

"No, I do not belong here. I simply wish to speak with you."

Tangwen's eyes assessed Claerwen. "You have nothing to say here. And I have nothing to say to you. Leave."

The woman started away then stumbled mid-stride. Her basket tipped and some of its contents spilled.

That shift, Claerwen was sure, had been a change of mind about which direction to take to the heart of the colony. Tangwen would take a misleading route instead—to perhaps confuse a follower into getting lost.

Claerwen rushed to pick up the dropped cuttings. "Please…" She held them out. "I mean no harm."

"Just knowing of Excalibur is harm enough. Leave it be." Tangwen warily took the cuttings and turned away.

Claerwen caught the woman's arm. The desire to blurt out her frustration and ask what Excalibur was rattled in her like rocks bouncing in a metal tray, but she slammed a door on her curiosity. "There is something here that belongs to another who will need it soon. You know what it is."

A frown rumpled Tangwen's brow.

Confusion, Claerwen noted. "You know *where* it is."

Tangwen's eyes, wide and sad, looked young in spite of her age. "Who are you?"

"Myrddin Emrys prophesied long ago of a king yet to come." Claerwen felt the bond of fire in the head ripple between them. "One who will be strong and wise enough to unite the feuding tribes of Britain against the Saxon hordes. You know of this prophecy, don't you, Lady Tangwen? You know of the sword that was hidden for safekeeping—"

"Speak no more of this," the woman cut her off. "The sword no longer exists. Now leave!"

That was a lie. Claerwen was certain of it. The vehemence in the voice had been out of place; her anger from fear, not indignation. She watched the woman run away through the trees.

The sky had lowered and was so dark it looked like nightfall was coming on quickly. Thunder rumbled again, closer. Had the time already come to meet Marcus? Or was it still too early? The storm-laden sky was too thick to read time by the sun or the angle of shadows.

No use to stay now, Claerwen thought. Marcus was right, she should have waited, but she had been too distraught with him and needed time alone, needed to have something of her own to do while she sorted out her thoughts. And all she had done was create a bigger problem. She could never gain Tangwen's trust now, and the only other person who possibly could know anything was Handor.

"Eh…" Claerwen hissed at herself. Handor. How could she have ruined so much so quickly? With her hand pressed against her heart, she closed her eyes.

Lightning raked across the blackened sky. Claerwen missed it. Instead she saw water, roaring water that pushed against her, filled her head and seared her lungs.

The memories faded. She opened her eyes. The gods were warning her. But a warning for whom? Herself? For Marcus? Tangwen? Or someone else? Claerwen's hand dropped. Her breath came hard in shallow puffs. By the light, she needed to breathe. So many times the images had come and gone and left her choking and sick. Her skin crawled and she thought: this must be how she was going to die.

Chapter 26

Rheged
Summer, AD 476

MARCUS limped to the inn's entrance. His hair, greyed again in thick streaks, hung in straggles half over his face, and his cloak showed splotches of dirt. With his shoulders rounded into a slight stoop, he plodded through the leather drape hung in the doorway.

Inside, he waited for his eyes to adjust to the dark interior. Gods, he loathed inns. The overwhelming stench of rotting meat, stale beer, animal dung, sweat and urine stung his nose, and several bleary-eyed men turned to stare through the pall of smoke that filled the crowded common room. When they saw he was a stranger, they quickly returned to their conversations. An ongoing argument roiled at the far end of a long, central table.

Marcus found an unoccupied stool and sat down at the nearer end of the table. "How's the ale here?" He spoke in a gruff, thick northern accent to a man seated next to him.

"Good enough, stranger," the answer came with a skimming glance.

"Enough t'ease a day's troubles?"

A scruffy boy, likely the landlord's son, set a ceramic cup in front of him and filled it from an enormous skin of ale. Marcus scrutinized the dark liquid as it sloshed into the cup. "That's not watered down, is it? I've no use for piss water."

"No," the boy mumbled, his face cautious at the piercing glare he received.

"Good!" Marcus thumped a fist.

"Food, sir?"

"No use for food, boy. Just plenty o' drink." He slid a piece of copper across the table's surface in payment. The boy snatched it up and continued on his rounds of filling cups.

"What's the problem?" Marcus dipped his head towards the other end of the table.

The man beside him had returned to his own drink and was listening to the rising voices. "Eh? Oh, land dispute."

"Ach, if it isn't cattle, it's land," Marcus complained between gulps of drink. "Whose land?"

"Who else's? Lord Ector's."

"Ah, I've heard that name. So this's where his lands lie."

"Aye—prominent nobleman 'round here. Lands straddle Rheged's border with Strathclyde. You must be from the north? Orkney, from the sound of it?"

Marcus nodded the lie. "Traveling t' meet kin south o' here. Now I know I'm going right. So, tell me o' this dispute."

Pleased to have fresh companionship, the man besieged Marcus with an extensive tale of land disputes that had spanned generations. The tract on which the inn sat, once part of Lord Ector's clan's holdings, had been claimed by the landlord's great-grandfather at the time the Roman occupation ended. Another family also claimed ownership. Ector—and his father, and his father's father—as the prevailing overlords of the region, had been forced to mediate the endless dispute.

"It looked like they were finally going to settle—just a few days ago," the man said after more than two hours of talk and draining cups. "Until that one, there, started to interfere."

Marcus squinted down the length of the table. His eyes, like his mind, had trouble to focus. He was drunk at last—truly drunk, by the light—and it felt bloody good. If only it could erase the memory of the hurt in Claerwen's eyes from that morning. He knew she would have learned about the terms eventually, but why had he let it slip out then?

He looked at his tablemate. What had he said? Marcus drained his cup again and called for another, then remembered. Someone had interfered. The man who had been pointed out argued intently with his neighboring patron. His hooded head was lowered and turned to the side; a small, plain rock dangled from a leather thong around his neck. One hand periodically clutched at it, and a finger from his other hand poked so hard that the plank he struck rattled each time.

Blinking, Marcus tried to focus his watering eyes. For some reason the man's habitual gesture of playing with the rock annoyed him. Few men wore ornaments around their necks, unless they were noblemen and wore a torque to show rank. He rubbed his eyes and blinked again. The man straightened and turned on his seat to speak with someone to the other side. Light from the fire pit caught his face.

Marcus set down his cup and cocked his head a bit to one side. "You bloody, slimy, miserable piece of dung," he slurred too softly to be heard. Handor's wolfish face scowled out from the hood.

"I'd give a good wager they'll try to change the boundaries again," Marcus's neighbor picked up his talk once more.

"Huh?"

"They haven't tried diverting the river yet." The man laughed at his own jest. "I heard such nonsense mentioned this morning. Let's see who makes the best guess." He gave Marcus's arm a light punch and whistled at two other men at the next table. "Come here, and bring that dice with you!"

The landlord's boy appeared again to refill the cups and greedily accept yet another copper. Marcus gambled with the men. By the time the hours had passed into early evening, they began to make up words to bawdy songs. They heaped ridicule onto the feuding parties with the new lyrics and didn't even remember why they were doing so. When food and empty cups started to fly in response, the landlord finally roused himself from the kitchen long enough to order them to quiet down or leave.

"Aw, d'we have to stop?" Marcus said and rose, but he finished bellowing a line from the last song he had started with the others. Gods, he felt good. Someone pushed him towards the doorway. Barely able to stand, he wobbled a couple of steps then stopped.

The leather drape was caught up on a hook next to the entrance.

Outside, daylight had dwindled. Brilliant light flared into the room, a jarring crash of thunder followed. Seconds later, rain began to pound on the roof.

Confused and momentarily blinded, Marcus saw only darkness through the open doorway. He turned back to the other men. Handor. He had forgotten Handor. Where was he? He squinted at each face from one end of the table to the other, then the entire room, once, twice. The assassin was gone.

Marcus tried to speak. Only one foul expletive came out.

Claerwen took off her shoes. Afraid they would be ruined in the marshy ground, she stuffed them inside the small pouch strapped around her then cautiously started down into a reed-filled hollow near the east riverbank. At the bottom, liquid mud sat in a pool. Her bare feet kept slipping on the wet earth, and she eased around to the other side where the ground rose again, slightly steeper and dryer. She settled in to wait.

The sky continued to darken. Farther south, lightning skewered the blackened sky, over and over. A fierce one, she gauged, and guessed the storm was now over the inn and dropping a deluge. If it followed the river northward, as it appeared to be, it would reach her within the hour. Cold water slowly rose around her ankles—rain from the storm that was swelling up from the riverbed. She gathered up her skirts and cloak and held the small pouch in her lap. The water crept higher.

"Where are you?" she whispered into the increasing winds. Though unable to tell time from the obscured sun, she was certain Marcus should have been waiting for her by now. Unless he was in trouble, he was rarely late. But with the severity of that storm, he might have had to wait it out.

Claerwen edged up the depression's incline every few minutes. The water continued to rise. If she moved much farther, she would become visible above the reeds, and if the rain reached her before Marcus did, she would need to find another place to hide then hope to intercept him when he finally did come.

Minutes streamed by. White froth leapt above the level of the riverbank. Claerwen's knees pressed into the softening mud and she grew more awkward on the mushy, uneven surface. Stretching up, she gazed again into the south, but mist was quickly rising and cutting off her view.

"Please come soon," she said. The sense of isolation made her shiver. Then, a dark shape moved in the mist, not far away, directly in the path she had chosen if she needed to flee the hollow.

In the instant she hoped Marcus was standing there, the shape emerged and she recognized Handor instead, in a ragged, dark brown cloak.

Why? She sank down again. Why did he always have to be there, in the way? She didn't dare move. Think, she told herself. What could she do to distract him?

The assassin stared towards the river, then scanned around in the direction of the inn. His gaze ran back and forth as if he observed the progression of the water. He also seemed to be waiting for someone. For Marcus? In ambush? If only she knew where Marcus was, if he were coming soon, if she could coordinate a distraction to not only draw Handor away from her but to warn Marcus as well.

The assassin backed several steps and stopped again. Claerwen held her breath. Would he go? But the water was rising faster. A steady current flowed now into the hollow. The storm, feeding the river, fed the ground water as well. It was either move and die, or stay and drown…

"Please," she prayed in the direction from which Marcus should come.

Handor moved back another few steps, more quickly now. With his neck stretched, he scanned once more from the inn and on around to the lake and the grove. Then he smiled in the chilling, bitter, sly leer that was the closest semblance of a smile he ever gave. He turned and sprinted away.

Claerwen pushed up. Her motion and weight sank her into the mud, up over her ankles. The water was now above her knees and still rising. Shocked, she abandoned caution. In one place too long, she could no longer free her feet by merely pulling them out.

Claerwen threw herself against the slope where grass grew above the normal water level. She grappled the turf with her hands, dug in with her elbows, and strained up with all her strength and leverage and grit. Grunting with each small increment, she gradually wrested one foot free. A little farther, she urged herself, just a little more. Then the other foot slithered out of the slime.

Claerwen crawled up the incline. At the top, she lay flat. Beneath her, the earth vibrated. The sound of swift moving water had become a low, growling rumble that grew unbearably ominous within seconds.

On her feet, she turned towards the river, but the rumble didn't come from there. The roar grew louder. Claerwen turned again. It was coming from the stream that flowed down between the fells behind her. The smell of mud and freshly cut wood and grass swept her on a rush of air. Doom, she sensed. A single tear traced down her cheek.

Cold water struck her straight on, and the leading spray streaked through her hair at the temples, the full force of the flood an instant later. It rammed her face and body, and she was lifted, thrown backward, hurtled through the fluid terror and tumbled mercilessly. Silty water filled her nose, mouth, ears. Bark stripped from trees, leaves, grass, rocks—all scraped her. Please let it end soon, her mind cried; her lungs burned in agony.

She was thrown again, and her face broke through the churning surface. Gulping, she tried to catch the smallest bit of air, but her body needed to eject the water inside it first. She gagged violently and was spun around and around then thrust against a solid surface she never saw, flattened against it in the unrelenting current. Pain crashed into her chest. What breath was left in her expelled. She slid, pulled inexorably along with the shifting flow of the channel. Pain overtook all her senses, blinding, sickening, thick and heavy. Then the relief of blackness melted it all away.

Flushed, dizzy, Marcus's stomach caved downward, but not with the nausea that came from too much drink. The sensation was different, like his gut was dry and empty and about to split into a thousand pieces of crusty soil. His head ached, indeed, his whole body hurt. The inn was quiet. He could not tell if the sickness had closed off his hearing or merely if no one spoke.

A flash of lightning, thunder. Then his mind went blank and was filled with a scream, distant and unintelligible and reverberating inside him so violently his head threatened to explode. As quickly as it began, it died away. The cup slipped from his fingers and crashed onto its rim. It shattered into a thousand shards.

"Did you hear that?" he whispered.

Those around him stared. One by one they shook their heads. No one had heard anything.

Marcus struggled to make his mind work. Was he *so* drunk? Or was he delusional? The storm thickened, its sound more like a stream in full spate than rain. Somewhere deep within the gushing he thought he heard his name called. He knew it was not sound. It had come from inside his soul.

His boots crunched the broken cup into smaller pieces as he stumbled to the doorway. Lightning forked across the mottled charcoal sky again. Thunder, thick with evil, crashed hard enough to hurt the ears and leave them ringing. Silver rippled across the deep green earth, a roar like the ocean behind it.

Marcus charged out of the inn and smacked directly into the downpour. He halted in astonishment. "Damn you, bloody sea," he harangued the water.

Hooked by the wind, his hood whipped back; the downpour soaked his hair and ran inside his tunic. The cold rain slapped a degree of alertness into him.

"Eh-uh…" Marcus wiped a hand over his flushed face. Midway between the inn's front door and the stables, he watched water run across the turf towards him. He stumbled back. This was not the sea that engulfed his feet, but the river overflowing its banks.

He spit an oath and ran to the stables; each heavy step sprayed water. In the dark, he reached the horses and fumbled for the saddle on his animal. He grabbed at the wooden horns on the front and back, slipped, tried again and leaned his brow against the seat. Gods, he wished his head didn't feel like a block of moldy cheese.

"Claerwen," he said. It had been Claerwen's voice calling him, her scream he had heard inside him. He was sure of it. He knew, somehow, the bond that tied them together had cut through the other voices and noise and confusion that rattled like infuriated bees inside in his head. He shook it, trying to dislodge the woolly-mindedness, and pulled the horses outside. He tied the second animal's lead to his mount's saddle, vaulted up and bolted from the stables.

Marcus raced as if trying to outrun his own drunkenness. He was late. Damn, he was late. Sweat poured off him, hot and steamy beneath the cold rain that rilled over him. He hoped both the hot and cold would purge his neglectful stupidity as well. If only he had not craved the drink so bloody much, but he had, how terribly he had…and he still did.

Unable to use the track along the west side of the river, Marcus skirted the overflow. The storm, stalled over the inn, was quickly becoming spent. He soon passed its outer reaches. By the time he approached the low-lying hollow that sat on the river's opposite side, the concentration of clouds was already thinning and the late evening sky lightened.

Slowing, he stared. His scalp crept. Sickness filled his stomach again. In paralleling the river above the flooded area, he had been able to discern his location. The overflow had not been more than a hand's span in depth, and with the dissipating rainstorm, the water level was already dropping. But here he halted at an utterly decimated landscape. The placid burn that descended through the fells to the east and met the river above the lake's southern end ran in a spraying, raging cascade, more like a gale-driven sea than a flooded stream. The hollow had been obliterated.

"Bloody—" Marcus started. The diverted stream had been no rumor, and Handor's interference had been the cause. He turned the horse in a circle to scan the hills. "Where are you, Claeri? Where did you go to save yourself?" His voice was lost against the roar.

He rode up the closest fell to study the waterways. He would not be able to cross the river for some time. Then he gazed at the lake. Its level had risen as well. Floodwater ran broad and swift into the grove.

He turned again to the devastated confluence. A chill gripped him in the belly that wrenched the ale-fed bile. The diverted stream had nothing to do with any land dispute. It was in the wrong place. Instead, it had flooded the women's colony.

"*Could* you save yourself?" he asked.

His hand went to the oilskin-covered bundle hidden beneath the other gear on his horse. He found the shape of the Iron Hawk's sword, its hilt. He tightened his fingers around it in the need to feel its strength.

"Damn you, Handor. You shame your father's name and your clan and yourself with every breath you take." He stopped short of invoking the gods to lay their wrath on the assassin. That task would be his alone. His hand released. "Damn myself, for not having seen what you were going to do."

The deepening twilight would not last long. Marcus needed light, and in the severe dampness he would not be able to make a torch that would burn. He glanced at the western sky and hoped the sunset would break through the last of the clouds. Then he could search, at least for a while.

He muttered another curse and turned the horses uphill. In a broad sweep to the west, he inspected the fells as far as he thought Claerwen might have fled. He found no sign of her. Then, close to the receding river, he followed the muddy shore north from the confluence. With painstaking care, he examined every niche, every lump of debris, every mud or water-filled crevice for a half-mile, then turned back and searched once more.

Again at the confluence, and close enough to the over-spilling stream to be showered with its spray, he tore away piles of long, soaking grass and broken, twisted twigs. The stream's spate showed little sign of slowing. Until the diversion was repaired, the rush would not ease.

Exhausted from the effects of the ale, Marcus sank onto his knees, the horses' leads in his hand. He would have to cross the river as soon as it dropped to a safe level and flow. But how would he ever find her without daylight? By morning…

He could not allow himself to finish the thought.

He glared at the place where the hollow had been and tried to calculate: if Claerwen had been there as planned, she could have been either forced to retreat a fair distance or swept away. But which way? Which had come first? The river's overflow? Or the diversion?

"Damn," he spit and ground the heels of his hands into his eyes.

If only he could think clearly. Again he tried to reason: if Claerwen had avoided the flood, she would most likely have fled up the steep-sided, flat-topped hill on the other side of the river. He shook his head. She would have seen him and come down by now. Nor would he have experienced the anguishing cry inside his head.

He rose. "You could be there, in that," he said to the ravaged piece land then turned to the lake. "Or you could have been swept…there. Gods, what have I done?"

One of the horses nickered, a soft, comforting rumble in its throat. Marcus stroked the animal's rough, wet neck. He clicked his tongue and tugged on the lead. He would go north again, this time to the lake.

The horse stalled. He pulled on the bridle. Stubborn, the animal balked and slapped its tail hard. The other horse held still as if in agreement. Frowning, Marcus eyed his mount. Though neither frightened nor spent, the animal refused to move.

The horse nickered again and dipped its head. Marcus exhaled and shook back his damp hair. He did not need an uncooperative animal now. Perhaps the water had confused it, and he pushed the horse around until it faced away from the river.

The dusklight waned, and a partial moon was rising amid the last of the clouds. Marcus gazed past the horses at the water. Its ripples belied a deep, swift current that could carry away tree trunks and cattle. Perhaps by midnight it might be down enough, but he doubted it. In the dimming light, he watched more debris float from upstream. The diverted burn pumped it onward and packed it into a crook of the riverbank.

Amid the blacks and dark greys of the evening, a whitish patch glowed against a rock embedded in the turf. How brutal that water could rip apart something as strong and earthbound as a tree, and leave its wood torn in twisted fingers. He turned away; the sickening bile churned in his stomach again.

Once more the horse nickered.

Fingers.

Marcus's mouth dropped open and he swore at himself again. Would this bloody ale never let loose of his mind? Fingers. Not of wood. He whipped around, threw off his cloak and slogged through the creamlike mud.

"Claerwen!" Each step threatened to send him sprawling flat, but he closed in on the pale glow. He was right—fingers, human fingers, slender and fragile. Fingers that had clawed at the black rock and were now frozen in stillness.

"No... Please, no." He knelt and slid on his knees in the struggle to keep upright. He swore again and reached for the hand. Amazingly, the water had washed it clean.

Covered in layers of silt, Claerwen was nearly invisible, and would have been even in daylight. She lay facedown in shredded tree bark and reeds, crumpled awkwardly, her head jammed against the rock, her right arm twisted back and up. Her neck was arched over so sharply, it looked broken. The small pouch she had taken was still strapped around her.

"Please, be alive," Marcus prayed. He was afraid to touch her, but she had to be moved should the water rise again. He held his breath and gently laid his hands on each side of her, felt for any signs of life. No motion filled her chest with air. The first tears stung his eyes. He slid his hands underneath her and pulled slowly, and freed her from the debris.

He sat down in the mud and rolled her over into his lap, cradling her, and wiped slathers of blood-streaked filth from her nose, her mouth, her eyes. She slumped against him, limp like wet rags. He still felt no breath in her, and when he placed his fingertips to her neck, then his ear to her chest, no heartbeat thumped even faintly.

The tears hung on his lashes, in wait to be pushed over the edge by new ones yet to be formed. No more came—the shock was too much. Rocking, he bowed his head, his arms clutched about her. If Handor, or anyone, were to strike a knife into him at that moment, so be it, he thought. He would gladly accept the task of passing to the Otherworld, or to the next life, or into an unknown universe, if only he could pursue Claerwen's soul.

But no one was there except the horses and the water and the sliver of moon. He lifted his face to the darkness, filled his lungs and roared, roared a horrible scream meant to cast the gods from the earth and the sky and the bloody sea and anywhere else they might be hiding.

CHAPTER 27

Rheged
Summer, AD 476

IN spite of the roar of water, Marcus heard nothing. With Claerwen draped like soft clay across his lap, he sat in the cold, wet mud, and simply stared. How still death was. Where had her soul gone by now? Was she watching? Watching with those eyes that had glared stinging hurtfulness at him that morning?

He dipped his hand into a tiny pool of clear water that was within reach, collected a handful in his cupped palm, and drained it over her face, again and again, until the silt and blood were washed away. He grieved for every scratch and bruise revealed on her cheeks and forehead, dark and ugly against the pallor of her moonlit skin.

"How could I have been so…?" His question was pointless. He had ruined everything.

Claerwen's left arm rested on his knees. It slowly slid down and her hand flopped onto the surface of the mud. He pulled it back, tucked it against his chest, and he turned her just a little. Her face pressed against him; water trickled from her mouth and nose.

Consciously Marcus knew he could no longer sit there. He would have to find a cart and take her home. What else could he do? But he remained. What did he care anymore? The tears stung again but still refused to fall. He closed his eyes and slowly swayed; a low moan in his throat rose like the gradual deep howl of the wind. Out of it, a slow, poignant song took shape, one that wept of the heartache of all that had ever been lost. He had heard it so many times in his life, sung amidst the horrible keening of women for the dead each time one of his clan passed. He had heard survivors on battlefields sing it to their fallen compatriots, and in his nightmares, he had heard it for those who had never had a chance to pick up a weapon against the brutality that had befallen them.

By the gods, his only sense of peace was now gone.

His grip gradually loosened. He saw Claerwen's fingers had slid under his belt as if to hold on. How? Her knuckles pressed against his belly, but his belt was only loosely tied.

He caressed her fingers lightly. One twitched. Nerves. Always the nerves gave up last. His stomach churned.

Then a drawn-out, sickening gasp erupted from her chest, a choking, gut-loosening wheeze, and she slipped a little more.

His eyes widened. Had she taken *in* air? The sound was not the same as when a body expels its air. He had seen enough of death to know the difference. Water continued to drain from her nose and mouth.

"Claerwen?" He rocked her slightly.

Her fingers jerked against him then tightened around his belt.

"Claerwen!" Heat swept him in a racing sequence of surprise, thrill and terror that her tenuous hold on survival would last only moments. With her in his arms, he struggled onto his feet and scrambled for higher ground.

He laid her facedown in a patch of clean grass, then straddled her on his knees, his fists pressed beneath her in the hollow just above her stomach. He pulled up gently and forced more water out of her lungs. Shortly, she started to cough, a strangling, congested sound at first that turned into full hacking.

Marcus steadily pumped, encouraged her, prayed. When the water finally stopped draining, Claerwen's breathing slowly eased into a raspy moan. He rolled her onto her side. Her hands drifted up to her chest and clenched together there.

"Claeri, can you hear me?" He cradled her head in his hand and lifted a little. "It's Marcus. Can you hear me?"

Her eyes barely cracked open. Tears full of dirt ran from them.

"Can you hear me, Claeri?"

Her eyes found him and steadied but showed no coherency.

Marcus doubted she recognized him, but at least she had responded. The way she clutched her hands to herself worried him. Each shallow, labored breath seemed to bring her pain.

He smoothed her mud-caked hair. "I'm going to take you out of here. Claerwen? Do you understand? I'm going to take you where it's safe."

Her eyes flicked towards him faintly then closed. Marcus hoped she had understood, safeness being precious to her. He retrieved his cloak and wrapped her in its warmth, then, with the horses' leads tied to his belt, he lifted her. By the gods, how fragile and listless she hung in his hands.

"I'm going to take you to a house I saw," he said in his most comforting voice. He bundled her closely. "There's an empty one, on the west side of the lake; it's in woodland and has dried bricks of peat and rushlights inside. And a pen for the horses. I found it when I was scouting, before I went to—"

He never wanted to think of that inn again. He went on in his softest voice that she would soon be warm and dry and most of all safe.

The house was not far, a little more than a mile downshore, but he feared it might have been flooded. Though close to the lake, it stood on steeper ground than the grove on the water's east side. When he came upon the squat, round house of daub and wattle, he found it had been untouched. Why it had been abandoned, he could only guess, but for now, he counted its presence as a blessing.

He slipped the animals' leads from his belt and trudged to the doorway, ducked under the low lintel and pushed through the leather drape closure. The stale odor of mold from the sagging roof of thatch stank inside. He gently laid Claerwen on the earthen floor.

Marcus continued talking—perhaps the sound of his voice would help her focus, he hoped. In truth, he didn't know, and he wondered if he were only helping himself. He rushed to fill the dust and ash-filled fire pit with peat bricks. Lit, their pungency quickly filled the house.

Claerwen moaned softly and tried to turn onto her side, but she could not push herself over. Her breathing was not improving and her hands were still curled up against her chest.

"Let me see, Claeri," Marcus said and knelt. He opened the folds of the cloak. The fire pit's light revealed that her overtunic and shift had been shredded in the ordeal, and the filthy, wet cloth beneath her hands was congealed with blood. He gently took hold of her wrists.

Now he remembered—he had seen her hands like that not long after the vision. She had looked terrified and in pain, and each time she spoke of the images, that fear returned.

"Ah, Claeri—you saw this coming, didn't you?"

She moaned again when he pulled her hands down. He knew he was hurting her. He slipped his fingers into one of the tears and pulled. The fabric gave easily.

Aghast, Marcus felt his stomach cramp. A massive bruise spread across her, from the *clavis* bones down over her breasts to her belly. In the center, directly over her heart, her skin was purpled with tiny, bleeding cuts, many filled with splinters. The blunt end of a broken tree branch must have struck her, he guessed, and had left behind pieces embedded in her.

So horrified, Marcus could not think of a curse harsh enough to bother saying. He clamped his mouth shut—then silently thanked the gods the wood had not been pointed like the branch that had impaled his shoulder.

Her hands came up again. "No, Claerwen, you cannot touch this." He caught them and leaned down, his face close to hers. With one hand he held her cheek and pressed his other hand around her fingers. "You have wounds I need to clean. It will hurt. Can you understand me?" He squeezed her fingers lightly.

Claerwen's eyes slit open. He could see her green-blue irises move back and forth, unable to focus. Her lips, already parted in the struggle to breathe, moved, but formed no words. Then one finger pushed against the fleshy heel of his hand. Marcus's chest tightened. Tears were welling in her eyes. One slipped away, and her lids closed again.

He hoped his efforts to extract water from her lungs had not damaged her more. "May the gods bring you strength, my Claeri," he whispered. "And steadiness to my hands."

He rushed outside for the pouch with rudimentary medicinal

supplies. The animals were tired as well, he saw, and he relieved them of their loads, moved them into the horse pen, and promised extra grain would come soon.

Inside again, he worked through the night. With painstaking care, he extracted every splinter he could locate, cleaned each wound and salved them with an ointment made from marigold. Throughout, Claerwen drifted in and out of consciousness. She never truly cried; rather, she continued to moan. When he finally finished, Marcus pulled the ruined garments from her and examined her for other injuries. He suspected that bruising he found on her left side meant cracked ribs, but his probing told him none were broken through. Aside from the scratches on her face, he found only a few other minor bruises. Then he bathed her from a tiny wooden bowl he had discovered and dressed her in a shift and over-tunic from her spare clothing.

When dawnlight began to scatter the night, Marcus prepared a simple broth from dried meat he had ground into powder and set it on the coals to heat. Claerwen was gradually becoming more alert and he thought she now recognized him but was still unable to speak. Her breathing had grown more labored since midnight and when she descended into a fit of coughing, she seemed to experience a lot of pain. He wondered if water was still in her lungs, though he had been certain all of it had been expelled the night before.

Seated on the floor, he lifted Claerwen half-upright against him and cradled her head in the crook of his arm. He dipped the wooden bowl into the cooking cauldron and took a small amount of broth.

"Drink some, Claeri. You will feel better." He held the bowl to her lips. Her breath, in short, shallow bursts, rippled the broth's surface. "Please, try it."

She let him trickle the warm liquid into her mouth. Instinctively, she swallowed.

"Good," he said and repeated the act until the bowl was empty, then reached to fill it again.

Her hand lifted, bumped his arm and dropped again. Marcus gazed into her face with hopefulness. Her eyes were open, bloodshot, squinted against the firelight and showing pain. She struggled to speak.

"No need to talk, Claeri," he said, a smile in his eyes.

Her lips formed his name. Air pushed less than a whisper through them.

He reached again to fill the bowl, but her arm jerked. She couldn't lift it this time. She was trying to say more than his name. Her voice was too scratchy. "Wait a bit," he said. "Until you've had more of this. It will help."

Her eyes squinted urgency into his face and she cleared her throat several times, tried once more. "Bring…Tangwen."

"Bring Tangwen?" he echoed. His brows bent down sharply.

"Need…Tangwen. Please, bring her to me. Help. She is…healer. Help me."

The weakness in her voice wrenched inside him. "But we cannot trust her."

"Must…Marcus, must bring her to me. She is…master healer. Like Myrddin."

He tried a smile. "I will take care of you, Claeri. We cannot trust her."

"Marcus," she panted, "you can't. You know…not enough. I…too weak to tell you how…make treatments. Know not enough…myself."

He hesitated. He didn't dare argue with her. She could not afford the distress. But Tangwen? How could he dare trust Claerwen's life to that woman? Anyone with knowledge of the healing arts, master or apprentice, could easily turn a remedy into poison.

"No, Claerwen." He smoothed her hair. "I'll find someone else who can help. I'll take you to Lord Ector's—"

With great effort, she flung her hand up to his arm. Her fingernails bit his flesh. "You must bring Tangwen. I need a…*master* healer. If you don't, I will die."

Marcus hated to leave Claerwen alone; no choice had been left to him. With no help, she would die—she was right, he could sense it in her—but he feared he would never find that help in time. He emerged from the house's gloom, fatigued and light-headed from hunger and a full day and night's continuous wakefulness. He dragged his fingers through his hair and gulped in the cool morning air. Disbelief rankled in him that his next task was to find Tangwen, but the anguish, pain, and heartache in Claerwen's halting words had been worse than a twisting knife.

Marcus reached for his horse's lead. He glanced past the lower side of the house at the same time and missed the rein. A coracle leaned against the wall, an oar propped up beside it. He eyed the horse, then the coracle, then gazed towards the lake. The sunrise illuminated mist in brilliant white drifts across the water's surface and he caught glimpses of it through the trees. His hand moved from the rein and extended to the animal's neck for a quick pat, then dropped.

He sprinted to the boat. In good repair, it even had the straps to carry it across the back of the shoulders. This would be faster, much faster than he could ride around the lake, especially if he could still not ford the river. And if the mist held, he could approach the grove unnoticed.

He lugged the coracle to the shore, and with one foot in the bottom, pushed off with the other. The boat bounced and spun, and he quickly sat and hung on. Usually meant to float on a current while fishing, the paddle only a guide, coracles were notorious for being awkward to guide cross-stream. He took aim for the opposite shore and started to paddle.

But would Tangwen, or any of the other women, still be there? He didn't even know what she looked like except from Claerwen's description. If Handor's purpose in diverting the stream had been in truth to flood the colony and force the woman to flee the grove's protection, she could be impossible to find. Worse, Handor could have her.

Marcus fought the current and his deepening fatigue and paddled with short, steady strokes, one side then the other. "If only Myrddin were here," he muttered. His dislike for the Enchanter mattered far less than knowing he could trust Claerwen's life to Myrddin's healing skills. But wishing for the Enchanter's help was useless now, and if the colony had been abandoned and no clues to Tangwen's whereabouts left behind, he would have to take Claerwen to Ector's stronghold. He hoped he was not wasting time.

In a heavy bank of mist, the coracle abruptly stopped with a harsh scrape. Marcus was lifted off the board seat and thrown onto his knees. Recovering, he saw he'd landed near a thicket of rowan he had guessed was within a half-mile of the grove's southern boundaries. The floodwater had receded, but like the rivershore, a thick, sludgy layer of mud had been left behind; only the rock shoreline had been washed clean by the lake's lapping waters. He climbed out and pulled the boat deep into the thicket.

Marcus bounded up a steep notch filled with small boulders where water continued to drain back into the lake. Above, the ground was soggy and his feet squished and sank or slid with each step. Heaviness plagued his tired legs, but he ran the half-mile to the grove on a path he judged would take him to the colony's center.

Drawing near, he heard voices drift through the wood—women's voices calling to each other. They must be attempting to clean or salvage what they could, he thought. From the depth of the mud, he doubted they could recover much.

Farther along, he caught his first view of the white-robed women. He slowed and wove through the thick summer foliage. The women milled among a small group of dwellings, most of which appeared intact but had been inundated with the ubiquitous mud. One of two large oblong-shaped buildings, close to the trees that edged the lake, had partially collapsed. Its roof now sloped from the middle down to one side. None of the women appeared to have been injured, but he saw no one he thought could be Tangwen. He hoped when he emerged with a shouted order to remain still that he would not spook them. He reached for his sword's hilt.

Mid-stride, Marcus halted. In the trees opposite, he caught a shadowy glimpse of a man watching the colonists. Handor—from his ragged clothing. Air hissed through Marcus's teeth. He had no time to fight or play a cat-and-mouse game.

His gaze switched back to the damaged building. Through a narrow gap in the broken wall, another of the women, her robes stained with muddy blotches the color of liver, gathered items into a basket. That could be her, Marcus hoped. She looked about the right height, weight, age, but she was too far away to see if her eyes were brilliant green. He shifted his gaze to Handor. Had the assassin seen her yet? Barely visible, Handor slinked slowly to the left, away from the building. He stopped every few paces to study the compound.

Marcus stalked to the right. He continued around towards the damaged building, an eye on Handor's progress, and picked up speed. At the back wall, he slipped through a wide rift beneath the slumped roof. There, he crouched in a dark corner.

The woman's back was to him. She was stretching across a fallen beam that had crushed a heavy plank table. A bundle of drying herbs clung to the damaged wall, but it was too far for her to reach; her fingers swept the fragile petals and dislodged half of them. The bundle fell into a crevice behind the beam.

The building had been her infirmary, Marcus realized, and she was trying to save what she could of her medicinal herbs. Little looked salvageable. That was not good for Claerwen's sake. He leaned back and glanced through the break in the front wall. Handor was still creeping along. Much farther, and his line of sight would connect with the woman.

On silent steps, Marcus traversed the muddy floor. With the knife from the back of his belt in his right hand, he circled his other hand around and clamped it over the woman's mouth. She jolted up, and he pulled her backward, pressure under her chin to keep her tilted off-balance and braced against him. Her wide-open eyes—as green as the hills in spring—showed panic. He backed with her into the fallen roof's shadows.

"You will come with me," he whispered close to her ear and lifted the dagger enough for her to see. "Don't make a sound."

The woman stiffened. Though frightened, she appeared calm enough, but when Marcus pulled her towards the gap in the wall, she planted her feet and started to struggle. Her feet slid, unable to find traction in the mud.

"Don't fight, Lady Tangwen," he said. "You will come with me."

She pushed against his arm and kicked at his feet. Frail, she was no match for his iron-hard muscularity. With her braced against him, Marcus jerked her around. The pewter religious symbol hanging from her neck swung and clunked against his elbow. He forced her to look straight through the broken front wall. "If you don't stop fighting me," he said, "the man you can see between the two hawthorns—over there—will take you instead."

Tangwen again stiffened. She had seen Handor, he knew; now she was shaking. Without another word, he dragged her backward, farther beneath the sloping roof, then on through the ruptured edges of the wall.

CHAPTER 28

Rheged
Summer, AD 476

"YOU said nothing of her," a woman's voice objected. She sounded impersonal, distrustful, old. "Leave me be."

If only they would stop arguing, Claerwen wished. She heard a scuffle behind her, and the words continued to shoot back and forth. Unable to remember how long she had been awake and aware of them, she was growing weary of the disturbance. In truth she was weary of everything, the pain, the cold earth she lay upon. She recognized Marcus's deep voice, hushed, strained, tired, and very insistent. How long had it been since the pain had begun? Since she could pull in a full, comfortable breath? What was this place and who was the woman? If only she could remember what had happened. If only they would stop arguing.

"My wife will die without a healer. She needs your help."

"You said nothing of her," the woman's objection came again.

More scuffling. The voices quieted but continued to exchange, stubborn against stubborn. Marcus had found Tangwen, Claerwen came to realize and wanted to lift her head to see, but she was unable. It had taken all her strength earlier, while he had been gone, to roll onto her right side. She had hoped it would ease the pain and her breathing, but neither had improved. Instead, she had succumbed to the racking cough that sent dizzying agony all through her. She squeezed her eyes shut and fought its rising urge to start again.

"My wife is dying. Can you not see that?"

Claerwen felt Marcus's hand on her hair. He was kneeling next to her and stroking it. She could smell the leather of his belt and baldric. He hovered above her, his thick black hair close around his face, the hilt of his sword above his right shoulder. He looked up at the woman, anger in his face.

"She asked for you, Lady Tangwen. She knows you are a master healer."

Silence followed. Claerwen closed her eyes, and her hope drained away. Tangwen was about to refuse and bolt. Marcus would not attempt to force the woman into proffering her skills; force would only increase the risk of twisting healing into harm.

"Handor will find this place, don't you realize?" the woman said.

"I will see he does not."

"How?"

"That is not your concern now."

Claerwen felt his hand leave her hair. He was on his feet now. Her senses were fading.

"She said you are a healer. A *master* healer. It's true, my intent in bringing you here was to help my wife. Handor was a convenient excuse to get you to come."

The scrape of two steps indicated the woman was backing towards the open doorway. One more step, heavier, belonged to Marcus. "If Handor had found you first, he certainly would not have given you safe haven," Marcus persisted. "As long as you stay here, you will be safe."

No further steps scratched the earthen floor. Claerwen listened to the silence draw in again, broken only by her own rasping. She imagined Marcus staring down the woman, his iron grip on her arm to keep her from fleeing. Moments passed, and with them too much quiet. Now Claerwen wished the voices would start once more. Even the arguing was better than silence. "Please…"she said.

The steps approached again. Marcus. She felt his hand cup her shoulder.

More silence.

"You need to turn her onto her back," the woman finally said, "and prop her up, just a little. She will be able to breathe better."

Claerwen forced her eyes to open. She wanted to feel relief sweep through her, but instead, pangs of fear shot through her muddled mind. Tangwen stood over her with a face of cool distrust.

"What happened?" the woman asked. "How long has she been like this?"

"She was caught in the flood," Marcus said. "Last night." He collected pouches from their gear and stacked them in a wedge, the softest on top. He raised Claerwen, his arm around her shoulders, and settled the pouches under her until she was sitting up halfway. He indicated where he had found the splinters. "I think she was hit…here."

Tangwen knelt and listened, first to his explanation of how he had treated the wounds, then to Claerwen's chest. She nodded slowly. "Her breathing has eased a bit. The bone, here," she pointed where the uppermost ribs came together, "may have been pushed in and is pressing on her heart. That is why you need to keep her partially upright, to ease the pressure while it heals. If there is damage to the heart, she will need much time to regain her strength."

Claerwen squinted up at Marcus and waited for his reaction. He stared downward, his lips parted to speak, but he said nothing. He looked exhausted, and in the few moments of clearer thought brought on with easier breathing, Claerwen realized how long it must have been since he had rested. Propped up, she could see enough of him that he was filthy and bedraggled, his clothes mostly covered with dried mud. Then he looked across to Tangwen.

"*Will* she regain her strength?" he asked.

From the deep apprehension in his eyes, Claerwen was sure he had meant, "Will she *live*?"

Another long pause. The distrust in the older woman's face had not diminished. She met Claerwen's eyes. "I will examine her. I will give you an answer when I have done so."

Marcus's brows lowered. He remained kneeling.

Tangwen's eyes narrowed at him. "I will not harm her if that's what you suspect."

With an effort Claerwen thrust her hand towards Marcus. She was able to reach his knee. "Rest now," she whispered. "Rest."

He picked up her hand and held it. She watched his glare of warning drop away from Tangwen and turn into sadness. He rubbed his eyes with his other hand then his palm wiped down over his face. "I have need to attend to something," he said then gently laid down her hand.

The sadness in his face changed back into the disturbing hatred again, but in the haze of pain and weakness, Claerwen could not untwist her mind enough to understand why—why now. He rose and turned away. Her blurred gaze followed him. He crossed to the wall where the rest of their gear was stacked and gathered up the bundle wrapped in oilskin. Cold and distant, he ducked through the open doorway.

Claerwen sat up halfway. "What are you—?"

Tangwen gripped her shoulders and pressed her down again with a caution not to make such sudden movements. The pain caught like a hook. Claerwen sank down into semi-consciousness again, and never heard Marcus's footsteps pace away from the house.

"Do you remember what happened to you?" Tangwen asked hours later.

Claerwen drifted between wakefulness and the exhaustive slumber that injury caused. The unclear voice must have spun up out of a dream. The words meant nothing, and she tried to descend back into the comfort of sleep.

"You are awake," Tangwen said. "You need to drink some of this broth. As much as you can, to build your strength."

The woman's voice, though soft, jarred Claerwen closer to waking. Her mind garbled the words. She struggled to open her eyes.

"What did you say?" Claerwen doubted she had made sense herself.

"You must drink this."

Claerwen stared into the thin, brown-colored liquid. Her eyes blurred. Her mouth already tasted as bitter as the broth looked and smelled. Willow bark was in it—for the pain. She licked at its familiar taste on her lips and guessed small amounts had been trickled down her throat while she had been asleep. She felt

Tangwen's hand on the back of her head. It lifted, and the bowl pressed against her lower lip. She sipped.

"Do you remember what happened?" Tangwen repeated.

Claerwen swallowed. It was a medicinal infusion, not merely a tepid broth. It contained more than willow bark, but she could not think clearly enough to identify the other ingredients. By the light, she was tired. Sick. Her chest felt like ground meat, her lungs rattled. She laid back her head and tried to speak. Nothing came out.

"You don't remember the flood?"

Claerwen frowned up at Tangwen and slowly shook her head.

"Your man said you were caught in the flood. A stream was diverted. You don't remember at all? The rainstorm? If you were thrown against a tree, or if something hit you?"

Claerwen cleared her throat twice and still could not find her voice. The effort agitated the pain and she leveled her hand just above her chest.

Tangwen nodded. "The pain is the worst there, is it not? Take more of this." She held the bowl to Claerwen's lips again.

Claerwen sniffed at the broth. This time she hesitated. If only she could clear her mind. What else was in it?

"It has willow bark, yarrow, and leaf of dandelion," Tangwen said. "It was all I could find within a few paces of this house. Hawthorn berry should have been in it as well, but it's too early to take them for harvest this time of year. All I had prepared was probably ruined in the flood."

Claerwen drank. The liquid eased the dry scratchiness in her throat and she was finally able to rasp out a few words. "Dried berries…of hawthorn?"

"Aye," the woman answered.

"Then…my heart?"

Tangwen nodded. "You must have been struck hard in the chest. Splinters tell me it was a broken branch. Aside from the possibility of broken ribs, you have much pain there and you feel sick in your stomach. You also feel inordinately fatigued, don't you?"

Claerwen nodded.

"From the symptoms, I think your heart may have been damaged. It may recover. It may not. It is too soon to say. Your man said you were not breathing and he could find no heartbeat when he found you. If he had been perhaps a few minutes later, he would be taking you to your clan to bury. The gods were with you that night. And he did well in treating your wounds with what he had. They should heal properly, no fever. When he returns, I will look for something more useful for the pain."

When he returns? The phrase confused Claerwen. She vaguely remembered begging Marcus to bring Tangwen to help. And he had been there, arguing. Before that, she only remembered pain—sleeping, waking—always pain. Nothing more came to her, and the effort to plod her way through the muddle-headedness was too exhausting.

She turned her head to one side, then the other. The house was completely unfamiliar, and mostly empty except for the pouches stacked along the wall. Groping, she found she was lying on freshly cut reeds built up to keep her elevated instead of flat. Marcus's cloak covered her. She had no notion of how long she had been in the house. The open doorway showed dusk.

"Where is Marcus?" she asked.

"I don't know. A bit more."

The hand lifted Claerwen's head again, the bowl at her lips. She drank the last of the bitter liquid without hesitation. "Don't…understand," she said. "Where is he? Why…" She dropped back, too exhausted.

"Don't you remember him leaving?" Impatience laced Tangwen's tone.

Claerwen closed her eyes and shook her head. He must have had a task he needed to tend to, but why couldn't she remember anything? She wanted to pummel the inside of her head to make her mind focus, but the mere thought made her reel.

Stay calm, she told herself. She knew the wobbling in her head would ease only if she lay very still. She listened to Tangwen move to the fire pit, poke at the coals and set a new brick of peat among the withering flames. Claerwen drifted. Perhaps she could sleep some more. Then, the image of Marcus with the Iron Hawk's gear bundled under his arm floated into her memory. And the icy look that had been in his eyes meant he was descending into the warrior's dark persona.

Her slight intake of breath induced abrupt silence in the house. She opened her eyes.

"You remembered something." Tangwen stared at her. "What was it?"

Claerwen dared not to answer.

"What did you remember just now? Your husband leaving? Do you know why?"

"No."

"He said you had asked for me."

Claerwen nodded.

"Why?"

The question stabbed and the silence that followed made it even more pointed. Claerwen wondered how Tangwen could ask such a thing. Was it not obvious? She tried to ignore it and turned her face away, but the question's accusatory taint suddenly brought direction to her mind—Tangwen expected another confrontation about Macsen's sword.

"Why?" the question drilled again. "Why not a healer from Lord Ector's court?"

A boot scraped outside, and Claerwen turned her head. Marcus stood in the doorway. His eyes shifted from her to Tangwen and back, and though he seemed less covered in dried mud, his face was as haggard as ever. Relieved he was there, Claerwen guessed he must have crossed water somewhere and had washed off some of the mud, but he still had not rested.

"What goes on here?" he demanded. He swung two leather pouches from his shoulders onto the floor next to her. His eyes bored into Tangwen. "Answer. What goes on here?"

The woman's green eyes stalked Marcus. Even in the dimming light they appeared bright. "I've done all I can for now. She must rest. I can do little more without the proper herbs and many are not available at this time of the year. Those that I can find will take time to prepare."

He dipped his head towards the pouches. "Look in those. Hopefully most of what you need is in there." He knelt down and placed his hand to Claerwen's cheek.

"You took this from the infirmary?" Tangwen bent and stared into one of the pouches. "How did you—well, you must have forced your way."

"No one is there," he said. "They are all gone."

Tangwen glared at him. "Why?"

"Can't say. Perhaps they gave up trying to save it?"

"That is such nonsense," Tangwen countered. "They would never—"

Marcus twisted around and caught her by the elbow. "Do you care if my wife lives or dies?"

For the first time, Tangwen's impersonal evenness dropped enough to reveal fear. She shook free and snatched up the pouches, retreated to the other side of the fire pit. She sat and began to rummage through the bags. Her demeanor returned to practicality—not a hint of thanks or gratefulness for his retrieval of the herbs.

Claerwen slid her hand around Marcus's arm. The anger and hatred and sadness all smoldered in his intense eyes, and she felt she was looking through a portal into his dark side. He had never aimed his animosity at her, not even indirectly, and she trusted he never would, but he had become so difficult to reason with in the last few days. Last few days? What was she thinking? She didn't even know how long it had been since…since when?

She wished she knew why he had taken the Iron Hawk gear. Perhaps he had only hidden it, but from his worn appearance, she doubted that. And he had said, "I can't say," not, "I don't know." He must have done something at the empty colony, but what? Though he was right not to trust Tangwen, Claerwen wished he would swing the gate shut on his dark side once more.

Then she saw his hands. His palms were reddened to the point blisters had almost formed. A fresh, shallow scratch, straight and clean like a knife cut, ran diagonally from his left wrist across his arm. A matching cut split his sleeve. He had been fighting.

"Marcus," she slurred and fumbled for more words, but the pain dragged at her mind and she laid back her head. She needed rest, lots of rest. Though any memory of the flood eluded her, she did recall her dismal failure in the grove. She glanced at Tangwen. How would she ever be able to find the wits and strength to rectify that awful mistake?

She gazed up at Marcus again. His mouth was in a flat line, a hard, hollow look in his eyes. By the gods, she wished she could just get up and comfort him. Her eyes filled with tears. How would she ever be able to help him complete the quest? If only her mind would clear enough to think. If she could only survive long enough…

Her hand dropped from his arm. She had to give in to the exhaustion and the sickness. She could no longer stall it. He was calling her name, but everything turned black again.

The days that followed fell into a vague routine. Though she slept much of the time, Claerwen knew Marcus had begun to hunt nearly every day in the early mornings and at dusk. She also knew he patrolled at the same time, a way to search for any signs that Handor had returned. In between he dried meat, prepared meals and helped her to eat. Because she was too weak to walk, he carried her into the woods where she could relieve herself while she leaned limply against him. At night he sat propped against the wall while he drank from a wineskin and waited for her to fall asleep. The hollowness never left his eyes.

Tangwen remained coldly efficient. Occasionally Claerwen tried to enjoin her in talk, but the woman abruptly disengaged from every conversation ever started. She continuously went out on short excursions and each time returned with new cuttings that she prepared in a makeshift laboratory she had set up. Oddly, she never took her meals at the house, and Claerwen guessed the woman ate while foraging. Most of the time she was absent or working with the plants, and avoided Marcus altogether, her way of affecting an uneasy truce with him.

The days turned into fortnights, a month passed. Dawn came again. The first rays from the rising sun streamed through the open doorway. Claerwen listened to the quiet. So peaceful, she thought. And no pain. Her body seemed at rest as well. She must have slept comfortably—for the first time—and wondered, had Tangwen put chamomile or some other herb in the last infusion, something to help induce sleep? A bit more lucid, though still feeling dull-witted, she remembered no fitful dreams of pain. Still, she was afraid to move much, even to stretch, fearful of starting up the tortuous agony once more.

To her right, the fire pit smoked profusely, a swirling column of pale, sunlit silver rose and escaped through the smoke hole in the roof. Beyond, curled on her side against the opposite wall, Tangwen drowsed on her reed pallet, her head on her arm.

She knows, Claerwen thought. The woman knows the day will come when she must speak of Macsen's sword. Was it *so* painful? *So* horrible? Claerwen wished that day would come soon. Then she and Marcus could finish their quest and go home and she could get well again.

She also pondered the story Marcus had told of Blaez. The Frank had sounded likeable and kind, and the woman described as gracious. Even Beornwulf, who had never met Tangwen, had the impression of a kind woman. Claerwen had felt immediate sympathy, but now, gazing at Tangwen's face, she could not conjure up sympathy at all, not even with the bond of fire in the head. Perhaps Blaez's betrayal had created the coldness in her even though she must have realized it had saved her life. To Claerwen, the woman was singularly impersonal, and she wondered how Tangwen had ever taken to the healing arts.

Claerwen looked to the other side of the house. Shadows gloomed the place Marcus slept every night. She could barely see him there, sprawled flat on his back on the bare dirt floor, a wineskin in the crook of his elbow. He snored lightly. In another time and place, she would have let laughter claim her at the comical way he looked, but now she only felt his loneliness. She wondered where he was getting his drink.

Rustling came from Tangwen's side. The woman had wakened and was circling the fire pit. Kneeling, she pressed an ear to Claerwen's chest in the daily examination of her heart and breathing.

"A little stronger today," she reported. "Continue with the hawthorn berries, along with the other herbs."

The woman said that every day, Claerwen thought in frustration and disappointment. The improvement was minimal overall—one day a little better, the next day worse again, and her stomach still had the feeling it had sunk clear through to the floor beneath her. In the beginning she had thought that meant she was hungry and eating would ease the nausea, but solid food had not helped at all. Claerwen was beginning to wonder if she had made an assumption she shouldn't have about how well the woman truly knew healing.

"Your heart is getting stronger, even if you don't believe me," Tangwen said. "You should start to walk a little everyday. It will help you regain your strength. Get him to help you." She cocked her head at Marcus. "He should make himself more useful."

Claerwen resented the judgmental tone. Sure, Tangwen had produced medicines, but Marcus had done all the rest of the household chores.

Tangwen rose. She poured more of the hawthorn and willow bark infusion into the small wooden bowl, the same as she did three times every day. She set it down next to Claerwen.

"The women are returning to the colony," Tangwen announced. "I saw them across the lake late yesterday."

"You're going back to them? Now?"

"I must."

Pangs of uncertainty rattled Claerwen. "You can't go. Not yet."

"Your man can help you."

"But—'tis not safe, is it?"

Tangwen's brilliant green eyes bored into Claerwen. "Handor has not been seen again. I am leaving for where I belong." With that, she whisked out through the doorway.

Disheartened, Claerwen gazed at the bowl and felt like an animal that had just been provided its daily ration. She looked over at Marcus again. Several days' worth of beard darkened his face. Grey salted it like his hair. He had missed his usual morning hunt and was still sleeping. Too much to drink again.

She considered the bowl. Left without supervision, she had been given a challenge. Or was it a threat? Medicine? Or poison? She glared at the doorway and wanted to call the woman ugly names. No use.

The bowl sat within an arm's reach. She would have to sit up without help to pick it up and drink it. Her whole chest still ached constantly, and when she pressed her hand lightly to the bone between her uppermost ribs, it felt like gravel lay underneath and brought a mild sense of palpitation from her heart. She believed the ribs had fused again to the bone, but rough movement could dislodge them before they had a chance to truly heal.

"Marcus?" she called, her voice still as weak as she felt. No movement from him. Ah, well, the time had come to try to sit up alone anyway, and she did feel more alert. Perhaps this one small achievement, if she accomplished it, would signal the beginning of new strength.

Claerwen fisted her hands and pressed her knuckles down into the reed bedding a little behind her hips. She adjusted both until they were comfortable, closed her eyes and readied herself. How simple—sitting up, or walking, or running, or tumbling across the grass with Marcus once was. Pangs of loneliness gripped her and she looked once more to him. Still no movement. With a sigh, she pushed.

It was easier than expected. Though her heart raced with the simple exertion, she had succeeded. Now, for the bowl. She braced herself, one hand planted on the bedding, and reached. The distrust reared again when she picked it up. She sipped just enough to taste. It was the same as before. Relief. She drank it down.

In the same moment she set down the bowl, Marcus grunted and rolled over. Gradually, he gained his bearings and sat up. Claerwen watched his head come around. When his confused gaze crossed her, the strange hollow look came into his eyes again. She thought it looked akin to shame.

He surveyed the house and his gaze came back to her. The shame turned into surprise. "You sat up on your own?"

Claerwen nodded.

"This is so fine indeed," he said and crawled to her. "Perhaps then, by autumn, I can take you home—"

"She's gone, Marcus."

"Gone?"

"She said the women are returning to the colony. She's going back there."

He sat back on his heels. Astonishment, sadness and resentment mingled on his face. "Good," he said. "I reckoned as much from her, I just didn't expect her to go so abruptly."

"Then…you've seen them as well. She said there was no sign of Handor and thought it safe. Why would he give up so—" She regarded him. His eyes were growing grim again, and she smelled the mead on him. "That's what you did."

"Did?"

She took hold of his arm. The cut had healed but a thin scar remained, one among many. "The Iron Hawk fought Handor again, to drive him away. Didn't he? The women fled at the same time as well. Then you were able to take anything you wanted from Tangwen's infirmary."

"Handor doesn't matter now, Claeri. I will help you be strong again, and with luck, I can take you home before winter."

"No." Claerwen shook her head. Ceredig had used the same words about Beornwulf. "Handor does matter. We will finish what we started."

He stood and raked back his hair. "You can't be serious."

"I am, Marcus. If there is any chance to regain my strength, I will take it, and we will finish this. *Then* we'll go home."

"No. Nothing matters now, except to get you home and safe and well again. Not the sword, not Handor, nothing."

"Did the Iron Hawk kill Handor?"

"No."

"Then he does still matter."

When no other response came, she knew Marcus had no faith in her recovery, even if she were home and had all the time and help possible. She watched him turn away and walk outside.

Claerwen held her face in her hands. Why? If he thought Handor made no difference, why was he still so entrenched in the anger and guilt? What was it about that awful man that drove the pain and nightmares? If Ceredig was right, that Marcus had witnessed an unspeakable atrocity all those years ago, how could Handor have any connection to that? And even if Handor did, to kill him would not free Marcus. He would only bury the guilt inside himself again.

And if she should die, what would he do then?

CHAPTER 29

Rheged
Autumn, AD 476

THE awful smell was there again. Please, not again, Marcus wished. How many times was it now that he had stood in the old Roman building, a boy again? Somewhere, the screaming woman wailed with the wind and rain. Her shriek echoed over and over in raw, piercing agony.

Then silence. Only the beams above, invisible in the dark, moaned under the slow sway of the dead. The last of the shadows faded, and he was utterly alone, an adult now, suspended in an endless dark space.

He felt a sword in his hand, the familiar feel of the Iron Hawk's weapon. He glared through the masked helmet. Before him, Handor stood, eyes wide with terror, bleeding and barely able to stay on his feet. It had been a good, satisfying fight, the Iron Hawk relished. He reveled in the feel of strong heaving in his chest and the sweat running off him.

Behind the mask, he smiled bitterly. It was comfortable there, hidden, unreachable, untouchable. Now…for the final descent…

He tossed the sword up and caught it in a new grip, like a huge dagger. Arm cocked back, he thrust it with all his strength. The blade sliced into Handor all the way up to the cross-guard.

Handor stared at the sword in disbelief. Whether he was stunned that he was still alive or that he had lost the fight—and his life—the Iron Hawk could only speculate. He crossed to the assassin and wadded the neck of his tunic with one hand and gripped the weapon's handle with his other. "This…is for flesh and blood and bone," he hissed into the face that was quickly draining its color.

He twisted the handle to the left. A soft sucking noise told him he had torn deeply of the flesh. He turned it to the right. Scraping. He had hit bone. The face was blue, the chin quivered, streamers of dark red dripped from the mouth, and the stink of death was already rising.

By the gods, the stink of death again.

He pushed the dead man away and pulled out the sword as the body fell. Several steps away, he halted. Flesh and blood and bone. For honor? No, he thought. Bloodshed never spoke of honor.

Marcus dropped onto his knees. The helmet was gone. He watched rivulets of blood drip from the sword's edges into the grass—his own sword now, no longer the Iron Hawk's. Thick bits of flesh and splinters of bone stuck in the fuller. If he did not clean the steel quickly, the matter would congeal in the coating of blood. Yet calmness had come upon him and was too all-encompassing to disturb. He wanted to savor it. With aching slowness, he laid the sword on the ground.

He looked down at his own belly. A gaping hole with blood gushing from it had been gouged into him. He stared, just as Handor had. A most satisfying fight, indeed, he thought. Now, at last, with the life flowing out of him, perhaps he could forget how he had abandoned his soul. At last, he might be able to rest.

Someone was calling. The voice wavered.

"Marcus?"

He let the cold wind wash over him and cool the sweat that ran down from his scalp.

"Marcus? Are you awake? Are you—?"

He sat up and swore. Another nightmare. Same beginning, different end this time.

Claerwen was calling him. She was sitting among the supplies of herbs and medicines on the other side of the house. And she was staring at him.

"'Tis nothing," he muttered and shook his head to clear the mud and soot of concentration that clung to his mind. The image of his sword grinding into Handor's flesh refused to let go. He lurched onto his feet and crossed the floor.

Her face stopped him before he could ask what she needed. Even in the dim light of dawn, he saw her pallor could rival the whitest marble. The pouch in her lap was one in which Tangwen had stored herbs to be used only as a last resort. It contained a packet of foxglove and he could see she had been struggling to open the leather ties; her hands were shaking too much, her fingers unable to work loose the knots.

Kneeling, he touched his fingers to the pulse in her neck.

"Can't breathe," she gasped out. "Feel sick, so weak." She pushed the pouch towards him. Her eyes pleaded for him to open it.

"The foxglove is too dangerous," he said and took it from her. "We don't know how to measure it."

"Getting worse. My heart…feels like…jumping all over inside. No choice left."

The fear of losing her stung him. She had been doing well since Tangwen had left, and by the time Lughnasa had marked the beginning of autumn, she had been walking short distances without help. He had hoped she would be strong enough to travel soon, but now he realized she had been tiring more quickly and not eating well for several days.

"I'll go find Tangwen," he said and made to rise.

"No." She clutched at his arm. "I can make the infusion myself."

"It's too dangerous. You could poison yourself."

"I can—" She leaned and slowly coiled in on herself, in the way ashes curled when burned. Her knees drew up involuntarily, and she held her fist to her chest, as if willing the pain to stop. Sweat instantly drenched her.

Marcus called her name, again and again. She could no longer answer. He dropped the pouch and lifted her, carried her to the reed bedding, laid her on it. Without pause he darted beneath the doorway's low lintel and crashed through the thick foliage surrounding the house. A trail of yellow and russet leaves showered down behind him.

He knew where Tangwen probably was. Often, he had discovered her while he'd been hunting or patrolling. Not far from the house, she hid in the woods where several peculiar oak trees grew closely together. There she harvested rare cuttings that grew among them. The trees had been lightning-struck, and their branches twisted together and dipped nearly to the ground to create a bower. Marcus guessed the woman enjoyed privacy, even from the other women, and found comfort in the old trees. On the occasions when he had seen her, he had merely observed then left unnoticed.

Now, he burst through the woods in a fluster of leaves. He skidded to a halt not more than three paces from Tangwen.

She was seated on one of the oaks' low-bent branches, her eyes closed in meditation. At his disturbance, they opened with a withering stare.

"She is failing?" she asked.

Failing. The word hit Marcus in the gut. "Aye, she is."

Tangwen ran past him. Her robes flared and caught against the underbrush's protruding twigs in her rush. Marcus followed.

In the house, Tangwen dropped to her knees and bent over a gasping, white-faced Claerwen. "I was afraid this would happen," she said after a brief examination. Her brows dipped down at Marcus.

"Is there nothing you can do?"

Her sharp green eyes filled with a concern he had never seen before. "One more infusion." Her gaze dropped to Claerwen. "Different from the others."

"Foxglove?" He knelt.

"'Tis dangerous."

Tangwen's stare challenged him for permission to proceed. Marcus's stomach sank along with his hope. Foxglove, the beautiful purple flower that was capable of healing, but only when it reached a dosage close enough to kill. The slippage from one to the other was so tenuous even the most skilled healer could never be sure the measurement was correct.

"If I don't—" she began.

"And if you do? And it's too strong? Or she can't tolerate it?"

"It's her only chance—"

Claerwen's fingers brushed his knee. He leaned, his ear to her lips, but her whisper was so light he could not understand. She repeated, several times; finally he caught the words: "Let her do it.

Please."

He straightened, his eyes not focused. She was begging him to give permission. When he had pulled her from the mud-packed rivershore, he had fully believed then she had died. How could he see her like that again? He wiped a hand across his eyes.

Tangwen intruded on his private anguish. "She wants the infusion?"

He sat back on his heels and winced.

Claerwen's face turned slowly to Tangwen and her eyes opened. They looked as if they had sunken into her head just within the past few moments. "Give it to me," she mouthed.

Tangwen's gaze burned into Marcus. He knew the choice was Claerwen's. He had no right to take that away from her. She was failing. Minute by minute. He could hear it in her scratchy breathing, see it in her clenched hands. It was worse now than when he had first brought her to the house. How could he allow it? How could he not? He had done this to her with his need to control and protect, and she had complained, not only on the morning before the accident but many times. He was too sheltering. She had said he put her in worse jeopardy by blocking her from seeing danger coming. He had only wanted to keep her safe, the one need she had in her life. Yet now, because of his stubbornness, he could lose her.

"So be it," he said. "Do it."

He bowed his head, his face in his hands. She was failing. And he had just done the equivalent of signing her execution decree.

Singing. Someone was singing. A long way off. In an old language. Lilting, magical, soothing.

Marcus tried to raise his head but it was so heavy he could barely turn it to one side. A dream, he thought, it must have been another dream.

Night after day after night had passed, and he had kept vigil while Tangwen worked the foxglove formula again and again. Delicate, tiny flowers, he pondered each time she developed a new infusion. So deadly. And Claerwen's last hope.

If only it would work.

The singing became clearer. It was a chant rather than a song. How long he had slept? He could not remember lying down. He opened his eyes. Still night, and the house was black inside except for a soft red glow from the fire pit's coals. Between, an arm's length away, the silhouette of a wineskin blocked his view.

The chanting, he realized, had not been from a dream but from Tangwen. He listened, drawn in, and quickly became mesmerized. Her voice was not so rich and the words were in a language, though familiar in its sound, he did not understand. This was of the old ways, a voice of the ancestors. He had heard druids speak it, including Myrddin.

Marcus sat up. Tangwen had pulled her reed pallet near Claerwen and was sitting on it. She rocked with her eyes closed, engrossed in the chant. How many nights had passed since the decision to use the foxglove? Even Tangwen had lost count. The chant meant the foxglove still had not worked and the woman had taken to her last option. He watched Claerwen cling to a fraying thread of life.

The chanting stopped. Tangwen's exhausted eyes traced over Claerwen.

"She does not improve," Marcus said.

Tangwen laid a hand on Claerwen's brow, then her cheek. "Something has changed." She leaned to listen to Claerwen's heart, a motion that had become habit.

Light from the fire pit illuminated Claerwen's face. Marcus crawled across to her. "Is she conscious?"

"No. Her eyes are open, but she's not responding like one who is awake."

He watched Claerwen's eyes shift back and forth between slitted eyelids. She rambled in a low, constant mumble. "Is she talking?"

"The medicine can give bad dreams."

Or visions? Marcus questioned silently. "What does this mean?"

Tangwen settled back on her pallet. Head bowed, her face receded into her white kerchiefs. With her hands folded together, she began to chant again.

Marcus muttered an oath. He ignored the cold glance it brought him and listened to Claerwen's spirit fight. Her mumbling's pattern nearly matched the rhythm of the chant, but while the singing soothed, Claerwen's whisperings sounded distressed and were growing more so. Her eyes no longer moved but stared at the darkness above.

Marcus picked up her hand. "What is it, Claeri?" He leaned close. "What do you wish to tell?"

Her lips stopped moving and she appeared to drift, then her eyes closed. Soon, the words started to form again, more clearly this time. "Don't let Handor…"

Marcus glanced up at Tangwen. Had she noticed? The woman remained distant, unhearing.

"Don't let him," Claerwen said. "No, not the— Don't tell Handor."

A period of silence passed. "Tell him what, Claeri?" he whispered close to her ear.

"My father has it."

Confused, Marcus sat upright. Tangwen had gone silent again and frowned. "The foxglove can make her delusional," she said. "I don't think she can hear you."

"If you believed that, you wouldn't sing all night. It's supposed to ease her distress, isn't it?"

"The torque," Claerwen blurted. "He cannot know of it. My father—"

Marcus shut his surprise behind a blank face. He hoped Tangwen truly did think the remarks were nonsense and that his reaction was merely his patience chewed beyond recognition.

"You are not one of those of the new religion, are you?" Tangwen asked. "One of those who thinks this is evil because it belongs to the old ways?"

He scowled back at her. "No. Never."

Claerwen was silent now, the tension gone as suddenly as it had come. He stroked her hand. Dreams, Tangwen had called it. And delusions. No, she had sounded more like she spoke from a vision. Or the memory of a vision. She had once seen all the pieces of Macsen's Treasure in one, including the sacred torque.

"She can hear me," he said. "In her soul."

"She can feel your anger," Tangwen advised. "And your absence.

As if you're not inside yourself." She rose and walked out of the house into the night.

"My absence," he said and he smoothed Claerwen's hair. "You have all the right to have lost faith in me. I can't expect your forgiveness any more than from all the others I have failed."

He knew another nightmare would come that night. He could already sense the images bleeding through the cracks of the thick gates behind which he tried to keep them blocked.

No, he told himself. Not now. Not this night. He eased down and pressed his face to Claerwen's shoulder. He curled in as close as possible, his palm against her side. Her chest rose and fell unevenly, and he drew long and slow breaths. If she could feel him, perhaps she would try to match them. He moved up a little and pressed an ear to her neck. The blood coursed through her—slow, fast, slow, strong, weak. Mostly weak.

He closed his eyes and willed her to live.

Jostling woke Marcus. Fully alert, he had expected Claerwen's discomfort to disturb him. For anything she needed, he was prepared to rouse Tangwen.

But he was not prepared to see that morning had already come again and Claerwen had sat up—without help. She was tentatively testing her steadiness. In wonder, he watched her take a breath, deliberately shallow at first. No cough. She winced. Pain, but not the hard, face-wrinkling grimace as before. She took a deeper breath with caution, and let it out.

"Claeri?" he called softly.

Her eyes darted back and forth. Amazed that she was sitting upright, she turned to him.

Marcus sat up, cross-legged, and faced her. He allowed a smile to start. "By the light," he said and he reached to brace her up by the arms. Frail between his hands, she sagged, and he touched her as if she would shatter under the slightest pressure. Still, it was a step he would have never foreseen the night before.

"I will take you home soon," he whispered. "I promise you."

He hoped the thought would bring a smile and she would slip

into his embrace, but her eyes bored into his.

"Claerwen?"

She gave no response.

Marcus leaned closer. "I *will* take you home…where you will have all the time you need to be well again. And safe, Claeri. Soon."

He bit off his words when Tangwen appeared at the fire pit. She stirred the coals to life and glared at him, then at Claerwen in assessment. She was unsurprised by her patient's sudden progress. How long had the woman been awake and observing in her cool, uncaring manner?

"It will be a long time before she can go home," Tangwen said. "Even with the correct amount of foxglove, she needs to rebuild her strength as much as her damaged heart can bear. You see how weak she is. But if any change occurs in her, I will need to rework the infusion to match the change. Do not plan to leave before spring at the earliest."

Tangwen stood with her arms folded in defiance. "I'll be returning to the grove today." With that, she left the house.

Resentment spun up inside Marcus like a windstorm, and his eyes pinched tightly as if to hold it back from exploding. For so long he had wanted to fully savor the sweep of joy over Claerwen's mending health. Calm down, he told himself. Stay in control. She needs attention, not anger. In that regard, Tangwen was right. The anger had to stop.

In the days that followed, Marcus resettled into the routine of hunting most mornings and evenings. Though fragile, Claerwen once more doggedly began the long task to regain her strength. By early winter, she was able to walk unassisted and took over the cooking chores. Most of the pain had subsided.

Winter deepened. More weeks passed.

On another freezing afternoon, bundled in his cloak, Marcus stopped on his way back to the house and watched the pale sun fade between barren trees. He was early that day, having caught two hares. He stared grimly and thought of the holiday of Imbolc that had slipped by a few days before and marked the beginning of spring by the old calendar. He had already sensed the change coming. The last of the snow was only a few patches of dirty, brittle ice. Claerwen had been healing well, though she still tired easily. Soon she would be strong enough to travel. But what would that bring? She never spoke of going home.

A cold wind squalled and whipped Marcus's hair into his face. He opened his eyes. The sun was down and he had been lost in thought far longer than the few moments he had planned. He pushed back his hair, turned again for the house, and wondered if Claerwen was afraid of going home.

Spring, AD 477

Sunlight illuminated thousands of fluttering young leaves. Claerwen leaned back and raised her face to meet the warmth of the full spring afternoon, gentle as a soft lamb's wool blanket. Her hair, loose and damp, draped her shoulders and back. Like a creature at home in the woods, she sat with her legs curled under her while she let the air dry her skin from bathing. Seated on a cloak, her clothes next to her, she arranged its wide folds around her legs and hips to keep the damp ground from chilling her.

Claerwen breathed deeply of the earth's scents and the fresh green and gold light. The small stream she had chosen for bathing trickled a few paces away. The woods were thick enough to afford privacy, but she knew it was not truly safe.

Just a bit longer, she wished. The peacefulness was exquisite compared to the house filled with Marcus's incessant brooding. She sighed and heard her own sadness in the sound. Even now that she was clearly getting stronger, he still only talked of going home—when he talked at all. She could not understand his silence about the quest. That he had not confronted Tangwen about Macsen's sword by now with his usual bluntness or had planned a ruse to trick the woman into talking was so unlike him.

And his drinking, though it had always been abundant, baffled her in its chronic excessiveness. Oddly, that had eased a bit in the last weeks, but only by the increase in his brooding, as if he had forgotten a wineskin was within easy reach.

She closed her eyes and imagined if he were to come up from

behind, softly calling her name, then touch her the way she loved to be touched with his big hands. Little time had been left for affection between the end of exile and the accident, and since, they had carefully avoided anything that would tax her strength. She missed him even more now than during the exile—here she could see him, smell him, hear his voice, and not be able to give in to her craving.

"Claeri?"

She smiled at the sound of his voice, soft, gentle, commanding. Then she realized he was standing there, just as she had wished. She snatched up her undertunic in a clump in front of herself and twisted around. Wet and stripped to his loincloth, he must have been bathing in the same stream but far enough away that she had not heard him. His clothes were rolled together under one arm; his other hand held his sword, the bow, and the quiver of arrows by its strap.

"I didn't mean to startle you," he said and knelt. He set down the clothing and gear. His wet hair dripped over his shoulders.

When she met his black eyes, they were exactly the same as on the night she had first met him, somber and sad and so intense they seemed to keep her from falling away into the deepest abyss. The difference was the age in them; hardships had taken their toll and wiped away the hopefulness of his youth. It was like looking at his reflection repeated in multiple mirrors, each a little farther away, each from a lifetime in which she had known him, backward and forward, for all time.

She touched his face, then moved her fingers into his hair. She kissed him, full and heated; and when he tried to withdraw, she pulled him close again.

"Are you sure?" he whispered.

Her next kiss was far more fervent. When his hand slid beneath the undertunic, she could not help herself. His rough hands, warm and insistent on her breasts, rose chills that raced across her skin. Heat followed. The tunic dropped, and he pushed her back into the folds of the cloak.

Ever and forever, the vow made between them on their wedding day raced through her memory. By the gods, how she treasured this man. In the warmth of the sunlight pouring down, she gave herself to him without reservation.

Afterward, they dozed long into the early evening. To Claerwen, Marcus looked more content than in months. No other words had been said. None could be. She squeezed her eyes shut on tears of both joy and relief. No pain had returned or even threatened in the exertion, no weakness, no nausea. For the first time, she truly believed she was getting well.

When the first hint of coolness stirred the air, they rose and dressed. Marcus promised to return early and went back to hunting. Claerwen started for the house.

Not long, the walk back followed the stream she had bathed in then went on down through the thickest of the woods. Glimpses of the lake to the east were visible on clear days when the water sparkled brightly. Fells to the west rose sharply.

Claerwen was halfway down when movement caught her attention. She expected to see a grazing hart—Marcus had told her that more than one of the hills had been named Hart Fell for the magnificent male red deer found there.

But no deer grazed. Tangwen walked through the woods instead, her direction straight for the house. Claerwen watched from a stand of birches until the older woman was well away, then followed.

By the time Claerwen reached the house, Tangwen stood at the hearth. Cool assessment branded the woman's face. "You appear to be doing well," she said.

"Why are you here?" Claerwen returned her own appraisal.

The woman's brilliant green eyes bored into Claerwen. "'Tis not safe any longer."

"We haven't seen Handor since summer—"

"Not Handor. Meirchion. His soldiers."

"How do you know this?"

"I've seen them. Within the past hour. I counted twenty men marching south. I couldn't see how heavily armed they were. But they carry Meirchion of Rheged's standard."

Soldiers from Meirchion Gul? In the fells? Claerwen wondered what they could be looking for so far from Caer Luguvalos. Twenty was too few to have been raiding into Strathclyde. "Were they moving as if towards a destination?" she asked. "Or were they fanned out like they were searching?"

"They marched in a line. They seemed to have no interest in their surroundings."

"Probably an escort returning to Caer Luguvalos," Claerwen said. "But that doesn't mean more aren't behind them."

A lengthy silence followed. She wondered why Tangwen had come. Warning was not in her nature. Then, to Claerwen, it seemed the air inside the house was growing closer, like it was thickening.

"Do you remember what you said in the night before you finally began to recover?" Tangwen asked. Her voice sounded odd, as if it came out of the oppressive air.

Suspicious, Claerwen held the woman's eyes. She remembered nothing—except being sure she was going to die. She shook her head.

"You mumbled for a long time. You mentioned Handor."

"Foxglove gives strangeness to the mind. Perhaps I dreamed badly."

Tangwen's head swayed back and forth. "No, you did not. You clearly said Handor's name. Then you spoke of your father. And a torque. You said something like, 'don't let Handor know my father has it.'"

Fire in the head. Claerwen recognized the gods' presence in the house. It strengthened and held her shock in check. "I don't remember saying anything," she said and wondered what other secrets she had mistakenly babbled.

"But you know of the torque. You must. And if you know of that, you know of Excalibur as well."

If only she did know, Claerwen wished. And how much she should say. Here was an unexpected crack in the door she had needed to open for so long—the gods were handing it to her—but if she made a mistake like the last time… She calmed herself and drew on the gods' closeness for courage.

"The high king has the torque," she said. "As it should be."

"How could you know if the king has the torque? It was lost with the rest of Macsen's Treasure."

"The torque was not lost." Claerwen spoke, low, clear, with hope to pry the crack open a bit more. "It was hidden for safekeeping, like all the other pieces, until it was returned to the high king." She hardened her face to make the woman feel discomfort. "My father was the keeper of Macsen's torque."

The coolness in Tangwen's eyes fell away like a scab crumbling to reveal tender new skin. She rubbed her temples, and when she bowed her face to hide her new astonishment, she inadvertently pushed back the kerchiefs. Already loose, they slid down around her neck.

Claerwen had never seen her without them. The woman had white hair, pure white, not tinged yellow the way aging hair often became. And it was smooth and soft as feathers. Its clean lines contrasted sharply with the common notion of an aging woman healer—a grizzled, haggard crone.

Claerwen was reminded of a cat, a beautiful, fine-boned white cat with huge bright green eyes. She studied Tangwen's face, wide-cheeked, short chinned, the delicate, crinkly skin of a woman well past her fiftieth year. She had no notion of Tangwen's true age. But as their eyes met again, she had the sense they had known each other before in some ancient time where they had shared another meeting begun in distrust and anger and uncertainty.

Claerwen drew the woman to sit at the hearth. "Handor's name brings you fear. The way it brings Marcus hatred and anger."

Tears slowly filled Tangwen's eyes. "I am so ashamed of him. He was different when he was young."

Claerwen was surprised their acquaintance went back so far. "What happened to him…after his father was killed?"

The older woman's eyes snapped up. "His father?"

Claerwen nodded slowly. "Aye, I know Hywel Gwodryd was his father. I also know Meirchion Gul of Rheged murdered Hywel. But that's all I know."

Tangwen's shoulders drooped as if she were relieved. "Handor fled after…Hywel…was killed. I went back to the colony to hide, I was so afraid of Meirchion. More than a year later, I heard it said Saxons had captured Handor and enslaved him somewhere on the Saxon Shore. How he got away and why he came back here, I don't know. He's grown into a man so cold and bitter, I fear him as much as Meirchion."

"Because you witnessed the murder? And that's why Meirchion's name brings you fear as much as Handor's?"

The green eyes widened then grew sadder.

"Do you know *why* Hywel was killed?" Claerwen asked.

A narrow shake of the head.

"The rumors say," Claerwen tested, "that Hwyel knew Meirchion planned an uprising that would damage Rheged."

"You ask too many questions."

"I must, Lady Tangwen. 'Tis no longer a matter of choice." She lifted her hands, palms upward. "The gods are within this place. You know this, don't you? You have fire in the head, just as I do." She paused to let her words take hold. "It's Macsen's sword the prince wants, is it not? We have come to believe Meirchion learned Hywel was the sword's keeper, and he's using Handor to find it because Hywel was his father. But Handor never knew anything about the sword. He believes you do."

The tears fell down Tangwen's cheeks, one by one in silvery lines. "How can you possibly know all this?"

Claerwen held back from speaking of Beornwulf or Blaez. She had already said enough, and now she found herself fighting her own tears. Here was the woman described to Marcus.

"I don't where the sword is," Tangwen said. "I only told you it didn't exist to make you leave me alone. I cannot remember."

"But you knew at one time?"

"I was perhaps five-and-ten summers. My mother was still alive. She belonged to the colony as well and was teaching me the healing herbs. I wandered away from her to find some of the plants on my own and saw a young man digging in the woods...burying a sword."

Claerwen touched one of Tangwen's trembling hands.

"I told no one of what I had seen," the older woman went on.

"But you don't know where? If it was close to the grove?"

"I never tried to find it again. He buried it at the foot of a stone—one of those carved to look like the place's spirit. Except this stone was odd, it had a strange shape. The carving looked incomplete—"

Claerwen drew a sharp breath that stopped Tangwen. "Does it

look like an anvil?"

Tangwen shivered. "You've seen it?"

"Only in the fire. I don't know where it is. But I've seen it in visions."

"By the light..." Tangwen looked like she was going to be sick. "Have you seen if Handor still wears a small piece of metal hung from his neck?"

Claerwen shook her head.

"Hywel gave him a piece of metal—it's raw iron actually—on a leather thong, years ago, when Handor was quite young. It has a mark on it that matches one on the anvil stone. He always wore it."

"Does Handor know what it means?"

"I'm sure he does...not." Her eyes lifted to the doorway.

Claerwen turned. "Marcus..." she breathed. She felt his presence fill the house, as if the gods had abruptly withdrawn in order to allow him to enter. Anger stood in his eyes and he dropped his hunting gear. She rose.

Tangwen got to her feet as well. She caught Claerwen's arm and stepped past her. "I want to know—when you brought the medicines from the grove, did you go there to kill Handor?"

His eyes shifted from Claerwen to the older woman. "No."

The coldness in his tone jarred Claerwen.

His glare grew harsher. "Too many questions would have been asked if his body were found. I would not kill him on Lord Ector's lands. Not then."

He brushed past Tangwen and stood before Claerwen. His black eyes burned into hers, and his fingertips traced a lock of her hair, from her temple to her shoulder. "Stay here," he whispered so faintly she barely heard him. "I'll be back soon."

He turned from her and strode through the doorway.

"Marcus!" she called after him.

Tangwen grabbed her arm again. "Let him go."

"No, I must—"

"Let him go."

Claerwen stared at the empty doorway. "Why?" she whispered. The abrupt change in him was stunning.

Tangwen tugged on her arm. "Has your man seen Handor?"

Claerwen stared at her blankly. "Handor… Now? Here?"

Fear shook the woman, and she gave a single nod.

Claerwen sensed the power of the gods had reclaimed the house, and that was how Tangwen knew.

"Will your man kill him?" the woman asked.

Chills quivered on Claerwen's skin. "By the gods, I don't know, but he very well could. Did you hear what he said? 'Not then.' He didn't kill Handor *then*." She surged forward into the doorway. "But Meirchion's soldiers— If he hasn't seen them—"

"What will you do?" Tangwen came up behind her.

Claerwen pushed her back. "Stay here. I'm going to warn him."

"But if your heart is damaged further, it could cost your life."

"If I don't go," Claerwen said, "I could cost Marcus his life. I will be fine enough. Douse the fire pit. Either stay in the house, or better, hide in the woods. The colony won't be safe. If Handor is out there, don't let him find you."

Claerwen rushed out. In the horse pen next to the house, she heard the animals rustle. One was saddled, ready to give chase, but still inside the pen. She could not imagine Marcus had gone after Handor on foot—unless Handor had been so close that a horse was unnecessary…

She ran to the fence. No sign of Marcus. Instead, metal gleamed, out of place. His sheathed sword lay along the house's wall, the cross-guard caught in the deeply angled late afternoon sun.

Claerwen opened the gate and crossed the pen. On the ground next to the sword, she found a cloth—an oilcloth—had been carelessly thrown down. "No," she breathed and picked it up. A scattering of old, moldy thatch dropped from it and led her to look up into the roof's eave. A slender hole showed where he had been hiding the Iron Hawk's gear.

She hugged the cloth. Short of breath, she pressed a hand to her heart and willed it to slow down. Exertion or worry, she could not tell which drove it. "By all the stars in the heavens, Marcus," she said but was afraid to finish her thought.

Chapter 30

Rheged
Spring, AD 477

DEATH *to you… Your choice…*

Words from the effigy pried into the Iron Hawk's calculated thoughts. Crouched behind a low, sharp-edged ridge of stone, he studied the scruffy gorse and heath-covered fells—from the steep slope on which he waited, down to the trickling stream at the bottom and up the opposite hill. In the fading light, Handor refilled a small waterskin at the stream's brink.

While he watched, the Iron Hawk pried up a small stone with jagged edges. Aye, he wanted Handor's death. Like no other he had ever wanted, but he could not name what it was in the man that created such steel-bound hatred. It dug farther into his soul than mere revenge for the attempt on Claerwen's life. It had started before then and was more scarred, more dredging. *Death to you,* he glared through the helmet's eye slits. Stay and fight, or run again. Make a choice.

Darkness was closing in, just enough for the Iron Hawk's black leather armor to blend into the gloom. He crept crablike down the hillside and kept to the heath to soften his footfalls. From behind a sprawling gorse bush, he took aim and pitched the rock.

He was up and running before it struck. The assassin jerked when it did, and before he realized what had happened, the warrior rammed a fist into the back of his head.

The assassin dropped, stunned but not unconscious. The Iron Hawk heaved him over and confiscated a sword and a knife, threw them far across the heath, then rifled under the neck of the man's tunic. A frayed cord ran loosely around Handor's throat, a small stone hung from it. The warrior tore it off and stuffed it inside his tunic.

Handor moaned. The Iron Hawk stood. Then he pulled his own sword.

"Wait!"

The Iron Hawk spun around at the shout. Intent on his quarry, he had not heard the muffled thud of hooves descending the hill from the opposite side. He swore. Claerwen rode towards him.

"Go back!" He punched a fist in the direction of the lake.

She kept on towards him. "You must come with me!"

"Go back. It's too dangerous!" He caught the bridle and forced her horse around.

Claerwen backed the animal before he could slap its rump. "Listen to me!"

He dragged her off like she was a sack of grain, his arm around her waist, and he half-carried, half-dragged her up the hill. He pulled the horse behind them. A stand of trees loomed at the top, bracken in the spaces between that spilled out and down to meet the heather. Behind a broad oak, he pushed her up against the trunk.

"Do you know what you've walked into?" His voice dropped to a harsh whisper. "No, don't answer now. Just stay here." He started to turn away.

She took hold of his arm with both hands.

"Stop, Claerwen. Let me loose."

"Listen to me—"

He shook free, but she sprang again and hooked one hand in his belt, the other gripped his baldric. She hung on with all her strength. If he moved he would have to drag her with him.

"Please… Marcus—"

He tore off the helmet. "You know better than to call me that when—"

"Marcus, soldiers are out there. *Meirchion's* soldiers. They're coming this way."

He held still, glaring, and glanced at the sky through the tree-tops. If the assassin wakened and tried to run, was enough time left to hunt him down? The twilight was nearly gone and deepening fast into nightfall. Too fast.

"Listen." Claerwen loosened her grip. The sound of marching feet neared. Shouted orders and the jangle of gear accompanied them.

"Quarter of a mile," Marcus estimated. "And moving fast." He turned a notch at a time in a half-circle to listen for direction. "Heading southwest. Strange they haven't made camp this late. The question is, are they in league with Handor? Or against him?"

"Or don't even know he's here," Claerwen said.

An instant later, the answer came. The king of Rheged's standard appeared above the next hill's profile before the first soldier could be seen. Handor wobbled onto his feet, caught sight of it, then stumbled away. He gradually gathered speed.

"What does it matter, except that they *not* find you?" Claerwen asked.

Marcus gripped her arm. He steered both her and the horse farther into the woods. In a deep fold in the hillside, he directed her to find a place to rest.

"We'll have to wait until complete darkness," he said and tethered the animal. "He's likely going back to his own camp, wherever it is. You should not have come."

He pulled on the masked helmet and retreated into the warrior's dispassionate, cold remoteness. There, he could be silent and alone, and he climbed a few paces up the hillside to a thinner section of trees. With eyes of stone, he prepared to keep vigil.

Below, he heard her settle in, her movements fatigued. Perhaps she was even light-headed, he guessed. He could just see her, knees drawn up, arms folded around them, her face resting on her arms.

His thoughts trudged on like a millstone that ground its rough surface against his mind. Once more, he needed to regain control. Claerwen had probably just saved his life. Again. Against twenty soldiers, even the Iron Hawk was still only one man. And she had risked her own life.

"Would that I had not caused you this," he murmured.

Her head lifted.

He pulled off the helmet again and went down to her. He knelt, his face level with hers.

"Would that you had not caused…what?" she asked.

His hand pressed her wrist. "You don't remember, do you?"

"Remember?"

"The flood. The accident. And why."

She shook her head. "Only what you told me, which was little. That's not a memory."

His hand retreated and he settled more comfortably, straightened his left knee to relieve the pain. He cradled the helmet and stared at it. "That night…I was late coming from the inn…because I was drunk. Bloody, filthy drunk."

His eyes closed and he gathered his thoughts to go on. When he opened them, light from a sliver of moon crept from behind the tree crowns and gave more definition to Claerwen's patient face.

His anger was rising again. He felt it grip the set of his mouth. Control, he told himself. Why could he never stay calm?

Claerwen touched his arm and tilted her face close enough that he felt her breath. "And you think you caused my accident, because you were late?"

"I did. Handor was at the inn. But—"

"You were not the cause of my accident."

"How can you say this?" He lifted his gaze again.

"It was Handor's fault."

"No…no…I could have stopped him if I hadn't drunk so much. But I liked it too bloody much—"

"You've always liked the drink. And you've drunk heavily as part of ruses before. That's not new."

"Not like this," he said sourly. "If I had been alert at all, I would have followed—"

"*Please*, the blame does not lie with you," she said. "I was angry. First because of how you wrote the terms of the exile and that you didn't allow me to at least know this, and then because you tried to stop me from confronting Tangwen. I failed there, Marcus. Badly. You were right, I should not have gone, I was too distracted. It was *not* your fault. This would have happened anyway."

Happened anyway? He frowned grimly at her and opened his mouth to deny her reasoning again. But he stopped. There was no reasoning. She had seen the accident coming. The fire had told her. And he had even seen clues—in her fear, in the fist she kept holding to her heart. If the gods had deemed it to happen, neither he nor Claerwen could have changed it.

"Marcus?" Her fingers tightened around his gauntleted wrist.

"He was wearing this." From his tunic, Marcus withdrew the cord with the stone. "I overheard Tangwen tell you about it."

Claerwen held it in her palm. "You…the Iron Hawk took this from him just now?"

"Hide it." He could not focus on her. He felt distant, cold, and he wanted to retreat deep within the warrior's persona again, even without the helmet.

"You *wanted* to kill Handor," Claerwen said softly.

"Leave it be," he warned.

"When I came down that hill, I could see it in you, in the way you moved, in your gestures. I have never seen it so in you before. For the few times you've actually crossed paths with that man, how can he warrant so much hatred?"

"It was not my intention to kill him. Only take that stone. Leave it be."

"If you had already taken it, why did you stay there? With your sword raised over him? You've never *wanted* to kill anyone. You've always hated the taking of a life. What is it that has changed in you?"

He gave no response. He couldn't, not without letting the anger loose again, and Claerwen was neither its source nor its target.

"Ceredig told me a story," she said. Her tone was still low, gentle but prodding. "He told me of a Saxon raid…when you were quite young. In an abandoned Roman fort near Dun Breatann."

Marcus stiffened and he dug his fingers into the helmet's leather. "Ceredig knows nothing."

"He doesn't know the details. But he knows how it affected you."

The Saxon atrocity invaded his memory. He rose and strode a few paces down the hillside, the biting anger in each step.

Claerwen lunged after him, caught his arm. "I won't ask you of the raid…what little Ceredig said was enough. But that's where the dreams come from, isn't it? It's why you took on this kind of life.

And the Iron Hawk."

"Stop it, Claerwen." He shook free and turned from her. She was getting too close.

"No, Marcus. Can you not see? The Iron Hawk went after Handor to take that piece of iron. But why the Iron Hawk? You didn't need him."

"Of course I did—"

"No, you did not," she said, calm, clear. "You know the fear that identity creates. You've said so yourself. In truth, it was only to make it *more* dangerous, to satisfy this…this seeming need for—"

"That is enough!"

"Why?" she raced on. "Why? Every time Handor is out there, or anyone else you've ever had to chase down— Has your life become so worthless to you? This rage, this…this brooding has you shackled worse than the irons Vortigern put on you."

"End this now or—"

"No!" She smacked the helmet out of the crook of his arm. The horse whinnied and sidled when the headgear bumped its legs. She gripped his tunic and clung.

Her outburst fueled his anger. He whisked her around and pushed her back until she dropped into the ferns. Braced against the hill with one knee, he caught her wrists and leaned over her.

"You *will* leave this alone, do you hear me?" he spoke through his teeth.

"Is this your true nature? Is the disdain for killing just a mask to hide it, a nature you won't admit to himself except through the Iron Hawk?"

He sat back. His jaw gnawed air and he let go of her hands. Raking back his hair, he rose and turned away. He fully expected her to lash out again, but he heard her sit up and choke out an apology.

Could it be, he wondered, that she never spoke of going home because of him? He couldn't blame her—who would want to live with the disagreeable oaf he had become? Gods, if he could just stop hurting her.

"Forgive me," he whispered. "Please." When he turned back to her, she threw herself into his arms.

Marcus was waking. He had no desire to yet—the night had been very short—but something had disturbed him. Rustling? Go away, he thought, and he rolled over. Beside him, Claerwen slept soundly, motionless. He snuggled closer.

More stirring.

Tangwen again? At barely daybreak? His face rumpled in annoyance. No one else knew of the house. But the noise was different—not the way Tangwen usually sounded.

Abruptly alert, he sat up and grabbed his sword, but before he could lurch onto his feet, he realized the rustle came from inside. He twisted around then froze.

"Oh, fine indeed," he muttered under his breath, half-relieved, half-aggravated. Myrddin Emrys sat on the other side of the hearth, dim light from the smoke hole on his face. He wore the same mantle of black feathers as he had years before. His hair, now almost fully grey, thinning, and very long, straggled over his shoulders. To Marcus, he simply nodded.

Marcus was reminded of a bird sitting on its nest. He bit his tongue to stifle the sarcastic remark and laid down the sword. An intrusion was not what he wanted, not now, not with Handor somewhere close, and not when Claerwen was still unconvinced that they should go home.

"How did you know—?" The question was meaningless and Marcus aborted it. The fire had brought Myrddin out of hiding, if that's where he had been all this time.

Undisturbed, Claerwen slept on. Marcus crossed to the hearth. He rekindled the fire and filled the small iron cauldron halfway with water, set it among the flames, and located the bundle of packets of foxglove Tangwen had measured out for Claerwen. He emptied one into the water.

"Has that willow bark in it?" Myrddin asked.

Marcus observed the Enchanter's eyes trace to a half-empty wineskin then return questioningly, an assumption that too much had been drunk. He shook his head and slid a stick under the cauldron's handle, lifted and gave the vessel a slow rotation to stir its contents before he set it on the fire again.

"Where have you been all this time?" Marcus asked.

Myrddin picked up the empty packet. Frowning, he sniffed at it, then at the cauldron. His frown deepened. "Foxglove?" He stared at Marcus. "I smell foxglove. But that's only for severe—"

Marcus hushed him and glanced at Claerwen. She showed no movement except slow, deep breathing. He moved the cauldron to the pit's outermost ring of stones, then picked up his baldric and sword and signaled for Myrddin to follow him.

"She'll be waking soon," he said once they were outside. "Let her rest as long as possible." He walked past the horse pen into the woods, Myrddin following. Without revealing the circumstances of the quest, Marcus explained the accident, the injuries and the resulting illness.

Myrddin's face sagged. "This is so bad?"

"It is."

"And the damage is permanent?"

"Aye. The healer from the women's colony believes it so. Claerwen will gain more strength as long as she takes care of herself, but she will never have the endurance she once had. She tires so quickly, well, it's bloody troubling."

Myrddin's gaze lowered to the ground, genuine hurt in his eyes. Marcus had never seen a more candid moment of humanness in him and stepped away to give him time to reflect. He buckled on the baldric and waited, but the growing daylight prickled his impatience. He had to resolve the problem of Handor, and soon. He turned back. "Why are you here?"

The Enchanter's face regained its aloof, all-knowing expression. "The Iron Hawk has acquired something that may be of interest to me."

Marcus glared coldly at Myrddin. So, the Enchanter had seen. Then he had seen Claerwen's intrusion as well and followed the trail back to the house. More importantly, he also knew of Handor and the small lump of iron. And how long, Marcus wondered, had Myrddin been in Rheged?

"The Iron Hawk, you say? Indeed." Marcus eyed the mantle and flicked a finger at the feathers. "Is this what all wise men of the woods are wearing of late? Perhaps I should have one made for myself. Would make a fine disguise."

"You can never resist, can you?" Myrddin sniffed. He held out his palm. "You took something from him. What is it?"

Marcus folded his arms. "Why are you here?"

"Must we always play this game?"

"As long as you won't talk straight up instead of in riddles."

"You're being rather stubborn about this, aren't you?"

Marcus gave a twisted smile. "And isn't it rather so convenient that you should reappear now. Why now? Why *here*?"

"Only you—and Claerwen will—know this."

"And there's a reason why this is so, I would presume? You *always* have a reason."

"Just as you *always* do. How did you know to come to Rheged all those years ago?"

Marcus gave a short, bitter laugh. "I'm sure you remember the whispers at Uther's coronation. If Gwrast couldn't come for the homage ceremony because of his health, then where were his sons? They never did swear fealty to Uther. And you were in the midst of all that talk—no don't deny it."

"Such talk plagues every kingdom," Myrddin said. "Why did Rheged become so important to you?"

"Why are you here?"

Myrddin lifted his gaze to the sky. His condescending demeanor turned into a frown. "Have you not learned yet that all is intertwined? That once you have placed yourself into the path that the gods have shown you, you will follow it all the way to the end? You began that path years ago."

Marcus felt like a child being taught a lesson. "Wait here," he said and turned back for the house.

Claerwen still slept. Entering quietly, he fished through the pile of gear and retrieved the effigy. It was even more grotesque than the day it had been left for him to find. After years of being flattened inside traveling pouches, the dried blood and ink on it had cracked and peeled in places, and the dagger was tarnished.

Outside again, he found Myrddin waiting by the horse pen. Marcus laid the effigy on the top fence rail. "It appears you know of the man called Handor, who delivered this to me during Uther's coronation. A warning from Octa."

Myrddin translated aloud from the Latin, "'Death to you. Two sons of the north or two of the White Dragon. Your choice. Beware...Excalibur.' A warning, you call that." The Enchanter's lips started to curve into a smile but he caught himself.

The near-smile prickled Marcus's sense of caution. "What else would you call it?"

Myrddin again evaded the question. "Handor doesn't know Latin."

Marcus's suspicion grew. That was a detail, and an important one only someone who knew quite a bit about Handor could know. How much *did* Myrddin know? And, if the effigy was in truth not a warning, what was it?

"I assume Octa wrote it," Marcus said. "The wording isn't quite right."

The comment brought no response. Instead, Myrddin stepped away. He frowned at the sky again and turned slowly, his arms held out as if to question the force of the wind.

"Excalibur," he said softly. "I suppose it's an odd sounding name, isn't it? I believe it was given in Macsen's time, nearly a century ago when he claimed the high kingship after beating back the Saxons then. I don't honestly know what the word means."

Marcus found a touch of amusement in the Enchanter's lack of knowledge. "I tried to reckon that myself once. But what is—"

He stared at the effigy, and the connection between the word "Excalibur" and Macsen's sword suddenly became clear. It was a name, a name for the sword. And on the cloth, set off a little by itself, it was a signature as well. The sword was telling him to beware. It *was* a warning. But it was more than that.

A bitter smile crossed Marcus's face.

His gaze swept to the doorway. He had left the drape open and could see Claerwen. She had curled up on her side and faced away from him. Peaceful, she appeared to still be asleep, and he wondered how she would react once she knew her friend had used her. He turned back to Myrddin.

"You arrogant bastard. Excalibur is the sword. *You* wrote this, didn't you? Deliberately in poor Latin so I would think Octa wrote it. To have me find a way to stabilize Rheged. And to find the sword as well?"

Myrddin nodded. "And to keep you from interfering at Tintagel, so Uther could find his way to Igraine."

"And you could not have merely discussed this with me?" Marcus's left eyebrow crept upward.

Myrddin left the question unanswered. He stared through the doorway.

"You thought I would send her home?" Marcus lightly batted the Enchanter's arm. "She couldn't possibly have been safe there. Dinas Beris would have been the first place Handor'd look. He would have taken her hostage, to get to me. She had to come with me. If you just would have talked."

"There were too many ears listening in Winchester."

Marcus grunted. "But bring Handor into this? Why him? No…wait. Let me guess. You made a bargain with him. He delivers this to me in exchange for…for what?"

"Handor was imprisoned with Octa. I offered him freedom if—"

"Oh, freedom," Marcus cut in. "And you turned him loose?"

"Your name had been mentioned. Several times."

"Ah, now that makes sense. Find a man besides Octa who hates me enough that he'll cooperate with your plan. Then hope he doesn't act on that hatred before he delivers the message? Did you realize he wants me dead even more than Octa did?"

"I didn't know for certain. But your swordsmanship—"

"He was a bloody good swordsman himself."

"But not a swordmaster like you." Myrddin gazed at the effigy. "Handor must have added the dagger—I never saw it before now. And he wore a small rock on a thong around his neck, a piece of rock the Iron Hawk took. Why? What is its significance?"

"You mean to say the gods don't tell you everything?" Marcus smirked. "You shouldn't even have needed an ant to tell you how that beautiful, fine woman in there has paid with pain and—"

Unable to finish, he turned away and scraped his fingers through his hair. He wanted to say something horribly bitter and cruel, but it would serve no purpose other than to lose the last of his control.

Not now, he told himself, not now.

"There is a purpose to all that happens—" Myrddin started.

Marcus turned back to him when he did not go on.

The Enchanter was staring into space. "Distress," he said. "Something is wrong."

With his hand already reaching for his sword's hilt, Marcus bolted for the doorway, Myrddin behind him.

The house was empty.

CHAPTER 31

Rheged
Spring, AD 477

MARCUS spit a curse and yanked his sword out of its sheath. He had heard nothing, no rustling, no footsteps. Nothing. He glared at Myrddin's questioning face and instantly knew the Enchanter had heard no sound either.

"Is it *her* distress you sense?" he asked.

"No," Myrddin answered. "It's not. Does someone else here have the fire?"

"The healer from the grove." Marcus spun around and began to search the ground near the house's entrance. Shortly, he found fresh footprints in the damp earth and pointed them out to Myrddin with the sword's tip. "Only one set. She is alone."

That Claerwen was by herself brought no relief to Marcus. She was barefoot, each toe perfectly defined with every step, and she had not been careful to hide them. If it was Tangwen's distress Myrddin sensed, Handor was likely the cause and Claerwen could easily be walking into a trap.

Her route led to the lakeshore. Once in less closed in terrain, Marcus watched more broadly for the assassin, but he found no sign of Handor. He and Myrddin followed the tracks up the shore and within a half-hour found Claerwen nearly a mile from the house. The women's colony lay across the lake. Another wood, so thick it appeared impenetrable, rose up the incline behind the place she stood. Absorbed, she was examining a small plot of ground like she was searching for something she had lost. Marcus approached with caution.

Claerwen paused in her task. No sign of fire in the head showed in her face when she looked up, but shadows underscored her eyes and her cheeks had a waxy pallor that warned Marcus she needed rest. Her gaze passed from him to Myrddin's face with no surprise, as if she had already known he was there.

"It's the labyrinth," she said. Hope lit her green-blue eyes and she squinted out over the surface of the lake. The ends of a frayed cord trailed from her hand—the lump of iron from Handor.

"What labyrinth?" Marcus questioned, but she didn't hear him. From Myrddin, he received only a faint shrug. "A vision years ago," he said. "Complicated. I thinks she remembers something from that."

"If this comes from a vision," Myrddin said, "she will find what she is looking for, but you will have to give her time."

Of course Myrddin would say something so, Marcus thought. To the all-knowing seer, nothing mattered except that all must pass as it should within the gods' order of things. Fine enough, but that had little to do with keeping Claerwen safe, especially when Handor lurked within close range.

"I need to find the labyrinth," she repeated, her eyes locked on the water. Her hand moved in a pattern in the air.

Marcus assumed she was tracing the sacred labyrinth, a series of concentric near-circles that connected at the outer ends. The only one he had ever seen lay in the south at Ynys Witrin, one of the holiest places in Britain. Her hand was shaking, and though he did not wish to disturb her, he caught her wrist.

"You should go back and rest," he said. "Let me look for Lady Tangwen."

"Not Tangwen." She withdrew her hand and spread her fingers to ward off the interruption. "There," she said to Myrddin and pointed at a flat rock embedded in the earth. "Stand on that, please."

Myrddin calmly fulfilled her request. She studied the water a few more moments, then turned and walked past him up into the wood.

Marcus's warrior's sense began to prickle. Again he scanned for signs of Handor but found nothing of concern. "Do you still feel it?" he asked Myrddin.

A nod from the Enchanter, then…nothing but cryptic silence.

He scowled at Myrddin. "I wonder how you can be so bloody calm," he muttered then followed Claerwen into the trees.

She had not gone far. After pursuing her for fifty paces through heavy undergrowth, he emerged into a clearing nearly double the size of Winchester's courtyard. Claerwen was nearly all the way to the opposite side and had stopped. Green saplings, strangled in vines, soared like a wall beyond her, thick bracken spread out below. She gazed up, then waded into the bracken.

Uneasy, Marcus eyed the surrounding trees with care and began to cross the clearing. Shortly, Myrddin appeared behind him.

Nearing Claerwen, Marcus saw she had knelt as if before an altar and was tying the cord's ends together. She hung the piece of iron from her wrist for safekeeping, then placed her hands between the long, trailing vines to part them. "Here," she said and reached in farther. She pulled out clumps of rotting leaves and grasses. "She is here."

"She?" Marcus's brows dipped sharply. *Had* Tangwen been killed? And now the fire was leading Claerwen to the body? But an air of calm curiosity radiated from her rather than fear or sadness. He could see nothing through the vines.

"I saw her in my vision, all those years ago."

"Her? Who?" Reluctantly, he put up the sword, knelt and reached in to help. His fingers scraped on a rough surface. A squarish block of stone, black with muddy rot and splotched with lichens, loomed below his hands.

"This is the Lady of the Lake," Claerwen said.

The decayed weeds Marcus held fell from his fingers. He stared at her.

Myrddin, having come up behind them, dropped onto his knees on Claerwen's other side. He examined the stone and came up smiling.

"Aye, this is the spirit stone of this lake." His hand ran along the closest edge. "See—it's carved here. It fell facedown." He lobbed a look of superiority at Marcus. "All lakes have a Lady spirit."

Marcus ignored him. "It's not so big," he said and got to his feet. "I'll set it upright." He squatted down and grappled the front corners. Pain needled his left knee, and he readjusted his stance to ease it. He pulled, but roots had grown around the edges—he suspected all underneath as well—and were unwilling to give up the stone. With the dagger from the back of his belt, he cut into the tangle, as far as the blade could reach, then handed the knife to Claerwen. He tried again. The stone slowly tore loose. Now upright, it settled and leaned back slightly with a mild crunch.

Squatted again, Marcus helped peel layers of roots and filth from the façade. Once it was fairly clean, Claerwen slipped the piece of iron from her wrist again. "Can you see it?"

Marcus took it, turned it one way then the other. He saw nothing. "Didn't Lady Tangwen tell you this had a marking that matched one on the anvil stone?"

Claerwen shook her head. "I think she doesn't remember quite right. I was studying this when I woke up. It's not a symbol, but a carving. Hold it like this." She turned it in his fingers but he still saw only a lump of iron.

"May I?" Myrddin asked. He held it next to the carved stone in the way Claerwen had at first. "Of course," he said. "It's the same Lady."

Marcus took it back, and this time he caught the configuration, as clear as shallow, motionless water. He could not reckon why he had missed it. Now it was obvious. "But this is a Lady stone," he said. "Where is the one shaped like an anvil?"

Silence followed. Myrddin stood and stretched his legs. Claerwen gave no answer. She sat back on her heels and her shoulders sagged. Disappointment dragged at her face, all her enthusiasm gone.

Marcus expelled his breath. He placed the lump of iron in her hand and gently folded her fingers around it. "We'll try again another time," he said and stood.

"It *must* be here." She rose and started to push through the saplings. "Somewhere…"

"Perhaps something else Tangwen said will…come to mind…or…" Marcus's voice trailed off. Myrddin had followed her. Left alone, he shrugged and surveyed the clearing once more.

"Did I hear right?" Marcus heard Claerwen's voice, suddenly

low and harsh. He glanced between the saplings. She was glaring at Myrddin.

"Did I overhear you tell Marcus that *you* sent the effigy? *You* wrote the warning?"

Myrddin stalled.

"Did you?"

Another hesitation, then, "I did."

Marcus heard her take two steps. By the time he reached the saplings, he caught a glimpse of her fist punching up. She clipped Myrddin squarely across the mouth. The Enchanter backed, his fingers pressed to a split lower lip.

Marcus thrashed his way between the trees and pinned down her arms before she could do more damage.

"How dare you?" She struggled to free herself. "After all the years of friendship. How could you be so cold, so cruel to send my husband—?"

"Stop, Claerwen." Marcus held his face against her hair. "You cannot blame him."

"But you were nearly killed…" She turned in his arms and faced him. "The fall, then the exile, and—"

"Claeri, even without the effigy, all the talk at the coronation and all the misgivings we learned about Rheged's internal problems—I would have gone anyway."

Confusion crossed her face.

"I know, I'm always the one blaming Myrddin while you defend him." He smiled crookedly at the irony. "Perhaps it would have happened differently if he hadn't used Handor, but that man would have surfaced sooner or later because of Meirchion. I would have gone anyway."

The disbelief in her eyes tore at him.

"Do you remember how angry he was when he came north from Tintagel?" Marcus met the Enchanter's gaze and held it. "I would wager he'd say—once he had calmed a bit—that he had been a tool of the gods. Like me. Like you."

Her anger drained as quickly as it had come on and her shoulders slumped beneath his hands. He released her.

"I should know this," she said. "I am sorry."

"Don't be." Myrddin dabbed at his lip with a fingertip. "Though I expected this from him instead." He smiled thinly, then the smile turned into another frown at the sky.

Marcus gazed between the trees at the clearing again. Wind gusted, obscuring all other sound. Minutes passed. Nothing was there, but the hair on his neck continued to tingle as if lightning were about to strike.

"You're so tense," Claerwen whispered. "What is it?"

"I like this not," he said, and a sudden, colder gust struck him in the face. Movement stirred on the other side of the clearing. His scalp crawled. Then he saw why. Unmistakably, Tangwen, with Handor, moved slowly across the grass.

Marcus stalked sideways until he could see the woman better. Claerwen turned, then Myrddin, looking for what had drawn his attention.

Handor had gripped the ends of Tangwen's kerchiefs where they crossed around her neck and had pulled them taut. Forced to lean back awkwardly, she flailed her hands in an attempt to keep her balance. He pushed from behind, and when they reached the center of the meadow, he forced her down onto her hands and knees. The woman tried to loosen the kerchiefs, but they were so tight she could not get her fingers underneath.

From a belt sheath, Handor produced a Saxon knife. With slow deliberation, he pressed its edge to her throat.

"Where is the sword?" he shouted down at her.

The woman winced but said nothing.

"You must have told them where it is. Where have they gone?"

"I need to distract him," Marcus whispered, but before he could decide on a diversion, he heard the vines and saplings slap together where Claerwen stood. He jolted around, grabbed for her. She was gone, already running out into the open, off to the right at an angle. Myrddin followed her example and was walking out to the left.

Marcus heard Claerwen demand Tangwen's release. He swore and shoved the vines out of the way. She had stopped midway and Handor's searing glare drilled across to her.

Myrddin commanded a similar plea. Without moving the knife, Handor jerked at the unfamiliar voice. His eyes widened at the strange man in the feathered mantle.

It was not the distraction Marcus had wanted, but it would have to suffice. He squeezed out between the trees and assessed each figure's position and vulnerability to Handor's control. Claerwen's hands were curled into fists, her knuckles pressed against her legs. Myrddin stood as stiffly as a dead tree. Of Tangwen, he could only determine that she had not been cut; her face was still downcast.

"Trinity." The word escaped Marcus, remembered from the lessons of his boyhood. He had not thought of it in years, but the three figures with fire in the head reawakened the concept in him. Love, knowledge and truth, three rays of light from which springs justice. If any one element was missing, there could be no justice. Justice for Handor? Appropriate, certainly. But who would play the administrator?

The wind hissed in his ears. Handor's cold eyes lifted. Marcus met them and held with his own glare of ice. His skin crept. Fire or no fire, the warrior in him rose instinctively, and in that instant he knew that only he could be the administrator of justice. In truth, he had already known it for years, since the night the effigy had been delivered and he had looked into the hatred on Handor's face that first time.

Handor's ever-present smirk deepened. "Well, you had to be here somewhere, didn't you?"

Both Claerwen and Myrddin glanced. Marcus signaled a warning to them to stay still. He took two strides, halted, folded his arms, and again assessed the scene before him. Claerwen's worried eyes told him she was frightened behind the mask of bravery she showed.

Handor released his grip on Tangwen's kerchiefs. He stalked around to her side; the *seax* pivoted flat-bladed on top of her shoulder. Proud of his domination, he planted his feet widely.

"It's me you want," Marcus called out. "Let her go."

Tangwen's head came up. Tears streamed down her face, but she showed remarkably little fear. Marcus wondered if she were already resigned to dying. She blinked, and her gaze moved from him to Myrddin to Claerwen, then strained upward at Handor.

"What happened to you?" she asked in a voice soft and brittle.

"I…I want to know."

Handor scowled down in contempt. "Why would you care?"

"Please. Tell me what became of you, all those years ago."

The tension in the assassin's sword arm eased, but the blade remained on her shoulder. Why, Marcus wondered, why would she be asking this now? Did she truly want to know from a man fully willing to kill her? Or was she stalling, allowing time for her potential saviors to find a way to approach?

Marcus regarded Claerwen. She seemed closer to Handor than before, and he realized she had been edging towards him. Worse, he saw a knife gripped in her right hand, held down in the folds of her skirts. He reached behind to the sheath in the back of his belt. Empty. Damn, he swore silently at himself. He had handed it to her and not taken it back.

"I would like to know what happened as well."

Refined and clear, a new voice boomed from the edge of the clearing behind Tangwen. It jarred Marcus—he recognized it. "Blaez?" he murmured to himself, and watched his tall friend step out of the trees. The Frank wore a long, beige, sleeveless robe over his tunic and breeches. Unless hidden, no sword, no daggers were evident.

"Go away!" Handor roared. He pressed the knife to Tangwen's neck again.

Blaez halted. His gaze traveled from one side of the clearing to the other and took in each participant. Lastly, his eyes crossed Marcus's and paused, widened for an instant, then went back to Handor.

"What goes on here?" he demanded. "Why in the gods' names do you hold this woman as if you were a brigand?"

Unnoticed, Marcus eased his sword from its sheath and gained another stride closer. He dreaded Blaez's reaction once the Frank realized who Handor's hostage was.

Handor ignored Blaez. "Where is it?" he growled at Tangwen again.

The woman's catlike eyes glowered. "I will tell you nothing."

He pressed the blade tighter. "Where is it?"

She winced again.

Marcus watched in an arc from Myrddin across to Claerwen. Though she had gained another step as well, she could never overpower Handor. Even distracted by Blaez, the assassin was too aware of his surroundings, too well ensconced in the habit of reacting with violence, too good a fighter. Teeth gritted, Marcus dared not call her—a whisper would alert Handor, and she concentrated too deeply for him to catch her attention with a hand signal. And worst of all, still near the Lady stone, he was too far away. Even at a full tilt run, he could not reach Handor in time should the assassin turn on her.

Handor glared over Tangwen at Blaez. Blaez glared back. The two men reminded Marcus of Roman statues fated to stare at each other for all time across a forum. Then Blaez's eyes moved down to the blade.

"Stop this now, Handor," he said, his voice low, hoarse.

Blaez knew him? Marcus took another step and lifted his sword.

"No." The Frank held a hand up in objection.

Handor spun. The *seax* swung away from Tangwen.

"Let me talk with him," Blaez said.

"Talk?" Marcus questioned. "He was Octa's assassin! Now he kills for himself. He—"

Before he could finish, Tangwen twisted around behind Handor. Her gasping cry of a name when she struggled to her feet brought a wrenching pang in the pit of Marcus's stomach. Frozen, Blaez stared widely at her, unable to react.

Handor swept back around.

"No!" Claerwen shrieked. Her left arm rose, fingers outstretched as if to stall Handor. He rammed the butt of his weapon's handle against Tangwen's temple. The woman crumpled.

Blaez jerked. Handor stood defiantly over the woman, his arms coiled back, the Saxon blade aimed to slice across her neck.

"She doesn't know where it is," Claerwen shouted. "*I* do."

Blaez stared at her, dumbfounded. Marcus swore. He watched her fingers grip and re-grip the dagger's hilt. Though the weapon was still down against her leg, her arm was tense, poised to use the knife. And she would use it, he knew. But that dagger against a *seax* was no match. He eased forward a few more steps and came even with Myrddin.

Handor eyed Claerwen with annoyance. "Ah, aren't you courageous now?" he mocked.

"Is that all you know? To kill?" Carried by outrage, Claerwen took another step.

"So righteous," Handor sneered. The *seax* pulled back another hand's width.

"All *you* want is to steal the sword," she kept on. "For your own selfishness."

"Selfish? I say not! Macsen's sword will go to Octa's successor, Aelle. Soon, he will come with more warriors than this cursed island has ever seen!"

Myrddin drew in towards Marcus. "Aelle? Octa's successor? Who is he?"

"First I've heard," Marcus returned in a whisper. He flexed his fingers and repositioned them more firmly around his sword's hilt.

"But before Aelle gets it," Handor went on, "I will kill *that* man with it, for allowing my father to die." He jerked his head at Marcus.

"You *are* a coward, Handor ap Hywel," Claerwen said. "Your father would be ashamed of you."

"You know nothing of my father!"

"I know enough. That he was held in high enough trust to be the keeper of Macsen's sword."

"What use is trust?" he shot back. "Trust betrayed my father. Octa gave me more reason to trust than any Briton ever did."

Blaez's face darkened. "*Trust* did not betray your father. Prince Meirchion did. And you are doing so now."

"My father's dead," Handor hissed.

"No. He is not."

Palpable silence followed the revelation. By the gods, Marcus swore to himself, Hywel Gwodryd—alive?

"Impossible," Handor finally said.

"*Not* impossible," Blaez countered. He dipped his head at Tangwen on the ground and took another step towards her. "By the earth's soul, Handor, how could you have done that to your own mother? *She* recognized me."

Complete disbelief swept Marcus. The man he had known for

years only as Blaez? This was Hywel Gwodryd—Hywel of the Flowing Verse? Court bard of Rheged?

Handor's face puckered. "You? Imposter! My father's neck was broken."

"Meirchion killed my brother, your uncle," the older man said. "Then I was forced into exile for more than ten years. I *am* Hywel Gwodryd." He held Handor's gaze then moved it on to Marcus. "Now you know who I am."

Marcus nodded acknowledgement. It fit. The length of Blaez's exile matched the length of time Hywel had been supposedly dead. He watched Handor struggle with confusion and shock. Then a smug leer crossed his face. "Prove it. Show where the sword is."

"To you?" His father shook his head with slow deliberation. "Never. Why, Handor? What happened to you in all these years?"

Handor was going to lose control. Marcus recognized the signs—the flinching scowl, the nervous fingers on the weapon's handle. Moving to his left, he hoped to draw the man away from Tangwen and Hywel.

"Aye, Handor," he said. "Tell what happened to you. Did Octa treat you *so* well? As a slave, so I've been told."

Handor's face reddened.

"Apparently *not* so well," Marcus said when the intervening silence carried on too long.

"It was *your* fault," Handor suddenly bellowed and pointed the knife. "You will pay—"

"Pay for what, eh?" Marcus sidestepped a bit farther. "What do you think I have need to pay for?" He saw Hywel understand the ploy and begin to ease towards Tangwen, intent on pulling her to safety.

Handor's wolf-like glare filled with menace. "You! If you hadn't meddled, my father wouldn't have gone looking for you. Meirchion wouldn't have—"

"But no one killed your father," Marcus cut him off. "He is alive. Right there, as you can see. There is nothing to pay because it never happened."

Handor's rage grew increasingly focused on Marcus. Hywel slipped across the space to Tangwen. He reached her and pulled her up onto his shoulder, then turned back for the woods. His steps skimmed the grass as he stole away.

"You are not only a coward, but a traitor as well," Claerwen said. She took another step.

That she was angry rather than scared seemed to intrigue Handor. His lips curled and he tossed away the *seax*, slipped the tie of his cloak. It dropped to the ground. A second weapon, a full-sized sword, hung from his belt.

"Say that you *do* know where the sword is." He swerved to face her.

Marcus jolted but stopped short. In the same instant a small rock whipped through the air in a shallow arc. It cracked against Handor's skull and scraped across his left eye. He yelped and clapped his free hand over the side of his face.

Myrddin swore. "Get over here, boy."

Boy? Marcus scanned across the clearing in search of the rock's source. Hywel had reached the woods and was no longer in sight. It had not come from his direction. Then, a brown-haired boy bopped up from a patch of bracken off to the side, midway between Handor and Claerwen. Unafraid, he studied the others one by one with calm assurance.

"Now, Aradr!" Myrddin insisted. "Your foster-brother and guardians will be looking for you." A moment later, shouts of the same name reverberated from beyond the clearing.

"Take that boy out of here yourself!" Marcus ordered. He watched Handor frantically smear drops of blood and tears from his face. The assassin was cursing his scratched eye and everything else he could think of. Soon, he would understand Hywel and Tangwen were gone. Then he would recover his nerve and lash out.

The boy scrambled across to Myrddin. In astonishment, Marcus saw vivid blue eyes flash past—vivid blue eyes full of intelligence and that were a perfect match to the high king's. The name "Aradr" had to be a deliberate corruption of the boy's true name. Myrddin swept the child away, and when Marcus glanced at Claerwen again, he knew she had realized who the boy was as well. He hoped to all the gods the assassin had not.

Handor drew his sword, brandished it. "You will pay for all the years of pain, Marcus ap Iorwerth. You will pay—*mid flæsce ond blode ond bane!*"

The words cut into the ironclad part of Marcus's being where he kept his nightmares and regrets and ugly memories full of the stink of guilt and hatred. The words released it all in a rush like thousands of bats from a cave; those same words heard so many years ago, over and over in warning, their meaning lost in a language of which he had known nothing. Now the translation came without effort. Flesh and blood and bone. The people would pay with flesh and blood and bone. And they had, most gruesomely, for his lack of understanding the words.

In the fleeting moments the memory gouged through Marcus's mind, Handor surged forward, weapon raised, but after only a few steps he shifted and lunged for Claerwen instead.

"Run!" Marcus roared at her, but she stalled, her fingers clenched around the knife's handle. Hurtling across, Marcus aimed straight for her. By sheer luck, he was faster than Handor, and without slowing, he barreled into her. She flew off her feet and fell hard well out of Handor's reach.

Marcus veered back; his feet dug for traction on the turf. "Hrrraaahhhhh!" The war cry tore from his throat and sliced through the wind-roiled air. He drove in with every muscle and sinew strained to the fullest; his sword sheered an arc that crashed against the other man's blade. Unable to withstand the fury, Handor staggered backward.

Marcus blocked out all else. His warrior's instinct overtook him and rose above the soldier's trained drills of strike, feint and parry. He was descending into the nightmare of his own creation, the horrible dream of savagery from months earlier. There would be no coming back—he would follow it all the way to the end. One of them—perhaps both—would die that day.

His footing regained, Handor stormed in with ferocity. Marcus deflected the strike, and the stinging shock vibrated up his arms into his shoulders. He backed two steps to allow himself space to maneuver. Handor charged in again. Blade clanged against blade, up, to the right, down and left, back and forth, over and over.

In a rare gap in Handor's defense, Marcus rammed a heel into the man's hip. Handor spun back on the verge of falling. Marcus moved in for the next blow, but the assassin suddenly found his balance and swung fully around, his sword level with Marcus's neck. Marcus dropped and rolled to his right in the opposite direction of the slash. Bounding up, he thrust for Handor's vulnerable left side, but the man twisted in anticipation. The sword tip tore through the cloth of his tunic below his left arm.

Handor hurled himself into the reverse of the same twisting motion that had saved him. With his full, solid weight, he slammed himself backward into Marcus, his bent elbows in the lead.

Pain bolted through Marcus's gut. He reeled and fought to keep his balance. Handor whipped around, his blade in a diagonal slash. Marcus felt the rush of air swept before the sword; it brushed up from his left knee across his chest. He recoiled, lost his footing and fell.

His left thigh stung hotly. Marcus swore. He had been cut but had no time to even glance. He flipped aside, and the assassin's blade drove into the earth where he had just been.

Handor tugged at his weapon, lodged deeply in the soil. In the momentary delay before it pulled loose, Marcus pounded up with his feet. One heel struck the center of Handor's chest. His other foot thrust in hard below the man's chin. With a squeaking gasp, Handor flew backward and skidded.

"That was for Claerwen," Marcus yelled and rolled up onto his feet. He chased after the flailing figure.

Handor gagged for air. Barely able to stand, he met Marcus's blade with an awkward slap of his own weapon. He lunged and slashed without thought. He was weakening—the breath scraped through his crushed throat like a muffled scream.

Marcus backed then swung in again with an upward strike and caught his cross-guard on Handor's. The weapons locked and he pushed, turned them to the right, pressed downward against the assassin's waning resistance, harder, harder. An instant later he released pressure. Handor wobbled. With a swing back to the left, Marcus slapped the inner point of the man's elbow with the flat of his blade and caught the sensitive bone there. The strike, almost delicate in its precision, sent painful tingling down to Handor's right hand and loosened his grip, and when Marcus swung hard right, he knocked the weapon into a skitter over the grass.

Panicking, Handor swung a wild fist. It caught Marcus in the head. He went down on one knee; pain and dizziness sickened him. Get up, he ordered himself. Get up now. For an instant he believed he heard war drums thudding somewhere in the distance—like Uther's war drums from years before. It was his own blood pounding in his head.

Marcus gave his head a rough shake. His eyes slowly focused on Handor. The man had retreated several paces and was near to collapsing. He had not even tried to regain his sword. Instead, he held his hands to his damaged throat and squinted back, mouth agape, pain in his eyes each time he tried to capture enough air to remain conscious.

Marcus forced himself onto his feet. Sword lifted, he swayed and nearly fainted. He spread his feet wide, drew in a dozen deep breaths, and prepared for the end.

The man's face stopped him. Crushing disappointment, dread, the sense that all was lost had filled Handor's face. Was it a ploy to gain time? Marcus could not gauge if he had actually hurt Handor as badly as it appeared, but something had changed, something was very different. But this was not the time to leave anything to chance. Marcus advanced, his weapon raised.

Handor backed. The dead look of despair haunted his eyes.

Marcus stopped again, his sword cocked ready. "Give it up, Handor," he ordered.

The despair deepened. Handor slowly shook his head. Then he strained to pull himself up straighter.

"This…this you cannot…take…from me," he choked out. A small dagger appeared in his hand, pulled from beneath his sleeve. He closed his eyes and tipped his head back. In a motion so swift that it was done before Marcus could react, Handor raked the knife across his own throat. A rush of blood from the deep gash he had opened soaked his tunic. His head drifted forward; the dagger dropped. He crumpled into an awkward heap. His neck, no longer able to support his head, twisted when his chin hit the ground. His face turned to stare blankly across the clearing.

In awe, Marcus watched as if he had never seen death before in a world where he had observed far more carnage than he could ever count. He could not help himself. It was a different nightmare than expected—he had survived—yet it was the same as the old one in its finality, the sightless blue-white face, mouth open, the stench of death, so familiar, so sickening.

By all the gods… Marcus began a thought, but his mind went blank. His head pounded where he had been struck, and his left knee ached like it had been hammered. The scratch on his thigh stung. He closed his eyes and tried to will his senses to settle, but they rolled like a ship in foul weather. Gods, how he hated the sea.

Overwhelmed, he dropped to the ground.

CHAPTER 32

Rheged
Spring, AD 477

SOMEONE was calling his name. So far away, it seemed, like a feather should sound as it drifted on the wind, if a feather could make noise. Must he return to his senses just yet? Marcus wished only for quiet, for stillness. Where had he just been? He vaguely remembered sitting down hard, then nothing more.

Someone was pulling him up, hands under his arms, straining to set him upright and murmuring words. He knew it was Claerwen's voice; she spoke so softly he could not understand what she said. Her hair draped down over him as he felt her tuck herself in behind him, her arms tight around his chest. Moaning with newfound comfort, he took hold of a handful of her hair and held it to his lips. She pressed her cheek to his. He could have sat there with her forever, silent and calm, eyes shut, the wind on his face.

"It's over," he heard Claerwen breathe. His mind hooked onto her words. Had she said that several times now? How he wished the sentiment were true. Nothing ever truly ended, not for him, not as a spy, and not for her, because of him. Yet through all the years, through all the hardship, they had remained resilient.

A loud, ringing, echoing croak jarred Marcus loose from his thoughts. He opened his eyes. Out of the churning grey sky, a huge, sleek raven wheeled on the shifting winds. He watched it gradually spiral down and land near Handor's body. Settling its wings, it eyed its new prize and croaked again to announce the discovery.

Resilience, he thought again. Only a few gave up. Like Handor.

Marcus sat up fully and gazed at the seeping, gored body. A fleeting smile crossed his lips.

Claerwen shifted around to face him. When he met her eyes, he knew she had seen his smile and her gaze sank deep, deep into him, as if to pierce him to his soul's core. He cupped his hand alongside her face and leaned close, his brow to hers. "You were right," he said. "I wanted to kill him."

He watched her gaze drift away and fall to his sword on the ground. His dagger lay next to it. She had brought it back to him. "Did I hurt you?" he asked. "Are you feeling ill?"

"No. Only tired." She touched his leg. "Does this hurt?"

"No." He stretched out the limb and let her examine the scratch. The cut had only broken through the cloth of his breeches in sections, like a dashed line with bloodstained edges. "The breeches need more repair than I do," he said.

"And this?" She lightly touched the side of his head, behind his ear. "There's a lump."

He winced. "I'll be fine enough." He watched the raven's mate circle down to land.

"You always say that."

"I know. It's my nature." Marcus stuffed the dagger into its sheath and dragged the sword closer. His head throbbed, but he eased up onto his feet, the sword for support. "Stay here," he said.

His senses reeled as he walked, but he collected the cloak Handor had dropped and draped it over the corpse. Displeased, the ravens launched into the air and fluttered into the treetops. He watched them until his head stopped spinning. "Soon," he said. "Patience."

"Now I know who *you* are."

Hywel's voice. Tired. Full of numbing shock. Marcus still wanted to say "Blaez." He dropped his gaze from the treetops. Hywel stood at the clearing's edge, breath drawn to speak again but he held his tongue. He stared grey-faced at his son's covered body.

A resemblance, Marcus thought. That was why he had once thought the man looked vaguely familiar. He was Handor's father. Marcus pulled him away.

"He took his own life," Hywel said.

"You saw it?"

A long pause. "Why?"

Marcus stared at the cloak. Blood was soaking into portions of it. "I don't know. His hatred seemed to be his only reason for living. To him, I was the symbol of that hatred. A target. Perhaps when he learned you were alive, he was forced to lose his reasons for hating me. If that makes any sense?"

"And in the fever of that loss, he slit his own throat?" Hywel shook his head. "Is that what Octa taught him? That kind of hatred?"

Marcus wanted to say that perhaps Handor had already learned such hatred even before Octa manipulated it for his own purposes. Meirchion could have taught him that. But to offer such a bitter image to Hywel would serve no purpose other than to hurt. "I am sorry—"

"At least you were not forced to kill him," Hywel cut him off.

"No… I suppose not." Marcus leaned on the upright sword and gazed dully at the ground. "Has Lady Tangwen come around?"

"Aye, but she's not coherent yet," Hywel answered. "Your friend with the…feathers…believes she will be right again in time. He arranged for her to be taken to one of Lord Ector's strongholds for help. We will leave with that boy's guardians shortly."

"Good." Marcus hoped for Hywel's sake that Tangwen would recover well. More than ten years they had been separated. He was grateful that he had lost only five with Claerwen. Only five? That in itself was too long.

He regarded Hywel. Something more was different besides the name. Then it came to him—they were speaking in Cymraeg, the language of the Britons, not Brezhoneg. And Hywel had the accent and dialect of the northern kingdoms.

"You're not a Frank at all, are you?" he asked.

Hywel shook his head.

"A ruse?" Marcus straightened. "All those years? The accent? Everything?"

Hywel nodded. "I convinced you, a master of disguise."

"Damn." Marcus squeezed his eyes shut. The pain in his head would not ease. "And your nephews? Are they with you?"

"They wait at the old farmstead."

Marcus's lips flattened. Now he knew the grave he and Claerwen had found belonged to Hywel's brother.

The bard laid a hand on Marcus's shoulder. "I came back to tell you something you need to know."

Marcus opened his eyes. "Macsen's sword?"

Hywel's face saddened. "I wish I could tell you where it is."

"You were the keeper, no?"

"My brother and I, together, but we decided it would be safer if only one of us knew its location. He hid it."

"And he never told you?"

Hywel slowly shook his head. "When Meirchion made so much trouble and Gwrast hired you to stop him, I had fully intended to seek you out and tell you to find my brother. I had a token to give you, so he would understand to pass the sword's location on to you."

"Was Handor close to him?"

"My brother lived many miles away. When we visited, I usually went to him."

"Then Handor had little contact with him."

"Aye, and when my brother was killed, everyone thought it was me—we looked much alike. Meirchion wouldn't tell—he was just as guilty for killing my brother. Then I was forced into exile. To protect my wife, I let the mistake remain. But I don't know where the sword was hidden. I am sorry."

Marcus wiped a hand down over his face and turned to look for Claerwen. If she had been disappointed earlier, she would be even more so with this news.

"Perhaps it is just as well," Hywel said. "If it's forgotten, no one will fight over it anymore."

So many had fought over it already. Marcus kept his thought to himself. Across the clearing he saw Claerwen had waded into the bracken again and was staring towards the Lady stone. Patience. Resilience. Persistence. She was all of those—she was not going to give up looking for Macsen's sword. She had her reasons, good reasons, and she could be as stubborn as he. No, she would not give up, in spite of fatigue, sickness, disappointment. Her tenacity, along with her compassion, he admired most about her. He smiled.

"Is she the one you protected with your silence all those years?" Hywel asked.

"Aye," Marcus said quietly. "My wife."

Rustling shook the trees from the direction of the lake. Myrddin appeared at the clearing's edge and signaled that Ector's men were ready to leave.

"I must go," Hywel said.

Marcus clamped a hand on the older man's shoulder. "Have them take you to one of the northern compounds. You'll be across the border into Strathclyde and fall under Ceredig's protection, and with hope, be out of Meirchion's reach. I will come talk more after you've settled."

Hywel nodded. He tipped his head towards Myrddin. "I'm curious. Who is he?"

Hmm—how to explain Myrddin the Enchanter, Marcus wondered. "I'll tell you another time," he said, "when we've many, many hours to spare."

Hywel smiled sadly. "And you. Master spy. Master swordsman. Master of disguise. And I wonder, master of what else?" He took a long, final look at Handor's draped body. "That boy was master of nothing." He walked away without another word.

Marcus watched Hywel take the path into the trees. What would the man think some time in the future when he remembered back to this day, and that the young boy with vivid blue eyes who had traveled with him to one of Ector's strongholds turned out to be the next high king, proudly carrying the sword long believed forever lost? If it could ever be found…

With a glance to Myrddin, Marcus strode across to finally join Claerwen. She was about to slip between the saplings next to the Lady stone again. He heard Myrddin's soft footfalls closely follow.

"So that you know this," Myrddin said when he and Marcus reached her, "the boy only knows me as 'Emrys.' He doesn't know who I am, except as a 'wise man of the woods,' as you would say. Likewise, he doesn't know who *he* is. Yet."

"To protect him?" Claerwen asked.

"Until he is old enough."

Marcus closely regarded the Enchanter. "That's what you were doing all those years ago. The boy wears Ector's insignia. You were setting up a place to hide him, weren't you? A fosterage in a remote noble house—common enough to avoid questions. You could disappear from the rest of the world and still have access to him. He gets a foster brother in Ector's son for companionship—Cei is his name, isn't it? Clever enough. But why not in Strathclyde instead? It's more stable than Rheged…"

Marcus's words trailed off. He held Myrddin's all-knowing gaze. Stabilizing Rheged. That had been the task all along. "Ah, bloody," he started then clamped his mouth shut. To argue would accomplish nothing. He tramped through the bracken back to the Lady stone.

"It would have been fine indeed if this had been the one shaped like an anvil." He shook his head at it. Why could it not have been the right one? With one hand on top to steady himself, he pushed aside the curtain of vines next to it again. In the same moment the stone twisted faintly, settled a bit more. His hand slipped off. Unable to catch himself, he stumbled and his fingers jammed against a hard surface behind the stone.

Swearing and annoyed at his own clumsiness, he withdrew his hand and shook out the pain, then squeezed through into a small space behind the carved stone. He wanted to know what he had struck. It had felt rougher than the smooth bark on one of the young trees. In the gloom, he only found what looked like a huge lump of dead leaves.

The shape reminded him of a fat squatting monk. He smiled wryly. That was a silly thought, just to distract himself. Probably an old tree stump was underneath. He batted away a layer of the leaves. If only Hywel had known where the sword had been hidden, even just a clue. Pressing his fingers down, he found a solid surface beneath the leaves. It was rock, not rotting wood.

He scooped away more debris and began to trace the top surface with his hands. It was flat, rectangular, and roughly tapered at each end. The sides below curved inward deeply into a pedestal-like shape that flared out again at the base. It appeared to be of solid granite.

Straightening, he explored the top again more thoroughly and discovered a small hole filled with soil. Chills raced up his spine. The hole was similar in shape, depth and placement to a tool holder, like an anvil would have—an anvil. Could it be?

"By the light," Claerwen said, only an arm's length away. Caught in his curiosity, Marcus had not heard her. Myrddin observed from behind her. Absolutely still, she stared at the stone.

"This is it, isn't it?" Marcus already knew the answer from her eyes.

He continued his examination. In spite of its shape, he quickly realized, it was too small to conceal any sword of significant size. But in the talk he had overheard between Claerwen and Lady Tangwen, the sword was supposedly buried at the foot of a stone. Should he dare hope Tangwen had remembered that correctly?

He drew his largest dagger and poked the tip into the earth all around the base. The blade only penetrated the width of a finger before it hit a solid surface again. He knelt and scraped. The base, he discovered, sat on a longer, wider platform that had sunk into the damp earth. Base and platform made a seam, and when he dug the knife tip into it, he was sure the seam could be pulled apart.

"Huh," he grunted and sat back on his heels. He tapped the knife's handle against the pedestal while he considered if he could move the upper portion. A slight echo rang with each hit. He tapped more, bottom to top. The pedestal was hollow.

He rose. "Stand aside." He put up his knife. Half-crouched, he curved his arms beneath the outer ends of the stone.

"You won't be able to move it," Myrddin said. "It's too heavy."

"You think iron is light?" Marcus heaved. "I've moved enough anvils in my life to champion those bloody old Roman wrestlers anytime." The exertion made his head swirl. He backed and straightened, dragged in air to stop the spinning.

"Marcus, you shouldn't—"

He shook off Claerwen's concern. The stone had given slightly. He had expected to need several attempts, but it had shifted with little resistance and was no heavier than any other anvil. With barely enough space to work, he maneuvered it off the base and eased it over on one side until it rested at an angle against a pair of stout saplings' trunks. Kneeling down, he caught his breath and waited for his head to clear again.

His eyes slowly focused on the platform. An oblong, carved-out space inside it had been revealed, and he brushed his fingertips across a dark object within. Cold and clammy, it felt like the black, rich earth he knelt on. But as he groped from end to end, he detected a texture, the feel of old, oil-soaked cloth and the shape of a heavy sword. It was as long as the Iron Hawk's.

When he looked up again, he saw Claerwen—pale, hopeful, brimming with anticipation. She peered down into the opening. Myrddin hovered next to her, his aloof acceptance radiant in his eyes. Marcus imagined his own face reflected the same hope as well.

With a hand under each end, he lifted a little. From the weight and the balance, he already knew the sword was expertly made. The oilcloth, intact, had been bound at every handspan, but most of the leather bindings had rotted or been eaten away, only their impressions left behind. He laid the bundle down again in its crypt and unfolded the wrappings.

He heard Claerwen's soft gasp. Even in its scabbard and in dim light, the sword was magnificent. Intricate gold chasings and cabochon jewels on the hilt matched those of the ceremonial crown, torque and spearhead Uther had displayed at his coronation.

"The smith who made this was a fine master indeed, in both steel and gold," Marcus said. He raised it, one hand on the hilt, the other around the center of the scabbard. Gently, reverently, he drew it.

"And Excalibur is its name," Claerwen whispered. "Its true name."

"Oh, how I would love to practice with this," Marcus said. "Just for a few minutes." The blade gleamed even in the dim light.

He wondered how they would ever transport it safely to the high king. Uther spent most of his time chasing down Saxon war bands. To catch up with him could be difficult. And, once they located Uther, the need to protect a priceless ceremonial sword could be a hindrance to the king that far outweighed its symbolic inspiration to bolster morale among his soldiers.

The other option was to hide the weapon. But where? Winchester was not safe. Close to the Saxon Shore, Uther's capital was highly vulnerable to attack. Ynys Witrin crossed Marcus's mind again. The

Isle of Glass, sometimes called Avalon, in the Summer Country to the south, had encompassed the most sacred earth in Britain since time out of mind. Even respected by the Saxons, it was the only place he could think of where the sword might be safe.

He felt Claerwen's eyes on him. Looking up, he saw tears of relief quivering in them, her face lit with fascination. She still shook. Smiling, he held the sword flat across his hands and lifted.

In wonderment, she studied it. Her slender fingers traced lightly from hilt to tip and back. Done, she nodded.

Marcus passed his gaze to the Enchanter, quiet all this time, arms folded, his face as unreadable as ever. "What say you, Prince Myrddin?" Marcus asked. A sardonic grin hinted in his eyes.

Myrddin took a step forward. "Perhaps," he said with a wave of his hand that encompassed the clearing and ended over the sword, "it is only within the dark that we find the light."

The notion of "trinity" sprang again to Marcus's mind as if commanded. Love, knowledge and truth, three rays of light from which springs justice. Then he thought of Handor, drained of blood in the clearing. There was the dark side. It struck him then that no one could have been the administrator of justice, none of them who had been in the clearing that day, especially not himself, and not even Handor, whose hand had split his own flesh to spill his life. Rather, each had been given a task to perform, a path to follow, such that they would all meet at the end.

Marcus now recognized that Myrddin had always known this and had merely been a guide. In that infernal all-knowing gaze lay the easy acceptance that the gods interwove the substance of lifetimes into a pattern, a series of intertwining paths that only they created. His exile had to have happened, to lead him to Hywel. Claerwen's accident brought her Tangwen and a clue to the sword. Aye, he thought, to place oneself into one of those paths and follow it all the way to the end, through all the terrifying darkness, sometimes took a bloody lot of courage.

By the light… How could he have ever thought of himself as a giver of justice? He had not been that day, nor any other day, not as himself, not as the Iron Hawk. He never could have been. Handor's destiny had been sworn the day he was birthed.

Marcus slowly lowered the sword. He felt Claerwen kneel next to him, place her hand on his arm. She said something softly, but he could not look at her, could not listen. He stared at Macsen's sword lying across his hands.

If his duty could not have been as a giver of justice, he realized, neither could he ever have been a giver of freedom. All those years ago, in that crumbling Roman fort near Dun Breatann, the destiny of those who had died there had been sworn as well, just as his had been. To free them from their fate could not have been his task.

"Marcus?" Claerwen's hand squeezed.

Was this what all those nightmares had been trying to tell him? There was nothing he could have done. Nothing. Even had he known the Saxon language. He winced and gave a single, hushed, "ah," drawn from deep within his chest.

"Marcus?" she called again. "What is it? What's wrong?"

His gaze lifted to her. She was touching his face. What had she said?

"Sword of light, born of fire," Myrddin interrupted.

Marcus looked up. He fully expected fire in the head to show in the Enchanter's eyes, but Myrddin's irises were dark brown, not the amberish color they took on with the gods' power.

"Forged with strength of ancient magic," the Enchanter continued.

Where had he heard those words? Marcus asked himself. Then he remembered—they were lines from the prophecy, Myrddin's prophecy of the great king to come.

"Cries both with life and with death. Cast to stone, sword of fire." Myrddin met Marcus's stare. "You are a blacksmith."

Marcus nodded.

"The sword is for the king who will be our future," Myrddin said. "He will be the light that comes out of the darkness. You are a blacksmith. You know of dark and light, fire and iron. And now you know of the anvil stone and its secret."

Out of darkness, into the light. Marcus felt his head suddenly clear of the grogginess and pain, like a clean, fresh breeze had swept through it. Though it had been Claerwen's path to find the Lady stone, it had been his to find the one shaped like an anvil. He had recognized its contours, even in the dense growth and gloom, and he'd had the physical strength to move it.

The Enchanter swept his hands over the sword as if presenting it to the gods. "The sword of our high kings," he said. "For the future. For Arthur. Alone."

It was the first time Myrddin had said the boy's true name. "You'll not take it to Uther?" Marcus asked.

Myrddin shook his head. "Uther is caretaker of the kingship for now. He holds the crown, the spearhead and the torque in trust. When the time comes, they will pass to his son. But Excalibur is for Arthur alone. I believe you wished to ask what we should do with it now?"

Marcus nodded again.

"I say, leave it lie where it has been all this time. It will keep there a few more years. When the boy is old enough, at the correct time, I will bring him here. When he draws the sword from the anvil stone, he will know who he is."

Without another word, Marcus sheathed the sword and carefully wrapped it once more, then placed it back in its crypt. Rising, he began to maneuver the anvil stone onto its platform. The saplings he had leaned it against, strong and spring-like, aided him in raising it into position. Claerwen spread dead leaves over the top, and they restored the surrounding foliage as close as possible to how it looked before any of them had touched it. Silently, they returned to the clearing.

Claerwen held her palm open. The small piece of iron lay in it. "Rightwise king of all Britain," she said.

Standing close, Marcus felt her shudder.

"Should anything happen to us," she went on and folded her fingers around it again, "the Lady knows where the sword is. She is its protector. She will not let it be forgotten."

"So be it," Myrddin confirmed. "I will be on my way now. The gods be with you."

"Next time," Marcus said, a bit of impishness in his eyes, "if you want me to do something, come talk to me, will you? No more effigies?"

Myrddin smiled, his dark brown eyes swathed in riddles.

"Remember, there is still the grail...should you wish to seek it." He gazed into the sky. Then he laughed, a low rumbling that ascended into a sound akin to a soft cackle. He held out his arms and swept in a circle until the cackle left his throat and rose into the distance. A sudden beam of sunlight broke through a split in the clouds, and the black feathers of the mantle shimmered. One feather fluttered loose to land nearly at Marcus's feet. Then all went silent, and Myrddin walked away.

Marcus picked up the feather. Wise man of the woods, he mused. And a bit of madness to go along with the wisdom.

"You had the strangest look on your face when you held that sword," Claerwen said. "I thought you were ill, but that's not it, is it? Something happened to you."

He twirled the feather between his fingers. Her eyes were studying him, looking for an answer, and though he met them, he was not ready to talk. He had need to think first, think long and deeply on what he had learned. The guilt was still there, inside, embedded in his soul like maggots, and after he had burdened her with his brooding for so long, how could he burden her with this as well? How ironic that Myrddin, of all people, had evoked this new understanding and not Claerwen, who had tried for so long. Perhaps it was not ironic at all, just another step on his path. Path to where? No, he shook head, he needed to come to terms with this on his own.

He held up the feather, the impish glint again in his eyes. "Myrddin's molting," he said.

Off-guard, Claerwen burst into a round of giggles.

Marcus pressed his face into her hair and hugged her tightly. Her laughter was worth more than all the pieces of Macsen's Treasure put together.

Over her shoulder, he gazed back at the place Excalibur lay hidden. Barely visible, the Lady stone peered out. Even in the gloom of the woods, she seemed alive—a protector of the symbol of the future, a symbol that a young boy named Arthur would one day carry as a man, a warrior, a king. Marcus hoped to all the gods that Myrddin's long-awaited prophecy was coming true, and that out of the flames that forged steel and from the tearing cries of pain and charred remains of war, the light of peace would finally rise.

He released Claerwen and turned to look back at Handor's body. The ravens had landed again and were yanking on the cloak. Soon, they would drag it off the corpse. More birds clamored above.

"The ravens are gathering," he said. "But not for us."

Epilogue

Near Dinas Beris, Gwynedd
Lughnasa Eve, AD 477

"I want to wait here for a bit," Marcus said. He watched clouds skim the mountain peaks.

Claerwen pulled up her horse next to him. "Until the mist clears?"

He shook his head, dismounted and stalked a few paces up a ridge of sharp-edged boulders. From there, he gazed down into the next *cwm*. A deep blue tarn filled the basin of the steep, cone-shaped valley.

He shook back his hair, damp from the mist. It was the eve of autumn. In another day, he and Claerwen would be home. In the weeks since the fight in the clearing, he had grown far more at peace with himself than he had been for years. His nightmares had subsided, and now, though he still refused to talk about them, he was able to face the memories in his waking hours.

He pondered how the dreams had often distorted the memories, yet he still clearly saw all the faces of death—in the blank stare of those who had passed and in the haunted daze of those who had survived. War, starvation, torture, illness, abandonment—he had seen it all so many times, through both his own eyes and the ghastly eyes of his memories. And by creating the Iron Hawk with the intention to assuage some of that horror, he had only made it all worse.

He listened to Claerwen's footsteps come up the slope behind him. Her smile of joy and relief at coming home faded when he met her eyes.

"You're so serious," she said. "You're thinking of...*them*...again. Aren't you? I recognize it now."

He grimaced. Gods of the earth, how many had gone so pitiably while he had survived and was now given the chance to go home at last, and with his wife, to find days of comfort?

"I was thinking," she went on when he gave no answer. "All of those people have gone on to the Otherworld and then on to their next lives. Myrddin says they will be rewarded for the hardships endured in this life."

"Hmm," he grunted. The next life. What would he and Claerwen face in the next life? What reward would there be, if any, for their hardships? Or would they even be together? Reward meant nothing without her and the peace she inspired in him. And so much was still to be done in this life. He dashed away the thoughts and caught her hand, pressed his lips to her palm. He needed her touch, her warmth.

He kept her hand folded in his and closed his eyes. In truth he could find no words to describe what it was he felt now. The notion that he had taken on the Iron Hawk's soul to fight Handor but without the armor and trappings of the secret identity had been gaining ground in his mind. Except for his own weapon, he had faced Handor in the simple garb of a farmer or craftsman, tattered, unkempt and most of all, vulnerable. Regardless, he had become what he had always been—an implacable warrior bent on extinguishing an enemy. Then Handor had denied him that act, and the realization that dispensing justice was not his task had followed. Ever since, Marcus had come to wonder—why had he always been so full of arrogance?

"Handor screamed strange words," Claerwen said. "Just before the fight. They were in Saxon, weren't they?"

Marcus opened his eyes. Had she read his mind?

"They crazed you with anger," she said.

He ran his fingers through his hair. For days after the fight, he had let the Saxon words repeat silently in his mind, something he had never allowed himself to do since the first time he had ever heard them.

"Handor said the same words when he delivered the effigy,"

Marcus explained. "I think it was a Saxon war creed he picked up during his years with Octa."

He studied her hand, still in his. He had not answered her completely and had no desire to speak further, but she deserved more than the same meager explanations and cold-eyed silence he'd given her for years.

"There was a Saxon woman," he said, "who had been a slave in Dun Breatann. A native Briton bought her freedom and married her. When the Saxons raided…that night…she screamed those words over and over. They were meant as a warning. But she cried them in her own tongue—she was too panicked to switch to her adopted language. Then everything went silent. I tried to find her. I couldn't find anyone."

He stopped. He could not say the rest.

"And then you went inside the abandoned fort?"

Marcus winced. "The Saxons were coming back. I ran, but one of them hit me so hard I fell down an embankment to the beach. When I finally came to and reached Dun Breatann, it already was too late."

"They burned it all?"

He lifted his gaze. "Everything."

"Ceredig told me you were about one-and-ten winters then."

He nodded again.

"And you began working as a spy at five-and-ten?"

Another nod.

A tear fell down her cheek. "And the Iron Hawk?"

He released her hand and picked at a wrinkle on his sleeve, folding and smoothing it, over and over. "Within a couple of years," he said. "It was never enough to merely spy on people and pass on information. I always had to do more, go deeper, fight harder. Try to die sooner."

She wrapped her arms around him then. He breathed in the scent of her hair. It smelled of fresh grass and rain. How he cherished her closeness, her compassion. He emptied his mind and watched the tarn's water ripple. The peacefulness gradually filled him again.

"The mist is lifting," she said to break the long silence. "It will be a beautiful sunset. I wonder."

"Hmm?"

"The grail…the final piece of Macsen's Treasure. I wonder why Myrddin laughed like that."

Marcus grinned into her hair. "You don't know?"

She straightened, returned his smile. "No one knows what goes on in his mind, not even me." Her smile became a challenging look. "What has changed in you?"

"Changed?"

She studied his face. "You've been making jokes, teasing again these past weeks. Ever since Myrddin talked about dark and light, and you being a blacksmith. Something changed after that. Something you won't talk about."

Indeed, he thought. Something had changed. Along with the lesson about tasks and paths, the beginnings of a secretive notion had taken root soon after he had held Macsen's sword. In the fortnights that followed the idea had grown more solid while he silently considered it. He was split whether it was right to do or not.

She tapped his brow lightly with her fingertips. "Something is rolling around in there. I can feel it."

He met her eyes. Tenacity. There was another of her tasks. She had refused to let him stray from the path to find Macsen's sword, in spite of her injuries, in spite of his sourness, in spite of Handor's threat.

Handor. What had been his journey in all this? To spread lies and hate? If anything, the assassin had opened up old wounds and—

Marcus smoothed his moustache. Opened old wounds. Wounds that needed to be drained and salved and healed. To stop the festering. He smiled wryly. Another path. This one to a decision.

"I will make an offering," he said. "In the way of our ancestors."

Claerwen pulled back, her arched brows knotted in question.

To answer her, he walked down to his horse and flipped up the edge of his cloak. From the Iron Hawk's gear, he freed the sword. With the tip up, he rotated it around, back and forth to catch the blade's gleam in the sunset.

"I wish I knew the ancient tongue," he said. "Somehow, a prayer would seem to carry more power if spoken in it, I think."

He watched her eyes widen at the realization he was going to make an offering of the sword. He tipped the weapon over and held up the hawk-shaped pommel. "You were right, Claerwen," he said. "I don't need him. I never needed him. I will burn the armor, and when we go home, I will do the same with the other set of gear."

Claerwen stared at the tarn. "You're giving up the Iron Hawk? For true? Forever?"

The astonishment in her voice made him smile, though with a touch of sadness in it. "Aye, for true."

Her eyes shifted to the distance, across the mountains. "But not your work as well?"

"No, no. Only the warrior's identity. Uther will have more than enough trouble with this new incursion of Saxons. I will help him, as needed, in my own way."

She touched the sword's pommel. "This has been a part of you for a long, long time. Are you sure you can live without it?"

She was asking if in truth he could live without the guilt that had created the Iron Hawk. He hoped so. He had to. And he still did not quite understand the sense of peace that filled him more each day since Handor's death, as if it had taken up residence in his soul. The memories were still there, as horrible as ever. Perhaps he needed both, the pain balanced with the calm, perhaps that was the only way he could live with it.

"I will find a way," he said.

"That is good…good."

So little enthusiasm? Marcus frowned. She had always dreaded his work. "What's wrong?"

"A battle." She stared again at the water. "Here."

"Here? Where? By the tarn?" He waited for his warrior's sense to prickle but nothing came to him.

She shook her head. "*Cwm y Llan.*"

"Valley of the church? There's no place with a name like that here."

Her face lifted. "There will be. Or a name like that. It's not clear."

Marcus saw the light of fire in the head flicker in her eyes then fade. His jaw clenched. "When will this happen?"

She mumbled a few words he could not understand, but he thought he heard something about Macsen's sword. "Long after we are gone," she said louder then shivered, like she was shaking away dust. "It's gone. If it's important, it will come again." She shrugged.

Unnerved, he grunted. After so many years, as he had told himself a thousand times, he should be accustomed to her visions, but no matter how he trusted the fire, he still was not. He probably never would be. He shook his head faintly at himself and strode back up the ridge.

He took another long look of admiration at the Iron Hawk's beautiful weapon. The best he had ever forged. He could always make another, but never again with the hawk symbol.

"Go to the Lady of this water in peace," he said and with a great heave, sent it soaring. It flipped end over end in a slow-moving arc, as if reluctant to leave the world. A last sparkling turn, a pause, and it dropped, tip first to slice into the deep water.

The sun disappeared. The end of the day, the beginning of another. The release of light into darkness that would revolve once more into light. Another day, and they would be home after six long, difficult years. To Claerwen, he turned and took her face between his hands.

"*You* are my freedom," he said. "You always have been. Ever and forever."

Acknowledgements

WHEN I pick up a book in search of historical information, I not only recognize the tremendous effort of the author(s) who has researched and assembled a multitude of facts in an interesting and credible manner, but that the author has drawn upon the work of a whole army of people in search of the past. The same holds true of all interpreters and preservers of history, from museum curators to archaeologists. Their work resides in books, libraries, museums, archaeological sites, classroom and e-mail discussions and countless other venues, all to be discovered and enjoyed. It is to all this work that I go to find the broad spectrum of information needed to write a historical novel. It is such a shame to be unable to name these hidden contributors. To all of those people out there who have contributed in some way to our knowledge of fifth-century Britain and the Arthurian legend, as well as history in general, I am grateful beyond words.

I also wish many thanks on a more specific basis to Kevan White for his wealth of information on Roman wigs and Romano-British forts; to Peter Morrison for his vast expertise on medieval battle and combat; to Dr. Sonia Peltzer for her help with medical and herbal questions; to Judith Simpson for describing the sound and feel of an approaching flash flood; to Steve Pollington for translating that critical phrase into Anglo-Saxon; and to Paul Bonnifield for his patience, even during a bitter snowstorm, in teaching this townie girl about the behavior of horses as well as for his tips on a lot of other things I never would have thought to ask about.

To Harriet and the Thursday gang: thank you once again for coming along for the ride with me on this adventure. The fearless critiques, tidbits of knowledge, suggestions, encouragement and friendship are invaluable and treasured.

And the biggest thank you to my husband Peter who has had to put up with me all through this and will continue to do so. His unique insights collected from across the world have brought inspiration to this project.

About the Author

AWARD-winning novelist Kathleen Cunningham Guler is the author of the four-part Macsen's Treasure series, that includes *Into the Path of Gods* and *In the Shadow of Dragons*, which won a Colorado Independent Publishers Award for fiction in 2002. The author has studied Celtic history and Arthurian legend for more than twenty years in both the United States and Great Britain and has published numerous articles, essays, short stories and poetry. A descendant of the Celtic nations of Wales and Scotland, the author is a member of the Historical Novel Society and the International Arthurian Society. Visit her website at: http://kathleenguler.com.